A Kangaroo Court

A Triumph of Mediocrity

Shankar N Kashyap

> *Declaration;*
> *All the characters and events in this book are purely fictional. Any resemblance to any individuals, living or otherwise or events is purely coincidental*
>
> *Shankar N Kashyap*

DEDICATION

I dedicate this book to my dear departed father, whose life I have striven to emulate. He was an honest, kind man who saw goodness in everyone. I still remember his words 'There must have been goodness even in the devil himself'.

ACKNOWLEDGMENTS

I would like to thank Geetha, my wife who stood by me in times of obscurity and my children who had faith in me. I would also like to thank my dearest friends, Sashi, Ananda, Chandrika, and Upma for all their help. Extra thanks for Sashi who designed the front cover of this book. I cannot forget Lisa, Teri and Dawn without whose support I could not have come through. Joe was there as a 'Rock of support' for me at all times. There are countless numbers of people, who have helped me, stood by me, and believed in me. My deepest gratitude to one and all.

Foreword

It was a childhood dream. To become a doctor. To become a surgeon. To heal by the knife and to change people's lives for the better. The path that leads to this dream is one of tireless dedication hard work and unforgiving obstacles. It is a joyful celebration of that expended energy to achieve this ambition.

To practice this hallowed profession abiding by the Hippocratic Oath is what most doctors seek to do throughout their vocational life. The physician was for the longest time revered in society and was the very embodiment of respectability. His word was infallible; his judgment unquestioned.

As the innovations in medicine progressed so did the awareness and information amidst the public about available treatments and alternatives. . So much so the age, old role of the "Physician" began to change and there was a demand for accountability and regulation of this profession to "protect the public from poor doctors"

The General Medical council in this country performs this function. Their aims are to put patient safety first, support good medical practice, promote fairness and value diversity and respect the principles of ethical regulation: proportionality, accountability, consistency, transparency and targeting.

There is encouragement at every level to report a "rogue" doctor and an elaborate bureaucratic set up to investigate the complaint.

The annals of the predatory press are rife with juicy accounts of doctors, who have been reported to the GMC and there is no apology made for any havoc they may unleash either professional or personal.

While Dr Shipman and the Bristol enquiry have captured the imagination of the press and the attention of the public, there is little written about the personal agony and humiliation that is undergone by a doctor who is wrongly accused.

It could be argued that the public may well be protected by the well meaning actions of this regulatory body, but what of the hapless doctor who may well be the victim of a malicious slander or target of a jealous colleague.

For someone who has practiced his vocation with honesty, integrity and undoubted skill this unexpected accusation is a devastating life event.

1

The laborious workings of the General Medical council dealing with a malicious complaint against a competent surgeon are explored in intricate detail in this narration.

As the story unfolds, the question of the age renowned adage of "innocent until proven guilty" is thrown to the winds and under the pretext of "patient safety", the physician is "guilty until proven innocent". There are further doubts about the ability of the regulatory body to conduct a fair and unbiased enquiry as stipulated in their manifesto. A simple complaint that should possibly have dealt with at a local level develops momentum of its own, that spins out control.

The harrowing months turn into years while the General Medical Council utterly insensitive to the time elapsed, carries on its "investigation". The description of the hearings is almost comical, and the complete disconnection between the various parts of the proceedings, do nothing to inspire any confidence in the reader about the ability of the regulatory body to carry out its aims.

The author vividly portrays the effect of this ongoing saga on the doctor's personal and professional life. The sense of isolation, being an object of pity or patronising behaviour is deeply hurtful to someone who once commanded respect. Human behaviour in this situation is no different to animals that prey on an injured one.

While in the larger scheme of things, compared to tsunami's and earthquakes one man's injustice may seem trivial but to that one human being this event is just as cataclysmic. The reader will be touched by the description of the doctor's state of mind and his assessment of the relationships of all those near and dear to him in these troubled times.

In conclusion, any fair judicial process demands a clear delineation between the various parties involved in the deliberations but here it would appear that the medical council has assumed the role of the Judge, Jury and Executioner.

Chandrika Roysam

Consultant Anaesthetist

1.   Life Is Not Always, What It Is

'Can you get me a size 36 mm Delta ceramic head with standard neck, please?' I asked Helen, who was assisting.

Sinnie, who was on the floor said, 'Did you bring it in?'

'Of course I did. You should know better than to ask' I was just tapping the femoral component into the femur as I spoke. The satisfying change of sound as the implant gets its position is music to any hip surgeon's ears.

'One more little tap and we are done. Come on open the damn thing!' I said smiling.

'Yes Mr. Kasyapa. Here, Helen, it is a 36mm Delta Ceramic, standard neck. Expires March 2018.' Sinnie said with a tone of sarcasm in her voice and showed the box to Helen.

Helen repeated the words on the box, and confirmed the expiry date. Deborah then showed the box to me to read and confirmed what was being read. She opened the box and handed the implant in its sterile cover to Helen. Once the implant was opened, I was asked to read out the etched details on the implant again to confirm the right size. This was such an elaborate procedure but moved with the ease and precision of a well-oiled machine. It is repeated every time any implant is used in surgery. It is done hundreds of times daily, and it reminds me of a pilot's checklist before he starts the aircraft engines.

'Here you are Mr. Whiplash!' Helen said with a twinkle in her eyes. We got along extremely well. I loved it when Helen scrubbed to assist me. Any potential pressure is off, and everything moves so smoothly and is entirely stress-free. The head of the prosthesis was slid on to the trunion of the femoral component, and a gentle knock to lock the head on to the femoral component completed the procedure.

'Come on Helen. Let's see you reduce this without any sweat!'

"You just see how easy it is" Helen said as she reduced the hip into the joint with a satisfying clunk as the ceramic hit the ceramic of the acetabular cup. Just as, she got the hip reduced, I heard the theatre door open and Alstan's dulcet tones.

'That is 28 minutes Upaas. Is that your record?'

'No. I had this blonde assisting me to slow me down!' I laughed.

'Don't be rude in front of your guests!' and he went on to introduce that day's guests from Florence, Italy.

'This is Prof Conti from the University of Florence'

'Buongiorno Professore. Come stai?' I wanted to try a bit of my Italian.

'"Bene grazei. Piacere'

'And this is Dr Cesare from Lucca' Alstan interjected.

'Buongiorno Il Dottore. Piacere'

'Bene grazei' Dr Cesare replied.

'I am almost finished, and I will be with you in ten minutes. Alstan, would you mind taking them to the coffee room please?'

Alstan nodded his head and ushered the guests out of the theatre. I could see Helen giggling under the mask.

'And why are you giggling?' I retorted.

'They looked shocked when Alstan said 28 minutes. You should have seen their faces' Helen could not contain herself any longer it appeared.

It did not take terribly long after that to close the wound, dress and transfer the patient. I walked into the coffee room, 'Here is your coffee, Upaas. I knew you would not be long. It is not cold' Alstan smiled.

Prof Conti said 'What time did you start this morning?'

'Knife to skin at about 9. Why?'

'It is only 9.40 now. That is extremely fast for a hip replacement,' Prof Conti said with some surprise.

'Well. I do have five more joint replacements to finish by the end of the day.' I said.

The two of them looked at each other and nodded their head.

'Do you use two theatres?'

'No we are not that lucky. I have to finish all cases in one theatre'

'We were hoping to discuss your technique of revision hip replacement. Any of the cases today revisions?' Dr Cesare wanted to know.

'Unfortunately, no. All the cases today are primary hip and knee replacements. However, I can do the next best thing. I have a copy of my last presentation to the Dutch Arthroplasty Association on my laptop. And, we can go through that.' I was trying to be helpful, and I knew we had some time before the next case as our Anaesthetist; Tom Quinn was training a junior doctor today.

'That would be very kind.' Prof Conti added.

We spent the next twenty minutes going through my presentation showing my technique, of using bone graft to build up the deficient bone in revision hip surgery and my results of the procedure. They appeared duly impressed.

Just as we sipped our second cup of coffee, Sinnie walked through the door, 'Are you coming? The patient is on the table. We do not have all day you know. It is all right for some to sit and drink coffee.' It was always a pleasure to work Sinnie and Helen. The day went quickly and smoothly with no hassles. All of us followed Sinnie back into theatre. I introduced the two guests to all the staff and Tom Quinn before scrubbing up. Daire Thorne, our Theatre Manager, came through the door with relevant papers for the guests to sign before they could scrub up as well. She checked the consent I had taken that morning from the patient to allow visitors to view the surgery scrubbed up.

There were many questions during the procedure, and the discussions were in both directions. They used to slip into Italian now and then and apologise quickly.

'Allora. Nessuna problema. Capisco tutto. Non parlo bene' I would say to calm them down.

I wanted to know how their systems worked and about their techniques of doing hip arthroplasty surgery. I always believed that you learn while you are teaching. I always managed to pick up pointers during discussions with numerous visitors to my unit. The smooth running of the unit impressed them, and by lunchtime, we had finished three joint replacements with considerable ease. We went out to the hospital canteen, gloriously named Queenellies out in the surgery centre foyer for lunch. They were particularly keen for me to travel across to Florence, and perform a revision hip replacement surgery to demonstrate my technique of impaction bone grafting at the University Hospital in Florence. Sacha Bess, who was our Rapid Recovery Programme Coordinator joined us for lunch, and I left them with a promise to arrange my visit to Florence, to carry on with the rest of the list. Sacha would take them around the centre to show them how the system works which we had pioneered in the hospital. They were due to catch the late afternoon flight back to Florence.

'Where have you been?' Helen wanted to know as soon as I entered the unit. 'Next patient is on the table. Get scrubbed.'

As I checked the x-rays on the computer terminal and templates to get the implants I wanted for the case, there was a message from my secretary to call her back. It was Aaron Mcduck, my PhD student trying to get hold of me to discuss the visit to the Gait Lab at the University later that day. I promised myself that I would call him as soon as I finished this case and arrange to go after the list today. We had to finalise the Force platform that we had designed between us to assess the gait of patients before and after total hip and knee replacements. It was an exciting project, which would answer several questions regarding the efficacy of different hip replacements and knee replacements in relation to the patients benefit in their activities of daily living. It would give an excellent thesis to Aaron for his PhD and would be a feather in my cap as, yet another pioneering research in the country. I managed to get the list finished by about 4.30 that afternoon. My junior trainee, who I had not seen all day, was waiting to go around all the patients operated on that day. Nowadays these junior doctors have become a rare commodity. You hardly ever see them when you want them. By the time the ward round was finished, Aaron was waiting for me in my office. I offered him a coffee and sat down to go through hundreds of emails that needed response. I was thrilled to note that yet another of my papers on Revision Total Knee Replacements, using impaction bone grafting technique had been accepted for publication in a leading international journal. There also an invitation by ESSKA (European Society of Sports Traumatology Knee Surgery and Arthroscopy) to write a chapter on minimally invasive surgical technique for total knee replacements! This was a prestigious organisation, and they were asking me to write this chapter for a book to use for their exit exam! Everything seems to be happening today.

It was nearly six in the evening when we set off to the university. Deakin Manlan, the Senior Lecturer in Biomechanics at the university was waiting for me along with a couple of technicians. Aaron set up the Force platform, force plates, and started the software programme, which would run the recognition of gait in patients. We used Deakin as a guinea pig and taped all the Teflon marker balls on to his body. The cameras would recognise these markers and follow their movements to plot the activity of hips, knees, and ankles at different phases of walking. All of us knew that hip replacements and knee replacements got rid of pain in the arthritic hips and knees. However, there were no objective measurements of the functional activity after joint replacements. Particularly, as there were numerous different types of hip and knee replacements on the market, we need to know how they differ in their functional outcome as far as the patient is concerned. It would take three years to complete and would give a considerable insight into the workings of hip and knee replacements.

It was after eight in the evening before I could finish at the university and set off home. As I was driving home listening to some soothing Indian classical music, I was going over everything that happened that day. Moreover, I was extremely happy with the way life was treating me so far. The mobile going off disturbed my thoughts. It was Swayambhu.

'Hi Upaas. Where are you? We are waiting for you to start the music concert'

'I am just over the bridge, and I will be there in ten minutes.' I had forgotten the concert, where Sanvi and Shuchi were performing that night. I am going to get an earful from Lopa for sure!

Therefore, it was a late start to the concert and late finish. All of us trooped down to Swayambhu's house for some wine and dinner afterwards. There were animated discussions about the concert, and plenty of wine was being drunk at the same time. All was well with the world, and I was smiling.

2. Did The Sky Fall On The Head Or Was It Pushed?

There I was going through life totally oblivious to invidious nature of the beast. I was of the same opinion as the inimitable Gauls – only afraid of the sky falling on the head! I had an excellent job, fabulous family and a circle of friends, an envy of everyone. I had my vicissitudes but always came out on top. I believe it was a Greek philosopher, Epicurius, who said as long ago as the third century BC, 'Do not spoil what you have by desiring what you have not; remember that what you now have, was once among the things you only hoped for'. This helped me keep smiling all the time, no matter what the world threw against me. I used to think that this philosophy gave me certain 'invincibility!

The life, as I saw it was good, and I had nothing to fear. I was the hero to many of my patients and staff alike and I could not do anything wrong. Whenever I was away, people would wait for me to come back to be treated. Everyone from the lowliest worker in the hospital to the chief executive wanted me to treat him or her. My career was going up, and there did not seem to be an end to the heights I would reach. I was the toast of international conferences in exotic places like Rome, Vienna, Naples, Copenhagen and Barcelona. I was travelling the world demonstrating latest techniques of surgery in knee and hip replacement. My ego was getting bigger and bigger constantly being fed every day of the week. I had invitations to travel and teach from across Europe and beyond. The only fly in the ointment was a locum consultant causing unrest within the hospital I was working in. He was gathering a small clique of people around him who were essentially hangers on to support him. I was the clinical director of the department, and it was inevitable that there would be people, who were not happy with the way I ran the department. I always held patient care as the ultimate aim of any doctor, and I strived to develop the hospital and take it into the 21st century. As a consultant orthopaedic surgeon, I worked extremely hard to achieve my goals and unfortunately, ended up treading on some toes. Lopa had a marvelous job, and she was thriving in it. The children were blossoming, and Shuchi had just been appointed to a prestigious academic job in Oxford. Sanvi was excelling herself in her veterinary course, and Akshaj was coming up well in Amsterdam. The life could not have been better. All three of them had excelled not only academically, but also in sports and music. The family were the talk of the town, and everyone wanted us in their house.

We were travelling the world enjoying the family to the limit. We had just returned from climbing Kilimanjaro, and I had nearly died in the effort. That is another story to be told elsewhere. We did the Serengeti safari in Tanzania and enjoyed the delights of Zanzibar. The year before, we had savoured the delicacies of dishes from different countries on the spice road in Moscow and tasted the life style of the Czars in St Petersburg. That summer we had climbed Himalayas to savour exquisite flora of the Valley of Flowers at 16,000 feet. I had plans for future trips across the world to enjoy ourselves to the limit. We had taken up skiing in earnest and looked forward to our annual trip to La Thuile. As far as I was concerned, nothing could go wrong with life.

It is said that the life teaches you lesson now and then, particularly when you are least expecting it. Judging from the smoothness with which the life was strolling along, I should have guessed that it was my turn. I was totally oblivious to what was around the corner. I had considered my life 'unsinkable' like the Titanic, and just like the ill-fated ship; I was soon to hit an iceberg!

The sky did fall on the head one dull December evening as I came home from work! There was a white nondescript envelope marked 'Private & Confidential' from the General Medical Council (GMC) for everyone to see. First, I did not think much of it as I opened the envelope with some trepidation. The letter was a bland statement telling me that they have received a complaint from a Mr. Serpe about my work. It went on to say that, they are investigating the matter and would get back to me when it is concluded. This obviously had me worried to some extent and I tried to think of all the issues that had taken place over the previous two tumultuous years at the hospital. This man had complained first to the hospital trust, which had investigated his complaints thoroughly and cleared me. I was firmly under the impression that these allegations were investigated fully by the Trust authorities and laid to rest as a malicious rumour. That had made him complain to the regional adviser in surgery who also had investigated and found nothing wrong. I sent a copy of the letter promptly to the Medical Protection Society (MPS) and thought nothing more of it.

Nothing happened for nearly two years, and I was beginning to think that the GMC had forgotten about it. Just as I was settling back into a routine and had almost forgotten about the letter from GMC, there came another letter saying that the GMC would be investigating the complaint with a random selection of my cases. This to me was again extremely disconcerting, to say the least. Nevertheless, I was not unduly worried. I tried to get hold of the notes that were being sent across to this consultant in Glasgow for an assessment. Unfortunately, despite my best efforts, I could not get hold of them. There was a thick shroud of secrecy around the whole deal, which would shame the Nazi Gestapo intelligence during the war. About four months later, I was sent a report by the GMC. It said that I had to agree to a 'Performance Assessment'. Otherwise, I will be referred to the Fitness to Practice Panel with automatic suspension. Somewhere along the line, the Gestapo had changed to the SS!

That was the first time when I started to get an inkling of the seriousness of the situation. Here, I was basking in the adulation of my teammates in the hospital and by the international faculty, when my livelihood itself was being threatened. My first reaction was one of anger and sheer frustration. I read and re-read the letter and the enclosed document several times just to make sure what was happening. I called the Medical Advisor at the MPS for advice.

'I am frightfully sorry to hear the news. The MPS will help you through this. I would not worry too much about the letter.' Dr Smiths tried to calm me down. 'It is a process faced by many doctors, and we will work on this together. Do not reply to the letter until we have discussed it in more detail.'

He asked me to come and meet him later that week, and he would help me draft out a response.

It took me a good few days before I could start to analyse the document that was sent, as a 'Report of Assessment.' This consultant had been sent twelve sets of notes, identified by Serpe along with x-rays. First thing that struck me was that two of them were not my patients; one was treated by Serpe himself! Second thing to note was that the consultant who was performing the assessment was not an expert hip surgeon. According to Dr Foster's directory and the Royal College register, he was a retired orthopaedic surgeon from Glasgow with self-professed interest in fractured hips. By all accounts, he did remarkably few if any hip replacements and he had been asked to review 'complications' of my hip replacements! How valid his observations are for anybody to guess. It became clear very soon that his knowledge of hip replacement was poor and rather outdated. He had made certain dubious remarks about the cases that he had seen. Finally, his recommendations were that a more thorough audit of one hundred random cases should be performed, as there was a 'cause for concern'. However, the GMC officers took a different view and felt that as a call for a more detailed 'Performance Assessment.' The GMC sent me an 'invitation' to undergo a 'Performance Assessment.' The term 'invitation' is a misnomer. It was more of a 'threat' rather than an 'invitation.' If you did not accept the 'invitation,' it turns out that one would be suspended from the register and face Fitness to Practice Panel.

Later that week, I drove all the way to Leeds to meet up with the Medical Advisor, Dr Smiths. As I entered the waiting room, Dr Smiths came down, introduced himself and shook my hands.

'It is extremely nice of you to come down here. It will be lot easier to discuss the various options.' He took me up the stairs to an office, where another gentleman was sitting. He introduced himself as a 'legal adviser'. Both of them went through the document, and their advice was that I should take the Performance Assessment, as it is an extremely straightforward assessment set at an extremely junior level.

'You should not have any problems passing it.' Dr Smiths said.

He helped me fill the long-winded questionnaire with all the questions that were being asked by the GMC. He went through the system of assessment and showed how unhelpful the council can be with any queries. I had so many questions, but unfortunately, he did not have all the answers. He told me that he had several doctors going through this assessment process without problems. He tried to explain the whole process to me, how it worked, and how it had changed since the Shipman fiasco. Much of Britain's legal structure concerning health care and medicine had been reviewed and modified as a result of Shipman's crimes, especially after the findings of the Shipman Inquiry, which began on 1 September 2000 and lasted almost two years. Dame Janet Smith who headed the enquiry, said, the General Medical Council 'was an organisation designed to look after the interests of doctors, not patients'. Since then, the General Medical Council changed its motto from 'Guiding Doctors' to 'Regulating Doctors.' It was also the start of a system, where the GMC Panels included lay members, who had never been anywhere near a hospital before except as patients. They knew remarkably little about the way the health service worked. This proved seriously detrimental to numerous doctors and curtailed the way everyone worked. It soon became obvious, that we were living in a 'vigilante society.' Doctors began watching doctors and patients who came into the hospitals with the sole idea of suing doctors. This became the norm, than the exception. It was a free-for-all against doctors everywhere. It reminded me of McCarthyism during the height of the Cold War. The report said 'Suspicions were often given credence despite inconclusive or questionable evidence, and the level of the threat posed by a person's real or supposed leftist associations or beliefs was often vastly exaggerated. Many people suffered loss of employment, destruction of their careers.' Many doctors were referred to the GMC. They faced losing their registration to practice and essential destruction of their careers and lives. Looking through the GMC website one could find at least ten to fifteen cases active any given day, including weekends.

In response to the Shipman report, Sir Liam Donaldson, the Chief Medical Officer, published a report titled *Good doctors, safer patients*, which appeared in 2006. Sir Liam Donaldson echoes concerns about GMC FTP procedures and other functions of the Council, which had been widely suspected before but never voiced publicly. In his view, complaints are dealt with in a haphazard manner, the Council cause distress to doctors over trivial complaints while tolerating poor practice in other cases. It accused the Council of being - 'secretive, tolerant of sub-standard practice, and dominated by the professional interest, rather than that of the patient.'

All these characteristics of the GMC would become clear to me much later. Former President of the General Medical Council, Sir Donald Irvine, called for the current council, to be disbanded, and re-formed with new members. In 2007, Professor Sir Tooke led the inquiry into Modernising Medical Careers (MMC), the new and current post-graduate training structure for medical doctors in the UK. MMC has become extremely unpopular amongst the majority of medical professionals in the UK, and as a result, the Government set up an independent inquiry into the situation. In February 2008 the Secretary of State for Health, Alan Johnson, agreed with recommendations of the Tooke Report which advised that GMC should merge with the Postgraduate Medical Education and Training Board (PMETB). This hopefully is due to come into being sometime in 2010. Whether, it would be old wine a new bottle, remains to be seen. Judging by the way health service reforms go, I suspect it will be moving officers around, from one chair to another – a sort of merry go round. At the end of the day, it would be the same people doing the same job with a different title and doing it as badly as before. We moved from Family Practitioner's Committee to Fund-holders to Trusts, without seeing any effective change in the patient services or hospital care.

His parting words were -

'For someone of your caliber and experience, it should be a cake walk.'

I was very thoughtful as I drove back home. I had some misgivings about this assessment despite Dr Smiths' reassurance.

By now, I had managed to get hold of all the notes and x-rays of those patients assessed by the 'independent' surgeon. I went through them with a fine toothcomb several times. The only thing that came out of that was a rather poor grasping of intricacies of a hip replacement by the assessor who had done the report. I decided to get an independent opinion about these cases. I took anonymised copies all the x-rays across to the next international meeting in Rome. There were more than a few internationally acclaimed surgeons at the meeting. I was on the faculty, and a couple of the top hip replacement surgeons from the USA and Europe were there. One evening, towards the end of the meeting, I asked them to give a critical opinion on the x-rays that I had carried with me. The ruse was that I had been asked to comment on a Trainee's work. None of them could find any faults with any of the x-rays that were criticised by the so-called independent assessor from Glasgow. That filled me with confidence in myself but produced immense misgivings about the GMC, and its assessment process. I thought, what a pity I could not use the comments by these internationally acclaimed hip surgeons for my defence.

At that time, little did I realise that this was to be the start of a long drama with several episodes and numerous vicissitudes. I also did not realise that it had the potential to take over my life and literally destroy me. I used to read about doctors referred to the GMC Fitness to Practice Panel and suspended for several years. I always felt that there must be something wrong with these doctors as I had complete faith in the GMC and its role and functions. As far as I was concerned, I paid my dues every year to keep my registration and let me practice. It had been ingrained into me as some-what routine. Apart from those news items, I read in the ubiquitous Hospital Doctor journal or the British Medical Journal, I had never given it another thought. There were some high profile cases such as a Professor of paediatrics, Prof Meadows where the GMC had it totally wrong and had paid for it. A brief search in Google showed literally hundreds of cases of injustice done by the GMC. I found that there were websites wholly dedicated to helping fight the GMC injustice. The incompetence and sheer bureaucracy in some of these cases had been exposed in several websites. Obviously, these sites were the brainchild of those doctors who had been seriously wronged.

There were rumblings in these journals about the unequal number of overseas doctors hauled in front of the GMC. Several organisations including the Overseas Doctors Association and (British Association of Physicians of Indian Origin) BAPIO were actively fighting against this imbalance.

However, that did not concern me. Just like most of us, I was not affected, and all I was doing was, heated discussions over cups of coffee or a bottle of wine in the evenings. Just like most of us, I never gave it a thought during the daylight hours and did anything active about it. Even when one of my friends was implicated in a similar scenario, all I did was write a letter of recommendation and a small testimonial and washed my hands off.

Being a Doctor, I had been told was a 'job for life.' One was respected and placed high in society. One should have leadership qualities, and should be a beacon of the establishment. Need I go on? Well, anyway I was going to be shown that being a doctor is not all-that secure. In fact, it is probably one of most insecure jobs on the land. You spend all your life studying, working hard and training to be one. There is no time to learn or do anything else. Half of your life is spent on becoming an 'established' surgeon. You do not envisage and no one tells you to expect that the career might come to an abrupt end just when you think you have made it. Doctors are a peculiar breed, who are not geared to be anything other than a doctor.

The medical field breeds a type of people, especially in this country, who cannot stand anyone else being successful. Your colleagues go out of their way to pull you down and destroy you. The medical fraternity in this country encourages mediocrity remarkably successfully, and woe begets anyone who does not conform. We excel in mediocrity and thrive in a humdrum existence unless you belong to the 'inner circle' of political doctors. This is a breed of doctors who know how to talk and well known as the 'brown nose brigade'. They were identified very early in their career and fly through the training process, attached to one of the 'leaders' in the group. Their knowledge is well short of being acceptable, and any surgical skills, if required are substandard. That does not stop them from being 'successful' politically and go on to become consultants unusually quickly. Majority of them go on to administrative roles, chairing committees and heading organisations with singularly little clinical input. It is an unwritten saying that if you cannot operate, becomes a Professor! Our renowned NHS is filled with men and women who thrive on mediocrity. They go through their entire career blissfully ignorant of how poor their knowledge is. As long as you conform to this norm and do not rise above it, you can go through your entire career without getting into trouble with the council. I can only say that not a small number of patients get better, more because of their good fortune and the human body's propensity to get better, than the skill of the doctors treating them. The human body is a miracle of evolution, which can take a lot of abuse and still function as it does.

However, I digress. I had no inkling to the competence of the GMC until I received a letter from them informing me of the constitution of the Assessment panel and the process of assessment. The letter simply gave the date of the hospital visit and the names of the Assessment Panel. Within a few weeks, another letter arrived saying that the panel would have to be changed 'due to unforeseen' circumstances and hence the assessment would be postponed. At the time, I did not think much of it. It was another three months before a third letter arrived giving me the details of the assessment panel and the dates of their visit to Seaport. The only difference I could find was that there was one change in the assessors. Only then did it strike me that the assessor who was changed was the same person who had performed the 'independent assessment' of my cases! I wonder if this was a coincidence or was yet another blunder on the part of the council. I was to find out that this was only the beginning of a catalogue of mistakes.

I tried to look up the Assessors who were coming as a part of experts on the panel, who were coming to assess me. The first surprise was the chairperson of the panel – he was a practicing General Practitioner. I failed to understand how a General Practitioner could assess a consultant orthopaedic surgeon of nearly fifteen years standing and of some international repute. When I dug deeper, it turned out he was also one of those 'committee doctors' who sat on several Primary Care Trust Committees, chaired few organisations and also acted as an Assessor for the GMC. That made me wonder, where did he find time to practice medicine or treat patients? The next surprise was the second name on the panel – he was a retired foot and ankle surgeon. I was not too sure how he could understand all the nuances of a hip replacement, let alone a revision total hip replacement. A little more digging revealed some shocking facts! He was a consultant for less than five years and had spent the majority of his career at a middle grade level working under a consultant. He would not have been able to do any substantive work as an independent consultant. Therefore, his knowledge of a consultant's work or quality of such work would be severely restricted if he had any at all.

The third panelist was even better – he was a retired hand surgeon. According to the sources that I searched, none of them had operated on a hip or knee in the last ten years. They had all stopped practicing at least two years before the assessment. Where were experts in hip and knee surgery who were supposed to assess my surgery? These experts would be so far behind in the knowledge of current development in orthopaedics that they would be no better informed than the layman on the street.

The Council had sent a bunch of doctors who had not done any joint replacement surgery in at least five years, to assess a surgeon who had performed more than 3000 joint replacements, and was regarded as an international authority on the procedure. If I had not been in such a serious predicament, I would have laughed.

A trawl of various search engines, looking for the names of these three 'experts' failed to reveal a single publication, in any peer-reviewed journal that could relate hip or knee surgery to any of them. This again proved my point. The medical fraternity is divided into two groups – one who works his socks off treating patients, operating on them, making them better day in and day out. Then there was the other group, who could cut their way out of a paper bag, talk, sit on committees, and tell the other group what they can and cannot do. Obviously, the three assessors belong to the second group. I am quite sure this anomaly occurs in other fields of several service industries as well.

This is only the beginning of the catalogue of decisions by the GMC. I had to face during the following three years. Things were going to go from bad to worse and would make me curse the day I agreed to help Pakshar get a job in our hospital. When you help someone, the least you expect is that someone would not harm you. Well, this gentleman obviously had not read that bit about humanity or gratitude.

What I did not realise at that stage was the effect it would have on my life, my career and my family. The next three years would show me another side of human nature to which I had not been exposed to before. I would see rampant ineptitude in an organisation which I had the highest regard for, and which essentially controlled the medical fraternity in this country. It is an organisation, which decides the rights and wrongs of our profession and dictates the ethics of behaviour among the doctors. Over the years, the council had written the tenets of every doctor's do's and don'ts. Over the next three years, I would see how it treated everything it stood for with blatant disregard for the effects it would have on people.

I would also experience a new emotion and feeling of being treated as a criminal without being tried for any crime. The helplessness of fighting a behemoth of an organisation would hit my face at every step. I would see differing attitudes and changing behaviour of people around me. The next three years would show me facets of life, which I had only read about in novels and watched them unfold in movies, but never had experienced before. I would find out who my real friends are and why they are my real friends.

3. The Nightmare Begins..

I remember the day very well. It was just another ordinary day, which was coming to a predictable end. As the BBC Evening News finished the telephone rang. It was one of the girls phoning from the Accident & Emergency Department. They had been visiting each other in their respective universities when one of them had taken seriously ill.

When the call came through, my daughter had already been given morphine, and for obvious reasons, I wasn't allowed to talk to her over the phone. This was a reoccurrence of an ongoing, mysterious complaint, but this time it was serious enough to warrant hospitalization and further investigation.

On hearing the eventual diagnostic test results, we were immeasurably concerned and set off without delay early the following morning. Fortunately, she was in a stable condition for the moment but required surgery. She was booked in as an "Urgent" procedure the next week rather than as an emergency that day. Her Senior House Officer recommended that in the interim, she should have absolute rest and to stay away from any stressful situation. We decided to take her back to Seaport and bring her back to hospital the following week for surgery.

As we walked slowly to the car park, there was a phone call from none other than Clark, the Chief Executive of the hospital.

'Hi Upaas. This is Clark. Where are you?'

'I am in Oxford, Clark. Is there a problem?' I was a bit surprised by his questioning.

He wanted to know where I was as apparently my colleagues (the four consultants – Pakshar, Serpe, Carmit, and Foster) had come to see him at lunchtime to complain that I had left the fracture clinic unsupervised! I was shocked, to say the least! I explained the situation to him, and he was extremely sympathetic and said not to worry. I called Stanley to find out what had happened in the morning. Apparently, he had requested Pakshar to send his registrar to give my middle grade doctor a hand explaining the situation to him. Instead of giving my middle grade a hand, they had gone to see the Chief Executive complaining against me. He was taken aback as he had apparently explained to Pakshar about my daughter's illness and my emergency trip to Oxford. He also knew that there were plenty of people to give a hand in the clinic.

On my return, I called Pakshar into my room, confronted him with the issue of his complaint to the chief executive, and asked him if Stanley had not explained the nature of the situation to him. His answer was 'Yes, he gave some cock and bull story of your daughter's illness' and walked out. Things deteriorated from then on and became unbearable. I discussed the issue with my chief executive and said the situation may improve if I step down. He was quite adamant that if I stepped down, it would be a 'moral victory for the troublemakers' and will not achieve anything. He insisted that I stay on, and try to salvage the situation as best as possible. He offered to help in any way he can. However, the situation did not improve, and I was getting more and more frustrated. I discussed the situation again with a couple of my other colleagues and resigned as a Clinical Director of the department.

The same year we went home to India for holidays during December. The day I returned to work, I had a phone call from the chief executive asking me to meet him urgently. I went to the meeting with some trepidation as I did not know what to expect. As I entered the room, I was surprised to find it full of senior management including the director of human resources and the Medical director. That got me even more worried. The chief executive explained that he had received a phone call from the Regional Adviser in surgery regarding a complaint from Serpe. He went on to say, that he will have to investigate the matter as the complaint is extremely serious about high complications rates for my patients and that I was not in clinics and not supervising junior doctors. I was devastated and speechless for a moment. I did not know what to say. After a lengthy pause, I said that I thought the allegations were baseless and welcomed any investigation the trust wanted to undertake into my practice. I also went on to say that he could have access to my database of all the joint replacements done by me in the hospital. Both the chief executive and the Medical Director reassured me that they were not suspending me at that stage, as they were not concerned for patient safety. I would be informed of the progress of their investigation in due course. I asked all the correspondence from Serpe and the Regional Adviser, to be given to me and informed them that I would be taking advice from the Medical protection Society and the British Medical Association. They appeared to be quite content with that option.

As it turned out, the British Medical Association was not tremendously useful in this instance. I received a rather bland statement informing me that the issue was to do with the Medical defence organization. Just to think of how many thousands of pounds I had paid the BMA made me furious. I had been a member ever since I started working over twenty-five years ago and paid my dues diligently. First time I had asked for help and I get a cold shoulder! The least I expected was some guidance from an organisation, which professes to represent you, is a bit of advice. As usual, such organisations I find are filled with politically savvy doctors who are not particularly successful at what they do and are there only to build a career outside medicine and only looking at stepping up the ladder. I was so disgusted with their attitude, that I cancelled my membership immediately.

Serpe was well known through the region as a senior orthopaedic surgeon, and had developed some reputation as a teacher, and 'do-gooder' of sorts. He had the reputation of performing a complex operative procedure for children with severe leg and hip deformities, which made them virtually wheel chair bound. The procedure was complex and developed by a Dutch surgeon, which allowed the children to walk with prosthesis. It was widely believed that he was the first one (and probably the only one in the country) who could do the procedure. Only later, I found out that it was all a remarkably well fabricated story. The procedure was performed by his colleagues along with the help of the Dutch surgeon. As far as I could find out, his participation was admitting the patient under his wing. For this procedure, he was awarded a Variety Club award. As it turns out, he was eventually made a Professor without a chair at the local University. I am sure there would be fascinating stories behind how he managed to get the title. He had retired from service at his hospital, and his request to extend his contract was turned down by the Trust. He had left the hospital under a cloud and under rather unpleasant acrimonious conditions. It was much later that I found out that he had changed for the worse, since his health problems started, and he needed surgery. The term used by his colleagues was that he had "regressed" and was making outrageous decisions on patient management and was restricted in his practice by the trust management.

We were looking for someone to fill a vacant consultant post, when we found out that he had just 'left' a locum appointment at South Side. Two of our colleagues happened to have been his trainees in the past, and they suggested that we should appoint him to the vacant post for a short term. Unfortunately for me, I agreed with them, and arranged with our Trust Management to arrange for his appointment. That was the start of my troubles.

Within a few weeks of starting working with us, we found the behaviour of my colleagues had changed to a significant extent. None of the consultants would attend the morning meetings, and it transpired that there was a regular gathering of Serpe and his three cronies at his local pub every week. I am sure this is where they started to plot against me. Two weeks after the appointment, the Medical Director of South Side called up our Medical Director and said that Serpe had been asked to leave and again under a cloud. It is typical of our so-called leaders at the top – he would not put that down on paper and he went so far as to say that he would dissociate with any statement linking him to that fact. Serpe had goofed up a knee replacement operation and it had to be revised within a couple of days. The clinical director had reported him to the Medical director, and Serpe was allowed to operate only under supervision. Unfortunately for me, this did not come to light till very late after his appointment. Things gradually deteriorated within the department. There was a gradual polarisation, and I did not get any support in running of the department from my colleagues. Serpe turned out to be extremely manipulative and rather malevolent person. He took both of his apprentices under his wing and added a new younger consultant to his clan as well. The four of them gathered every week at his local pub and obviously the younger colleagues minds were gradually being poisoned by Serpe.

It was not too long before Serpe made his first complaint – to the Medical Director about my 'clinical practice'. The allegations were made to the Medical Director verbally backed up with a written statement. I was informed of the allegations, and I was told that to be seen to be fair, all the consultants work will be investigated by our Senior Nurse Manager, who had just returned from working as an Audit Facilitator for two years. I thought, who better than someone trained in audit. All the consultants work was audited, both clinical and operative. This showed that I was obviously doing the bulk of the work, but the complications were less than everyone else. It also showed that I was seeing many more patients per clinic than my colleagues. This also showed that Serpe's practice was seriously flawed. However, this finding was obviously not what they looked for and disappointed the lot of them. When the Medical director informed Serpe of the findings, he was not particularly pleased. He was also warned of his clinical practice, which did not go down particularly well. I am sure this had something to do with Serpe going away to meet the Regional Advisor in Orthopaedics for further complaint. The persistence with which he pursued his malicious intent was phenomenal. He went through the theatre register over two years, struggled through numerous data sheets from the Theatre Surgiserver printouts and spiced up the figures and added a few imaginary cases of complications (some of the cases turned out to be his own) to produce a document of complaint to the Regional advisor. It took him nearly a year to do this. The tenacity with which he pursued this would shame the worst plotter in history of the dark ages.

The three junior consultant colleagues became his lackeys and yes men. None of them had a brilliant background, and I am sure they were trying to cement their position, and get rid of any opposition and possible threat. i.e. me. The biggest surprise to me of the triumvirate was Pakshar. This was a man who owed his career in this country partly to me, to say the least. I still remember the day when I went to see Prof Borgeoer in Stefan Port to discuss the possible return of 'Trainee Registrar' to our unit. He was extremely sympathetic to our cause, and he listened patiently to all the improvements that I had made in the department over the previous two years. He was particularly impressed by the training programme and assessment programme I had devised for the juniors in orthopaedics. He wanted my permission to use some of it in the Royal College Training programme in orthopaedics he was designing at that stage. He agreed to get the representatives from the Specialist Advisory Committee to do an interim visit to our unit for an assessment and reinstatement of training status to our hospital. As I was leaving, he asked me if I would do him a favour. He told me of this young orthopaedic surgeon in India who was struggling, and was doing menial tasks for his boss, despite having suitable qualifications and training. He wanted me to find him a job in our hospital. He gave me his Curriculum vitae, and I said I would do my best and left.

At the time, Joseph was the clinical director of the department. I met him the next day and debriefed him about my meeting with Prof Borgeoer. He was quite pleased that the Specialist Advisory committee would be doing an interim visit. I brought up the subject of a job for this orthopaedic surgeon from India. He wanted to know if I knew him personally. Obviously, I had to tell him that I did not know him from Adam, even less about his orthopaedic skills. However, we both felt that doing a favour to Prof Borgeoer would help us in our endeavour to get our training status back. We decided to take up the matter with our hospital management as soon as possible. We met up with Clark, our chief Executive the following week and discussed creating a job as an Associate specialist in orthopaedics for our department. We had spent a fair amount of time preparing a business case for the request. Clark listened to us patiently, and muttered a few objections about cost, and how we are way over budget, and should we not look to save some money somewhere. Some creative accounting by Stanley, our service manager, had created enough resource in the system for us to afford the new appointment. In fact, we were able to show that it would be beneficial to the department and the hospital if we were successful in regaining the training status through this appointment. He said that he would give 'careful consideration' to our request and let us know. Normally, in management speak, that is a 'no' in polite terms. However, we were quite surprised to hear three weeks later that the appointment had been passed by the central team and finance was agreed.

Both Joseph and I felt that the Training status was already in our lap. I rang Prof Borgeoer to give him the good news. He promised to let this doctor in India know and ask him to send all the documents along with an application for the post. It was about two months later; Joseph walks into my office holding on to a sheaf of papers from the Department of Labour and dumps it on my desk.

'What is this?'

He smiled and said

'We might have laughed too early.'

He was being cryptic. Joseph was one of those men, who are permanently pleasant, and it took a lot to unnerve him.

'The department of Work and Pensions want us to fill this exhaustive document before we can get this surgeon into the country.'

I said, 'Leave it to me Joseph. I'll see if I can get the form filled in' with singularly little knowledge of what is required to fill the long-winded form. He just smiled even more widely and wished me luck before going out.

It took me about half an hour to go through the first reading of the document. It was during the second reading when it dawned on me that we could not answer many of the questions that were being asked. Some of them were regarding probity, integrity, and skills that none of us knew anything about this person. It was nearly two hours later; I called Prof Borgeoer with a splitting headache and asked for his help. I put the questions directly to him and asked him if he would answer them. He very cleverly hedged the questions and gave me guarded answers, just giving me enough information to fill the form. I took the damned thing home and spent a few hours toiling over the form. Lopa was not impressed when she found out what I was doing. By the next morning, I had finished filling the darn form, and it was on its way to the Department of Works and Pensions, after being counter signed by someone in the personnel department. I had a rather uneasy feeling once it was sent off. I had committed myself to someone who I had never met before and did not know anything about. I had a long discussion with Joseph again the next day.

He tried to comfort me with, 'if he is good enough for Prof Borgeoer, I am sure he will be good enough for us. He would not sell us a pup.' Only now, we know how wrong he was and how wrong all of us were. I think it was august that year, when we saw him for the first time, as he walked into our seminar room brought in by the erstwhile personnel officer. She introduced him to all of us. He had one of those cheesy smiles and looked pleasant, if a bit quiet. 'Not bad at all' was the general consensus, except Dougie Speirons who said he did not like his smile. He was allocated to another consultant, Spock Gelts, to work with. He appeared to settle down reasonably well, and we breathed a sigh of relief.

The Specialist advisory committee visit came and went. We were duly given training recognition provided we increase our trainer complement by one more. That was typical of an establishment filled with self-appointed people full of self-importance and remarkably little substance. I would have a lot to do with similar kind in time to come. It was nearly two years later, when the men in ivory towers decided that they needed more trainee registrars, and in their wisdom said, that they will assimilate 'good quality' surgeons in non-career grades into the training programme at a higher level depending on the experience of a doctor. By this time, Pakshar had been working with three consultants in the department. All of them were reasonably impressed with his skill and knowledge, and it was again left to me to recommend him to the regional training committee for possible assimilation. I called Pakshar into my office and asked him if he would want to become a trainee registrar. He did not jump with joy but nodded his head. I gave him the relevant documents and asked him to fill them in. I asked him to go and meet the director post-graduate training in Seaport, and the head of regional Specialist advisory committee. Four weeks later, I found out that he had not done either of these. I asked Joseph to see the head of the Specialist advisory committee, and I went to see the Director of Post-graduate training. To cut a long story short, eventually, Pakshar was assimilated into Specialist Registrar Training Programme and he soon left us to work in different hospitals.

It was yet another two years before we heard from him again. This time he came into my office on one Friday morning, looking rather glum and depressed. I asked him what the matter was. Everything came tumbling out, slowly at first with gathering speed like an old steam train. The crux of a half an hour dribble was that he was being denied access to sit the 'exit exam' as he had not published any papers in any peer-reviewed journals. Without getting through the exam, he would not be able to apply for a consultant post anywhere in this country. He only had a few months to achieve this near impossible task before his training period finishes, and he would be left on a rubbish heap of 'failed trainees'. I tried to console him and dug out one of my papers, which had not been submitted for publication yet on Keller's arthroplasty for bunions. This was some work I had done a couple of years previously, and never got around to finishing it and submitting it. It needed minor work in the form of literature search and corrections before submission. I took him across the corridor to see George Cooley who had by then moved from University Hospital. I explained the situation to him and asked him if he had any outstanding papers that Pakshar could put his name to. He was understanding and said he did have a paper on the approaches to the elbow he had been working on for a while. Both papers were given to Pakshar to finish off and submit with his name attached to the work. Low and behold, to everyone's delight, both papers were accepted for publication within three months, and he was allowed to sit his exit exam. The rest is history, as one would say.

4. Comedy Of Errors

It was a wet September morning when I got a letter informing of the details of the Assessment. The details were rather sketchy and informed me that the assessors would interview my colleagues, four to be nominated by them and five by myself. I was not too sure what they were looking for, and who to choose. Back to Dr Smiths, from the MPS. He was particularly useful, and advised me to choose from as broad a range of specialties in the hospital as possible. I chose two of my consultant colleagues, one operating theatre sister, sister in charge of outpatients and my chief executive. Dr Smiths was quite pleased with the selection. I spoke to all these people personally and explained to them the situation. First response was one of shock from everyone. It slowly began to dawn on me that I was held with high esteem by almost everyone in the hospital. Notice the 'almost' and not 'all'. That was because I was to find out later that some of my colleagues had their own little agenda. They would not admit to anyone being better than they are. There had been more appointments to the cadre of consultants by now, and obviously, they were trying to build their own little empires. Anyway, they all agreed whole-heartedly to come and support me and give statements to the assessors and agreed to be questioned by the assessors.

The second part of the assessment was an initial interview and a final interview, where I could bring a 'supporter' with me. It also included a 'case based discussion', where they would choose a certain number of my case records, and I would be questioned on those. The last part of the assessment was something I could not understand. It was titled 'Core knowledge test' and it would be held in London. This filled me with considerable apprehension – it was seventeen years since I had faced any examination. Back to trusty Dr Smiths. He tried to explain to me what it entails. The more he tried more I worried I became. I had chosen George to come with me as a supporter for the interviews. I have to say something about George here. He was a very kind man, but absent minded like hell. If his head were not screwed on, he would leave it somewhere. It surprised me that he had not agreed to marry more than one girl at the same time. He is notorious for giving appointments for at least three people at the same time in three different venues. I had telephoned his wife to remind him about the interview and made sure that he had not given the same date and time for other people.

It was yet another wet Sunday afternoon. As usual, George was late coming in. He breezed in five minutes before the interview was due to start and we rushed in. There they were sitting behind a desk grinning like the three stooges. That was my very first impression and I had difficulty getting rid of that image from my brain. The girl from the GMC who had ushered us in introduced me to the chairperson and he in turn introduced me to the other two members. I introduced George to them to make it all official. It was all extremely friendly and amicable. A lady walked in a couple of minutes later, all apologetic for being late. She was introduced as well, as 'Lay assessor'. Within minutes, I was wondering what all the fuss was about. Wolf in sheep's clothing comes to mind at this stage. Little did I know how these people would behave later. They began by questioning if I were comfortable with their enquiries. A lion asking the sheep if it would be comfortable sitting on his dinner plate! They took me through my training, qualifications, my work environment, and my colleagues.

Dr Dawkins, the lead assessor, was a portly man who looked like he would be more at home behind a rickety old desk in a local government office, in a backwater town, in northern England than a Doctor. He appeared to have some difficulty in breathing and vocalising his thoughts. There was more than one occasion where I had to ask him to repeat his question. He introduced himself and tried to explain his role and his remit within the assessment panel. He was at pains explaining to me that he was not an Orthopaedic Surgeon and that his colleagues were the 'experts'. Among his mumbles was the fact that he undertakes a lot of such assessments and sits on quite a few administrative panels, for the PCT (Primary Care Trust). I started to wonder if he ever saw any patients to treat in his surgery. By the time, he finished introducing himself, he was beginning to sweat. He had that cheesy grin which looked more like an uncomfortable apology than a smile.

He went on to introduce Mr. Amoshin. He was not a complete surprise to me. When I tried to look him up in the Dr Foster's website, he came out as one of those failed orthopaedic surgeons who were clutching at straws by becoming a member of murky organisations and committees nobody would be seen dead in. He had somehow got himself on to Basic Surgical Skills course as a teacher and called himself to be on the faculty of one of the medical schools in London. It transpired that nobody had heard of him in that school, as he never taught anything. He looked like a little weasel trying to look important. I half expected to see him with a printer's cap and ink smudges on his fingertips and a smell of new paper! He looked exactly like one of those permanent Locum Staff Grade doctors who go around the country trying to earn a living. I had seen numerous such people in my own hospital and would not appoint them again, if they were the last one available. They would go from one job to another never getting better, never progressing and try to hide their blunders behind statement such as 'I was never given a chance,' 'I was discriminated against' etc. First thing that struck me was that he would not get a job as a staff grade in our hospital, let alone a consultant. I was to find out from his detailed CV later, and I was proven right in my assessment to a large extent. His claim to be an expert was that he had done some hip replacements several years ago as a Staff Grade. Now he was a retired foot and ankle surgeon.

Next on the table was Mr. Crouper, a retired Hand Surgeon. I nearly asked him how he found himself qualified to assess a Hip and Knee surgeon. I bit my tongue and held my thoughts to myself. He was introduced as the other orthopaedic expert. I was beginning to get the feeling that the GMC had an entirely different definition of an 'expert'. From what I could gather from the Dr Foster website, he had retired from service as a full time hand surgeon the previous year. His knowledge of hip surgery could not be more than my knowledge of hand surgery. He looked fairly benign, and he had 'old school' written all over his face. His demeanour was that of someone who had been forced to do this job. Only to find out how wrong I was later on! He smiled at me and looked away. Strange I thought. Was he hiding something? Why did he not want to make eye contact? Rather unnerving I thought and looked at George. George looked decidedly puzzled by then. I could make out that he was utterly bemused by the composition of the assessment panel. He was mouthing the words – 'Surely this must be a joke by the GMC.'

The elderly lady who came late was sitting in the corner of the table sitting rather quietly and trying to keep herself awake. Throughout the proceedings, she was twiddling her pen in her hand and decidedly looked uncomfortable and out of place. She was again introduced to me by Dr Dawkins as the 'Lay member of the panel' – a Miss Mildred. She turned out to be a retired Lawyer. She apparently had been involved in a few assessments in the past. He took pains to explain to me, that she was there, to make sure that there would be a 'balance' in the proceedings. To this day, I still do not know what he meant. She smiled and did not say very much.

By this time, I could see sweat pouring down Dawkins's face. He went on to try to explain the procedure for the 'Assessment'. He said the first part would be an Interview, followed by 'Third party interviews' of the colleagues, chosen by the panel and me. To be followed by a 'Case based discussion' and finally a 'Second interview.' He did not go into details of any of the segments at any time. It was only later that I found out that they should have explained to me every segment in detail before asking me any questions. It would be well into this nightmare before I fully understood the convoluted and bizarre nature of the way the GMC and its servants worked.

Dawkins began again with his cheesy grin,

'Mr. Kasyapa, let me reassure you that this is an exploration and not an investigation.'

I looked at George as I could not make out what he was trying to get at!

'Thank you. That is reassuring.'

The questioning started in earnest. It looked as if they were ticking some boxes and writing something down furiously. It was not until quite late in the process I was to find out that there should have been a short hand writer at that interview. I did not see any sign of a short hand writer in the room. I was wondering how the conversation was being recorded for future reference.

By this time, I was quite relaxed and thought this will be over before we know what is happening. All this effort and work was for nothing. Little did I know how things were going to unfold in a few weeks. Dawkins continued –

'Tell us Mr. Kasyapa, why do you think this has happened?'

I was not entirely sure how much they wanted to know and how much they already knew. I was not sure if I could mention names and situations. There was no guidance of any kind by either the panel or the GMC. I looked at George for some help and started gingerly saying how good the department was and slowly picked up speed as they kept writing and nodding. None of them lifted their heads for a while. I went on to say how I built up the department from a small unit of three consultants to large unit with eight consultants and how I had built up an international reputation not only for myself, but also for the hospital. I explained how I helped the hospital achieve the waiting list targets set by the government three years early, and how I managed to achieve the model of excellence almost single handedly with the help of George. I was getting into it, as they did not seem to want me to stop.

Once or twice, I could see Crouper lift up his eyebrows and once I saw Amoshin prompting me to go on. Gradually I switched my tack towards the whole situation being a witch-hunt, started by a colleague who was jealous of my success and worked in cahoots with a couple of my colleagues to bring this case against me. I tried to explain that this had been investigated by the hospital three times, and my name had been cleared. None of the panel appeared to show any interest in this. They had stopped writing down, and were just staring at me. Very disconcerting I thought.

Crouper started with my experience and training.

'Tell me Mr. Kasyapa, how your theatre day works. Give me a snap shot.'

I went on to explain how my theatre works – spoke about the 'team work,' 'all hands on deck' and 'quick turnaround time.' I tried to tell them how I could easily get through six total joint replacements in one days list. I could see Amoshin raise his eyebrows on more than one occasion during this soliloquy. He obviously was not convinced.

'Do you mean to tell me that you can do six major joint replacements in one day?'

He was quite astonished. I could see the way he smiled at me when he said that and turned to look at his colleagues with blatant disbelief. I was wrong; it was not a smile but a grimace.

'Yes Mr. Amoshin. And we did that routinely every Thursday.'

'Can you cope physically with operating on six joints in one day?'

Sarcasm in his voice was undisguised.

Dawkins was mumbling something by this time.

'I Beg your pardon' I piped up trying extremely hard to hear what he was saying.

'When I was working in anaesthetics before I became a GP, there was a lot of time needed between cases and we could get through only three major cases in a day'

Scepticism in his voice as he looked at his two 'orthopaedic experts' was obvious for everyone in the room. I could see Crouper nodding his head from the corner of my eyes. The little lady in the corner looked with wide eyes just like a rabbit in bright lights. She obviously did not have a clue as to what was happening. I looked at George for support and he was sitting there nodding his head vigorously. However, none of the panel was even looking at him. For all it mattered he may not have even been there. He was almost entirely ignored throughout the session. I was becoming a bit nervous at their incredulity at what I was describing as a fact of life as far as I was concerned.

Dawkins continued,

'Do you have the same anaesthetist through the day? And do you have the same team all day?'

Was he not listening to me? Was I talking to the wall or the table in front of me? I could feel my ears starting to get warm, and the hair behind my neck starting to stand up. I took a deep breath and said to myself (calm down, this will do you no good).

'Yes Dr Dawkins. I did say this in the beginning.'

Crouper piped in

'Quite extraordinary'

The questioning about the work in theatre did go for a while before they finally gave up. I nearly said that they should come and watch me do a list next Thursday. However, again I held my counsel to myself. I could see the look of disbelief when I told Amoshin that I filled in the data on to the National Arthroplasty database as well during the theatre work until recently.

'So, now who enters the data into the register?'

The sarcasm in Amoshin's voice was competing with the size of grimace on his face.

'Two Nurse Practitioners have been appointed to do this now' I replied.

'Where is the data kept?' Amoshin would not give up. He was positively smirking now as if he had caught me in the act. I could see George staring at him with such a disdain, that I was sure they would pick that up, if they saw his face.

'It is entered into a database on the internet and obviously stored by the National Arthroplasty Register somewhere safe'. I could not believe that he would ask such a question. It was quite obvious he had no knowledge of the arthroplasty database. He was just trying to show off to others on the panel. Unfortunately, even this reply did not wipe the smirk off his face.

They went on to ask me about questions on Audit meetings, Teaching and Clinical Governance. They wanted to know if there were any such meetings in the hospital and if I attended any of the meetings. At this stage, I brought up my own arthroplasty database of which I am immensely proud. It was my belief that it must be one of the very few such databases in existence in the country at that time. It had details of every joint replacement performed by myself since becoming a consultant orthopaedic surgeon in 1995. Follow up data was independently collected by the nurse practitioners and entered into the database. I was proud to say that I had almost complete data for over 80% of all my joint replacement operations.

'When do you enter the details into your database?' Dawkins questioned.

'In the theatre after every case as well as in my office for follow up data' I replied.

'What is your end point?' Amoshin again smirked.

'There is no end point for data collection. It is a continual collection of data and can be used for any audit one wants to conduct' I answered. I might as well have been talking to myself.

'But what it is your end point for your audit?' Amoshin, now with a grimace and 'now I have got you smile' looking around at others in the room.

'I repeat, there is no end point for a data collection. If I were doing an audit, I would choose either revision or failure as the end point for that audit. But this is not an audit data.'. I was getting more and more irate. They did not appear to differentiate between data collection and an audit. I do not know how many times I calmed myself down, and how many times I wanted to get up, shake him by the shoulder, and shout 'can you not understand? Are you stupid?' All I could see was that they were scribbling away on their notes, and there was no expression on any of their faces.

Dawkins had picked up the 'portfolio' the GMC had sent me to fill and return. There was certainly no guidance as to how to fill the 'portfolio' from the GMC. All it said was, if I did not understand, I should take assistance from the defence organisation. However, I had filled it in as best as I could do, and sent it off due to the unusually short deadline given by the GMC for return. I had assumed that they wanted to know if I had done all things they were asking me. Crouper went through some of the questions and downgraded some of the answers. I had to explain to them that there was no guidance for completing the 'portfolio' and I had filled it from my own back. I assumed that they had understood. Obviously, like everything else I had assumed wrongly.

It was getting quite late by then. Dawkins looked at his colleagues and raised his eyebrows and said 'Any more questions to the Doctor?' All of them nodded their heads to say they did not have any more questions. He turned to me and said

'I hope you are satisfied with today. We have no more questions for you for today but will have some more questions for you at the second or final interview. Do you want to say anything at this stage?'

I could see other three looked seriously at me. Throughout the proceedings, Miss Mildred had had singularly little to say, and was busy writing most of the time. There were hardly any questions from her.

'I would like it to go on record that this investigation is based on baseless allegations made by individuals purely out of jealousy and vindictiveness. And there is no basis for this investigation to continue.'

All they did was nod their heads. I simply carried on.

'I would like to know what exactly the 'core knowledge test' is, as it has never been explained to me by either you or the GMC'.

'Don't worry doctor. It'll all be explained to you in good time.' Dawkins concluded.

'I want to know how I should prepare for the test.' I repeated.

'You don't have to read any books or prepare. It is primarily about your day-to-day work at the hospital.' Dawkins responded.

Finally, he turned to George and asked him if he had anything to say. George was clearly taken aback by this as he was entirely ignored throughout the proceedings that day. He said he did not have anything to say. I suppose that was also a cue for us to leave.

As we walked back to the car, even George was deep in thought. I wanted to know what George's assessment of the situation was assuming that he would have some insight into such hearings. It turned out that he was quite bemused by the events of that afternoon as I was. He could not make any useful suggestions as to the outcome of the meeting. One thing we both agreed on was that the assessors were not giving anything away. In fact, we both felt that they made extremely light of the issues that were being discussed. I came away with the impression that this will blow away real soon, and I will forget the whole episode, as a bad dream.

George turned around as we reached home, in his inimitable style 'I think this is just a storm in a tea cup old boy. It will blow over.'

He did sound pretty confident. He came in to have a cup of tea and started to talk a little more freely. He felt that the Assessors looked like a decent lot, and they would understand that this was a 'put up job' as he put it, and I should stop worrying. When he left an hour later, I felt quite relieved and was more reassured than I was that morning.

It was quite late that night when I got a call from Salaam, an old friend of mine now working along with Pakshar in a neighbouring hospital. He had heard that Pakshar was going to give a statement to the assessors the next day. He offered to mediate between Pakshar and me, to bring some truce. He was prepared to work through the night. Apparently, he had been in contact with Pakshar several times regarding this issue, and had just spent a couple of hours with him discussing the question of propriety and integrity of being a colleague, and someone who had helped in the past. Pakshar had apparently finally promised him, that he would not go in front of the panel of assessors, to give any 'evidence'.

Salaam went on to say –

'Upaas, he is quite remorseful and was not very sure why he did what he had done in collaboration with others. I am sure if you talk to him, he may even change his statement.'

'That is not honestly going to help me now. He has done the damage and the wolves are at the door, baying for blood. It is too late for negotiations or discussions. If he wants, I am quite happy to talk to him' I retorted. I also said a few things about him, which cannot be printed here. Just before disconnecting the phone. Salaam said –

'Not to worry, he is not going to give any form of evidence tomorrow.'

It was nearly midnight when Salaam came back with the news that Pakshar did not want to speak to me. Salaam reiterated that Pakshar would not make any damaging statements to the assessors tomorrow.

However, that did not fill me with a great deal of confidence, as I was more familiar with the behaviour of the man than Salaam was. I firmly believe that once a man shows his true colours, it can never change, no matter what happens.

I went to work the next day as usual, got myself busy, and engrossed in a busy operating list and a clinic that afternoon. I knew in the back of my mind that my archenemies were being questioned by the assessors – both Pakshar and Serpe. Every time I thought about it, my heart used to go faster, and I used to get hot. It was pure helpless rage at how one human being can mean harm to another. I still have not understood the behaviour of some people, when they go out of their way, to cause harm to people. How can one sleep at night knowing full well that his actions that day might have harmed another human being, who has a life, feelings, family, and a career just like anyone else. I am yet to understand human behaviour of aggression against another human being. We are supposed to be better than animals in evolution and have power of thought and reasoning. How is it then that I get more loyalty and friendship and love from my dog than a lot of my fellow human beings?

The operating list that morning was particularly busy, and my mind was too preoccupied with my work to think about the assessors in the morning. There was no way of knowing what happened that day, in the old Greys Inn hotel, in Seaport. Tuesday was again extremely busy with outpatient clinics and meetings. There was a telephone call from the 'Panel secretary' asking me if I could come and review the case notes that had been identified, for the Case Based Discussion on Wednesday. This phone call came when I was in the middle of a clinic. As usual, the GMC had all the finesse and tact of a prized bullfighter. It was intriguing that the phone call came around three in the afternoon, and they expected me to drop everything and review all the case notes before five that afternoon! For me, all those patients, waiting for months to see me that afternoon, and again that evening mattered. When I tried to explain this to the Panel secretary, there was a kind of 'snort' on the other end of the phone. The nursing staff in the outpatient clinic sensed something was happening and tried to stay out of my way and make the clinic as smooth as possible. I had a rapport with my staff either in the outpatient clinic or operating theatre or even in the wards, which made me immensely happy to come to work every morning. I treated all of them as my friends and did not differentiate one from another. I could not understand some of my colleague's contention that they are 'staff and should be kept at a distance.'

One of my colleagues told me, that my downfall would be because of me being 'too nice'. 'They will take advantage of you.' 'You will not get them to do any work for you'. Finally, 'it can have a serious effect on patient care'. That to me is utterly incomprehensible.

When I said that I would not be free until late that night because of an evening clinic, the secretary just mumbled,

'In that case, you will just have to see them before the interview in the morning'

It was quite late by the time I got home that night after finishing yet another evening clinic finishing after eight at night. I was quite shattered and did not have much strength or patience to discuss the issues at home with Lopa. It was a hellish restless and fitful night. Even though I was extremely tired, I did not get much sleep that night.

I was expected at the hotel for 'case based discussion' for nine in the morning. I was there promptly to be faced with a large bundle of photocopied papers and x-rays. There were sheaves of pages – copies of few pages of notes belonging to 12 of my patients, some of whom I could recognise by their notes. They had given me an hour to get through all the notes and x-rays in an hour before they would question me on them. I was in no position to protest. I glanced through the notes and x-rays, to familiarise with them as much as I could do. I was not sure what I was looking for. The grilling started at about ten in the morning. It started to get interesting then. They gave me the same photocopies of few pages of notes and asked me questions on them. It was bizarre, to say the least. They apparently had found several pieces of records missing – clinic notes, operation sheets and pre-assessment notes. When I protested that I could not find them in the few pages that had been given to me, Mr. Amoshin retorted,

'We have had a good look at it, and we cannot find them. It is not there.'

My come back with that I would find them if they gave me full set of notes did not go down terribly well. There was a distinct air of chill as the questioning progressed. They were asking me about events that had happened ten years before –

'Why did your staff grade not discuss this case with you?' – An event, which had occurred about ten years previously.

'I cannot remember'

'Why did your middle grade ask for an x-ray of this patient?' pointing to an episode, six years earlier.

'I don't know.'

These are only two examples of the questions, which I had difficulty in answering without looking at the entire set of notes. The events in question had taken place from between six and ten years before! The whole process went on for the entire day with a short lunch break. It was extremely harrowing as they were asking me questions on patients with only half a dozen pages of notes in front of me. I had to guess at most of the answers. By the end of that day, I was utterly drained. If this was not an 'investigation', they were giving a remarkably good impression of it being one. I now know how those caught in the Spanish inquisition, felt like. One of the interesting things about the case based discussion was that there was no short hand writer to take notes. All four of them were busy scribbling copious amount of notes on large sheets of paper.

Something else became abundantly clear during the questioning. The knowledge of current day hospital working in general and orthopaedics in particular was non-existent, especially in the field of lower limb joint replacements. They appeared to have no knowledge of technique of joint alignment in knee replacements using jigs, without having to depend on the position of the hip. They had no knowledge of the audit process or statistical analysis whatsoever. They kept confusing data collection with audit, and my attempts to explain the difference was met with a bland stare, and I could see myself to be sinking more and more.

When it came to day-to-day handling of patients, I might as well be talking to a wall. They would not or did not want to understand the current practice in the hospitals up and down the country.

It was quite late that night, when I got a call from Salaam again, only to tell me that Pakshar had in fact gone, and he had given evidence to the assessors. It would be another couple of months before I got a transcript of what he said. Salaam had hoped that Pakshar would have given a positive slant on the events. I was not too hopeful. I knew by now that he would have vilified me to justify his association with Serpe. I still could not understand how the panel or the GMC expected him to tell them about my current practice, as he had not worked with me or seen my work for the previous three years. They should also know that he would be biased against me by his association with Serpe in the complaint received by the GMC. The only thing to do now was to wait and see what he had said in the transcript. I was not looking forward to the next day, for the supposedly 'final interview'. Partly because George could not be there as a supporter, and I had to depend on the highly unpredictable Peter as a 'supporter'. In hindsight, I think that was a big mistake.

On the next day, I picked up Peter from the hospital and made our way back to the hotel. I had many misgivings by now, but it was too late and there was no one else I could have taken on that day. Again, the interview started reasonably well with pleasantries all around. This time, the questioning was on day-to-day orthopaedics – management of wrist fractures, broken hips, and general management of patients. There were also questions about departmental policies. Throughout the process, Peter sat like a lost gold fish in a big pond. I did not think he knew or understood what was happening. He nodded his head a couple of times and did close his mouth once or twice. Towards the end of the session, I was convinced that it was a complete waste of time bringing him along as the assessors again paid scant attention to him.

Many of the questions were repetition of what happened on the first day, probably a bit more structured. They were more specific in their questions than before – How many cases did I operate on in a typical day? What time did I start? Who worked with me? etc. I could see from their faces that they had difficulty in believing my version of events that took place in our hospital. It was as if they had come from a system altogether alien to what happened in the hospitals up and down the country.

At the end of the session, there was the usual –

'Any more questions for the doctor?'

Followed by the negative nods by all, Dawkins turned around to me –

'Do you want to ask us anything doctor?'

'Yes. I do. You still have not told me what the 'Core knowledge test' is.'

Dr Dawkins smiled and looked at his colleagues, Amoshin had his sheepish grin on his face, and Crouper could not be bothered.

'We will let you know nearer the time. There is nothing to worry about. You don't need to read any text books and you don't need to do any preparations.'

Then he looked at Peter and asked him if he had anything to say. I would have been extremely surprised if he had anything to say. He had spent the whole time sitting with his head drooped to one side. He just nodded his head and it was time for us to go.

I dropped Peter off back at the hospital and made my way home. I could not make anything of the whole saga of this part of the 'assessment'. To me, it was like going through a grilling about my knowledge and practice, but the assessors kept on insisting that it was 'not an investigation.' I would never find out even after the end of this nightmare nearly three years later.

By now, the entire hospital knew what was going on, and I did not know what response I should expect when I went back to work. I need not have worried so much. It was as if nothing had changed. I continued working at the pace I had done for years, and everyone else worked with me as if nothing had happened. Unfortunately, this was not going to go on for a long time. About two months after the assessors visit, I had to go down to London for the next part of the assessment – Core knowledge test. It coincided with my visit to Vienna, and I had to travel directly from Vienna to London. It was my regular six weekly visits to Vienna, where I taught in the Department of anatomy, the technique of minimally invasive surgery in total knee replacement using cadavers. The course had been running extremely successfully for the previous three years. It had attracted from senior registrars and consultants to eminent professors of orthopaedics from across the world. The delegates for that meeting included two professors in orthopaedics from two eminent universities in Europe. I had spent the whole day demonstrating nuances of minimally invasive techniques, and discussed the learning curve and pitfalls in the technique, with the best in Europe.

I had booked myself into a hotel near Heathrow. Met up with both Sanvi and Shuchi as both appeared to have some free time. We did not discuss anything about the coming assessment and decided to ignore the whole thing as a farce.

Next day, I took a taxi to the GMC building in central London where I was ushered onto the third floor where the test was due to take place. I was quite apprehensive as I entered the building, which got worse when I realised that I still do not know what this test was about. At about ten in the morning, I was taken into a room by one of the faceless functionaries of the GMC. I was met up with the three assessors as well as the lay assessors. Dawkins's first words were,

'I am sure you know the format of the test?'

I looked at him astounded. I had no clue what the test was about as he had refused to explain to me what the test was despite repeated questioning.

'No Dr Dawkins. I do not know what the test is about. I did ask you several times during the interview, and you did not tell me.'

He looked at his colleagues and gave a wry smile.

'It consists of a written test followed by a practical test where you will be asked to perform some activities. The written test has two components, one for Core surgical knowledge, and the other for your specialty, which is orthopaedics. We want you to write your current practice in your hospital. We are not expecting didactic essays.'

He also said that the lay assessor will stay in the room, to answer any queries and that I could take more time than allocated if I wanted to.

I opened the question paper with some trepidation. I read all the questions and reread them to make sure. At the back of my mind was Dawkins's statement 'write your current practice in your hospital.' This should not be difficult, I thought. I answered all the questions as much as I could and still had some time to spare. I went through all the answers again to be sure. When I said that I had finished, the lay assessors took my papers away, and I was asked to have a lunch break with lunch provided for by the GMC. It looked as if I were a captive for the duration within the glass, and aluminium mausoleum.

After the lunch break, I met up with the assessors again to be told that I have to face two clinical scenarios with actors. One was a disgruntled patient whose operation had gone wrong, and the other was a patient waiting for a total hip replacement. I did not think either of them was difficult and handled both the patients with no problems. I thought the first one was an excellent actor, who was a very disgruntled patient with complications, after a minor operation, and wanted to know why he was not told of the complication. She was extremely irate and kept insisting that she would 'take this up further.' She wanted to know 'how many patients have been messed like me.' To top it, the clinical notes were missing. Despite that, I managed to calm the patient quite well. Once the two interviews were finished which were being watched by the assessors through a camera in a different room, I was taken to a row of cubicles with surgical stations.

Crouper appeared to do most of the talking, and he said that instructions would be given before each station. I had to perform the task that is set out for each station. It seemed straightforward enough until I started on the tasks. There were problems with almost all the stations. The equipment was inadequate with parts of them either missing or the wrong type. When I pointed this out, I was told,

'It has been noted.'

The tissues that I was asked to use, had dried up long ago, and were almost impossible to handle. A couple of the stations had procedures, which I had never even seen let alone done them, as they had nothing to do with orthopaedics. When I pointed this out to the assessors, I was asked to just -

'Complete the task the best you can.'

At one of the stations, it was nearly ten minutes into the test before the technician realised the equipment had been positioned upside down. The so-called experts who were supervising the test had not realised there was anything wrong until then. I was asked to leave the room, while they re-arranged the equipment – so much for the 'experts'. Here, I was being expected to show a flawless performance while the assessors themselves had made a serious blunder in the process. No one can question his or her incompetence or mistakes. Another thing that struck me was that there was no one recording any of the tests – no short hand writer and no recording of any of the events that day. It was essentially going to be my word against theirs. When it came to one of the orthopaedic tests, the most crucial part of the equipment, a camera, was missing. All they said was just

'Do the best you can'

I had to use a technique, which went out of practice about twenty-five years ago – doing an arthroscopy of the knee without a camera! The end of all the stations, I was taken into a room where all the four were sitting across a table. They asked me if I had anything to say about the way the day went.

'I am not entirely happy. Some of the tasks I was asked to perform were inappropriate. I had never done some of the tasks I was asked to perform today, in my entire life.'

I objected about the quality of the equipment and the type of equipment that was provided to me. All they said to all my objections was,

'We have noted your concerns.'

The whole episode finished by about five that evening. At the end of the day as I was walking towards Central train station, I felt extremely uneasy about the entire day. I had a distinct impression that I had been stitched up well and truly. The train journey back home to Seaport appeared to take longer than usual. I tried to read a book I had bought in Vienna airport, but could not concentrate. It was quite late by the time I reached home, tired and exhausted. I did not have the strength to discuss the day in detail with anyone. I went straight to bed after a bite to eat.

The next few weeks went by, when nothing happened, and I was beginning to think that it was all a nightmare, when a thick envelope dropped in through the letterbox one day from the GMC. It was over 100 pages long. It was the transcript from interviews, with nine of my 'colleagues'. I did not pay much attention to it first as I was busy preparing for some talks in Rome the following week. It was not until that weekend I had a chance to read the transcript. As I read the statements and answers from each of my colleagues at the hospital, it restored some confidence in humanity. As I read interviews with Serpe and Pakshar, worse was to come than I had figured. The lies that these guys were stating as facts stunned me and I could not believe my eyes at the content. Serpe went so far as to say that, he 'can tell a dodgy doctor when he sees one', and that I was a 'dodgy doctor'. What struck me was, that the assessors had not asked for any proof for any of the scandalous statements these guys were making. The outrageousness of some of the comments the two had made was beyond belief. Both of them had made criticisms about my work in clinics and operating theatres without ever being in the clinics or operating theatres with me at any time. Pakshar had shown his true colours. He had lied through his teeth at several stages of questioning. Reading his statement made it quite clear, that he was trying his best to destroy me. I thought back to that night before his interview with the assessors – he had promised Salaam that he would not make any damaging statements. It turned out that he had no intention of telling the truth either to Salaam or to the assessors. After I finished reading his evidence to the assessors, I lost all faith in humanity, at least temporarily. Here, is a man who owes his livelihood in this country to me, by all accounts, and he is making his best efforts to destroy me as his pay back. When one help another human being, the least one would expect was, that he or she would not harm oneself. To me this went against all the tenets of humanity and essence of human behaviour as I have been brought up to expect.

What struck me later was that none of the assessors thought fit to ask the all-important question – had they seen me examine a patient or operate on any one? Both of them had quite outrageous comments about my work and no one had asked them for any proof of any kind. There were statements such as, 'he was never in the outpatient clinics', 'all the decisions are made by nurses and junior doctors', 'nurses ran all the clinics', 'there is no teaching in operating theatres', and 'junior doctors are left with no supervision'. The fact that this was totally the opposite of the statements from seven other people who were giving evidence did not make a penny worth of difference to the assessors. It should have warned me at that stage that all this was just eyewash and the decision to punish had already been made.

Reading of the entire transcript of the interviews took me the whole of the weekend, and it took me two readings, before I could digest what was being said about me by my colleagues. It was heartening to note that all my present colleagues, particularly the nursing colleagues and doctors of other departments felt that they would have no hesitation in recommending me as their surgeon for themselves or their families. Some of the comments made by two contemporary consultant colleagues in the department were rather guarded, to say the least. One of them, was particularly cagey about everything he was being asked. He went to pains at length to make them believe that he was better than I was. The interview appeared to be more about him than me. However, it was probably my naivety that made me oblivious to this at the time.

It was gratifying to note that the Chief Executive had admitted my role in improvement to the hospital, and highlighted the fact that I had treated his family with excellent results. All of them, except the two complainants and the two consultant colleagues said that they would be happy for me to treat them or their families.

5. The Interim Orders Panel

It was six weeks before the 'assessment panel' produced its report. To say it was a revelation of how warped human thinking could be is an understatement. I could barely recognise the statements made by the report. My first impression was that the assessors had totally ignored all the witnesses who were working with me at the time, and taken the words of two disgruntled individuals who had not seen me over the previous three years let alone seen any of my work. The report was scathing about practically everything about me and my work. It was a statement by orthopaedic surgeons of a bygone era who thought every innovation was a product of evil.

Some of the statements made were so outrageous that I had to read them three times before I could believe what was written. The first reading of the long document was rapid, and not much of it registered. I wanted to see how it ended and what the conclusion was. I rushed to the end only to be utterly dismayed. They had failed me in almost every aspect of clinical care and assessment modules.

They had concluded that I was not safe and that patient safety was at risk. They had made draconian recommendations, which included that I 'cease operating immediately'. My heart sank, and I had to sit down to digest what was said, and try to understand the implications. What they had said was the realisation of one of anyone's worst nightmares. I was facing losing my job, which would mean lose my livelihood, lose my house and essentially everything I held dear to me. Being a doctor was the only thing I could do. If I lost my registration, there was nothing else I could do. This is a profession which does not allow one to train to be anything else. There is no time or the energy during your working life as a surgeon to learn any other skill. The quality of 'leadership skill' is so ingrained into you that you cannot accept any other job, which does not allow you to be at the top. Moreover, having spent nearly fifteen years at the top of the surgical ladder as a consultant had made me virtually useless for anything else. So many things went through my head at that moment that my brain was utterly jumbled. I had to clear my head fully and extremely quickly. It was crucial that I needed to get my brain back into gear to try and salvage the situation as best as I could do.

First thing to do was to find out the immediate implications of the report. That night was an exceptionally long and painful one. I could not sleep and could not get any rest. As soon as I thought it was a reasonable time, I called Dr Smiths at the MPS. I could not get hold of him until late morning. Luckily, I did not have any clinical commitments that morning. It was nearly eleven in the morning when I finally got hold of him. He had already seen and read a copy of the report. He tried to reassure me and was extremely sympathetic.

'I simply cannot believe this report. It is a gross miscarriage of justice. Do not worry we'll fight it and win.'

That was all very well, but I wanted to know what happens now. He said,

'What the assessors have said is their opinion of their assessment and their recommendations. It is up to the GMC to take whatever actions they need to take.'

I was still not clear.

'What does it mean to me now today?'

'Initially you will be asked to appear before an 'Interim Orders Panel' which may or may not impose some restrictions on your registration, before the GMC decides on your case'.

He continued.

'We will instruct solicitors who in turn will appoint a Barrister to represent you in front of the IOP. We will have to meet up before that to discuss the issues and take it forward.'

My concerns were still not entirely resolved.

'But the recommendation was for me to 'cease operating immediately?'

Dr Smiths was patient and tried to explain to me again.

'That is their recommendation, and it is up to the GMC to take any action if they want to. They may accept the assessors' recommendation or they may not. Your hospital will have had a copy of this report, and they also cannot take any action based on the report, as it is not the decision or recommendation of the GMC.'

That helped to settle my mind to some extent. The panel of assessors had looked at my practice and come to a decision, whether right or wrong did not appear to matter. It was an obscure Greek philosopher from the 6th century BC who said, 'Justice is simply advantage of the stronger'. I was just beginning to understand the power of the GMC, and this was my first step into the complex machinations of the organisation. Let me try to make it comprehensible if I can. When a doctor is referred to the GMC, it sends a team of investigating doctors to assess the complaint. The team or panel will report their findings, and the GMC then sends in a team of performance assessors, who will visit the place of work of the doctor, to assess the victim's work, and produce a report. This doctor now is referred to something called Interim Orders Panel, which control or regulate the doctor, while yet another panel called the Fitness to Practice panel, does its own investigating. At the end of it all, exceptionally few people understand what happened to them and even less have the will to continue to fight. Usually, one is totally demoralised at the end of it, and many doctors either leave the country or stop working altogether even if they are successful in clearing their name. This process has destroyed so many careers and families over the years that it can be seen as nothing less than a modern Spanish inquisition.

Dr Smiths continued.

'We will have to respond to this report at some stage. Not right now. We will see what the Interim Orders Panel does before responding to the report.'

'What do you want me to do in the mean time?' I queried.

'I want you to go through the report and let me have your comments on the report.' Dr Smiths replied.

That meant I would have to go through assessor's report with a fine toothcomb and write my comments on the report. Judging by the fact that the report went on to over 300 pages, it was going to take me some time. This task filled me with dread. I was not looking forward to it. I cancelled everything for the next three weekends to work on this. This was only the start of downhill trend of my income, which would accelerate extraordinarily quickly over the ensuing months.

That weekend, I sat down early Saturday morning to read through the report. It took me nearly four hours and several cups of coffee to do a thorough reading. By the time I finished, I was exhausted and thoroughly drained. There was a mixture of incredulity, anger, and despair at the end of it. I simply could not believe what I was reading.

I could not believe that they had failed me in Basic Surgical Skills test and the surgical knowledge written test. I simply failed to comprehend that they were saying that I lacked 'basic surgical skills'. How could I have operated on thousands of patients over the last twenty-five years or so, without serious mishaps happening all the time? I was being blamed for missing notes, missing typing and missing x-rays. Their argument was that, as a consultant, it is my responsibility to make sure that all these documents are available all the time. I should be not only looking after the patients and operating on them, but also look after the typing, file the typed letters into the records, get all the investigations reported, file the reports. I also had to make sure the nurses record their notes, check that the nurses, and other doctors have written in the notes, keep records, and make sure the x-rays do not go missing. The GMC was telling me that I should be a doctor, surgeon, typist, secretary, record keeper, porter, manager and stores manager – all in one. There was one place where they had criticised me for one patient not attending his clinic appointment. If my livelihood was not at stake, it would have been hilarious reading.

The recommendations were contradictory, to say the least. The first sentence said that, I 'should cease operating immediately' and then go on to say that I should keep a record of all the operations done by me. It said, 'Mr. Kasyapa is an extremely hard working doctor' and said he does too many operations. I was being criticised and punished for being hard working and honest. Overall, it was a damning indictment of all hard working doctors across the country. What it was essentially saying was that you do not have to be a good doctor as long as one records everything in the patient notes. They do not want you to treat many patients well. I was being told that I should not listen to patients requests for treatment if there is the slightest risk involved, even if the results of the treatment is excellent. I should refuse treatment for those poor individuals who had medical problems and deemed 'unfit' and 'risky' by others. Innovation is seriously frowned upon and one is punished for it. It did not matter that this innovation is being hailed as the saviour of thousands of suffering patients and is considered by everyone across the world as the way forward.

One Saturday morning, I sat down with the assessor's report on the floor with all the other documents from the GMC over the past year spread out in front of me. I was trying to see if what I did was wrong and where did I go wrong. I must have done something seriously wrong to fail this assessment. I tried to see what information I had been given by the assessors before the assessment, and what in fact, transpired. That was the first time when I realised that I had walked into a well-laid trap. The most obvious fact was that the assessors had duped me into believing that the written test was about my everyday practice. However, the assessment of the written test showed that the questions were from a professional Royal College of Surgeons exam and it needed preparation and response of a much more detailed exam style. Their statement at the time of the test was, 'write what you do in your hospital practice' was far from the truth. It took me two full weekends to go through the assessment. I found numerous faults, and at times incompetence on the part of the assessors.

Dr Smiths called a few days later to tell me who my solicitor and barrister were. My solicitor was from a firm of Smith, Gore & Sons, called Nancy Charlston and the barrister would be a Derek Bail. Nancy turned out to be an ebullient young lady, full of enthusiasm and always looking on the positive side of anything and everything. This was the start of a long and close relationship with several ups and downs over the following three years.

I drafted a response to my solicitors at the MPS and after several corrections sent it off as an email. They had made so many mistakes in their assessment that I did not have much difficulty in picking them off. The amazing thing was, in every aspect of their assessment there were significantly more positives than negatives, but they still considered them to be of concern or unacceptable. Some of the errors were so serious that it was beyond belief. They had picked up one case of reconstruction of a fused hip joint to a total hip replacement and said that it was something entirely different. As that procedure was rather rare, there were remarkably few done anywhere in the country. Nevertheless, the assessors felt that I had not done enough Revision hip replacement surgery and that I should stop all revision hip surgery. They had ignored the fact, which was clearly shown in my data, that I had done hundreds of revision hip replacement surgery, and I was involved in several large studies on the subject. This also highlighted the ignorance of the field of hip replacement surgery by the assessors. The catalogue of their blunders was so long that I could fill a book with it.

It was an exceptionally long response as I had dissected out every criticism made by the assessors, and was successful in destroying their criticisms – or, so I thought. It will become obvious much later how wrong I was. Nancy was quite impressed by my response and she, along with Dr Smiths, made some changes and sent it back to me for approval. This was duly sent off to the GMC. I was waiting for a reply from the GMC, which was not forthcoming, and I soon forgot all about it.

It was one of those wet and dark March afternoons when I landed in London, to meet my barrister before the impending IOP hearing. I was obviously quite stressed out, as I did not know what to expect. As I walked along the busy London streets towards the chambers, I was deep in thought and barely noticed the constant and slow drizzle. I was quite wet by the time I reached the chambers. I was ushered into a waiting room. It was not long before Nancy and Dr Smiths came along. That was the first time I met Nancy – in the waiting room of the barrister's office in London. As I entered the offices, I saw another lady sitting and waiting rather anxiously in the foyer. When I went to the reception to announce my arrival, she got up and introduced herself to me. I was surprised to see Nancy dragging this huge suitcase with her.

'That is a big suitcase! Are you planning on staying in London for a while?' I quipped.

Nancy smiled and said

'No. The suitcase has papers and documents for the case.'

That worried me even more. She looked at my face and tried to reassure me. We all went down the stairs through a singularly impressive looking old building, full of character and charm. Our barrister, Derek Bail was waiting for us. He had a fair amount of papers spread over the large conference desk in front of him. He introduced himself, and I must say he was everything I expected a barrister to look like. He was suave, smart and had an aura of authority around him. He started with reassuring me that he was there to help me and that he will do his best to help me with the process. We went through the assessors report in some detail over the next three hours. It was extremely painful to listen to someone else read the report where I was being crucified. By the time we were half way through; self-doubt had begun to creep in. There were times during that meeting I felt extremely distressed and defeated. I could not see how Derek Bail could convince anyone, that the assessors were wrong. We would be talking to lay people on the IOP mostly and certainly not to any orthopaedic surgeons. I suspect the barrister sensed this and tried his best to reassure me.

I said that I did not know what the IOP's job was. Derek Bail said they were 'watchman of the processes. They will consider the evidence and see if they can let the doctor continue to work while the GMC concludes its investigation. I wanted to know what the IOP would do or could do. Dr Smiths interjected at that stage.

'There are three options available to the IOP. One is obviously immediate suspension, second is to allow you to continue working with no restrictions, and the third was to continue working with some conditions on your registration. Obviously we will ask them to let you continue working with no restrictions.' He smiled as he said it.

I did not know the process of the hearing. I wanted to know if we could produce any witnesses. I was thinking that it would be like a court of law. I was so naïve I was still to be exposed to the unique methodology of the GMC soon.

'No. Unfortunately, you are not allowed to bring any witnesses.' Derek Bail explained.

I had a telephone call from my new chief executive, John Fitzgerald who had taken over from Clark about a year ago, as I was leaving to London that morning. He had said that he would like to come and give evidence in my support at the IOP hearing. However, this news disappointed me immensely. At this Nancy turned around and said we can request the IOP if they will allow Mr. Fitzgerald to make a statement. Derek Bail said that it was worthwhile exploring that option. It was nearly six by the time we finished the conference, and I walked slowly back to the station. The rain had stopped, but it was pretty dark and the streetlights were on. I caught the last train out of London. I had mixed feelings as I sat trying to read a book on the train. I could not concentrate on the book and felt utterly drained. I kept falling asleep through the journey and finally woke up as we were pulling into Durham station. I called up Lopa to see if she could pick me up from the station. It was quite late by the time I got in. I did not feel like eating anything that night and very soon went to bed to try to get some sleep. It was a hellish restless night with very little sleep. I got up the next morning with a splitting headache.

It was a couple of weeks before I heard from Nancy again. Apparently, the GMC had agreed to let my Chief Exec come to the IOP hearing. I passed the information to John Fitzgerald, who said he would be quite happy to come along,

'Anything to help Upaas. I think it is appalling what they are doing.'

The date of the IOP hearing came, and I was on tenterhooks by now. The hearing was posted for the afternoon, and I was told it should be finished by about four in the afternoon itself. I caught the morning train to London again to reach the GMC offices by lunchtime. This trip was becoming a routine now, and I felt like a long distance commuter to

London. There were nine hearing rooms at the GMC, and there were nine hearings going on that day. Nancy said, 'It is not unusual to have ten hearings in a day here.'

I was quite shocked. The number of doctors who were being subjected to this was astounding. We had to wait for the panel to finish an earlier case, and we were finally summoned into the hearings room at about two. It was a large rectangular shaped room with desks arranged in the shape of U. The Chairman was sitting at the head of the arrangement as it were with a secretary to his right and a Legal assessor to his left. There were two other panelists sitting there as well. The problem started as the chairman sat down and we all sat down.

He said, 'I can see a gentleman sitting in the visitors section. As you know this is a private hearing, and no one is allowed in.'

Derek Bail stood up and said,

'That sir is Mr. John Fitzgerald, the Chief Executive of the St Edward's Hospital trust who has come all the way from Seaport to support Mr. Kasyapa.'

'As you know Mr. Bail, we cannot take any evidence in this hearing. As it is a private hearing, that gentleman has to leave the room'. The Chairman would not have any of it.

'Sir, our solicitors have taken prior permission from the GMC for Mr. Fitzgerald to attend this hearing. He has travelled a great distance to be here to support Mr. Kasyapa, and it would be a great shame if he is not allowed to say what he wants to say'. Derek Bail protested.

There were whispered conversations between the chairman and the Legal assessor. We were asked to leave the room while they discussed the situation. It was nearly half an hour before we were allowed back in.

The chairman started again addressing Mr. Bail. He said that Mr. Fitzgerald can sit in the room in the visitors' gallery, but he would not be allowed to speak. He had noted Mr. Fitzgerald's gesture of support and that he would take that into account.

He then went on to introduce the panel and all the people sitting in the room. I was totally ignored. It felt as if I were transparent. The legal assessor spoke with a dry and droning voice reminding everybody what the rules were and what the panel is allowed to do. I was asked to say my name and the registration number, and that was the only time anyone spoke to me throughout the proceedings. I felt like a criminal sitting in the dock listening to the diatribe coming from the GMC barrister. The barrister acting for the GMC started and concentrated on the assessors report criticising my work and me. He was addressing the chairman all the time and never once looked at me. He called for conditions to be placed on my registration, to 'protect the patients and the public' and 'in the interest of the practitioner'. I would come across this statement of "practitioner's own interest" several times during the following three years.

I can never understand how a practitioner's interest is served by stopping him or her from working. It would also become quite clear to me, that the medical management could do anything it want with impunity if they use the term 'patient safety'. This term seems to me be like some magic mantra which can be used to whisk away all evils in healthcare. It is also a magic wand, which can be used to get rid of anything or anyone they do not like. This term is used across the board with some amazing results. This term has been used by individuals and organisations across the country to ruin numerous careers and lives. I suspect a proportion of the doctors affected did deserve it, and we do need someone to police the medical fraternity. There are doctors who get away with being less than perfect, and get away with pretty poor performance. Unfortunately, the system we have is not good enough or adequate enough to pick these poorly performing doctors. All it does is that, it throws an extremely large net where a large number of excellent doctors get caught, and there is no system of recognising these and to protect them. This reminds me of all those lovely dolphins, getting caught and dying in the fishing nets across the Atlantic.

Once the GMC barrister sat down, it was the turn of Derek Bail. He wanted to stand up to address the chairman, but he was asked to sit down to do his address. He did his best to defend me, by picking out the numerous faults by the assessors, and he highlighted the fact that they were neither qualified nor competent enough to judge me. He managed to show how biased the whole assessment process was, and pointed out the support I enjoy with my colleagues and staff, and stressed the fact that the chief executive had come down to London to support me. He asked that I should be allowed to continue working without any restrictions as the assessment was deeply flawed.

Once Derek Bail had finished, we were all asked to leave the room as the panel went into 'camera.' At first I could not understand what it meant. This was another term I would become very familiar with as time went on. We all trooped out to the waiting room and started to dissect the proceedings of the day. Nancy was decidedly positive and felt that there was no way the IOP would suspend me or put any restrictions on me. We spent the next hour waiting and drinking vending machine coffee that is so generously provided by the GMC. By the time we had all visited the loo, the third time, we were asked to go back into the room. As we all sat down, the chairman was reading some papers he had in front of him. He picked them up and just read the entire statement out. It was one of the most monotonous monologues that I had heard. The gist of it was that I was not suspended from practice, but allowed to practice with several restrictions. The panel wanted me to work with a named 'supervisor' and a 'mentor.' I was stopped from doing any complex surgery or revision hip replacement surgery. I had to attend a Basic Surgical Skills course run by the Royal College of Surgeons and work in an 'arthroplasty unit' for two to three weeks. I had to stop all private practice with immediate effect. I had to keep a record of all the operations I did, and produce a logbook signed by the supervisor two weeks before the next IOP hearing, which would be in about six months. These restrictions would stay on my registration for a maximum of eighteen months.

I was quite shocked and rather disappointed. It was probably because I did not know what to expect, and after Derek Bail address I was quite confident that I would be cleared. It was also probably because it had not sunk in at that stage that my career, and my future were at stake. Nancy was quite pleased, and said it was excellent news. She said that it was a good start for the process of defence, and she was quite confident that we could get all the restrictions lifted in time. John Fitzgerald sat there looking rather dumbfounded. The experience was all a bit overwhelming. All he said was, 'That was worse than the Nuremberg trials. At least the Nazis had a chance to defend themselves.'

I was not in any position to comment. I was a bit shell shocked myself. I could not understand how or why Nancy or Derek Bail were congratulating themselves. I had never imagined anyone would find my surgical practice to be anything but excellent, and I had just been told that there would be restrictions on what I could do and could not do. I did not see anything to feel OK about. I thought I had reached the pinnacle of my career only to be told that I have to work under a junior surgeon's supervision.

John went on to say, 'If there is anything I can do to speed the process of clearing your name, please let me know. I will do all I can. Let me reassure you that the entire trust board is one hundred percent behind you on this.'

He left us to ponder over his words, and I was extremely grateful for his presence, despite the fact that it did not make any difference to the GMC.

I thanked everyone and made my way back to Central station to catch the train back home. Once I was on the train, I started to think about the implications of what had just happened. The enormity of the IOP's conditions would not register for a while yet. I had hoped that this nightmare would stay private, and I could get through this without losing my name and reputation. Now it was all going to change. I was told that this IOP decision would be on the internet on open domain for everyone to see. The restriction on my registration would be on the GMC website. There was no way of keeping this under cover anymore. I did not know how to deal with restrictions on my private practice. I had a clinic at the local private hospital that Friday. My head was full of questions that I could not answer.

What would happen to patients who were coming to see me after recent surgery? What would happen to those patients who were due to have surgery the next day? What reasons can I give to my patients who are on my waiting list have their hip replacements revised? How can I face my colleagues and staff as well as patients with this smear stuck to my name? Who will look after my patients with complex problems? What would the Trust do with this restriction on my registration? I could not answer any of these or numerous other questions.

Suddenly it occurred to me that, at a stroke of his pen, the chairman of the IOP had taken away nearly a third of my income. I did not know how I would manage with this sudden decrease in earnings. It does not matter how much one earns, the expense catches up with one's income. With three children in university and a hefty mortgage to pay, my NHS salary was going to be woefully inadequate. It would be a few months before the effect of this reduction hit me. It was with a heavy heart that I reached home quite late that night.

6. The Humiliation Begins

When you are climbing a ladder of success, you never think you would be coming down, or you would have to do any of the tasks that you did on the way up ever again. Particularly in the medical fraternity, there is a set hierarchy and one does not naturally mix with junior doctors once you have reached the top. Consultant surgeons everywhere in the world are such a breed, that they depend on the juniors to do a lot of day-to-day looking after patients. It would probably come as a shock to the general public, if they knew how much, consultants depend on their juniors and colleagues from several other specialties for management of their patients. Now, I was facing a situation where I had to do the tasks, which I probably would have done with my eyes closed about twenty years ago.

First thing that happened when I got back to work, after that ordeal in London was that everyone was telling me what to do, or at least I felt that everyone was telling me what to do. All sorts of do-gooders materialised out of the woodwork. Self-styled leaders came around and set up an 'action plan group'. It had a manager, nursing officer, a director along with our clinical lead in orthopaedics and the clinical tutor in orthopaedics. They thought it would be 'good for me' and they will have to help me go through this period of stress with all their help. In fact, it was purely set up to keep an eye on me and my work. I had to sit in a meeting with this group once a month, and show them that I had been 'good boy'. Without as much as by your leave, they took over my clinics and lists. They had full control over my clinics and theatre lists. The theatre lists would be sent to the clinical lead every week for his approval, and the manager would keep an eye on the clinics. I had to record every surgical procedure I had performed and get it signed off by the Clinical lead who had been nominated as a 'supervisor,' even though he had been a consultant surgeon for less than two years. As to the clinical tutor who was acting as a 'mentor' less said the better. All these meetings and 'supervision' frustrated me enormously. However, when I sat down to think about it much later, I am sure they meant well and had my best interests in their hearts.

The upshot of all this was that the manager produced a 'report' after every meeting over the next two and half years. I must say this did come in useful later with the GMC. At the time I felt that the clinical lead and clinical tutor, both of whom were very much junior to me, took great advantage of the situation and made me feel small at every opportunity. It reached a stage of unacceptability when they suggested that I should undergo an assessment by them. That was the final straw. I met the medical director and asked the constitution of the group to be changed to reflect my seniority. After a painfully long negotiation, this was accepted, and the medical director himself agreed to be the mentor, and George Cooley who was much more senior to me as the supervisor. This made these interminable meetings be more tolerable than before.

One of the requirements of the IOP was for me to spend three weeks in an arthroplasty unit. When I discussed this with the Trust managers, I was faced with a blank stare. They did not have a clue how or where to organise such an attachment. I had to use my contacts across the country without being indiscrete to find a place for me to spend. Most of the senior arthroplasty surgeons across the country knew me as an 'expert' in both knee and hip arthroplasty. It would be an utter humiliation for me to ask for their help, and then to spend three weeks with any of them. After a lot of search and numerous telephone calls, my trusty friend Gautam managed to find a place down south of the country run by no less than the chairman of the regional training scheme who also happened to be one of the top hip surgeons in the country. I was lucky at the time that his research fellow had gone away for six weeks. He was one of the very few hip surgeons I was not closely acquainted with. When I started to get the paper work sorted to get there, I realised the bureaucracy involved. It took me four months of persistent phone calls and letters before I could get to my attachment in Marsden on Sea.

When I started to look for the Basic Surgical Skills course, I was quite surprised to find that there was a course almost every month somewhere or other. It looked like all the hospitals in the country were vying with each other, to run a course. I wanted to attend a course, which was as far away from home as possible, so that I do not run into anyone I knew. This is a course run for junior doctors setting out to become surgeons. They teach you the most basic techniques one needs to learn as a surgeon – such as suturing and tying knots. After sifting through various options, I trimmed it down to three centres down south of the country and sent off applications for registration. Eventually the selection was made for me by two of those centres cancelling the course due to lack of interest! I duly paid the fees, and waited for the course organisers to send me the course materials. When it did arrive, I was bemused to start with and then wondered why I am doing this. Going through the materials and the content made me realise that this was so basic that the junior most surgical trainees should be doing it. It was utterly humiliating to see the activities that were going to be taught to me in this course. The list of tutors made the feeling of utter humiliation worse – half of them were not even consultants. I was going to be taught by doctors, who were not too long ago themselves probably taught by someone like me.

I had managed to book myself into a hotel within ten minutes driving distance from the hospital where the course was being held. I was not looking forward to the course. I was filled with humiliation, apprehension and some trepidation. As I entered the ubiquitous 'Education Centre,' my feeling of degradation was utmost as I met some of the candidates registering for the course. Some of them were younger than Shuchi, just out of medical school. The introductions began, and I was trying my best to hide that I was a consultant elsewhere from others. The course chairman turned out to be a consultant vascular surgeon, who was most unlike the typical vascular surgeons that I had met before. She was kind, considerate and appeared to understand my position quite well. She was discrete throughout the course and so were the other tutors. However, this did not diminish the sense of mortification that I felt during that period. I was probably at my lowest ebb during that period. At the end of the course, there was a 'one to one' feedback session with the course chairman. She gave me my scores for the course, which were probably the highest for that course and was quite sympathetic towards me. It was odd that her sympathy did not make me feel any worse! My response to anyone showing me sympathy was to go completely into a shell and suffer in silence.

'I do not know why you are here doing this course Mr. Kasyapa. Judging from your performance during the course, you should be teaching in this course and not being taught. If you feel up to it, I would be gladly welcome you as a tutor in this course'. She said.

'Thank you very much for those kind words, but I will have to decline this time as I do have other commitments'. With those words, I bid her good bye and set off on the long drive back home.

I was home for just two days, before having to drive another 400 miles to the south coast to start my 'sabbatical.' I reached Marsden on Sea late Sunday night and had some difficulty locating the flat I had booked. The agent who had promised that he would be there was conspicuous by his absence. It took me half a dozen phone calls and a two-hour wait before he turned up with the keys to the flat. As we entered the building, I felt as if I had gone into a time warp, and landed somewhere in the sixties Britain. The lift had a metal gate, which had to be opened manually when the lift came down to get in. The decor of the lift itself was typical of the sixties with formica sheets covering the walls and a dull circular light with decals stuck on! As we reached the ninth floor and pulled the creaking metal gates open, we were in a dark corridor with musty smell and a solitary dull light with an art deco style lampshade. As the agent struggled with the keys, to open a rusty lock, I thought to myself, this does not look good. However, as we entered the flat, it was a pleasant surprise. It was quite a friendly, comfortable place with one bedroom, dining room/sitting room and Kitchen. There was a small, old fashioned box TV (must be one of the first colour TVs on the market), which did not have a functioning remote control and probably had broken a few years ago, soon after purchase.

Once the agent had taken me through the usual routine of showing how everything worked, I emptied my car. It was a nerve-racking event as the lift made such a racket every time I opened and shut the old metal gate. It chugged like an old steam train every time it went up and down. I thought this noise must have woken up everyone in the building. However, after four trips, there did not appear to be a soul in the building. It was an eerie thought to think that I may be the only resident in this old, ramshackle building. I half-expected ghosts to appear from the dark corners of the corridors as I walked down them. It was nearly midnight by the time I had warmed the food Lopa had given me, and sat down in front of the tiny television in the sitting room. I was thinking about the next day as I went to bed and did not get much sleep that night. It was unusually warm and sultry, and when I opened the window the fresh air was welcoming to start with. Soon I discovered that I was on the sea front, and the roaring of the rough seas was particularly disturbing. Instead of the gentle waves that would lull one to sleep, that night it was blustery and extremely loud. I was not sure what to expect from the new hospital or the consultant that I was to work with for the next three weeks. I had never met Mr. Bridge before and I did not know anything about the hospital, apart from the blurb in the website.

It was a bright and sunny morning when I reached the hospital. After parking the car, I started looking for the usual personnel department. It was not that difficult to find as the hospital turned out be a small one – a mixture of old and new. I was quite impressed by the staff. They had all my details, and it was not long before I had my photo identification badge, and a pass for the car park. I was not used to this efficiency in Seaport. Before I could sit down, Mr. Bridge was in the personnel department. He had come all the way down to welcome me! That certainly shook me. No one had shown me that kind of consideration in all my life. He was extremely kind and respectful. It was only later that I found out that he was the chairman of the regional specialty advisory committee for orthopaedics and advisor to the government,

British Orthopaedic Association among other things. He turned out to be an old-fashioned surgeon who was also one of the biggest hip surgeons in the country. I felt humble and deeply gratified in his presence. He took me around the department and the hospital personally and spent the whole morning discussing a lot of things. He took me to lunch in the hospital canteen, and we went to his outpatient clinic in the afternoon. It was such an enjoyable surprise to talk to someone who holds you in some respect. This was someone, who had never met me before, and he knew singularly little about me apart from the papers I had sent him in the post for getting a temporary job contract at the hospital. He treated me with equal terms and did not for a moment at any time make me feel that I had anything wrong with me.

After the clinic, we went across to meet his secretary, Ross who turned out to be another pleasant and remarkably efficient lady. She welcomed me to the office and showed me where Mr. Bridge kept his journals and books, and said I could come and use them whenever I wanted to. What a change coming from an environment of a pool of secretaries sitting in an office with no personal attachment. At the end of the first day I was content, and the turmoil in my mind had come to rest. As I drove back to the flat, I was reminiscing at what happened that day and I must admit I was relieved, to say the least.

The drive back to the flat was pleasant all along the promenade with the sea on my right side. I could see a number of surfers out as the waves were quite big and the day was bright and warm. I quickly got changed and went out on to the promenade for a long walk. As I walked east on the promenade, I reached the city centre and the pier with its amusement parks and gaming parlours. There was a gentle southerly breeze and the sun was shining down. There were a lot of young couples strolling along the promenade hand in hand mixed with retired citizens. It was such a sight to see these gentlemen with blazers, walking stick and golf cap, walking briskly along the promenade. Am I ever going to be like that? They did not seem to have a care in the world, as they weaved their way around the children playing on the walkway. There were a number of open-air restaurants selling everything from fish and chips and burgers to Chinese and Indian restaurants. There were cafes selling seafood cooked from freshly caught fish from the sea that morning. Lopa would love to come here, I thought. She loves fresh fish. I only wished Lopa was there with me. I thought with a heavy heart. It took me well over an hour to reach the end of the promenade, and it was getting dark. Therefore, I decided to trace my steps back. I could explore the city centre another day. As I walked back, I could hear the sea gulls in the distance and the sea was getting a bit noisier with higher waves. The bright lights of the pier came on and it was a fantastic sight to see. It was like Christmas in the middle of summer. Somewhere along the promenade, I could hear soft music wafting to my ears. Mixed with laughter of young couples and small children, it was amazingly beautiful and utterly peaceful. I took my time walking back, and relished every minute of it. As I neared the small park just abutting the promenade, I could see a band stand with a jazz band playing in the bandstand. It immediately took me back to my university days back in Bangalore. How many times I had stopped my bike in the middle of Cubbon Park to listen to a band playing in bandstand. This was a practice imported into India during the British raj. I had listened to brass bands, jazz, Indian pop music along with string quartets in the Cubbon park band stand on the way back home from the uni.

I stopped and decided to listen to the music for a while. The few park benches were taken by young lovebirds, and most other people were lounging on the grass. I found a dry piece of grass and sat down. The band was fabulous; particularly the guy with the trombone was excellent I thought. I could recognise some of the pieces they were playing and that made it even more enjoyable. The experience of listening to beautifully played jazz music with a background of the sound of the sea and the sea gulls now and then was out of this world. It is an experience that cannot be described, and it had to be experienced to appreciate it. My words are making an exceedingly poor attempt at describing an out of the world experience. It was past ten at night when they finished and I walked slowly back to the empty, dark flat. As I opened the creaky metal gate on the ninth floor, I suddenly felt rather lonely, and the entire place was eerily quiet. I sat down, tried to get the internet working on my laptop, and gave up after about an hour. I seemed to have taken the only spot in the south coast with no Wi-Fi access. I tried to read one of the books I had brought along with me, but could not concentrate. I finally gave up all attempts at being productive and went to bed around midnight.

It was just after five in the morning when I woke up. There was already bright sunshine peeking through the curtains, and I could hear the gentle waves of the sea. I quickly got changed, downed a glass of orange juice, and was on to the beach before you could say bless you. It was a fantastic experience not felt before at any time since coming to this country. There was bright sunshine, warm and hardly anyone in sight. The only things I could see were the sun, sea, and sand. I went for a long, brisk walk, and soon some joggers started to overtake me. The walk did me a world of good. It got rid of all the cobwebs from my brain and by the time I got back, I was tired and hungry, but feeling extremely fresh. I looked forward to meeting Mr. Bridge again, as we had a theatre list with one revision hip replacement to do.

It was just before half past eight when I walked into Ross's office. Ross had already been there for a while. As I sat down to look at some journals, she brought me a piping hot cup of coffee. That had never happened to me in the twenty odd years of my career in the health service. A few minutes later Mr. Bridge walked in all smiles. We walked down to the ward, to see the patient. By that time, the junior doctor had already consented the patient and marked the limb for surgery. It was obvious that the patient was immensely pleased to see Mr. Bridge. We looked at the x-rays and walked down to the operating theatre discussing how the case should be managed along the way. In the operating theatre, he introduced me to his other colleagues, nurses and anaesthetists as, 'This is Mr. Kasyapa, a leading arthroplasty surgeon from up north. He has come to see how we do things here,' He said with a smile on his face.

Not once did he mention it to anyone that I was there as a result of the decision of the GMC. We positioned the patient together talking all the time about the approach and problems we might face during the procedure. As he did the surgery, I was amazed at seeing the ease with which he handled everything, either instruments or people. The procedure took over two hours and went quite smoothly. Not once did he lose his composure or his temper, and it was a delight to watch him, and assist him. There were a lot of discussions during the surgery, and there was continuous give and take, during the procedure. Once we finished we went down to the coffee room, where I could immediately see the respect he commanded from every one. He sat down to write the operation notes and dictate the operative procedure. Within minutes, one of the nurses brought in a basket full of cakes, biscuits, and pastries. It was all overwhelming for me, and it took me back several years when the hospital service was as friendly as this. The camaraderie among the staff at all levels was particularly evident. This was an experience that would be repeated everywhere we went, wards, operating theatres or outpatient clinics. Moreover, it did not change during the three weeks I was there.

There were no commitments that afternoon and I went to the local supermarket to get some groceries. I had decided that I would cook some food that evening. There was the usual huge Tesco's just round the corner from the hospital where I spent an hour getting everything, including a couple of bottles of red wine. It was a pleasant evening with my favourite music from the lap top, delicious wine and beautiful weather. Once the cooking was finished, I went out again for a stroll along the beach and explored the city centre looking for an internet cafe. I spent the next hour browsing the net, checking my emails and answering them. The city centre itself was nothing spectacular and no different to any of the numerous mid size cities in the country. There was the usual pedestrian precinct with Marks & Spencer, Argos, and John Lewis among all the other shops mainly selling clothing and electronics. I thought it was disappointing after the walk down the pier the day before. I noticed a gym very close to the flat on the way back, and I walked in. It was rather dark and somewhat dingy. It reminded me of those places I had seen on the movie 'Get Carter' not too long ago. The people using it did not look as if they would be welcome in the Gentleman's Club in Oxford or Mayfair. It was a pretty basic gym, but did have what I wanted. I paid for three weeks membership and came back with a little piece of cardboard with word 'Member' handwritten and the edges curling in. It was probably a white piece of cardboard some years ago. Now it had some indeterminable colour – brownish black with a bit of green thrown in.

As I came back to the flat by about nine, the red wine had been left just about the right length of time for 'breathing' and was 'heavenly'. The food I had cooked tasted delicious as well, maybe because I was hungry by then. I spent the next couple of hours updating my files, and worked on a couple of research papers I was trying to write for a while. Wednesday was a 'free day' with no commitments at the hospital, and I had all day to myself. I had decided not to waste time during the three weeks, and I had set out a timetable for exactly these kinds of days. It would include the usual morning walk along the beach, visit the Internet cafe to check my email, work on research projects, and spend an hour at the local gym ending the day with an evening walk at dusk followed by a customary glass of red wine. To some extent, it was a godsend opportunity to catch up on all research projects that I had on the boil. By the end of those three weeks, I was ready to submit three papers for publication. I also finished writing protocols for the gait analysis project I had been thinking of for the past two years.

Shuchi's graduation came in the middle of those three weeks. I had been looking forward to that weekend for a few months now. It is not every day that your daughter graduates from Oxford. I was the proud father of someone who had the distinction having scholarships for three years in a row – a first in the history of Oxford! Lopa, Sanvi, and Akshaj came from Seaport, and I drove up from the south. Shuchi was tremendously excited, and so were we. This was one spark of joy in the midst of gloom and doom. All of us got ready in good time; even Lopa was ready on time probably for the first time. Shuchi had to go early for rehearsals, and we all stood in a queue to enter the hallowed halls of the Sheldonian theatre. As we shuffled along with all the other proud parents, we felt we were walking tall and swollen with pride. The whole assembly was quiet. No one was saying anything for fear of spoiling the sanctity of the place or the occasion. Once we were inside and took our places, we could not wait for Shuchi's name to be announced. I was ready with my camera to take pictures, and Lopa was ready with her video camera. The ceremony was brilliant and was full of pomp and circumstance. We went out for a celebratory dinner afterwards in the local restaurant. I made my way back to Marsden on Sea as Lopa and the others went back up north to Seaport.

Those three weeks that I spent with Mr. Bridge, was one of the most memorable ones in my orthopaedic career. In the outpatient clinics, we would discuss cases openly, and he would introduce me as one of his colleagues to his patients and all the other staff. He paid a lot of attention to what I said and took several suggestions on board. I learnt a lot from him, not only orthopaedics but also humility and humanity. Working with him in operating theatres was an eye opener for me. Most surgeons whatever field they are in develop their own way of doing things, from the way one scrubs to up to implanting prosthesis in hips and knees. I felt relieved and probably slightly flattered as well, to see that his technique mirrored mine in most ways.

7. The Hearing

I was not looking forward to the dreaded 'hearing'. There was a lot of 'guidance' and support from my friends. Messages from numerous friends wishing me well filled my SMS in-folder. My two daughters insisted that they would accompany me to the hearing for the first day. I changed the booking from a hotel room to an apartment. We (with Lopa and Sanvi) would set off from Seaport and Shuchi would join us from Oxford. Only Akshaj could not join us.

I had taken a week off for preparing for the hearing. I spent most of the time going through the assessment process report with a fine toothcomb, and managed to pick a few holes in their report. I went through my personal portfolio, which filled three enormous lever arch folders again and updated the logbook and the diary. The portfolio was now so voluminous that I was beginning to wonder that I might need a fourth Lever arch file. I had made up my mind that I would face the trial with an open mind and not dwell on it too much. I spent an hour and a half every day in the gym to get my mind off the intense concentration needed for the preparation. I found that it had 'burned off' the cobwebs that had covered my brain after a few hours of going through all the papers. I remembered one of my teachers during my college days telling me 'success in any project is to do with preparation, preparation, and more preparation'. I had decided a long time ago that this would be my leading project and wanted to succeed. I also remembered my teacher telling me that one needs single-minded motivation and an intense desire to win. The key for me is 'single minded motivation' and a wish to clear my name at all costs. I have now reached a stage that there was 'winning or nothing.'

There was a change of barrister for the Fitness to Practice (FTP) hearing. MPS had decided to go for someone much senior than Derek Bail and had appointed Fred Barnard. He was a QC (Queen's Counsel) no less and had well established chambers in London. He came with fabulous credentials and had experience of employment tribunals for over 30 years. Nancy had telephoned me towards the end of the week reminding me of the conference we need to hold on Sunday night with Fred, our barrister.

Nancy tried to be as reassuring as possible over the phone, and she was quite positive about the whole thing. I looked through all my files once more, and printed out all the numerous files I had created linked to the hearing. I remembered from previous outings that it was incredibly difficult to get any files printed once you are out there. I checked all the files, to make sure everything that I needed for the hearing was there. I took two of everything that I could duplicate as a backup. Gautam dropped in for a final briefing before the hearing. Between the two of us, we went through all the possible scenarios, and found there were certain issues that could be addressed by talking to his wife, Yadavi (special interest in epidural anaesthesia) She was a Consultant Anaesthetist at his hospital and Pavaki, Swaymbhu's wife (for assistance with perioperative management of diabetes), who was a Consultant in Cardiac Anaesthesia and Clinical Director at the regional Cardiac Transplant Centre. One of the criticisms from the assessment panel was that my answers in surgical 'core knowledge test' were wrong in management of post-operative pain. Both the assessors had criticised my comment on respiratory depression after epidural anaesthesia – called it 'dubious complication.' Yadavi produced numerous literature evidences to the contrary. Pavaki produced some detailed protocols for management of diabetes during the perioperative period.

We had planned to set off to Manchester soon after lunch. However, like every well-planned trip something did go wrong, the gremlins were at my GPS. The stupid thing decided to conk out just as I was feeding the hotel address in Manchester. I could not bring it back to life, however, much I tried. I had to ask Sanvi to get another GPS from the shops. We finally set off a couple of hours later. There was a lot of discussion about the whole process in the car and the way the investigation had been conducted. Both Sanvi and Shuchi were quite passionate about the unfairness of it all. Both of them had gone through the report and my analysis of the report at some length. Shuchi promised to look for a diabetes management protocol in surgery from patients coming in for surgery in her hospital on her return.

We arrived at the apartment by early evening, and I had to rush off to meet Nancy and Fred at the hotel. As I was driving into the car park, my mobile went off. It was Nancy.

'I was just wondering where are you were?'

'I am just entering the car park.'

'I'll come down to the lobby to meet you, and we'll go up to the meeting room.' Nancy replied.

The meeting went off quite well. As could be imagined I was quite apprehensive about the whole episode. Nancy put me at ease almost straight away by being confident about the outcome. Fred joined us a few minutes later. Nancy introduced me to Fred, and he turned out to be a fast thinking, and extremely clever gentleman of the old world. He would look to be well suited to be in one of Parry Mason's books. Both of them took me through the process of the FTP hearing. The way I understood was that it had three stages. The preliminary stage where there would be legal arguments between the two barristers on the legality of the FTP hearing. Fred took me through the arguments that he was planning to go through at the preliminary stage. The council had made so many mistakes in their own process of assessment, that neither Fred nor Nancy could figure how they could justify continuing with the hearing. The guidelines for performance assessment set out by the GMC, was quite clear in choosing the assessors – should be doctors practicing in the specialty that the doctor is practicing.

However, the lead assessor was a general practitioner, one orthopaedic assessor was a retired consultant in hand surgery, and the other one was a retired consultant in foot and ankle surgery. None of the assessors could be considered as 'experts' in hip and knee surgery. To top it, neither of the orthopaedic surgeons were currently practicing in orthopaedics. The assessors themselves had made numerous mistakes. They had not given me any information on the test of knowledge, had chosen two interviewees who had not worked with me for at least three years for the third party interviews, and a test that was set up was not geared towards a consultant orthopaedic surgeon with a sub-specialty interest in hip and knee surgery. As we were going through the 'disclosures' by the council, it turned out that the whole process was set in motion by a junior council caseworker. The reason they had given for referring me to the FTP was 'due to extensive concerns *raised by* Mr. Kasyapa'. When Nancy protested why I should be referred to the hearing for concerns raised by me, they had replied that the letter was a 'typographical error' and that it should be read 'due to extensive concerns *raised against* Mr. Kasyapa'. However, when all the 'disclosures' were looked at carefully, it turned out that the council officer had been less than honest all along. The series of emails made it clear that the case examiner (whoever he or she may be) was in a quandary at our protest, and appeared not to know what to do. It was quite clear in the emails released to us that the reason given in the first letter would be the right one. It seemed as if, 'how dare you protest at our process and you should be taught a lesson' I was being punished for raising concerns at their assessment process. It was assumed that one would bow to the almighty council, and tremble under their power.

Disputing their findings with a '95 page long document' is not the done thing. The caseworker said in his email to the examiner that 'Mr. Kasyapa has raised extensive concerns (95 pages long) and it is unlikely he will accept any conditions.'

We were understandably furious at the way the process had been carried out by the council, and Fred went on to say that he had never come across any organisation behaving in such an appalling way. Such behaviour would not be and should not be tolerated in a modern society. We discussed the various options available for us at this stage. Fred was quite clear that there had been an abuse of process, and the hearing should not go ahead, and if does it is a travesty of justice. He was quite firm when he said that if the FTP panel decided to go ahead with the hearing we should apply for a judicial review of the whole process. Nancy also felt the same, but said we should weigh up the options depending on the reasoning that may be put forward by the panel to continue with the hearing. She was being pragmatic, and I felt realistic. We needed to look at the situation taking emotions out of the equation. If the reasoning were bizarre, we should go for a judicial review. However, if the reasoning is not clear and fudged, as it usually is with the council, we should just carry on with the hearing as we are well prepared for it at this stage. Her point was that the judicial review would take at least another six to nine months, during which time I will be left in a limbo. The three of us finally agreed that we would regroup after the decision is read out before going forward. After that, we went through the emails once more before going on to the next stage of the process.

If the case progresses to the 'first stage,' it would be the case by the council who would be trying to prove that I was proven to be deficient by their assessment. They will call their witnesses, who in my case would be the three medical assessors. The three assessors will be examined by the council's barrister and cross-examined by our barrister. The council's barrister will be obviously trying to prove, that I was a 'poorly performing doctor' and he will ask for my registration to be curtailed or erased. He would bring out all the negative points as he sees it from the three assessors. It would be Fred's job to break down the witnesses and get them to accept, that they had carried out a flawed performance assessment and that there was no finding of proven deficiency in my performance. I had prepared an analysis of the entire performance assessment and picked out numerous holes and downright blunders by the assessment team. Both Fred and Nancy were quite impressed by the amount of work I had put into it and the results. At the end of the 'first stage' Fred was planning on applying for 'no case to answer'. The panel would then have to consider both the arguments and come to a decision whether the case should go on to the next stage, which is called 'impairment stage'. Both Fred and Nancy told me that the panel would have to deliberate for at least a day to come to a decision.

If the panel decides to turn down our application and go ahead further, we will have to bring in our witnesses. I will be questioned by Fred followed by cross-examination by the council's barrister. Curiously, I looked forward to that as I felt that I might get a chance to purge this feeling of 'un-cleanliness' that has surrounded me since this nightmare began. It would give me a chance to show the world (or at least the council) what I am, and how wrong they all are. I had had a feeling all along, that I had been victimised for my own success, and remarkably few people, if any, did recognise what I coul do, and achieve. It is not a feeling of helplessness, but rather frustration at not being able to make people understand my capabilities. There were a lot of comments from my well-wishers about 'not being a conformist' and not falling within the 'bell curve'. I could never understand why one should be criticised or not accepted if one falls outside the 'bell curve'. Every new invention, idea, progress in history has been achieved by someone working outside the bell curve. My contention was that one would develop into a well-established mediocrity by staying within the bell curve. Ever since, I found what I was proficient at, I have been striving to improve and set an extremely high standard in my achievement. I was prepared to work extremely hard for it and was willing to make sacrifices.

The meeting with Fred and Nancy went on till late at night. I was tired yet refreshed after the meeting as I felt that there was a sense of direction for everything that was happening now. I felt much more positive than before about the outcome of this ordeal. On the way back I called Gautam and we had a long debriefing. It is always reassuring to talk to him. I have always found him to be level headed, and one of the very few men who could think laterally, and at the same time get an overview of the entire situation without asking too many questions. It was a quality, which is quite rare, and often misused by people in power. He can look at the issues and come up with an analysis and more often than not a solution, which is not always visible at the outset. It needs an extremely sharp, analytical mind and forward thinking quite akin to a chess grandmaster.

By the time I got back to the apartment, Lopa and Sanvi had scouted the area around our apartment, and managed to get some take-away for a late dinner. We sat around the food and went through all the discussions that we had a couple of hours earlier. Lopa was a bit apprehensive about the judicial review with good reason. She sees most things in black and white and does not have a concept of the world being gray and rather amorphous. She was a remarkably strong person and had singularly rigid views of rights and wrongs about everything and everyone. She was the first one to warn me of Pakshar at the very first meeting. She had stood by me at all times, and got frustrated at not being able to understand the machinations of the council, or the legal process of this country. Justifiably she could not fathom how such a process can exist in a 'normal' society with clear-cut rights and wrongs! The discussions went on till quite late into the night.

Shuchi had not managed to get away from her work in time to reach Manchester that night, and she would join us in the morning. Sanvi had the whole itinerary for the next day well planned, as Shuchi can never be relied on for day-to-day planning. Sanvi has been here for me encouraging me at times of lows with fighting talk. She is someone who is probably more sensible and realistic than others in such matters. For some one of such tender age, she was showing maturity that surprised me at times. She is extremely sensitive, and I had always felt giftedly clever. She grasped the situation quite quickly and started to analyse various options with skill of a barrister. She felt that the council might not opt out at the preliminary stage as it may have disastrous consequences to them. It was finally agreed that we would wait for the nature of decision and the reasoning behind the decision before we could take it any further. I was tired and fell asleep the minute my head hit the pillow.

8. Day One; Monday, 28th April 2008

The built-in alarm woke me up at the usual time of five in the morning, but I stayed in bed till after 5.30 ruminating over the previous night's discussions, and the coming day's events. I had never seen the council building in Manchester and was not looking forward to seeing it either. I looked through the map, and made sure I knew where I was going. We set off on foot, as Nancy had told me that it would take about ten minutes. Lopa and Sanvi would pick up Shuchi from Piccadilly station and join me at the council offices. I had warned them that if they came too late, they would not be allowed inside. It just shows how little I knew about the extremely lethargic speed of the workings in the council.

As I turned the corner into the street looking for St James' building, I was a bit taken aback. It looked like one of the city centre streets with lots of eateries and shops.   It was not what I expected for the regulatory organisation of all the doctors in the country to be situated in. It is more suited for a shopping complex or at the most, offices for some commercial organisation selling insurance or stocks than headquarters of a regulatory body. It was not long before I spotted St James's building as I scoured the facades of all the buildings on either side of the street. St James's Building was built by Clegg, Fryer & Penman for the Calico Printers' Association in 1912. Built in the so-called 'baroque' style, it is an enormous seven-storey building (it contains 1000 rooms) it is clad in Portland stone, with 27 bays opening directly onto Oxford Street. It has an equally large central gable entrance with rising classical orders, broken pediment and topped by an octagonal lantern.   The frontage of the building was entirely covered with cafes selling sandwiches and pizzas and shops selling sweets and cigarettes.   The entrance to the building itself was reasonably impressive with an imposing marble staircase and a rotunda in the middle of the foyer. I was even more taken aback when I found out that the council occupied only a couple of floors of the building which also had, as I had surmised, companies selling insurance and finance brokers.   Once you are inside, it is just like any of the numerous government offices – drab and dull with a claustrophobic effect the government buildings are so adept at specialising in.

At the reception, I was given a 'visitor' badge with GMC written all over it and asked to go to the fifth floor. As I got out of the lift at the fifth floor, a nondescript, looking office reception faced me. There were two receptionists with all the interest and enthusiasm of an undertaker's attendant sitting with pencils in their mouth and an extremely bored expression on their faces. I announced myself and after briefly looking through their little 'diary,' the girl announced, 'You are here for the hearing, Dr Kasyapa.' loud enough for the people on the street to hear. I felt myself cringe with humiliation and an intense desire to throttle the receptionist. One thing that had become abundantly clear to me about the council was that you were a criminal until proven otherwise from the minute they receive a complaint. You are treated with contempt and made to feel insignificant. They will go out of their way to destroy one's self confidence, and a belief in oneself. I suspect they get training from the lowest menial to the president of the council, in abject humiliation of their 'subjects'. It is done in such a way that one begins to admire the subtlety sometimes used in humiliating one, and it has been crafted into a fine art.

I was lead into a glass-fronted office set aside for 'the defence' where Nancy and Fred were already waiting for me. The room had two large windows with locks broken and facing a derelict area at the back of the building, on either side of the Manchester canal. Nancy handed me a copy of the skeleton argument that Fred was going to use that morning. I skimmed through the document and was quite impressed with it. He had used examples of previous cases in courts of law, and had used what I thought was, an exceptionally strong argument for not continuing with the hearing. There was a veiled threat of a judicial review if the panel decided to carry on with the hearing. He had not minced his words in the document, and some of the cases he had quoted made me feel that the panel had to be either too stupid to understand, or too brave if they decide to go ahead. When I voiced this to Nancy, she said that more surprising have happened in the Council before.

Lopa and the girls joined me, just as I was getting worried that they would not make it on time. I need not have worried. The starting time came and went with no activity whatsoever. Nancy saw me fidget and she showed me the coffee machine down the corridor. I got myself a hot chocolate and a cup of coffee for Lopa. At long last we were called in, and we all trooped into the Hearing Room 4. I looked at the clock; it was close to ten in the morning. Most of the first hour was spent waiting around in the defence waiting room drinking coffee and hot chocolate, wandering up and down the corridor. I could see several people in the same predicament as I was. There were numerous secretary types wandering in and out of rooms carrying clipboards and 'looking busy.' I could easily make out who were the doctors in the same situation as I was – stress written all over their faces, repeated coffee trips and toilet visits. As time passed I saw some men and women in dark suits pulling along small suitcases slowly walking into the corridor smiling and cracking jokes. These were obviously the 'panel members' of the nine cases that were going on that morning. None of them appeared to be in any hurry even though most of them were already half an hour late for the morning start. They were all trooping into a large room marked 'Private' at the bottom of the corridor on the left. Staff in kitchen uniforms were seen to be going in and out of that room with cookies, pastries, donuts, croissants and fruit. It looked as if they were partying in that room. I would not have been surprised to find bottles of wine in there.

If I say that it was a farce of epic proportion from the beginning, I would not be exaggerating. After the preliminary welcome, Mr. Barnard said he had some preliminary arguments. I could see the look of surprise on the panel members faces. They wanted to know if there is a written 'skeleton argument'. Mr. Barnard handed a copy for each member of the panel. Lo and behold, they wanted to have a break to read it before Mr. Barnard could proceed with the case! I was beginning to think we were in a comedy musical. We were asked to leave the hearing room, and they went into 'camera'. I would hear a lot of this 'going into camera' over the coming months. All of us gathered our papers again and trouped back into the waiting room. It had lasted six minutes exactly.

Before I proceed, I better give a picture of the panel members and the hearing room. There were about nine hearing rooms on that floor, as far as I could make out. The hearing room we were allocated was a rectangular shaped room with broad windows along the entire length of one wall. The tables were organised in a 'U' shape with the chairman sitting at the head of the table along with a Legal assessor and the panel secretary – very similar to the set up of Interim Orders Panel. On either side of the end of the table were the two other panelists. There were name boards in front of all of them so that we could read who was who. That is there being a name board in front of everyone except myself. I would realise soon that any doctor that comes in front of such a panel was treated as guilty, and it was his/her duty to prove otherwise. I sat with Fred and Nancy at one end of the table, and the GMC barrister sat opposite to us. A short hand writer was sitting at the end of the table on the left of the GMC barrister. There was a small table and chair in the middle of the 'U' for witnesses to sit. On the tables there were sheaves of paper and exceptionally large lever arch folders. All along the back wall you could see more papers and folders. At the far end of the room, there were chairs for the visitors, which often included gentlemen of the press.

What can I say about the panel? The Chairman turned out to be a retired Philosopher – I could not figure out what a 'philosopher' did as an occupation? He was a mousy little guy whose eyes kept darting from one corner to another when he was not dozing. He always looked worried. His eyes darted from one end of the room to another, never looking at anyone in particular. That was when he was awake. We would see him nod off a number of occasions during the coming days of the hearing. It turned out that he was a lecturer in Philosophy before he retired. The GMC blurb said that he was an 'experienced panelist'. All that meant was that he had sat on a lot of panels. Whether he had any training to do this work, is an entirely different matter, and I would have been surprised if he had any training.

The second panelist was O'Neil – a General Practitioner from Scotland. He was also described as an 'experienced panelist'. We all took an instant dislike to him. He had this cheesy Cheshire cat grin on his face permanently and looked positively slimy. You would not buy a second hand car from him. He spent most of the time staring at the witness, as if to undermine the witness whoever it was, and scribbled little notes to the chairman. The chairman made it clear to everyone on numerous occasions, that he was the only medical member of the panel.

'He is against all doctors. He was a medical expert in a case last month, and he crucified the doctor on stand' Nancy said. 'He sits on a lot of panels and is also on some committees in the BMA.'

Let me get this right. This man sits on GMC panels, does performance assessment and sits on BMA committees. So when does he get time to see patients? The picture that was emerging was all too familiar. He is one of those committee animals who would be extremely uncomfortable in a clinical setting. His experience of a hospital set up in general, and orthopaedics in particular, would be next to nothing. We would see his true colours as the hearing progressed

The third panelist was introduced as Reverend Barker. Another retired gentleman – this time a retired lay preacher. He was also said to be an 'experienced panelist'. What he knew about patient management or hospital orthopaedic practice is anyone's guess. He had the typical beer-drinker's face with alcoholic blotches all over. He reminded me of the tubby Friar Tuck from the last Robin Hood movie. We all assumed that he would be a harmless bystander, as he spent most of time trying to stay awake. We had seen him carry what looked like bottles of wine in shopping bags into the dining room, on more than one occasion. It may have had something to do with his tendency to fall asleep.

The legal assessor was a lady sitting next to the chairman often whispering in his ears. She appeared to be a dour large lady with a severe lack of sense of humour. The role of the legal assessor was said to be an impartial observer of the proceedings, and there to provide advice to the panel in matters pertaining to legal issues. She is ostensibly there to see that all the rules of the GMC and the law of the land are adhered to.

The panel secretary is one of those busy bodies we see all the time in hospital corridors. Those ubiquitous managers walking up and down the hospital corridors with clipboards and files in their hands trying to look busy and influential. She appeared to spend half the time sitting writing things down furiously in her notebook and the other half typing something in the computer, which was set in one corner of the room. I never found out what she was typing during the entire hearing. The rumours on the web were that these panel secretaries double up as GMC officers and they write out the determination of the panel before the hearing start, and the chairman reads it out at the end. The hearing is only a show, and it does not matter what has been said or shown during the hearing. At that stage, I found that hard to believe to be true.

The GMC counsel was someone with an unfortunate name of Bill Sykes. He did impress me considerably. He was tall and suave and knew his stuff extremely well. He always spoke in a measured tone and never once appeared to lose his composure during the entire hearing. He was always polite but firm. We all felt that his arguing style was rather uncomplicated but in the end highly effective. He knew the panel and the people in the panel well. Where Fred Barnard was addressing a court with a senior judge in a high court, Bill Sykes was addressing a lay panel with remarkably little knowledge.

In the corner of the 'U' configuration was the Short hand typist who sat through the hearing. There were at least ten of these who took it in turn. There appeared to be some recording device in front of them, as well as short hand typing device on the desk in front of them. The only time they ever spoke was when they could not hear what was being said, or did not understand what was being said.

There did not appear to be any one helping the GMC barrister. We never saw the GMC lawyer appear at any time during the entire hearing. We could see him scurrying along the corridor copying documents and getting faxes etc.

The young lady who was the GMC usher came into our room. 'They are ready for you now' We followed her down the long maze of corridors back into the hearing room. That was when I noticed the sign outside the door, 'Cameras not allowed. Recording devices not allowed.' Once we were all seated, the chairman began 'The panel now has read the skeleton argument. Mr. Barnard, if you would like to address us please?' and looked at Mr. Barnard.

'Sir, thank you very much. Sir, as you know, this is a case concerning an assessment panel report, which is the substance of the evidence that the GMC seeks to rely on.' He continued and asked them to look at the copies of correspondence from the GMC. He directed them to look at the letter from the GMC referring my case to the Fitness to Practice (FTP) panel, and asked them to open the document titled 'case examiner's rationale'. He read out a paragraph in the document, 'Due to the extensive concerns _raised by Mr. Kasyapa_ the case examiners consider that the case should be referred to Fitness to Practise Panel for consideration'. He added, 'They are not relying on the findings against the doctor by the assessment panel but by referring to the concerns which he himself had raised' looking at the chairman.

'Sir, then the solicitors, Smith, Smith, and Gore, for Mr. Kasyapa probed that. They wrote a letter of 25 September, which you will find at page 10. In the second paragraph:

'We write to seek clarification in respect of the case examiners rationale. Which of the concerns raised by [the doctor] have caused the case examiners to determine that the case should be referred to the FTP?

In making this determination, to what extent has the substance of the concerns raised by Mr. Kasyapa, been taken into account?'

We note that in the case examiners rationale no reference is made to the points of substance raised in the letter from Smith, Smith and Gore to the GMC dated 13 July.'

Fred was getting warmed up. He then directed them to look at the response by the GMC case examiner. He was flatly refusing to discuss the issue'

'It is not for me to try and interpret that decision and offer you further clarification or request the case examiners provide me with further reasons. I regret I am unable to assist you further with this matter.'

He then pointed to the letter by my solicitors, to the effect that the rationale was, 'irrational and impermissible' which also threatened the GMC with legal action if a valid reason is not given. He was getting into his element now. Pointing to the internal correspondence within the GMC, he asked them to open the letter from the GMC secretary to the Case examiner asking them 'They have particular issues over the reasoning behind your decision to refer him to a FTP panel due to the concerns he raised over the performance assessment'.

Nancy had been busy over the previous few weeks, trying to get all the internal documentation from the GMC, using the Freedom of Information Act. Unfortunately, the GMC had released only about 40% of the documents hiding behind some obscure law set out in 1963. Even the documents that were released had large chunks blacked out. Fred asked the panel to read the response from the GMC secretary where it said that, the case examiners would not change their decision. However, they would like to change the wording in one of the paragraphs 'the first sentence of the final paragraph should read:

'Due to the extensive concerns raised <u>against</u> Mr. Kasyapa the case examiners consider that the case should be referred to Fitness to Practise Panel for consideration'. The secretary had just changed the word 'By Mr. Kasyapa' to 'against Mr. Kasyapa' thus changing the rationale completely around. He then directed to copies of some emails that we had been successful in getting using the Freedom of Information act. He pointed out to the email correspondence between the secretary and the case examiner –

'The GMC has lied to this Panel.

The basis of it appears to be an e-mail, which you have not looked at before, at page 14.

Mr. Harrison, having e-mailed the case examiner or examiners on 10 October in the terms that we just looked at page 13, the response is at the top of page 14:

> 'Dear Stephen
>
> Perhaps it would have been better to state 'due to extensive concerns raised against Mr. Kasyapa the case...' Can we discuss on Wednesday before replying.'

He proceeded to demonstrate the cover up within the GMC using copies of several letters and emails. There was one letter, which was rather telling of the way the GMC worked.

' . that the third person, 'Kasyapa,' has been converted to the second person, 'you.' It is not clear to us how this comes to be a referral from the investigating officer to the case examiners when this page would appear to be a set of charges against the doctor based on a decision which the case examiners must have previously made..'

This makes it quite clear that the GMC secretary had already made the decision and was asking the case examiner to rubber-stamp it. I was beginning to understand the hierarchical structure of the GMC now.

Fred went on to show several documents where it was quite clear that the decision to refer me to the FTP had already been made and they were trying to justify their actions. He highlighted the fact that the GMC tried to cover its tracks in several documents where they had simply used the 'cut and paste' feature.

He was looking at the Chairman when he said, 'Sir, in our submission, a referral to the Fitness to Practise Panel on the grounds that the concerns raised by a doctor, in his Rule 7 response, to an assessment report, challenging the qualifications of the assessors and the way that the assessment report was done is entirely legitimate for the doctor but entirely illegitimate for the GMC to cause that to be a basis of a referral to the FTP.'

The chairman sat impassively, O'Neil was staring at Barnard with that grin fixed on his face, and the Reverend was trying to stay awake. Fred had been talking for nearly an hour now and I was beginning to worry as to how much of all this was being absorbed. Fred was suggesting that the panel should call the GMC secretary and the case examiner to take a stand and explain their actions to the panel. He pointed out that the case has not been referred to the FTP using legal means and that they cannot continue to hear the case as it was illegal.

'If the allegations are not referred to you in accordance with these Rules you cannot entertain the case.'

He then went on to quote several cases to support his argument and said that it is irrational to continue with the hearing of this case, as the GMC did not have anything apart from the performance assessment report, which was over a year and half old. The cases of note were

'*Krippendorf v GMC, Cohen v GMC* (where the present chairman was involved as chairman of the panel and was severely reprimanded in the high court at appeal) and *Meadow v GMC*. The GMC do not have any further evidence to produce and that the panel cannot decide whether the fitness to practice is impaired. According to the GMC rules, 'The FTP Panel shall receive further evidence and hear any further submissions from the parties as to whether, on the facts found proved, the practitioner's fitness to practice is impaired.' He pointed to the fact that 'Is impaired' and not 'was.' He was trying to show how illogical it would be to see if someone's fitness to practice is impaired based on what happened in the past. He pointed out that despite the fact I took exception to the conclusion drawn by the performance assessment report, I complied with all the conditions recommended by the assessment report. He asked them to look at the interim orders panel report at the last three sittings for confirmation of the compliance.

By now, Fred had been on the go for over an hour and a half. The panel chairman as well as the reverend, were finding it hard to stay awake. He finished his submission by saying 'Sir, I am sorry to have gone on at such length but those are our two preliminary points. We invite the panel to, as it were, stop the proceedings there.'

The legal assessor wanted some clarifications from the submission after which the chairman asked the GMC counsel to make his submission. Obviously he would be opposing any moves to quash the hearing vehemently.

'Mr. Chairman, I'll need some time to digest what has been said and prepare my submission' Bill Sykes said.

We all could see the huge relief on the chairman's face as well as the reverend. It was finally agreed that there will be a short recess of 30 minutes and we were excused. As we walked back to the waiting room, I was quite buoyant and felt that the case was as good as finished and we should be going home that evening. As we entered the room, I said to Nancy. 'What do you think Nancy? I thought Mr. Barnard was brilliant. I cannot see how Bill Sykes can beat that one.'

'I have seen stranger things happen before. We'll just have to wait to see what Bill Sykes has to say.' Nancy was being a bit cautious I thought.

'Who appoints and pays the panel and the legal assessor?' I wanted to know.

'The GMC appoints the panel and pays them,' Nancy said with smile on her face 'I know what you are getting at.'

'Exactly. How can the accuser be the judge and the jury? If the panel is on the GMC's payroll, why should they give a decision against the GMC? They will be doing themselves out of a job in future.' I was flabbergasted.

'I understand Upaas. It is completely unreal. It does not occur in any other profession. But we can only hope that this panel is independent in its thinking and decision making.' Fred Barnard added.

'What happens with barristers, Mr. Barnard?' Shuchi interjected at that point. She was looking completely bewildered at this revelation.

'They are reported to the Bar Council and are investigated and examined by an independent judge. I have worked with other professions such as the police and similar thing happens. It is only in medical and nursing professions where the investigation and judging is done by their own regulatory body.'

This was not good news we wanted to hear at this stage. I was beginning to have second thoughts about the outcome of today's hearing even before GMC's submission. I cannot see why the panel would cut the hearing short, as they will be out of a job tomorrow. This is said to last two weeks and they will lose the whole two weeks salary. For a retired lay preacher or a retired philosopher that is not an insignificant amount of cash.

We had our customary trip to the coffee machine and waited for the usher to call us. When we walked back into the hearing room after the break, we could see Bill Sykes looking very serious and he had a pile of papers under his arm. He obviously been had talking to someone at the GMC and has had his instructions how to proceed with the case. With the information gathered from Nancy and Fred, everything looked different to me. The room looked different and the panel members and the secretary looked different. They no longer appeared impartial or independent. I did not see the point in continuing this charade as the decision was already made. We might as well go to the next stage.

The chairman asked him to start when he was ready. The counsel said that he would hope to use 'tempered language' with a wry smile on his face.

'With respect to Mr. Barnard, I think to fling around accusations of lying to the panel and deliberately misleading the panel are not appropriate unless there is a very powerful base upon which to do so and which there is not here.' Bill Sykes went on. 'Secondly, this panel has no power to act as a tribunal of review over a case examiners decision. You are not a court of appeal and you do not sit as an administrative court reviewing either Registrars' decisions or case examiners' decisions.' For a minute there, I thought he was having a go at the panel. He glossed over the obvious blunder by the GMC in changing the wording from 'by Mr. Kasyapa' to 'against Mr. Kasyapa' in less than 30 seconds! He completely ignored that crucial fact that the GMC had tried to mislead blatantly in writing which was supported by the internal correspondence, which was so well highlighted by Fred. He concentrated instead on the assessor's report. His argument for the case examiner's rationale was

'. the assessment team had decided, not only was, in certain areas of his practice, a bad surgeon, but was in fact, a danger to the public posing a risk to patients.'

He claimed that when the case examiner saw that conclusion he had no other option but to refer to the FTP. According to him, it was not only legal but moral as well. One of the tacks of his argument was that our lawyers had more than enough time to go for a judicial review to stop the hearing and which they have failed to do so. He conveniently forgot to tell the panel about the delays by the GMC in releasing the internal memo, which was the basis for our claim to GMC misleading everyone, and in fact, that it was released only after a threat of legal action under Freedom of Information act. The odd thing about hearings in GMC is that there is no place for argument. Fred Barnard could not stop him and point this out at this stage unlike a court of law. His argument failed to have any substance as far as I could see. He managed to elongate his argument by referring to an obscure point in the law quoting a case of *Peacock*, which he claimed was similar to this. I for one could not see any relevance whatsoever in the case he was quoting. The only thing that came out of a long discussion of that particular case was that the judge did not allow a petition because it was late.

He spent some time on saying that I would receive a 'fair trial' and that we are claiming that there would not be a fair trial. I failed to see in which part of Fred's argument this was said. He went on to claim that I have not fulfilled all the recommendations by the assessment team, despite the fact that he had not allowed us to produce the portfolio of evidence to show that I had. He concluded by saying again that the panel had no powers to stop the hearing and that the case should continue.

It was getting close to lunch and I could see all of them looking at the clock on the far sidewall. The chairman looked at Fred.

'Sir, may I make my reply? Would you prefer it after lunch?' Fred said

'If you are going to be longer than, say, 15 or 20 minutes then

perhaps.' The chairman had a cheesy grin on his face.

'No.'

'Then we would like your reply now, if you are prepared to give it now?' The chairman said reluctantly.

He went on to show the rules where it clearly states that the FTP does have the power to halt a hearing in 'exceptional circumstances.' He then went on to point out the delays by the GMC to answer our queries, which made it impractical to go for a judicial review. He again stressed the mistakes made by the GMC and the cover up. He tried to clear the point about fairness of trial

'I do not say that the doctor cannot be fairly tried. Of course, he can. This is a fair panel and it will try him fairly, no doubt'

When he came to the subject of the use of assessment report by the GMC counsel, he was clearly angry and his face was red –

'Mr. Sykes says that he is not going to argue that the defendant could not put in material to show that he had fulfilled the conditions and so on. It is unreal. It is clear what this case is about. This case is about the criticisms made by the assessors and whether or not the doctor has satisfied those criticisms. That fact is simply not in issue. Mr. Sykes has not challenged the evidence which the GMC have had which I see now was before the interim orders panel. The GMC has been in possession of the numerous letters from his employing authority, from his mentor, from his workplace supervisor and from the consultant with whom he did the sabbatical for three weeks, the time period prescribed by the Interim Orders Panel. It has had the certificate of completion of the basic skills training course. All that material has been furnished to the IOP Panels.'

Fred stressed on the fact that the GMC was in possession of all the material supporting our submission and still insists on continuing with this. He reiterated the reports that I have had from everyone universally –

'He did satisfy the conditions. He did undertake the basic skills course. He did take the three weeks sabbatical where he was placed with Mr. Bridge in Marsden on Sea to observe. There is a letter from Mr. Bridge showing that he was entirely satisfactory and Mr. Bridge was so satisfied that he would be happy for Mr. Kasyapa to operate on a member of Mr. Bridge's family. Perhaps you ought to have that material.'

However, the GMC counsel as expected objected to the panel seeing that material. He also objected to the panel considering the three Interim Orders Panel reports, which clearly had agreed that I had fulfilled all the conditions. That is yet another strange anomaly in the GMC. There appear to be many different organisations within the GMC and none of them talk to each other and none of them agree with the others decisions. This has to be unique in the entire world.

At this stage, the chairman wanted to know if there were any other matters, to which both the panelists raised their hands. Both of them were picking at the grammatical mistakes within the GMC correspondence suggesting clearly that the cover up was not a cover up but a mistake by an employee of the GMC! It was becoming increasingly clear to all of us that the result here was predetermined.

The chairman said that they would give the determination after listening to the legal assessor's advice after lunch. He said, 'We'll adjourn from now until 2.15.' Both Sanvi and I looked at each other, and the clock. That is an hour and half lunch break. In three and half hours of that morning's session, we were actually in the hearing room for around two hours. If we ran the health service this way, most of the hospitals in the country would grind to a halt and the NHS budget would be twice as much.

Once we were in the waiting room again 'There is a nice sandwich place round the corner where we normally go. You can bring them here to eat if you want' Nancy said.

'What do you think Nancy?' I was still curious to know even though I had given up hope of getting a fair decision.

'Judging by GP and Reverend's questioning, I suspect they have already made their decision' Nancy was looking decidedly unhappy.

We were all very quiet as we walked down to the Philpot's sandwich shop round the corner from St James' building. There was a long queue and took us a while, what with Lopa's 'fast' decision making to chose her sandwich and get back to the waiting room. The lunch was a quiet affair as we all had a lot to think about. It was nearly 2.30 when we were called back into the hearing room.

The chairman asked the legal assessor to carry on with his advice. It was short and she appeared to hedge her bet. She did not say that the panel did not have power to stop hearing the case, but said that '.. so far as I can see from the rules there appears to be nothing preventing this panel, if they decide to do so, from hearing this case.'

There were a few questions and answers between the legal assessor and the GMC counsel. It looked as if Fred had become weary and decided to let go by then. A few minutes later the chairman said

'Thank you all. The panel will now go into *camera*. I am afraid I have no idea how long this is going to take. If we see that it is going to take a while the panel secretary will get a message to you.'

That was about three in the afternoon. They made us hang around until four before saying that we had been excused until next morning. There were several things that occurred to me that day. The amount of time wasted in these proceedings was astronomical. A maximum of three hours were spent that day in actual work. Secondly, as far as the FTP panel was concerned, I might as well have not been there. I was not acknowledged even once by anyone from the GMC after the front receptionist let me in. As I said before, once a doctor is reported, he or she is treated like a lump of meat and he gets scant respect and is treated as a convicted criminal. The most important and rather worrying thing that struck me was that none of the panelists appear to pay much attention to what was going on during the entire hearing. Even though they appeared to be listening, apart from snippets, very little appears to have been absorbed.

The walk back to the apartment was slow and we spent most of the time talking to Gautam filling him on the happenings of the day. I was completely drained by then and asked him to speak to the others to give them the info. I just was not in any frame of mind to go over the events of the day again with all of my close friends. They would all have been waiting anxiously to hear the outcome, as we were extremely hopeful of a positive outcome very quickly after the previous night's conference with Fred and Nancy. Once we had freshened up at the apartment we went out into the centre of Manchester to the shops and a restaurant. There was nothing much to do that night apart from making sure all the papers that I might need for the next day were ready in my brief case. We were not really looking forward to the next day as we suspected what the outcome would be.

9. Day Two; Tuesday, 29th April 2008

We had been asked to be at the GMC by 9'O clock to have a briefing with Fred and Nancy. Fred was a bit late in arriving He was working on the submission for the next stage, and he suspected that the FTP panel had already made their decision against us.

'Good morning all' Fred smiled as he came in wheeling his trusty pilot's case.

'Morning Fred. Hope you have had a good night's rest. Where do we go from here?' I was still anxious, and there was a faint hope that he may tell me that we will win today.

'The panel's questioning was rather odd yesterday and rather worrying. I am not sure how they will play this, particularly as this involves interpretation of the law and they don't have any legal training'

'For a lay person, your argument looked very robust yesterday, and I cannot understand how they can give a judgment against us'. I said, rather annoyed.

'Unfortunate thing is that they can do what they want as they are considered 'independent'. They can come with any decision they want as long as they come with a reason.' Nancy joined in.

'If they get it entirely wrong, can we not report them to someone or take some form of legal action?' I persisted.

'The chairman of this panel was involved in the recent case which was thrown out by the Judge on appeal, and the panel was severely criticised for its action by the Judge. The Doctor was awarded an undisclosed amount of money. However, they were not asked to come in front of the judge, and I suspect they are utterly oblivious to the outcome of the court judgment.' Nancy continued twiddling her pen as she spoke.

'Did the GMC not get upset at paying out the money, and reprimand the panel chairman? How can he be allowed to continue if he got a case so badly wrong? What training do they get to be on the panel?' I was getting hot under the collar.

'No. He probably got a slap on the wrist at worst from the president of GMC. Nothing else.'

'Do you mean to say that they can do what they want with impunity? No one to regulate them or question them?'

'Unfortunately, yes. I don't know of any FTP panel or its predecessor being taken to court to answer their actions' Nancy said, and Fred nodded his head. Dr Smiths had joined us that morning.

'The MPS had lodged complaints about several of the panelists before, and the only thing we have achieved is stopping some of the panelists to appear on MPS cases. Nevertheless, they continue to work on other cases. It is extremely lucrative work for them as most of the panelists are retired.'

I was quite taken aback. It is like allowing doctors to work without any recourse to complaints or litigation. I thought it was appalling, that these people are being allowed to make decisions, on highly trained, and highly skilled individuals, affecting not only their careers, but also their lives with not an ounce of regulation. This not only affected the doctors that are being crucified but also thousands of patients who were being denied a much-needed service.

Nobody had noticed the time during this discussion. It was well after ten in the morning. There was no sign of activity in the corridors at all. Nancy sent off Natalie, the reliable assistant to find out. She came back two minutes later.

'They will be ready in a few minutes.'

It was nearly half past ten when the usher came in to collect us. We all marched into the hearing room behind Fred. The chairman was already there along with his cronies. He started off saying that he has a determination to read. It was a long drawn out soliloquy as is common with all the determinations with the GMC.

It was a farce, if there was one. The panel had accepted everything the GMC counsel had said and refused to accept anything Fred Barnard had said.

For Fred's submission of 'lying' by GMC, he said,

'The panel accepts that the GMC correspondence, which it has seen, is not as clear as it might be. The passage quoted earlier in this determination illustrates the ambiguity of expression to which you drew the panel's attention. The panel, however, does not believe that the GMC intended to mislead.'

I could see Fred's face getting red and Nancy was fuming. I sat there, numb, as I could not believe how blatantly they were getting away with it. How can changing the words from 'by Mr. Kasyapa' to 'against Mr. Kasyapa' can be considered ambiguous is beyond any sane person or me? How can recorded discussions between officers of the GMC as to how the wording should be changed to suit the decision can be construed as 'not misleading' is unbelievable?

The panel entirely ignored Fred's submission that I have fulfilled all the recommendations by mentioning it in passing – 'You have submitted that Mr. Kasyapa has complied with all the recommendations made by the assessment team and has complied with the conditions imposed by the Interim Orders Panel.'

It took him half an hour to read out the determination and concluded that the hearing will continue. Mr. Barnard wanted some time to discuss the decision with me before proceeding. The GMC counsel pointed out that the 'Specialist Medical Adviser' will be available for only part of the hearing. It is a rule that there should be a 'Specialist Medical Adviser' who was a specialist in the area of the doctor, who is being questioned throughout the hearing. The chairman said that we could have 15 minutes to discuss the issue and return with our decisions.

As we walked out of the room, Fred said, 'Don't say anything until we reach the room'. We walked in silence until we reached the room. As we entered the room, Fred uttered with exasperation 'It is unreal. They have not taken notice of anything I said.' He was genuinely angry. 'We now have to think whether we should let them carry on with this farce or go for a judicial review.'

Dr Smiths was of the opinion that we would not get a fair hearing, and we should go for a judicial review. Both Fred and Nancy felt that as we were already here fully prepared, we should give it a shot. They felt a judicial review would likely set back the case by at least six months. I looked at Lopa and Sanvi who were there to see what they felt. I did not feel like waiting another six months to go through this painful process. If we fail in judicial review, I will still have to face the FTP panel. Finally, it was decided that we should just go ahead with the case and see how it goes. We discussed the strategy that should be adopted over the ensuing days for the case. I was not happy that there was no "Specialist Medical Adviser" during the entire hearing, as the panel clearly do not have any clue as to the workings of a modern NHS hospital let alone specialist hip and knee surgery. It transpired that the GMC had 'forgotten' to appoint a specialist adviser, and realised it too late to find one suitable.

'I'll make sure that we register our protest at this lack of responsible behaviour by the GMC at the start. I don't think we should insist on an adviser now as that would mean adjourning the case.' Fred said.

'I don't want an adjournment at whatever cost' I was getting rather annoyed by now. 'I cannot believe the GMC is letting these three clowns decide on the career of a leading hip and knee surgeon. What do they know about my work?'

We trotted back to the hearing room. Even, though I had expected this result, I was extremely disappointed and rather crestfallen.

Once we were all seated, the chairman started. 'Mr. Barnard, can you tell us the outcome of your deliberations please?'

'I can, sir. I am very grateful for the time. I have no application that arises from my discussions about your ruling. Sir, can I turn to the next point which Mr. Sykes flagged up, which is the position of the Specialist Adviser?' Fred started. He went on to elaborate the rules of the GMC that dictates that a specialist adviser should be present at such hearings and protest strongly at the absence of one.

'The specialist performance adviser, who was selected is required to be present during the hearing, just as the panel members and the legal assessor is required to be present through the hearing. It does not say that in respect of panel members or the legal assessor, but clearly the rules are drafted on that assumption.'

'Mr. Barnard, I thought this was not an application.' The legal assessor interjected. She had suddenly woken up and decided to take part in the proceedings.

'No. It is not an application' Fred retorted, 'I am registering my protest to be on record.'

'What exactly did you have in mind?' The chairman wanted more clarification.

'All I want to say, sir, is I am not applying for an adjournment, but I would simply ask the panel to note that we are very, very unhappy that the arrangements were made so late in the day that it was not possible to have a performance assessor present throughout. Whether that is lawful or not is a matter about which I am not making submissions at the present time'. I could see Fred was trying his best to hide the exasperation.

The GMC counsel wanted to say his version of the GMC rules. '. The specialist adviser actually has to be present throughout. The specialist adviser has to be available in order to advise the panel as required during the hearing. You will have the advantage of having a specialist adviser. I accept it is unfortunate that he is not present throughout. Because of that, we have asked for daily transcripts.' Unfortunately, the legal assessor had her own interpretation, and said that the specialist medical adviser need not be present throughout the hearing. This was beginning to sound like a GMC version of carry on movies! After a bit more of this bickering they finally decided that it was time the case started and for the first time decided to talk to me.

'I need to ask the doctor to confirm his name and registration number. Doctor, would you do that, please? Just tell the panel your name and your registration number. Remain seated if you prefer.' For the first time in two days the chairman looked at me. I gave my name as Upaashantha Kasyapa and my GMC registration – it sounded like a soldier in front of a military court – 'my rank and serial number sir!.' After that you are not allowed to speak. As far as the panel is concerned, you do not exist.

The panel secretary, who had been busy throughout the hearing popping to her computer typing, read out the charges against me. These were essentially the conclusions by the performance assessors.

Fred turned around and said, 'We accept that the assessors did come to those conclusions but the conclusions they reached, we say, were the wrong conclusions.'

It suddenly occurred to the GMC counsel that we had admitted to all the charges and said the conclusion drawn from those charges were wrong. It meant that there was no case for the panel to carry on at this stage and go directly to the next stage where I can call witnesses to disprove the GMC's case. The GMC counsel wanted Fred to withdraw his admissions of the charges. Things appeared to be deteriorating into a charade. The arguments went on for a while and finally the GMC counsel said he would need to take fresh instructions from the GMC and discuss the issue with Fred. Yet another break for everyone. We trooped out into our waiting room for another half an hour.

When we got back, the GMC counsel said that the GMC refused to amend the charges and were sticking to their guns. It meant that the facts were not being disputed by us and hence the GMC cannot open the case to call their witnesses – the assessors – to substantiate their claim. It would be a blow to us as well as we could not show the panel that the assessors were wrong in their conclusion. We would have had to go to the next stage to prove my 'innocence.'

The discussions went on for a while during which time the chairman had several whispered conversations with the legal assessors who is supposed to be independent. The chairman's words 'I am going to interrupt you because, as you appreciate, I am beginning to find this a bit surreal' summed up what was happening. When Fred tried to clarify the issue and get the case starting, it was obvious to the chairman that he could not waste any more time and he tried to mollify Fred with 'Everybody is getting irritable and we are just going to try and get this moving forward.'

By around 12.30 the panel had had enough and wanted to go for lunch. 'Bearing in mind the time, I think the right thing to do is for the panel to go into *camera*, during which time the panel will take its lunch. I think we will resume at two o'clock.' With that the chairman wound up the proceedings for the morning.

We did not get called back till about 2.30 in the afternoon. It must be nice to have two-hour lunch breaks at work. I was beginning to understand where all our subscription money to the GMC was going. Finally, Fred had to introduce a fresh 'charge' as it were to let the hearing continue. If he had not done that, I suspect we would have been going around in circles for the rest of the week. The charge was that the charges that were on the charge sheet were 'warranted' and of course we would refute that charge.

There were further discussions regarding this and the appropriateness of the addition. Just as Fred suggested to the chairman that the GMC counsel should start his case, the chairman said that he had to read out a determination regarding the new charge and that the panel has to 'go into camera.' It was amazing, how the panel was trying to stretch out the case as much as possible. We all had to go out again for the panel to 'go into camera.' We were again called into the room by just after three in the afternoon. The chairman read out a two-line 'determination' about the new charge and invited the GMC counsel to open the case.

Bill Sykes started out giving the details of my training and when I became a consultant and when I was appointed as a clinical director for the department. He gave a fairly detailed history of the complaints by Serpe and glossed over the report by Stratford about my hip replacements who had claimed that there was a cause for concern regarding complications with cemented hip replacements.

He admitted, 'The GMC does not now rely upon that expert report, but it did trigger further action by the GMC. The GMC decided to invite Mr. Kasyapa to undergo a performance assessment, the particular areas of concern being his performance in cemented hip replacements and also his complication rates.' He went on to describe the assessors that were sent down and the assessment process that was followed. As he started to read out their qualifications etc, it became clear to everyone in the room that none of them were really qualified to assess my work as a senior orthopaedic consultant surgeon.

If it was a court of law, one could have asked why the GMC did not chose specialists in hip replacements to do the assessment. Unfortunately, in the GMC, there is no such option available.

He went on to describe the conclusions drawn by the assessors. Out of nine areas, they had found me 'acceptable' in five, cause for concern in two and 'unacceptable' in two areas. He then went on to describe the test of surgical competence and how the assessors had marked me as 'fail'. He obviously dwelled quite a bit on the 'unacceptable' and also the failure of test of surgical competence.

It is extremely painful and humiliating to listen to when someone is describing you as a 'failure' and generally incompetent and you do not have any way of defending yourself. Tom Sykes took about an hour to complete his submission where he was essentially saying that I was a poorly performing surgeon and not fit to practice. It must be one of the longest hours in my life. I could not wait for him to finish the harangue as it appeared to me. He concluded saying that the assessors 'found the doctor to be a hard-working surgeon who, as I said, the team considered his workload to be too high which was leading to patients being inadequately assessed.' His final statement was rather amusing – 'They also found that his management was, to some extent, at fault and there seemed to be an institutional problem of what they termed 'conveyor belt surgery." Somebody needs to tell the GMC and its 'assessors' how the modern health service works and also the benefits of the system to the patients, that was pioneered by several leading orthopaedic surgeons including me in this country and abroad.

As he finished his statement, Fred reminded both the GMC counsel as well as the FTP about the original complaint, which was conveniently left out by Tom Sykes.

'. original complaints made by Mr. Serpe to the GMC which are referred to in the assessment panel report as being about cemented hip replacements being inappropriate or inadequate as done by Mr Kasyapa and, secondly, that Mr Kasyapa had excessive complication rates. Both those allegations were not in fact borne out on the assessment.'

To which Sykes replied, 'I can certainly say they are not pursued now.' There you have it – it does not matter what the complaint is against a doctor, the GMC will do its best to discredit him/her using whatever means available at its disposal.

Now it was Fred's turn to do the opening submission. He wanted to tell the panel why we thought the extensive response was made objecting to the assessors report to start with. The GMC had done yet another 'deviation from the normal' by asking the assessors to do another report excluding the third party interviews giving yet again an adverse report.

He started with the complaint against me by Serpe to the hospital chief executive, which was extensively investigated to find no substance in the complaint. He also highlighted Serpe and Pakshar's complaints to the regional advisor, which again did not find any, fault, and went on to discuss the events, which lead to sacking of Serpe.

He went on to the assessment report, which was the sole weapon for the GMC. He opened with the third party interviews the assessors held with nine individuals at the beginning of the assessment. 'In reaching their conclusions the assessment panel appears to have relied heavily on criticisms made by Mr. Serpe and another former Trust employee Mr. Pakshar. Mr. Pakshar resigned from the Trust in October 2003' Fred started his defence quite strongly I thought.

'GMC did not conduct the performance assessment until Nov-Dec 2006 when the assessors interviewed Mr. Serpe, his knowledge of Mr. Kasyapa's practice, in so far that he had any direct knowledge, could only be up to February 2004' That is two and half years after Serpe was sacked. He went on to point out that Pakshar left in October 2003 which was over a three years gap.

He went on 'The judgment 'unacceptable' seems to be based upon the comments made by Serpe and Pakshar who had no knowledge of Mr. Kasyapa's practice at the time of the assessment.' Fred pointed out that apart from these two people everyone else gave extremely positive comments about my work, skill, and knowledge. 'When interviewing Mr. Pakshar conceded that he had never been present in Mr. Kasyapa's Clinic. He is simply not in a position to comment on Mr. Kasyapa's practice, even when they were colleagues up to October 2003…'

Fred was picking one point after another in the so-called 'unacceptable' conclusions by the assessors.

'The judgment of 'cause for concern' appears mainly to be based upon the comments of Pakshar and Serpe given in the third party interviews. In particular, the assessment team has recorded 'unacceptable' judgments in respect of comments made by Pakshar relating to Mr. Kasyapa's operating lists and comments made by Serpe relating to a failure to discuss problems with colleagues. Bearing in mind neither Pakshar nor Serpe has worked in the Trust for over 3 years, it is surprising that any weight has been attached to their comments when considering current clinical practice.'

The chairman interrupted at that point.

'May I interrupt you? I am reluctant to do so, but if you are going to read much more of this it would assist me to know what objection this is leading up to?'

'You see what the GMC have done. Instead of asking the assessment panel whether the exclusion or diminution of weight in relation to those two witnesses would have made a difference, they have asked for the exclusion of all witnesses, including of course the bulk of the witnesses whose evidence was favorable and supportive to Mr. Kasyapa' Fred tried to stay calm. I was beginning to wonder if I was sitting in the same room as the panel. They don't appear to have registered anything Fred had said so far.

'The response of the GMC is, in our respectful submission, unwarranted and disproportionate. The exclusion of all the third party evidence, including that which is favorable to Mr. Kasyapa, produces inevitably the result that since the bulk of the evidence was in his favor the addendum report converts what were findings of acceptable performance to unacceptable.' Fred tried to stress the point.

This argument went on for a while and the contention whether the statements by the two disgruntled had a skewing effect on the assessors conclusions was not settled after about an hour of discussion. It was finally decided to 'see how it goes.' The GMC counsel wanted to call his first witness which was Dr. Dawkins who had been wandering up and down the corridor all day. But what happened next was out of this world and gives you a taste of how things work in the GMC.

The chairman stopped Sykes and said, 'I am minded to take a short break. Is your witness here?'

Sykes looked a little surprised and looked at Fred as he spoke 'Yes he is and has been for a while now.'

'Can I suggest we take a 15 minute comfort break and resume promptly at 3.30.' The chairman insisted.

'In order that the witness is not kept going for too long would quarter to five be appropriate?' Sykes wanted to know.

'As you are aware, the panel sat very late last night. I was hoping we would not be late tonight.' The chairman would have none of it. For those of us mortals, the hearing finished the day before at just after five in the evening. I do not know what would be an 'early finish' for this panel! The chairman finally agreed that he would like to finish by 4.30 that afternoon. It was beginning to rain outside and it was decidedly murky looking outside through the dirty window of our waiting room. I hoped Lopa had brought an umbrella.

We were called in just after 3.30 and as we trooped back in after yet another session at the coffee machine.

Sykes started off by calling his first witness – Dawkins. He looked like a well fed middle aged clerk at the local council. He sat in the chair with solitary desk in the middle of the room. He was sworn in by the GMC usher. His CV was distributed to everyone in the room that is everyone except me. Sykes started off with his qualifications and career. He was a general practitioner in a 'large practice' according to him. When he started to list his other 'current posts', it came as no surprise that he is one of those 'non-clinical clinicians.' He was, among other things, an assessor for the NCAS (National Clinical Assessment Service), clinical adviser to the Health Care Commission, assessor for the GMC, expert witness for the GMC, member of the Primary Care Trust etc. One would wonder when he would get time to see his patients or be a general practitioner.

When he was asked as to how a general practitioner considers himself to be qualified to assess a consultant orthopaedic surgeon, his answers gave an insight into the workings of the GMC.

'Yes. In some specialties there is a shortage of lead assessors, so sometimes, particularly the GP assessors - because general practice tends to be sort of quite wide ranging - are asked to lead out-of-speciality assessments.'

What he was essentially trying to say was that no self respecting orthopaedic surgeon would stoop down to do this kind of work.
Sykes continued, 'Can we just ask something about your experience in leading assessment teams? How often have you conducted this particular type of exercise?'

'I lead about six assessments a year. Over the years I have - I have not got an exact count, but I have probably completed about 50 assessments' Dawkins answered. That was very interesting revelation about his work as a GMC assessor. My brain went into a math mode and started to work out how many days per year that would make. Judging by my own experience, each assessment takes eight days, meeting to write the report is two days. Leaving aside the days spent at the FTP hearings, which make it 60 days a year. What with time spent on the numerous committees and working with administrative organizations, I would be surprised if he could spend more than six months a year practicing medicine. One gets the picture of the type of doctors who are assessing hard working surgeons.

Sykes wanted to know the modus operandi of the assessment as Dawkins was the lead assessor. Dawkins droned on in his quite rather stuttering language about how they considered the background of complaint and the different stages of the assessment. By the time he came to the actual assessment best part of the afternoon had gone. Both the chairman and the reverend had had their short kips hoping no one had noticed them. I was sure when Dawkins was describing at some length how he had to sit down a whole day to write the report, both of them were fast asleep.

'Can you just help us, before we launch into the main body of the report, about how your judgments are formulated and how it works within the team?' Sykes was trying to pin him down.

'You will probably see through the report that under each heading of *Good Medical Practice* as we go through the assessments, the various things that are done like the review of medical records, third party interviews, we make judgments on information we receive in the elements of the report. Then they are tied together to come to an overall conclusion for each heading of *Good Medical Practice*.' Dawkins replied.

I could see Nancy lifting her eyebrows and looking at every one. We were all beginning to realize that it was going to be a very long hearing and as Sykes started with the people interviewed for the 'Third party interview,' we started to get some idea how subtle the GMC functionaries are.

'You also interviewed Mr Serpe, Mr Pakshar, Mr Charlton, and Mrs Slattery. May I just ask you this - because we will look at some of your assessments on the third party interviews - were you aware of the background within this particular surgical department at the time that you conducted these interviews?'

'From the papers we were given, shall we say we were aware that there was, or certainly had been, some friction within the department. We were aware of this when we interviewed people. We interviewed Mr. Serpe because it is fairly standard practice to interview the complainant.' Dawkins forgot to mention that Serpe had not worked with me for nearly three years and whatever he was going to say would be three years out of date and would be based on a dubious memory of a 70 year old. He also 'forgot' to discuss Pakshar who had not worked with me for three and a half years and Sykes also seemed to forget to mention his relationship.

'Page 15, I think it is, providing or arranging investigations, and your overall judgment in this was acceptable?' Sykes was putting words into Dawkin's mouth.

'Yes, it was.'

'First of all, you had two sources of information. You had third party interviews and what you term 'case-based discussions.''

'Yes.'

'The third party interviews you have dealt with already. You interviewed the various third parties. I think those interviews were transcribed?'

'Yes.'

'You also made notes of the interviews as they went?'

'Yes.' Dawkin's replies did not change significantly for a while. Sykes was doing a good job of producing a case based on his own statements without taxing the witness.

'I see. If we go please, to page 11 of your report, the heading is 'The Context of Practice.' We have looked at this briefly already. In terms of the man that you were dealing with and assessing, did you understand what his speciality was?'

'Yes' It was not surprising to anyone on this side of the court when Sykes did not pursue this matter any further.

'Case-based discussions, could you explain to the panel please, how that works?'

'Yes, the medical records are looked at and I think in this case a total of 42 records were looked at and out of those 42 records we pick a total of 12 to have a case-based discussion with the Doctor. These are not necessarily picked because there has been a problem with them. They were picked in this case by the orthopaedic assessors as cases that would allow us to lead into discussion about areas of practice.'

This was the first time Dawkins spoke at length and as he went on he became bolder and the answers became longer and longer. However, we could not see any sign of even the remotest interest by anyone on the panel.

'How do you come - and I am just using this as an example and we will deal with the others, I can promise you, much more quickly - but how do you come to your overall acceptable conclusion?' I do not think even Sykes expected what would come next.

'It is a bit of a balancing act really. Not all judgments necessarily carry the same weight and it is a matter of looking - we would always, for instance, give more weight to information which comes from a case-based discussion. Not always but that is, information we have from the doctor himself. Third party interviews can be useful but most useful information generally comes from the medical records themselves in the case-based discussion in this case. Therefore, I would look at all the judgments that were made to be acceptable, looking at the third party interviews first, and there were a considerable number of judgments that were all perfectly happy with the way investigations were made. In the next section, looking at the acceptable judgments made from the case-based discussion, for instance, Mr Kasyapa knew what investigations to perform, possible brachial plexus lesion, there was a reason why a CT scan had not been done in a particular case and, basically, the information from the case-based discussion was that there was an acceptable level of knowledge about what investigations should be done and, in general, what investigations were done. The reason for cause for concern on one judgment, because investigations had not been done, that was not marked as unacceptable. That was one case out of 42 and that judgment alone gave no evidence of a repetitive pattern. It was not maybe three or four cases where the same investigations had been missed out; it was just one instance, so it was marked as cause for concern rather than unacceptable. The unacceptable judgments were considered to be unacceptable simply because although it may well be the staff grades who were ordering the unnecessary x-rays, at the end of the day it is the consultant's responsibility for the investigation of the patients and that was something that would need to be addressed and the orthopaedic assessors, one of them certainly marked the interpretation of the x-ray as unacceptable because he felt it was a fairly significant - the x-ray was obviously showing severe osteoarthritis and appeared to be misinterpreted. However, when you put all of those together the weight of evidence was much more towards an overall acceptable performance in that section.'

When Dawkins stopped, I could see most people apart from probably the short hand writer had lost interest half way through this long monologue. The Reverend and the chairperson were struggling to keep their eyes open. Obviously, the wine during the lunch hour probably was not such a good idea today.

Sykes went through all the headings in the GMC's Good Medical Practice and asked Dawkins how they came to a particular conclusion. He was good, I thought. He was highlighting the conclusions so well but at the same time disguising the mistakes or oversights by the assessment team in general and Dawkins in particular, I could see Fred and Nancy writing furiously during the interrogation.

'Dr Jankoweicz said the particular weakness was that he takes on too much and not saying no. Was that something of a theme?' Sykes continued 'Yes. That is one of the most consistent themes that run through the peer review. There was a feeling from what we were told, what we discussed in the case-based discussion and really what we discussed looking at the initial interview, although judgments are not made in the initial interview, there was a feeling that we could perhaps say Mr. Kasyapa was perhaps too willing and had possibly been pressurised into doing more than was appropriate.' Dawkins answered.

Since when did it become a crime to work hard? This criticism would continue throughout the hearing. I could not remember anyone asking me at any time either during the 'assessment' or before if I was coping with the work I was doing. If I remember right, I had asked to do the work that I was doing and not the other way round.

'Now the numbers, just so this is clear, that we see at the side of those judgments refer to the appendix which at this stage I am not going into. It may be Mr Barnard will want to but I am not going to the core material. That appendix is not actually created by you, I do not think, is it?'

'No. What happens, most of the information that goes into the database is handwritten during the third party interviews or the review of medical records or case-based discussion. Information we want transferring to the database is handwritten and then a circle is put round it and a category of good medical practice and an A, C or U judgment given to it. Then the GMC office staff put that together into a database. So the report is based on that.'

Dawkin's reply surprised all of us on this side of the court. This is the first time anyone had admitted to the involvement of the GMC staff in the assessment process. The organisation is so secretive that it takes a court order to get even half the information one wants.

I could see Lopa totting something up. She appeared to be ticking a box every time a name was mentioned. Later it turned out that she was tracking the number of times various people were mentioned. Serpe was mentioned 41 times and Pakshar 26 time in the 40 minute of questioning. Out of the nine people interviewed, the other seven got a mention of seven times in total! This gave quite a clear picture of the bias in the assessment and by Sykes. I could understand why Sykes was using the antagonist's rather than my supporters to help his case. I would hope the FTP panel would recognise this overt bias in the argument. The fact that Pakshar and Serpe were the complainants and they would do their best to pull me down went unnoticed by Assessors or the panel. There was only a brief mention of this fact.

'May I just ask you this - because we will look at some of your assessments on the third party interviews - were you aware of the background within this particular surgical department at the time that you conducted these interviews?' Sykes questioned

'From the papers we were given, shall we say we were aware that there was, or certainly had been, some friction within the department.' Dawkins tried to gloss over.

By now, I could see the Chairman was getting quite fidgety and kept looking at the clock. We had been on the go for 40 minutes now and it was just after four, when Dawkins said, 'Do you want me to launch into those or pull stumps there? I am entirely in your hands.'

'I guess if it was going to take us beyond five o'clock, then I would prefer to stop now' The Chairman said hopefully. However, Sykes promised that he would finish before 4.30 and hence he was allowed to carry on.

The next 20 minutes were spent on trying to get Dawkins to say something about medical issues, only to find him repeating again and again to 'ask the orthopaedic experts.'

Promptly at 4.30, the Chairman stopped Sykes.

'I am a little worried about concentration dropping off and so on. It is not fair to any of the parties if that happens' And turning to Dawkins he said, 'Doctor, I need to remind you that you are under oath and you should not discuss this case with anyone until you are discharged.'

He then decided that it had finished 'late again' and would start at 9.45 the next morning. I do not know what these people would call finishing at eight at night and starting back again at eight in the morning as most surgeons in this country do.

Back in the waiting room, Nancy appeared to be deep in thought. 'I am not sure what to make of him.' She was obviously talking about Dawkins. 'The guy hardly ever does any clinical work and he was completely at sea when questioned about clinical aspects of his own assessment. He dodged all the questions and we have to depend on the orthopaedic guys for some answers.' She was looking at Fred.

'I think I have an idea of this guy now. I have some questions that he cannot evade.' Fred was a bit more optimistic. 'I think I better head back to the hotel. I have got a few hours of work to do before I confront him tomorrow.'

The rain had stopped by the time we got out and as we walked back to the apartment, the mood was rather sombre and unsure of what had happened that day. As we reached the apartment, the mobile rang. It was Swayambhu.

'How are you? How did it go today?'

'I am not sure. We finished early and are walking back to the apartment. I did not have to do anything today, but I feel drained. The hearing is continuing. The panel gave a determination against us saying that the GMC has not done anything wrong. The case has started with initial statement from the GMC Barrister, Bill Sykes and the GP Dawkins is on stand now.'

'Who is Sykes? Do they have to be sworn in when they start?' As usual, he wanted to know all the tiny details. My mind was rather numb and tired, but it was still worth it to get out of system by telling the details to him, it was as if I was purging the un-cleanliness of the day from myself. I gave a summary of the day's events. I knew Gautam would want to know the details as well. Therefore, I asked Swaymbhu to pass the details on to him. He promised he would.

As we sat down at the local Italian restaurant for a quick dinner, we realised that Shuchi had to go back that night. The dinner was cut short so that she would not miss the train.

'I'll just go from here to the station. You don't have to come.' Shuchi was being herself. Always the 'last minute girl.' I have never known her to be well on time to anything – trains, planes, or automobiles! We rushed through our dinner and ran across to Piccadilly just in time for the last train to Oxford. There was not much time to reminisce the day's event in much detail as we were all tired and could not wait to get to bed and get to sleep. It was a fitful night and a not much peaceful sleep.

10. Day Three; Wednesday, 30th April 2008

The next morning started pretty much the same as the day before. We walked down to the now familiar Portland Road to the GMC in quiet contemplation. The sun was out, and the day promised to be warm. It was early spring, but no sign of it in the concrete jungle of central Manchester. We reached our waiting room by about nine in the morning only to see it deserted. Natalie breezed in a few minutes later.

We found later that she had been there since early morning copying reams of documents for Fred. It was not long before Nancy made her way into the room looking fresh and ready for the day. During our trips to the coffee machine down the corridor, I had seen Amoshin wandering around the corridor looking lost and obviously enjoying the GMC hospitality at my cost. When I told everyone in the room about his presence, there were 'unlady' like offers of biffing him one by Natalie.

'What is he doing here today? He is unlikely to be called for a while at least.' I wondered aloud.

Nancy smiled and said, 'At probably a grand a day, I would not mind hanging around for a few days'

'At the rate Dawkins is going, he will be on the stand for the whole of today' I think my frustration was probably showing.

'Dawkins does go on, but he does not answer any questions directly. Fred will have to try and pin him down for some real answers,' Nancy said looking at the door expectantly. Lo and behold, Fred entered, wheeling in his trusty pilot's case, and balancing large lever arch folders under his left arm. I got up to help him.

'That is very kind of you. Morning all' He was beaming. 'Did all of you get good sleep?'

All of us nodded looking rather bemused by his upbeat behaviour. By about 10 in the morning, we were beginning to see some activity in the corridor. It was well after 10 when the GMC usher finally called us in. We gathered all the bulky folders and files and walked across to the hearing room 4. As we got into our seat, I could see the panel along with the legal assessor were exchanging the previous night's dinner problems and the quality of wine in some restaurant.

After what seemed to be an inordinately long delay, Dawkins was called back, and he took his seat in the witness chair, in front of the panel. He wore the same dirty grey suit as the day before and looked more like a clerk in the local council office, than a general practitioner.

Sykes started again with Dawkins. He questioned him about the test of competency, and as the day before, Dawkins could not answer a single question without going into a long ramble. Once the answers were deciphered, it turned out that he was asking Sykes to ask the orthopaedic experts! He took him through test of competency, review of medical records and case based discussions – probably more than 75% of the assessment. He could not answer any of them without saying 'you'll have to ask the orthopaedic experts.' Sykes started to ask some specifics.

'The surgery core knowledge test. As we can see from your report, I think the test comprised of eight questions. I have described those as eight exam-based questions. Is that fair?'

'Yes, that is fair.' I could see the worried look on Dawkins's face. He obviously did not know where this was heading or at least gave an impression as such. Fred had told us that none of these witnesses was 'schooled' by the GMC legal department or their barrister before taking a stand! And I am King Tut.

'Where do those questions come from?' Sykes continued.

'I am informed that they are held in a question bank held by the GMC that is based on questions used by the Royal College of Surgeons examinations'. Well well well! He knew about these questions but would not tell me about them, before the test. He did not repeat what he said to me before the test – 'questions about your day to day work in your hospital' or what he said at the end of the first interview 'don't need to study any books for the test.'

Sykes took him through scoring of the tests, and how marks were calculated. Most of the answers were obtuse, and I could see the panelists looked rather blank, and lost in the middle of Dawkins's verbal diarrhoea. Sykes wanted to know who wrote the report.

'When you come to this area of your report, is this something you all discuss together?'

'Yes' Dawkins was being brief for a change.

'At the end of the day, you actually wrote this report?'

'I wrote that. The discussion there was from the report-writing day.' Dawkins appeared to be proud of that fact.

Sykes's questioning was direct, and he did manage to drag everything he wanted out of Dawkins even though at times, I thought he was leading.

'Again, I do not want to lead you, but just making sense of that, however good his specialised knowledge is, what you seem to be saying is if his core knowledge is poor, then patients are potentially put at risk?'

'Yes.' Dawkins replied

'That is how you come to your unacceptable finding?' Sykes persisted as no one was allowed to stop him.

'Yes.' I could see Nancy's eyebrows lifting on several occasions during this questioning. I wonder if a Judge would allow this kind of questioning, where you answer your own questions. The only time Fred objected with,

'Sounds like a leading question.'

'It is stating the obvious. It is a leading question but it is also stating the obvious, with respect.' Sykes did not even stop as the panel chairman was not even paying any attention to this exchange.

When some of the faults in the assessment became known, I thought Sykes was slipping.

'The consultations were observed through a one-way mirror and assessed according to the structured schedule'. Sykes was asking about the clinical scenarios used with actors and observed by the assessors.

'That is an error. The template is normally being used for assessments done in other centres where..' Dawkins said and took Sykes by surprise.

'This was not a one-way mirror job?'

'No, it was not.' Dawkins was looking decidedly uncomfortable. Sykes being a sly Barrister wriggled out of it before anyone could take notice and quickly changed the subject and went on to the next topic almost seamlessly.

I thought Sykes's summary of Dawkins's statement and conclusion was telling; '- a summary of your findings at page 82, you explain that Mr. Kasyapa was required to undergo an assessment because of concerns about cemented hip replacements and complication rates. We have made it quite clear those were areas that the GMC are not pursuing.' I thought this summarised the attitude of the GMC quite clear. It does not really matter what the complaint about the doctor is, they will find a fault with him or her and ruin his or her life.

Sykes continued with Dawkins's conclusion

'His qualifications were acceptable. He co-operated completely, as you have indicated previously.' Sykes went on.

'Yes.' Dawkins agreed.

Sykes continued to read the script from the assessment report 'He is a hardworking surgeon in a busy unit.

He was capable of appropriately assessing his patients and following them up.

He made appropriate use of investigations.

His peers consider that he has appropriate surgical skills.

He is willing to ask for advice and help and has a good relationship with his colleagues. He is considered to be a good team member and is popular with everyone.

He is capable of keeping adequate medical records.

He works well with the resources available to him and he was instrumental in developing the present surgical centre.

He is capable of handling orthopaedic emergencies.

He is keen to keep up-to-date and enjoys teaching.

He complies with laws and statutory guidelines.

He is approachable and supportive and will listen to constructive criticism.

A departmental audit apparently showed that there were no problems with his work.

He is capable of acceptable communication with his patients. He is polite and respectful towards them .. accessible and available.' Sykes finished looking at the Panel Chairman, rather than Dawkins.

Nevertheless, the assessors still found things during their assessment to say that I was 'deficient.' The tirade after the 'But' went on for ten minutes with minutiae of faults the assessors had managed to, what I can only describe as 'create' during their assessment. As he concluded, the chairman was looking at the clock and it was nearly quarter to 11 in the morning. We had been at it for nearly 45 minutes. He wanted a break and so off we went out for more coffee and hot chocolates from the GMC's coffee machine.

As we entered our waiting room, we could see glorious sunshine outside and we could see couple of narrow houseboats navigating the lock behind the St James' building. Everything looked so calm and peaceful outside. I spent the time looking at the neat way the guy on the boat, handled the lock and moved the boat expertly through the lock. It was fascinating to see someone work on something and he appeared to be whistling a song as he did it. He obviously knew what he was doing as the whole operation was slick and was finished before you could say timber. What would I give to be on that boat right now, instead of the dreadful GMC offices?

On the way back to the hearing room, all of us were quiet. Fred had spent the whole break time going through Sykes's examination and jotting down points in red ink. By the time he had finished, the document was awash with red ink. Nobody had said much during the break as Fred was concentrating a lot and none of us wanted to disturb his train of thought.

Dawkins was called back into the hearing room and sat at the witness chair. Fred started his cross-examination. It soon became obvious that Dawkins was going to dodge as many questions as possible and not give a straight answer. Fred pointed out to him that he had not included several important documents in his assessment report. 'Dr Dawkins, you and your panel had some materials about the background to this case before you started, did you not?' Fred asked.

'Yes.'

'You do not actually identify what they are in this report. Is that right?' Fred persisted.

'I do not identify them as a list of documents available, no.' Dawkins was not very convincing.

'But you had, for example, some material from Mr Serpe relating to his complaint?'

'Yes.' Dawkins was actually looking at Sykes to see if he was going to intervene.

'There was a British Orthopaedic Association report into the orthopaedic department at this hospital. Were you aware of that?'

'I honestly cannot remember specifically. It is about 18 months ago now when I look through the papers. If it was in the bundle of papers sent in advance I will have read it, yes.' Dawkins replied looking somewhat uncomfortable. All of us could see that he was not telling the truth. He knew exactly what document was being discussed and he knew exactly what the document contained. It was a report by the British Orthopaedic Association, which was commissioned by the hospital in 2004 to look at the problems within the orthopaedic department. The report was scathing about the support by some individual consultants in the smooth running of the department and the difficult situation the clinical director was under.

Fred moved on to the way the assessment was conducted. He wanted to know why the GMC's rules of observing the doctor at the place of work were not followed.

'You subjected Mr Kasyapa to various tests at the GMC head office in London. Do you think, on reflection, it would have been more appropriate to have assessed him by observing his every day practice?' Fred was being polite.

'In an ideal world that would happen and if, for instance, we had been assessing a GP that would have happened. Unfortunately, and I will not go too much into the background, because of difficulties that arose with surgeons, surgical specialities do not get their practice observed. There are also issues of consent from patients, what you tell the patient about the other people in the operating theatre are. So, yes, in an ideal world it would be much better to observe the doctor but we cannot.' Dawkins was again lying. He had conveniently forgotten that surgeons visit other surgeons to observe surgical techniques all the time and there is never a problem with consenting from the patients. All the new techniques and advances in surgery are learnt by observing someone else operate in their own environment. Otherwise, no one will be able to keep up with the rapid progress in any surgical field.

Fred tried to find out why the assessors interviewed individuals who had not worked with me for years to know about my work.

'Mr Serpe was selected by the panel, was he not, as the complainant?' Fred asked.

'As the complainant, yes.'

'You say that has happened on previous occasions, has it?' Fred persisted.

'Generally, the complainant would be interviewed. It is often the medical director of a trust, or in the case of a GP it may be one the doctor's partners or whatever but, we would usually interview the complainant, yes.' Dawkins was beginning to waffle.

'Do you say it is usual to interview the complainant, even if the complainant had not worked with the doctor in question for a period of years?' Fred was now looking at the panel chairperson for effect. Unfortunately, there was no recognition in the Chairman's eyes.

'I think in this case the complainant had worked with the doctor. We take into account events after 1997 and Mr Serpe had worked with the doctor in that time, yes.' Dawkins was definitely waffling.

'Can we just test that? Mr Serpe was a locum consultant at the hospital whose employment was terminated on 23 February 2004. Is that right?'

'Yes.'

'So he had not worked with the doctor for two years and nine months before your third party interviews?'

'No, he had not.' Dawkins was not moved one bit. He looked as if he did not care.

Then Fred tried to dig some more information about Serpe.

'His evidence, therefore, was bound to be out-of-date, was it not?'

'Not necessarily.' Dawkins was brief.

'Mr Serpe was employed as a locum for what, 14 months before that?'

The fact that he worked with me for such a brief period was lost on the panel completely.

'I think it was that length of time, yes.' Dawkins was not going to stress on the period.

'Do you know why he left his previous employment?' Fred tried to be direct.

'I do not, no.' Dawkins was lying again. I had told the assessors that Serpe was dismissed from the previous job and my discussion with the medical director of that hospital during my first interview.

'Did you not know that he had been dismissed by his previous employer?'

'No, that is not something we would have asked of him.' I could not believe how this man could sit there and lie under oath.

Fred then tried to see how they could choose Pakshar as another witness when clearly he was malicious as well and had not worked with me for years.

'This letter, Dr Dawkins, was written to the GMC three months before your assessment and I think that you had this because Mr Serpe refers to it in his third party interview.'

'Yes, I think we did have this.'

'We can see in the second paragraph that Mr Serpe was concerned that it would be suggested that he had an ulterior motive or personal vendetta against Mr Kasyapa and, therefore, it would be appropriate for other consultants to be interviewed and he identified those consultants as Mr Pakshar and Mr Foster. Is it right that the assessment panel, in consequence of that, chose Mr Pakshar?' - This along with Carmit was the 'gang of four' who used to meet in the local pub to plot against the hospital and me on a regular basis.

'As far as I remember that was probably how we got his name as still a consultant who had worked in the department and was now elsewhere but relatively close by.' Dawkins continued to lie with impunity.

'Did you learn that Mr Pakshar had left the service of this hospital some three years before the third party interviews, in December 2003?'

'Yes. I am not sure of the dates but we knew he had left some few years before.'

'Dr Dawkins, it is not usual, is it, to allow a complainant to select a further member of the third party interviewees; in particular, where that person's evidence is at least three years out of date?' I could not understand why Fred was not stressing on the fact that he was malicious and vengeful. I had made that perfectly clear to Dawkins at the very first interview.

Fred tried another tack.

'Was the obvious request not for somebody who was currently working as an orthopaedic consultant in the department?' That would be an obvious thing to do in any impartial investigation one would think.

'Yes. If you notice we already had two of those on the interview list.' Dawkins was not going to be intimidated.

'Why not have another? You could have had Mr Cooley, for example?' Fred probed further.

'We could have done. There was probably a reason why not, but I think it is fair to say we considered that gave a better balance rather than just interviewing everybody who was working in the department at the time. We had a balance between the past and the present.' Dawkins was clearly waffling and was trying to justify a serious gamble that they had taken. They had obviously hoped that this clear bias would go unnoticed if it ever came to be challenged.

'Not a balance of impartiality to Mr Kasyapa, would you agree?' Fred persisted.

'No, I do not' Dawkins had been clearly coached not to admit anything dishonest. 'Their evidence is noted, but we do not base overall judgments purely on what they tell us.'

'We will look at that in due course. There is no question, is there, that Mr Serpe was prejudice against Mr Kasyapa?'

'I think it is obvious that he and Mr Kasyapa had their disagreements, shall we say.' Dawkins would not admit to the obvious malice from Serpe or Pakshar. His coach had worked very hard indeed.

'It goes further than that, does it not? It is clear that Mr Serpe was prejudice against Mr Kasyapa. Perhaps I should not use the word prejudice because it has racial overtones, but he was biased against him.' I thought Fred was fighting a losing battle here. Dawkins was not going to admit any underhanded deals by the GMC.

'He had his disagreements and obviously felt strongly enough to complain to the GMC.' Dawkins persisted like a dog with a bit between its teeth.

'Can we look at some of the things he said in the attachments that he thought the GMC ought to see before the assessment took place?' It looked like Fred was not going to back down.

Just then, the chairman intervened.

'Mr Barnard, I was just going to inquire if you are going to be referring to quite a lot of this letter, it might be advisable to take a few minutes to read it.' I could see that he was looking for a reason for a break. After another enforced break of fifteen minutes, we trooped back into the room to continue with Serpe's letter. It was only much later that, it became clear to me that the chairman was only trying out a diversionary tactic. He was trying to break Fred's train of thought, as Sykes would not have been allowed to object.

'The allegations that, Mr Serpe, raised on the first page of the notes of the meeting of 22 December with the chief executive and the director of health, development and modernisation are essentially the allegations he repeated to your panel during the course of the third-party interviews, are they not?' Fred started.

'Basically, yes.'

'If we go to the letter which follows the notes of that meeting, the letter dated December 31, 2003, we can see that the medical director of the Trust investigated the concerns which Mr Serpe had raised ten days or so earlier and concluded in the second paragraph that on the evidence he had seen and heard, it was his firm belief that: '..patient safety is not jeopardised and, as such, my recommendation would be that Mr Kasyapa is allowed to continue with his current scope of clinical practice.' Fred looked up to see the chairperson had a wry smile on his face.

'Yes' that was probably the briefest of replies by Dawkins.

'Mr Serpe repeated the allegations again. This time with the Regional

Adviser for Surgery, did he not?' Fred had managed to get back into his flow.

'Yes. He did.'

'Mr Charleston, the then clinical director went through the nature of the investigation carried out; complication rates in terms of early dislocation following hip arthroplasty and wound infection were looked at all of consultant orthopaedic surgeons working at St Edwards Hospital between January and December 2003. He also looked at clinical activity for all surgeons in terms of their presence in out-patients and their presence at trauma lists. The highlights were - we have read that. Upaas's complications, no higher than any of the other four surgeons, considering his high surgical throughput, no higher than 0.5 per cent, well below average. Did not consider this an area of concern. Secondly, the infection rate was no worse than that of the rest of the team, therefore gave no cause for concern.' Fred finished reading from the letter as he looked at Dawkins this time to see if he was following him. 'Just pausing there, did your panel see more than these highlights from that comparative investigation?'

'Not as far as I was aware' Dawkins was lying again without batting an eyelid. 'I honestly am not sure whether we saw the full investigations. I know we got this paperwork. I remember getting this in advance.' They had access to all the documents that Serpe had sent along with the documents from the hospital's investigations long before they came to the hospital.

'Did the assessors not think that it would be sensible to interview Dr Barbour, who had apparently investigated these allegations?' Fred tried a bit of direct questioning.

'Not necessarily' Dawkins would not be drawn.

'The allegations that Serpe made, which are set out here, notwithstanding

Dr Barbour's contrary findings, you have summarised at page 5 of your report, have you not?'

'Yes, they are the two headings that were given to us.' Dawkins replied.

'And you still insist that there was no reason to interview Dr Barbour?' Fred questioned this time looking at the Chairman. 'They are the two matters which the GMC thought merited a performance assessment?'

'Yes.'

'As I read your report, there is nothing to substantiate either of those allegations in it, is there?'

'You may be as well checking what the orthopaedic assessors - as far as I am aware, no, certainly not specifically those two areas. The report does not criticise the doctor on those.' Dawkins again was trying to be as evasive as possible.

'We can say this - I appreciate that this is not an answer for Mr Kasyapa - but the complaints which caused the GMC to call for a performance assessment appear, apparently, not to warrant it?'

'That is not for me to answer' It was slowly becoming clear that this whole charade was extremely well orchestrated and was meant to appear 'independent.'

Fred wanted to pursue this a bit further regarding malice.

'Now tell me Dr Dawkins, the agreement that where theatre lists and outpatient clinics clash, Mr Upaashantha Kasyapa should give precedence to the clinics. Is that something that you have found had occurred in the three years prior to your investigation?'

'I think you will find that looking at all of the report as a whole, as I kept saying yesterday and this morning, there is some evidence that, having been given too much work in theatre, meant that outpatients could still be a problem. I would not say necessarily. We were told it had been addressed, but I would not necessarily say that it had been completely addressed.' He conveniently forgot to mention the audit figures given to them at the start of the assessment.

'We will go to the point where this is raised in due course, but the evidence was that it had been a problem in the past, but the current situation was that it had been addressed and was being dealt with?' Fred could be persistent when he wants to be. I thought he was not going to let go until he got the answer he wanted. I am not sure if Dawkins understood that. If he did, he concealed that very well.

'No. It says here that it had been addressed, but we were looking at Mr Kasyapa's performance, as to what we found. We were given this as background, but because we were given this as background does not necessarily mean the problem has been addressed.' This was probably the first time I began to realise that he would change his attitude toward the evidence shown to suit his conclusion. At times, he would accept whatever was shown and at other times, he would come out with a statement of 'cannot believe everything that was said.'

'What it does mean is that you should be testing the up-to-date position rather than the situation as Mr Serpe and Mr Pakshar could give evidence about it three years earlier. Do you agree with that?' I am sure at that stage Fred thought he had his man. He had walked right into a cleverly built trap. Or did he?

'No, I do not agree with that. In a sense, where do you draw the line? Do you just do it as an absolute snapshot on the day, two days you are doing the assessment. We were inevitably aware of the background. We were aware of allegations that had been made, and you talked about Mr Serpe being biased. He may well have been, but he had still made the allegations, and the GMC had taken them seriously enough to pass it on to us to do a performance assessment, so we knew that background. We knew, shall we say, there was unhappiness in the department.' Dawkins's reply would gladden the heart of any veteran politician.

'In relation to Serpe, can I just confirm the extent of your knowledge? We see that the last of these notes, which Mr Serpe has attached, is 5 February 2004. Were you aware that, by a letter dated 23 February 2004, the chief executive gave Mr Serpe notice that he, the chief executive, had decided to terminate Mr Serpe's locum consultant post and would pay one month's pay in lieu of notice, the effect being that he was effectively paid up until 23 March?' Fred continued to try to discredit Serpe.

'I cannot honestly remember whether we actually saw that letter itself. We obviously knew that Mr Serpe no longer worked at the Trust.' Dawkins lied again. The assessment team was given the full documentation before they started the assessment, which included Serpe's termination notice.

'We have that letter and perhaps it is appropriate that we should hand it out' Fred waved that letter out. Nancy got trusty para-legal Natalie to hand out copies of the letter to everyone in the room including the short hand writers. He invited everyone to take a minute to read the letter and then asked if everyone had read it. Turning to Dawkins, he said,

'Did you see this as part of the documentation?'

'Yes, I think we did, yes.' I was impressed with the impassive reply. The fact that he had lied only a couple of minutes ago did not appear to affect him at all.

'Let us see if we can establish what this letter shows. It shows, number one, that the St Edwards Health NHS Trust chief executive had decided to terminate Mr Serpe's employment.' Fred continued to badger him.

'Yes.'

'It is quite clear too that he sought an agreement with Mr Serpe not to work, at least for a temporary period?'

'I am not quite sure how valid that is since we do not really know what the claims against Mr Serpe were.' Dawkins's reply did not fool anyone apart from himself.

'No, we do not. Thirdly, it is quite clear that if Mr Serpe did not agree that he would no longer continue in clinical practice, the chief executive would refer the matter to the Strategic Health Authority, who might decide to issue an alert letter?' Fred was trying to strike home a point, which was probably completely lost on the panel that was looking decidedly jaded by that point. The reverend was trying to keep his eyes open and had actually started to doodle on a piece of paper in front of him.

'Yes, I would suggest that the medical director would look into the situation properly and may or may not issue an alert letter.' Dawkins was again trying to move the point of interest away from himself.

'It is quite clear also, is it not, from the correspondence we have looked at, at rather great length this morning, that Mr Serpe was likely to bear a good deal of resentment against Mr Kasyapa?' Fred was getting a bit exasperated by the evasive answers.

'As I said, I am not privy to what was in Mr Serpe's mind. I am very aware that Mr Serpe obviously had some concerns. Whether they were valid or not, we were prepared to listen to him. He may well have been biased against Mr Kasyapa, but we were aware of this. Perhaps I am not quite sure of what your question is really.' I was finding this rather unreal, as did Nancy who was having some difficulty controlling her rage.

'Now Dr Dawkins, you have not agreed with me that Mr. Serpe bore grudge against Upaashantha Kasyapa. Let us go through his interview with you in some detail. Can we just look at some of the things that Mr. Serpe said to you and your colleagues in the third party interviews? Can we go to page 14, to the last four questions on that page?

'Q   How do his skills [compare] with those of his colleagues?

A   Poor.

Q   And, this is from your own experiences?

A   Absolutely. Absolutely. Surgical skills?

Q   Yes?

A   Poor. Surgical, technical skills?

Q   Yes?

A   Yes, poor. As I said to the medical director on one interview, you know having been in orthopaedics for 40 years, or qualified for 40 years, I can tell a dodgy doctor when I see one, and I am afraid that this was one.'

That was an outrageous and exorbitant criticism of Mr Kasyapa, was it not?' Fred looked up as he finished reading the transcript.

'I am not sure about whether your language is correct. It was a criticism of Mr Kasyapa that this doctor made.' Dawkins still refused to admit he had made a mistake and was feigning outrage at the language used by Fred.

'Did it occur to you to ask Serpe if he had seen Upaashantha operate or been in an operating theatre with him at any time?' Fred would not be cowered.

'No. As I said before we were not there to do an investigation.' Again play on words by Dawkins.

Fred moved on to some more false statement made by Serpe.

'Let's see what else Mr Serpe said to you about Kasyapa. Shall we?

'Q   How does Mr Kasyapa review and reflect on his own performance?

A   I have no idea. Well, I say I have no idea. I think he, from his computer he kept a record of his cases on his own computer.

Q   His own computer?

A   I think I have sent you a copy of that printout, which showed that he had a very low infection rate and an exceedingly low dislocation rate. So, I can only assume that, because I know that is not true, I can only assume that he did not do much personal reflection.

Q   You say that is not true?

A   Well, the printout from his computer is not correct, statistically.'

Did you ask him where he got the print out from? Was that not a print out from the hospital computer? It does say at the top of the first page 'Data from Surgiserver, St Edwards Hospital.' Is it not true that he had never seen Kasyapa's database?' Fred was pointing to the sheaf of papers he held in his hand.

Sykes intervened at this stage. He was worried about the way things were going.

'I am sorry. How can this doctor deal with that? This is an expert witness dealing with an assessment.' He was looking directly at Fred as he said that.

The chairman not unsurprisingly, agreed with Sykes and asked Fred to move on.

'You have been going on about this for quite some time now and I wonder whether we could take it that the panel has got the point and ask you to move on a bit.' He was jumping at the interruption for yet another break.

'I am just aware that the witness has been giving evidence for a little over an hour. If it would assist you to take a break now? Shall we take a somewhat early lunch break then and could we come back at quarter to two. Thank you very much.'

I instinctively looked at the clock and it was only 12.15. An hour and half lunch break seems to be a routine with this panel. The Reverend was fully awake now and looked decidedly tired. O'Neil had his plastic smile on his face and looked as if he was happy for the break as well. We gathered all the papers and trooped out to the waiting room. Nancy thought it was going very well and Fred was deep in thought as we walked along the corridors. We left our files in the room and made our way to the trusty Philpots for some sandwiches and a drink.

We had a long wait when we came back to the room. It was past two in the afternoon when we were eventually called in. As we walked into the room, first thing we noticed was the change in furniture settings. The 'visitors' chairs' had been moved to a corner which made it almost impossible to see Lopa from where I was sitting next to Fred.

The chairman started by saying, 'Two house-keeping matters before Mr Barnard continues, please. I have become aware there is a dramatic thermal imbalance in this room. Some people are very cold, some people are very warm, and it is more than just an irritation. My two colleagues have changed chairs. I do not know how much we can do about this. We will keep the blinds drawn and if anyone would like to remove his or her jacket please do so. The other matter is I am aware that visitors are stuck in a corner where the boxes seem to have pride of place and I have asked to have this adjusted but we do not want to move materials when solicitors and counsel may know where things are.'

I could see reverend and O'Neil had swapped chairs and the Reverend had his jacket off. Dawkins was called back in to the witness chair again.

Fred started off, 'In so far as Mr Pakshar is concerned, do you agree in his third party interview he was very upset about a paper called a 'Vision for the Future' which Mr Kasyapa had produced in 2002?'

'Yes.'

'So unhappy was he that he resigned the service?'

'I knew he had left the department. I presumed it was because of that.'

'I think he resigned in December 2003 and his resignation took effect in January 2004. Is that your understanding?'

'Fine, yes.' Reluctance in Dawkins's voice was there for everyone to see.

'Would you say he held a grudge against Kasyapa?'

'No. I cannot' I thought Dawkins was a bit too sharp with his answer. Was it because he was going over something he wanted to hide?

'Let us see some of his third party interview answers, shall we? He said to you, I quote 'Kasyapa is never in Clinic, they are run by junior doctors and nurses' and yet he tells you during the same interview at a different point that he was never in Kasyapa's clinic. He also said to you at one point that Kasyapa 'cuts corners during surgery' and again during the same interview later has said that he has 'never seen Kasyapa operate'. Is that not true?' Fred said pointing to the transcript of the third party interviews.

'Yes' was the short reply by Dawkins.

'So is it not clear from that, Pakshar has not told you the truth to deliberately mislead you in your assessment? Would you now not say that he had an obvious malice against Kasyapa?'

'No. I cannot. It is open to interpretation' Dawkins was still trying to avoid being caught out.

'Come now Dr Dawkins, what other interpretation could there be?' Fred persisted.

Sykes intervened at this stage again.

'How can this doctor answer that question? It is pure conjecture.'

As we expected the chairperson agreed and asked Fred to move on. It was becoming gradually clear to us how the rest of the hearing was going to proceed. If I were a betting man, I would put my money on the GMC winning the case.

'Let us move on to your report for a minute if you will please. Could you go to page 18, please? At the bottom of that page, there is a statement that:

'Mr K did not perform enough of a complicated operation (hip revisions) to maintain a skill',

- And reliance is placed on two judgments in relation to that and there in relation to patient number 161294. In fact, that parenthesis, hip revisions, is an error, is it not? This was a patient who had an ankylosed hip, which required revision, and the question that was posed to Mr Kasyapa was, 'How many of this kind of revision do you do?" Fred looked at the chairperson to see if he was registering the importance of the question.

'I have that documentation in front of me. If it refers to the more complicated hip revision, fair enough. It is just making the point, if I have transcribed it wrong, that Mr Kasyapa was doing a certain type of operation that the two orthopaedic assessors felt he was not doing enough of to be doing them, basically.' I could literally see Dawkins's brain working overtime to try to get out of this.

'Your conclusion is on page 19, five paragraphs up, two above the bottom hole punch:

> 'The assessment team were concerned that Mr K did not perform sufficient revisions of hip surgery to maintain the necessary level of skill.'

Do you see that?'

'Yes.'

'That is an error on your part because he was doing many, many revisions of hip surgery.' Fred was still looking at the chairperson.

'Yes. I have not got all the bits and pieces that you have in front of me but if that refers to a different sort of operation, that could go in and it would still have the same meaning in terms of not doing enough of a particular operation to maintain the skill. Though if you want to question the two who made those judgments you may be better off on that.' Dawkins was getting a bit desperate. Moreover, I could see that Sykes was starting to fidget. He was a cool customer and never showed his emotions. The only way to know that he was getting flustered was when his eyebrows started to twitch ever so slightly.

'This was no part of your judgment. Is that what you are saying?' Fred persisted.

'Mr Amoshin and, I think, Mr Crouper.' Dawkins conveniently shifted the blame on to the other two assessors.

'Yes. The difficulty is, Dr Dawkins, you have transferred the criticism in relation to a particular complication through to revisions of the hip generally, and that is reproduced at page 84 of your report where you see in the third line, that you and your colleagues have written:

> 'The assessment team do not consider Mr K performs sufficient hip revisions to enable him to maintain an adequate competency."

Fred was looking directly at Dawkins as he finished reading the transcript.

'As I say, you might need to check with Mr. Amoshin.' Dawkins would not budge.

'Dr Dawkins, somebody has written this report and translated it as we have seen at page 19 and at page 84:

> '..that Mr K did not perform sufficient revisions
> of hip surgery to maintain the necessary level of
> skill.'

Who is responsible for that?' Fred could not hide his exasperation.

'Well I was the one who has written it in conjunction with the other assessors. As I am saying, if I have made a mistake in transcribing it and it should have been a more complicated operation, the meaning is still there: the concern was that enough of a particular operation was not being done to maintain a competency. Now, I personally do not know how many operations should be done.'

'I am sorry Dr Dawkins, but how can you judge someone being incompetent if you don't know how many operations should be done to keep up the competence?' Fred was trying to get him to admit that they had that badly wrong.

'If I have put one word instead of another or one operation instead of another, I apologise, but I am sure Mr Amoshin can explain what he was meaning.'

'You are clear that the allegation that he did not perform sufficient revisions of hips each year is an allegation which cannot be sustained?'

Dawkins mumbled something under his breath. Both the short hand typist and Fred asked him to repeat what he said

'You are probably right' Dawkins replied.

'Let us turn now, please, to page 20 and look at the heading, 'Limits', which, overall, you found cause for concern. We will ignore the acceptable findings and go straight to those, which are recorded as giving a cause for concern. The first entry is:

'In a [third-party interview Mr Jankoweicz] said
that a particular weakness was that [Mr Kasyapa]
'takes on too much' and not saying 'no'.'

That is not really a fair summary of what Mr Jankoweicz was saying, is
it?'

'I am not sure. I have not..' Dawkins had started to mumble again.

'With respect, Dr Dawkins, the little judgments that you have in part 2,
for example, the one you quote at page 20 here, is meant to summarise
the evidence of the third-party interviews. The proposition I am putting
to you is that when you quote, 'takes on too much' and not saying 'no'
as a weakness, is it only fair to qualify it by what Mr Jankoweicz is saying
on the next page, his practice has changed?'

'For a start, when we are interviewing, we are writing these down as the
interview goes and making the judgments then. We do not wait for the
transcripts to come a few days later, and then go through them, and
make judgments. The judgments are made on the spot.'

Words were tumbling out as Dawkins tried to justify his report. He had
said not too long ago that the report was compiled at a later date after
analysing the entire data. Now he was saying that the judgement was
done on spot. I failed to understand how he could justify making snap
judgements without taking the whole issue into perspective. It looked as
if they were trying to get it all over with without using too much work.

'We see that Mr Pakshar has said that Mr Kasyapa would put six or
seven joints on a list with only one theatre. That was recorded as a
cause for concern. Can you help us as to what investigation the
assessment panel made of what the benchmark was for a skilled hip and
knee surgeon and the number of operations he would do on an
operating list?' Fred continued in the same vein.

'I think, again, in all fairness, you should ask one of the orthopaedic
assessors that. I do know that both of them were pretty clear that six
major joints on a list would be considered by most of their peers to be
too many. As to the actual evidence from that, it probably comes from
local surgeon work, and I am sure they can quote where they got that
from.' I am not sure, when the assessors went and enquired with the
local surgeon network to see their workload. If they had, they would
have found at least a few surgeons who had similar type of lists in the
region and several in the country. It does not pay to be better than an

average Joe.

'Mr Charleston gave evidence that the number of joints that Mr Kasyapa did on the list had been reduced after discussion, did he not, or do you not recall?' Fred continued.

'Yes, we were told some of them had been reduced. We were still concerned, after the assessment and having talked to everybody that we talked to and looked at, that Mr. Kasyapa had too much of a workload. In many ways, that could have been marked as unacceptable.' Dawkins replied.

'Let us see what Mr Charleston the current clinical director of the department said to you shall we? Over the page he says, at page 58, at the bottom Miss Mildred asks her usual question of strengths and weaknesses and under weaknesses he says: 'I think he, oh dear .. How can I put it? I think reverting back to the way he attempts to try and do as much as possible for his patients and the trust, that sometimes he is or was a little naive in the way he tried to deal with some of the problems.' The point I put to you, Dr Dawkins, is it is clear from Mr Charleston's evidence that Mr Kasyapa had moderated his workload from the time that he ceased to be clinical director. Would you accept that?'

'No. I do not accept that. I think it is clear that Mr Charleston thought Mr Kasyapa had taken on board what he had said, but I think it is still fair to say that, overall, looking at his workload there was a cause for concern raised' Dawkins was standing his ground.

Next Fred introduced John Fitzgerald's statement to the assessors during the third party interviews where he had said that the waiting list pressures were reduced as we had achieved the 2008 targets by March 2005 and that Kasyapa is doing the same workload as everyone else. However, Dawkins again defiantly refused to accept it. I could see Fred was getting exasperated and I was not sure how much of this was being registered by the panel members. We had seen the Reverend nodding off a few times already and the Chairman had his eyes closed a couple of times.

'Dr Dawkins, the point is that you have relied here specifically on the evidence of Pakshar, who we know had not been a colleague for three years and yet, the assessment panel have not recorded the evidence of Charleston and Fitzgerald that his workload had been cut down?'

'I think we have recorded that in the audit section as how he responded to things but ..' Dawkins's voice trailed off and it could not be heard by anyone.

'Dr Dawkins, I am sure you understand the point I am making.' I thought for a moment there Fred had given up. I had never seen such dogged resistance from anyone.

'All I am saying is that there is enough evidence, and we do look at all the evidence that we noted, to raise a concern that ..' before he could finish, Fred was on to him

'But with respect Dr Dawkins, did you not tell me a few minutes ago that the judgements were made on the spot without analysing everything?'

'No. I did not. What I meant was that the report is written later on a report writing day. My English is not as good as it should be.'

That came as a shock to all of us on this side of the bench. Here is an Englishman, born and brought up in the UK, studied medicine in the UK and professes to be a leader and member of several learned associations telling us that his 'English is not as good as it should be.' He, according to his own admission and CV, qualified, trained and working as a principle General Practitioner in England.

'What you failed to do as a team is to distinguish between the past and the present is it not? That is the long and the short of it.' Everyone in the room could hear the exasperation in Fred's voice.

'No, it is not. You may feel that but you cannot separate the past from present.'

'Now let's look at some other evidence you have put forward as 'cause for concern' Pakshar's evidence was that neither discussed cases with the other. Is that not it?'

'Exactly. The team are not criticising Kasyapa because Pakshar said that. He just said it and it has been recorded. I think there are perfectly good reasons why they would not necessarily discuss cases with each other.'

'The panel might be intrigued to know why it has been recorded as a cause for concern at all. Would that not be construed as a fault on Kasyapa' part.'

'Because it was said' Bland reply from Dawkins.

'Come now Dr Dawkins, you don't expect for us to believe that.'

It was time for the Chairman to intervene. I do not think they could have taken any more, particularly a post lunch session.

'Mr Barnard, the witness has been giving evidence for about an hour now. I have been looking for a convenient point to take a break.' It was decided to take a break for 30 minutes and return at 3.15 pm. In the waiting room, Nancy appeared to be getting a little jaded and tired. I also felt that we were probably not making the kind of progress we would have wanted to make. Dawkins was taking too long. Both Nancy and I wanted Amoshin to be on the witness stand for a considerable time so that his credibility and evidence could be destroyed. Dawkins had taken most of two days. I could see Fred was a bit fed up as well at the recalcitrant witness. I had sent feelers out through my orthopaedic network to find out as much as possible about Amoshin as the usual internet sources had revealed very little.

The last session started with Fred's continued questioning of Dawkins.

'Now Dr Dawkins, let us look at some of the judgements that you have said as 'Unacceptable'" I am reading down on page 21 of your report, 'The following judgments were recorded as unacceptable,' and the first entry is: 'In a TPI [Mr Pakshar] said that [Mr Kasyapa] would do more cases on a list than it was safe to do.' Can we assume that that is a reference back to the entry at the top of that page?'

'Yes, it will be the same area of the TPI.'

'It is the same point, is it not? Put it that way.'

'Yes.'

'I appreciate different references are made by different authors but they all listened to Mr Pakshar giving his answers in the third party interview and they are referring to the same point that Mr Pakshar was making.'

'Yes.'

'So not only is it a cause for concern, it is also unacceptable. Can you just explain to the panel how a criticism can be both a cause for concern and unacceptable? Surely it is one or the other, is it not'

Again, Dawkins mumbled something inaudible no one could hear. This time the chairman had to ask him to repeat what he said.

'It is difficult to say so long after the assessment was done. It is nearly two years ago now.'

'All right, I will remember that. Then the next sentence says, 'A knee replacement had not been done with the proper technique and there had been no postoperative follow up' That is 231 and 327 and they are the same two orthopaedic surgeons.' 'Yes.'

'Of course, I will ask them about that but let me ask you this: do you agree that Mr Pakshar brought no evidence in relation to the case of the alleged knee replacement done without proper technique and without post-operative follow up?'

'Yes, he brought no evidence along.'

'Do you agree that the assessment panel sought no evidence in relation to that allegation?'

What Dawkins said next came as a shock to me and I am sure many people will find difficult to understand as a part of investigation.

'We never ask for any proof or evidence for any allegations any one makes against the Doctor. We are not there to do an investigation.'

'Dr Dawkins, your assessment panel are relying on this as a finding of unacceptable performance for the doctor in circumstances where his registration might be erased?' Fred managed to show his incredulity both in his voice and in expression. He was probably expressing the disgust we all felt on this side of the room.

'We would not go out and seek further evidence from what a TPI says because the assessment runs to a pretty formal structure.'

'And this 'formal structure' is designed by the GMC, I suspect?' It was a rhetorical question, which bought severe objections from Sykes, and the Chairman asked Fred to refrain from making such statements. Fred did not look chastised. He was quite happy that he had scored a point.

'Let us look at yet another judgement that you have made. There is an entry:

'In another case Mr K could not remember when he had seen a patient pre-operatively.' That is patient 510132. The reference is 674, which is at page 256. Can we just turn that up at 256? It appears that the question was. 'When did you last see her?' The answer was, 'I cannot remember.' Is that basis for the cause for concern here?'

'I think the basis of the cause for concern is that - you may want to check this with Mr Crouper - that there was nothing - I presume from the medical records that there was nothing recorded about her being seen pre-operatively or for assessment, whether that was in the pre-admission clinic, and the cause for concern is whether, in fact, Mr Kasyapa had actually seen her or not. As I say, I am sure Mr Crouper can clarify that answer.' Dawkins was quite happy to pass the responsibility easily to someone else.

'This was a case from the year 2000, was it not?'

'I do not know. I have not seen the - I do not have the records in front of me. I presume that is ..'

'Just take it from me. If it was a case in the year 2000, you hardly expect the doctor to remember when he had last seen a patient six years ago, would you? You cannot remember this statement you have recorded two years ago?' There was very little Dawkins could say apart from mumbling about the time delay and the amount of papers to deal with.

Fred continued 'Then we come to the concluding parts of this and I think we have dealt with most of it already. Can we go over the page, to page 22? Can I take the last paragraph first: 'Mr K must work with the rest of his team to ensure that he has an operating workload that is safe for the patients.' There is no evidence that patient safety was put at risk by Mr Kasyapa's workload, is there?'

'No. That is a recommendation that an operating workload should be safe for the patients.' Dawkins continued to waffle.

'There had, in fact, been an audit, which you record at page 36 of your report in the second paragraph: 'A departmental audit has not highlighted any problems with Mr K's performance.' You had no evidence to doubt the accuracy of that conclusion?'

'No. I think that is the audit I was referring to that we were told about it being done.' Dawkins clearly had no idea what he was talking about.

'Let us look at your next conclusion. The proposition is, let us just read what you have recorded: '..Mr K is willing to take on an unrealistic workload in theatre, despite advice. Because of this our overall judgment is cause for concern."

'We have concerns Mr K is willing to take on an unrealistic workload in theatre, despite advice. We are saying we have concerns.'

'But have you no evidence. Indeed, it is contrary to the evidence, is it not?'

'No, it is not contrary to the evidence. There is some evidence. We have concerns. We cannot ignore them. We had concerns that Mr K was willing to take on an unrealistic workload in theatre, and it worried us, it worried the two orthopaedic assessors. We are not saying it is unacceptable, because there is not a lot of evidence, but we had a concern.'

'At the risk of incurring the chairman's impatience, let me put this proposition to you one last time: There is no evidence that Kasyapa was willing to take on an unrealistic workload in theatre despite advice. In fact, the evidence was to the contrary. Do you agree?' For the first time I could see a semblance of activity in the Chairman's eyes.

'I think we agree, that he had been advised about it and some people thought he had taken the advice. All I am saying is the fact that still raised a concern about workload. No matter how many different ways I put it, I cannot say anything any different to that.' None of us were sure if he had actually conceded that he had made a mistake or not.

'I am just having difficulty understanding why it is that you were not prepared to accept the evidence of the clinical director and the chief executive that the workload had been brought under control.' I could feel the anger in Fred's voice, even though well disguised.

'As far as I am aware, it may come up in other interviews - and it may have partly come from the initial interview, though I have not got a record of that here so I cannot swear to it. As far as I am aware, in particular, the orthopaedic assessors were still under the impression, as were the lay assessor and myself that Mr Kasyapa was still doing six major cases in an operating list and that was felt to be too much of a workload. His performance in the assessment section was unacceptable because in 2 out of the 42 cases, if we are correct, there was a completely inadequate assessment of the patient, which is 1 in 25 per cent, which means, potentially, a considerable number of patients would not get assessed.'

'In that case, can I ask this: All these conclusions the panel reaches about workload, and we have looked at it in two sections now, based on evidence in third party interviews which have been transcribed and so on, was this allegation ever actually put fairly and squarely to the doctor to see what he said about it? Namely, that his workload was excessive and was creeping up.' Fred asked.

'I would have to check back to the original documentation but I think his workload was discussed in the initial interview for the portfolio and there will be handwritten records of those interviews available.'

Fred would have none of it. 'Let me put it to you, Dr Dawkins, that he has never been asked to say what he has to say in his own defence against an allegation that his workload was excessive and that the measures that, it had been said had been put in place to control it, were not effective, and that that was having an adverse effect on patients to the extent that they were at risk of harm.'

Again Dawkins had very little to say apart from something about having to look at all the documents before answering. Fred decided to stop and invited Dawkins to read whatever documents he wanted to read overnight and answer them tomorrow.

I could see the reverend had woken up and was pleased as can be at the conclusion. I am sure he was looking forward to a cool beer in the plush hotel accommodation provided for by the GMC.

Dawkins had said that he would have to drive down to London the next afternoon for a Test of Competence. It later turned out the test was actually the day after next. It was my mistake to think that you should not lie under oath!

We spent a few minutes in the waiting room discussing the day's events and any preparation that needed to be done for the next day. Nancy had given me the page numbers of the TPI transcripts to read to pick up a few points and reminded me to get as much dirt on Amoshin as possible. We said our good byes and started walking back to the rented apartment near Piccadilly. As we reached the apartment and were chilling out, Gautam called. I went through the day's proceedings in some detail with him, as it had become a routine every evening. As I was talking to Gautam, sitting in that extremely uncomfortable but very fashionable high-backed chair with what could only be described as enormous blinkers on either side, Lopa came in with coffee and some snacks. Once you sit in that chair you could not see anything but whatever is directly in front of you. If we wanted to talk to each other, we had to sit opposite one another. We had to sit towards one edge of the chair at a certain angle to watch the TV. It must have taken me a good half an hour to give Gautam the details of the day's proceedings. He again emphasised the need to get as much information as possible about Amoshin and see if we could discredit him. He had sent out feelers as well and was waiting for response. Lopa had decided to cook a simple meal for the evening as we were getting a bit fed up of the restaurant food Manchester had to offer. Just as she finished cooking boiled rice and a simple bean curry, Swayambhu called. First thing he said was that he was driving down in the morning. I managed to persuade him to take the first train, as we would be driving back together on Friday anyway. Gautam had filled him in about the day's events and he had some news about Amoshin. It had turned out that one of my schoolmates from Medical School, Vishwa, was actually working in the same hospital Amoshin had retired from. Swayambhu happened to know him as well and managed to get his mobile number. I looked at the clock and it was only nine in the evening.

I decided to call Vishwa and dialed the number.

'Hi Vishwa. Remember me? I am Kasyapa from Bangalore Medical College.'

'Hi Kasyapa. Of course I remember you. I have not seen you since we came to your house in Staines Bridge in 1984. How are you? I have heard a lot about you. You have really gone up in the world.' Vishwa enthused. If only he knew what was happening right now. I decided not tell him the details of my problems and decided to create a fictional colleague who was in trouble. After telling him about the problems this colleague has had and being assessed by Amoshin, I wanted to know about Amoshin's background.

'Did you know of a Phata Amoshin, who retired from your hospital in 2005?'

'Yes. Of course I know him. I did not have much to do with him. He was a 'Clinical Specialist' similar to a Staff-grade for a number of years, until a few years ago they decided to make him a consultant to do some foot and ankle work. He did not do much during that period. Did some simple procedures like bunions and claw toes?' That was interesting information.

'Did he do hip replacements when he was a Staff grade?' I asked.

'Yes he did some under another consultant who was a clinical director at the time.' Vishwa replied.

'I have been told by my colleague that his CV says that he did regular lists for hip replacements and that he had done over 2000 hip replacements. We normally don't allow our staff grades to do independent lists in our hospital.'

'That cannot be true. He never had his own lists. He was allowed to do one or two cases in the consultant lists and he was doing small cases on the lists when his consultant was away, such as removal of metalwork and bunions. There is no way he could have done 2000 hip replacements. I don't think we have any consultant in our hospital that has done that many hip replacements on their own.' Vishwa was obviously surprised at my question. This puts a completely different complexion on what Amoshin has said in his CV that had been made available to us this morning. On the first day of the hearing, the GMC had said that they did not have any CV for any of the assessors. We were completely shocked by that revelation. Here you have a regulatory body of all the doctors in the land appointing assessors without looking at their CVs. These assessors are supposed to be 'experts' in the field to assess the doctors' competence. We failed to understand how the GMC decides to choose assessors without knowing their qualification and experience. It would be very interesting to see if Amoshin would swear to his CV when he takes the stand in the next couple of days.

I said thank you to Vishwa, asked him about his wife and children, and said we should meet up soon and hung up. Lopa had overheard most of the conversation and said 'Fred should completely discredit Amoshin. He is not fit to assess even a Staff Grade. How can he be allowed to assess a senior consultant?'

She was seething with rage. After dinner, I sat down to do the homework Nancy and Fred had given me with the transcripts. It was quite late by the time I finished and go to bed exhausted.

11. Day Four; Thursday 1ˢᵗ May, 2008.

I was up early in the morning, as I knew Swayambhu would be coming down by train and I would have to go to the station to pick him up before going down to the GMC offices in St James' building. As I was walking into the Piccadilly station, the 8.30 train from Seaport was just pulling in on time for a change. Swayambhu was one of the first ones out of the train. As soon as he saw me, he dropped his bag, gave me a hug, and shook my hand. Tears welled up in my eyes, but I hoped that he had not noticed it. I can say with some authority that I had one of the best sets of friends in the world. Gautam and Swayambhu, along with their wives, Yadavi and Pavaki, had stood by me at the worst of my times unlike anyone I had known. I can easily say that I may not have had the courage to carry on with what I went through without the support of my dear friends.

As we walked towards the apartment, Swayambhu had about a thousand questions. He was one of those who wanted to know everything in detail, the dots on the i's and crosses on the t's of everything. No detail was to be left out. It could be tiring sometime but necessary. As we reached the apartment, Lopa was ready to leave for the GMC. He hugged Lopa with a genuine feeling which cannot be described. The bags were quickly dropped, and Lopa asked Swayambhu if he wanted a cup of coffee. He would not have any of it. He was itching to go to the GMC see for himself the place and feel the atmosphere of the place.

We set off down Portland Road towards St James' Buildings. It was yet another dull day with overcast skies and a forecast for rain later. Swayambhu wanted to stop at the local convenience store, to buy a notebook for him and bought one for Lopa.

'We should write whatever is said in the room that we think are relevant. You never know when it may come in useful.'

'But there are short hand writers in the room.' I said doubtfully.

'Who pays for them to copy?' Swayambhu asked obviously knowing the answer.

'It is the GMC obviously' It suddenly occurred to me what he was getting at.

Swayambhu just smiled and pocketed his notebook after giving one notebook to Lopa.

Once we were in the building, we got Swayambhu his own ID badge from the lady at the front desk who barely took notice of who was coming or going. As we entered the waiting room, there was a lot of activity with Nancy and Natalie busy with lots of papers and Fred was apparently having a meeting with Sykes. They were apparently discussing some legal issue, which I could not understand despite Nancy trying to explain to me. I introduced Swayambhu all around, and Nancy explained the procedure again to Swayambhu. It was not until well after ten when the usher called us in. Fred did not have much time to speak to me, as he was busy with Sykes before we were called in to the hearing room.

First thing we noticed as we entered the room was a lady sitting next to the Reverend with a board in front of her proclaiming her to be Dr Feras Mercia. She was a rather severe looking woman, short with thick-rimmed glasses and with a distinct lack of humour. She reminded me of a headmistress we used to have in our school days, which nobody liked. She also had a wad of papers and a couple of large lever arch files in front of her. Before the chairperson could say anything I asked Nancy if she knew what had been happening over the previous three days.

'She should have been given the transcripts of the last three days. Unfortunately, the GMC have not been able to get the transcripts back to us and will not be giving it to us until next week. In short, she won't know what has happened over the last couple of days.' Nancy tried to explain in a whisper.

'In that case, how can she give any advice to the panel in their decision making process? I was getting a bit concerned. We had requested earlier that week that we should have sight of the CV of the Specialist Performance advisor. There was not any. The GMC apparently do not have any CVs of either the assessors or the Specialist Performance advisors. It looked like anyone willing to work for the GMC and has qualifications, as a doctor is sufficient for them to be an assessor or an adviser. It did not look like the GMC made any effort to get a suitably qualified person to do the job. My suspicion was that any suitably qualified surgeon would be too busy to spend their time in this charade.

The Chairman started the day with a brief introduction.

'Good morning, everyone. First, we have been joined this morning by our Specialist Performance Adviser, Dr Feras Mercia.'

Dawkins was eventually called, and he sat in his witness chair. Fred started at the same question where he had ended the previous evening.

'Dr Dawkins may I remind of my question yesterday to you; 'Can I ask this? All these conclusions the panel reaches about workload – and we have looked at it in two sections now – based on evidence in third party interviews which have been transcribed and so on, was this allegation ever actually put fairly and squarely to the doctor to see what he said about it, namely that his workload was excessive and was creeping up?'

And your answer was: 'I would have to check back to the original documentation but I think his workload was discussed in the initial interview for the portfolio, and there will be handwritten records of those interviews available.'

Now that you have had time to read through the documents, can we have your answer please?'

'I was asked on what evidence I was basing our concerns about Mr Kasyapa's workload, whether that had been addressed. I have not seen the notes of the initial interview. They are handwritten notes that I am not sure we could find easily, but ..' Dawkins knew very well what the answer would be in the notes. The legal assessor intervened with,

'Dr Dawkins, I thought the point was that you were going to look through the handwritten notes?'

Dawkins again rattled on about the concerns raised during third party interviews by Serpe and Pakshar.

Fred again stopped him. 'With due respect Dr Dawkins you are not answering a simple question. It is nothing to do with the third party interviews. The question simply was whether you asked Kasyapa about his workload. Let me take you through your own handwritten notes we have here.' He passed on the photocopies of the initial interviews with me in November 2006 to the chairman and the panel. These were hastily photocopied that morning by our trusty paralegal Natalie and stapled. Unfortunately, we did not have enough time to paginate them. This caused enormous confusion and Fred had to ask them to paginate themselves. That took some time as the specialist performance adviser was getting all her notes mixed up. I must admit that the whole scenario was so well orchestrated that the stress on the main issue was considerably diminished by all the confusion with interruptions by the chairperson, legal assessor, specialist performance adviser, and Sykes.

Fred finally tried to pin Dawkins down,

'Finally, can we go to page 20? The penultimate question on the page is, '5/6 joint replacements seem high in one day?' and the answer recorded is, 'The gap between cases is 15/20 minutes. Theatres sometimes go on to 6 pm. We start at 8.30 am.' The final question on that page is, 'You feel OK physically, coping with that workload?' and the answer recorded is 'Yes'? Given that, I put two points to you.

The first is that Mr. Kasyapa's workload at the material time was five to six operations in a list. Do you agree with that?'

'As I tried to say, I would agree that Mr Kasyapa says there that it is five or six. The evidence from other sources is that it was six, so I would agree six.' Dawkins was trying to say that I may not be telling the truth and he would rather believe others.

'Surely Mr Kasyapa, the man who is actually doing the work, is in a better position to know, is he not?' Fred pointed out the fallacy in his reasoning.

'If I can perhaps put how… I think I tried to explain yesterday how the assessment is built up. This is the initial interview with Mr Kasyapa and we clarified his workload. He said 'five or six'. When I say about workload in the report, I say throughout the report something like 'There is information that gave us concern about Mr Kasyapa's workload'. Now I have managed to tie all that together. I am not really arguing, if Mr Kasyapa said that it was five or six and other people said that it was six. What I am trying to say is that the picture that built up through the report – and when we are doing the assessment we do not have the whole report in front of us, obviously – this is when the database is tied together and the information comes into one place, and when it was tied together and I was writing the report and we had the report writing days, from the information we had from the third party interviews, as I said yesterday, we still had some concerns that there was a considerable amount of evidence that the workload was six major cases a day, and I think we agreed that that was something that the orthopaedic assessors could explain why they felt that was excessive.' Dawkins was clutching at straws.

'Perhaps there is little difference between us. It is quite clear on the evidence that everyone is agreed that there were plainly occasions when Mr Kasyapa was doing six operations in a list in a day?' Fred persisted.

'Yes.'

'There is simply no dispute, and that is what he was doing at the time, but you have pointed out this morning that that had been reduced by Mr. Kasyapa from doing up to eight operations in a list?'

'Yes. When I went through it, the evidence from the third party interviews quoted is that several years before when there were problems Mr. Kasyapa was doing eight major operations a day and he had changed down to six.'

'Can I come back to the question that I posed yesterday, which I have reminded you of today? The fact of the matter is that the allegation that his workload was excessive and was creeping up, which was the case that you made yesterday afternoon, was never put to him, was it?' Fred was reminding the panel rather than Dawkins as he was looking at the chairperson as he said it.

'Well, this is what I am trying to explain. We could not, because at the time when we were with Mr. Kasyapa we only had the bits in the report; we had not all seen all the evidence. It was when it was pulled together that we felt there was some concern. I do not really like the word 'allegation' because I am not necessarily trying to say that we are alleging that his workload was excessive. What I was trying to say yesterday was that when it is all pulled together, when several weeks or months after we had seen Mr. Kasyapa it was all pulled together, we had some concerns that there was perhaps an excessive workload in theatre' Dawkins replied.

'No, Dr Dawkins that will not do. Yesterday afternoon you told the panel that the reason you had found that this was a matter of concern to the panel and led to an unacceptable finding because of the pressure that it was said to put on carrying out assessments was a cause for concern in itself, was that you were concerned about the future and your fear that the workload would creep up?' Fred tried to pin down to admitting he was wrong.

'Yes.'

'The point is that the doctor never had a chance to answer that, to reassure you that it would not. Indeed, he did not even know that that was a matter in the minds of the panel until he read your report?' Fred tried to drive the point home.

'Fine. I am not quite sure how we were meant to be able at the assessment to bring up all these points. What I am trying to say is that that was based on the evidence in the database that we gathered. It is in the report. The panel will presumably make a judgment as to whether they think that is a valid point.' Dawkins clearly putting the onus on the panel to make their mind up instead of admitting that he was wrong. What happened next was quite unreal, if I may use Fred's words. Sykes objected to the statement Dawkins had just made saying we could not use material 'post 2007' as Dawkins had mentioned my portfolio in his reply. The legal assessor was asked for advice and she agreed with Sykes and the chairperson threatened to 'go into camera' if Fred did not agree with that. Fred reluctantly moved on.

'Let us look at the GMC's good medical practice guide, 2001 version. Is it right that this is the bible, as it were, for an assessment by the GMC?'

'Yes'

'The requirement is that Mr Kasyapa recognised the limits of his professional competence and worked within them?'

'Yes.'

'It is quite clear that he was working within what he recognised as the limits of his professional practice in undertaking five to six joint replacements in a day?'

'I think you are asking me presumably, in answering that, to state a fact. What I am saying is that there is concern and that you will be able to talk about it with the orthopaedic assessors who are better qualified than I to say what a sensible workload is in theatre. They felt that there was some concern that the workload was too high.' Dawkins replied looking at the chairperson.

'Can we look at paragraph 4 of *Good Medical Practice* on page 3? That reads:

> 'If you have good reason to think that your ability to treat patients safely is seriously compromised by inadequate premises, equipment, or other resources, you should put the matter right, if that is possible. In all the other cases, you should draw the matter to the attention of your Trust or other employing or contracting body. You should record your concerns and the steps you have taken to try and resolve them.'

The panel was aware, of course, that Mr. Kasyapa had put forward a paper entitled

'A Vision for the Future'. That is right, is it not?'

'Yes'

'That paper proposed the appointment of two further consultant orthopaedic surgeons. Is that right?'

'I cannot remember the full paper but I think it did, yes.' I suspect that Dawkins had hoped that Fred would not produce this document as evidence. At the time when we were under pressure to reduce waiting lists and achieved what was termed by the Government as 'Model of Excellence', I had produced a document termed 'Vision for the Future' and sent it out to my colleagues for comment before implementing it as a responsible leader of the department would. I had spent a considerable amount of time analysing the available resources within the department of orthopaedics in particular and the hospital in general. Taking the results of this analysis as the base, I had worked out the requirement to achieve this model of excellence. This model was a proposal by the Government to a group of selected eight hospitals in the country to see if we could achieve the March 2008 target by March 2005. The Government would fund such a project and the incentive to achieve this target would be funding for a major innovation project within the hospital, which in our case would be an NHS Treatment centre. Achieving this would have been a feather in the cap of any hospital in the country. The prestige associated with achievement of this to any hospital would be incalculable in terms of money. This document had worked out details of how many extra theatre hours and clinic time required along with personnel required to achieve safely the target set.

Briefly, it would need an increase of one qualified Nurse for every theatre session, two more consultant surgeons, one senior middle grade, and two nurse practitioners. It also detailed all the other personnel required such as increased clinic nurses, theatre nurses, and ward staff to achieve the target safely and on time. It had taken me over six weeks to get all the figures and costs etc to produce the document. The document was distributed to all the consultant colleagues in the department for comment before finalising it and submitting to the Trust Board. I had discussed the document informally with our service manager and the then chief executive informally. Both of them had shown a lot of enthusiasm for the document. Unfortunately, this did not go down very well with our colleagues, particularly Pakshar, Foster, and Carmit who with the help Serpe planned to scheme against me.

To the surprise of Dawkins, Fred did produce the document as evidence.

'This is the paper that caused Mr. Pakshar such concern, is it not?'

'Yes.'

'You agree that it proposes two further orthopaedic consultant surgeons and on additional middle grade to be appointed in the short term and additional nurse practitioner/clinical research nurse x 2. Is that right?'

Dawkins just nodded and did not say anything. I could see that the Chairman was looking a bit uncomfortable and the Reverend for the first time looked a bit alert and was fidgeting. He had stopped doodling on the paper in front, which he was doing all morning. Fred continued.

'Page 3, under the heading 'Short term'. The solution is in the immediate stage, short-term stage. We can see at a glance, without descending into the detail, that he is proposing a lot more staff to deal with the orthopaedic throughput, is he not?'

'Yes.'

'As we know, that did not meet with the approval of all the consultants in orthopaedics, did it?'

'No.'

'In fact, it was not put into effect as far as you are aware?'

'As far as I am aware, no.'

'But in drawing that matter to the attention of the Trust, was he not fulfilling his obligations under paragraph 4 of *Good Medical Practice*?'

'I just want to make sure that we are talking about the same thing. Yes, paragraph 4 of *Good Medical Practice* refers to the use of resources, and there is a section in the report on the use of resources. Do I need to say anything more other than Mr. Kasyapa's performance in the use of resources was found to be perfectly acceptable?'

'It is a bit more than that, though, is it not, Dr Dawkins? Here we have a chap who is doing a heavy list by any account, who is trying to help the

Trust to reduce its waiting lists at a time of great pressure, who ultimately reduces his list from eight operations to six, and who also has said to the Trust, 'Listen, guys, you need more staff here, you need more consultants'. What more can a man in his position do?'

'I am not quite sure what you are… I think I have said this quite a few times. The only issue as far as I can see that you are asking me about is that the assessment team had some concerns that Mr Kasyapa's workload in theatre might be too heavy. Now that came about on our advice from two orthopaedic assessors. I cannot answer this question any more. They are going to come and give evidence and surely they can answer it better than I can.' Dawkins had finally managed to twist the whole subject around and wriggled out of answering a rather crucial point by diverting it on to his colleagues. I was a bit disappointed that Fred did not push the issue further. He had him by the shorts and should have rammed it home. I thought he let him get away with it. I looked at Swayambhu who was very busy writing something in his notebook.

Fred moved on to the assessors criticisms about my note keeping. They had said that it was unacceptable that some of the notes were missing. According to them, it is every doctor's responsibility to make sure the secretaries type the dictation and add them to the patient's notes.

'Did he not say that there was a period after his permanent secretary had left when he had a series of locum secretaries?'

'I cannot remember offhand.' I nearly said why has he not written it down as he expected me to write everything down.

'The other point is this: in any NHS hospital notes and tapes from time to time do get lost, do they not?'

'I think it can be said that can happen in any NHS hospital or in any general practice. Nothing can be guaranteed 100 per cent, no.'

'If you go to the fourth entry in that second half of page 25, it says that Mr Kasyapa stated that he now dictated his operation notes or put them straight on to the computer. That is not quite right, is it? He said that he now put them straight on to computer operation notes?'

'I am sorry, I have lost the reference.' It had become Dawkins's habit now well recognised by everyone in the room, apart from probably the panel, whenever he did not want to answer a question or he wanted time to think about an answer to say this.

'On page 25, the second half of the page without the indentation, the fourth paragraph.'

'Yes.'

'The point that I am putting to you is that that is slightly inaccurate. He said that he used to dictate his operation notes but now he put them straight on to the computer?'

'Yes, I would accept that that might be slightly inaccurate. I mean it would not be a criticism of Mr Kasyapa if he did dictate his operation notes. I cannot see the...'

'You cannot see the significance of it?'

'No, I cannot see the significance.'

'Is not the significance of it that you did criticise him for dictating his notes where the dictation got lost or was wrongly transcribed?' Fred said. I wished he had said that how can you make wrong entries and expect Kasyapa to have 100% right entries all the time?

'No. The criticism was that when notes were missing... If you dictate notes, it is not a criticism of people dictating notes, because not everybody is happy on a keyboard and things get lost when you type things into a computer, things can disappear, as I am sure we have all found. The criticism was that if you dictate notes or you put them on a computer, you still have the responsibility for making sure that those notes are found, so that if dictation does not turn up at the secretary, there needs to be some system in place, somebody recognises that something has been lost and something can be done about it; and I think the criticism made about dictating – in fact, talking about yesterday – was that the problem was that it would be brought to someone's attention that dictation was lost maybe two or three weeks after it had been lost, and then you are relying on memory. You need a system that if the dictation is missing or an operation note is missing, the secretary from a list says on that day, 'I have not got this dictation' and it can be re-done while it is still fresh in people's mind.' Dawkins obviously lived in a world of his own, as did the other assessors to expect the typing to be done on the same day of the clinic or same week in the short-staffed NHS.

'This is just unreal, is it not, Dr Dawkins? What if the secretary does not get round to doing the typing for two or three weeks and only discovers it then? That is the reality of life in the NHS, is it not?'

'Well, it should not be.'

'It should not be, but ..'

Dawkins did not let Fred finish.

'It is not up to me to decide that that is the reality in the NHS. What I am saying is that there should be systems in place that things do not get lost. I mean general practice is in the NHS but I would be in trouble if three weeks later I was told that my referral letters had not been done, because I would not be able to remember what was on them. It may be a reality but it should not be a reality, and it is up to the doctor to make sure that patient safety is protected and do something about it." It would be interesting exercise if we can look at fifty of his patient records to see how many dictations were missing.'

'He did something about it. What he did was to decide that he would put his operation notes straight on to the computer himself. That is the point, is it not?'

'Well, as the point about half an hour ago, I am not sure whether I can refer to other things. What I would say is that the assessment found that there was a problem. Mr Kasyapa said that that had been dealt with, but there was a problem in the notes that we looked at where things were missing.'

Dawkins had been schooled enough not to admit to any such mistakes. I have suspicion this is probably the only qualification the GMC look for in their assessors, as it clearly was not interested in the qualifications or credentials of any of them as doctors or surgeons. I could see the chairperson had been looking at the clock several times during the past fifteen minutes and there were glances between O'Neil and the Reverend as well. Finally, when the Reverend gave a slight cough and that was it. It was also a point where Fred had Dawkins in a corner and could have scored some points.

'Mr. Barnard, I am going to start looking for a point for a convenient break. The doctor has been giving evidence for a while now. Could you guide me?'

'Could I take just a few more minutes to see whether we can finish this subject matter?'

'Thank you.' The chairman reluctantly agreed to the dismay of the reverend.

'Now Dr Dawkins, staying with the records, do you also agree with me that the entry halfway through the second half of page 25, 'Mr. K stated that he now dictated his operation notes or put them straight on to computer', is erroneous, I am sure inadvertently, but that it should say that he now, having dictated them in the past, put them straight on to the computer? Do you agree?'

'Yes. I have already answered that I agreed.'

'The conclusion on page 26 was that his performance in this respect was unacceptable because incomplete records make it difficult for another doctor to know what has been done as regards missing operation notes, which could be particularly dangerous for the patient. Was it not incumbent on the panel to point out that the doctor had changed his practice for the better in relation to missing operation notes that could be particularly dangerous for patients?'

'I could point out that Mr. Kasyapa said that he had changed his system for the better, but I suppose what I am trying to say, as I have already said, is that we had the notes in front of us that we were looking at from a reasonable period before. I mean you said the date of that operation was two and a half months before the assessment. I mean we are looking at notes. We ask for the notes to be made available. We cannot look at notes of the week of the assessment because of the physical improbability impossibility of getting them out. We look at what I would say are recent notes and found a problem. There could be a rider that Mr. Kasyapa said that he had changed his system, but we had no evidence that that system was changed.'

I wish Fred had reminded him that he claimed they were not doing an 'investigation' and hence why were they looking for 'evidence.' They had taken Pakshar and Serpe's words as gospel truth, but I needed to back my statements with evidence.

'But in assessing the doctor's current practice, was it not incumbent on you to call for the notes to check?' Fred was stating the obvious if not rational next step in any investigation or assessment.

'No. You are talking about the impossibility.' Dawkins's reply was brief and sounded final. I cannot understand why. If he can expect the secretaries to type the notes on the same day of dictation, it cannot be impossible to get notes of a patient operated on in the previous ten weeks. Fred decided to break at that point as he was clearly not getting anywhere with him. He could not get a reasonable answer or even a logical answer from Dawkins for the question of record keeping. Dawkins was clearly wrong but he was not going to admit to it come hell or high water. The reverend was quite relieved when we broke for coffee at about eleven ostensibly to return in fifteen minutes.

As we waited in the now familiar waiting room looking at the dull sky outside and a steady drizzle, Swayambhu said, 'This must be the most depressing city in the world. The buildings are grey and dark with grime from years of factory soot. The roads appear dirty and damp. There are boarded up premises wherever you look'

Natalie who was from Manchester did not like that one bit, but had difficulty defending it. She did try to talk up some of the 'finer points' of the city to no avail. Swayambhu would not change his mind. I felt the same way, particularly as everything looked depressing when you are being hauled over coal in public. Both Nancy and Natalie were busy making some fresh copies of the documents for the panel and writing page numbers during the break. We were not called back in till just before 11.30.

Fred continued into the next judgement of the assessors. They had said that there was a cause for concern about my communication with patients.

'Dr Dawkins, can we move on now to the penultimate section of this part of your report, which deals with communication with patients? It begins at page 40. The panel found that overall there was a cause for concern here?'

'Yes.'

'There were judgments recorded as acceptable, which I will come back to in a moment, and then there were judgments recorded as giving concern and judgments recorded as unacceptable. The overall conclusion – and it is in the penultimate paragraph on page 42 – was that current evidence from the case-based discussion would suggest that on occasion patients were not given full or correct information?'

'Yes.'

'You have explained to us that you have simply put down the judgments that you and your colleagues have made, whether for against, without any sort of weighing up, as it were, of those that are unacceptable against those that are acceptable, but I want to ask you about the first entry under the heading of judgments recorded as acceptable on page 40, where it says:

> 'In a TPI, AS (Mrs Slattery) said that Kasyapa would discuss treatment options as much as possible in the limited time available. There did not appear to be any problems in giving information to patients. His communication with relatives and carers was on a par with that of other consultants or anyone else. Communication was a strength. Kasyapa was willing to answer questions and explain things to patients.'

Is that right?'

'Yes.'

'Did you not think that Mrs Slattery's evidence was the best that you could possibly have of Mr Kasyapa's communication with patients?'

'She would be a good source of evidence on communication with patients, yes.'

'Can we just look momentarily at her third party interview? This is in D6, which is quite a thick document containing the transcripts of the third party interviews. Page 22 is the interview with Mrs. Ann Slattery. I think the transcriber seems to have missed out this lady's present position, because if you look at her first answer, she says, 'From 1997 – I have to think of this – prior to that I was clinical nurse', and what has been missed out is what she has been or what she now is. The answer to that is that she is the outpatient sister and manager, is it not?'

'I think that was stated at the beginning. Yes, she is the outpatient sister. We were told that she was the outpatient sister, yes.'

'Let us just see what her experience of Mr. Kasyapa is. She says:

> 'I have worked as a clinical nurse with Mr. Kasyapa and the other orthopaedic surgeons, I would say for 15 years. I do go into clinics to work with them. So I have known Mr. Kasyapa professionally working alongside him in his clinics and managing, as he did, any problems as all of the consultants have with space, and with things like that, you know, you do become involved with as a manager. There is never enough space.'

The next question is 'how often are you present when he sees patients? And her answer is, 'Not as often as I used to be. If he does evening clinics and I do his clinic, I will be with him when he is seeing patients. So, probably once every couple of weeks when he does an evening clinic and I am actually on that clinic.'

So this lady has long experience of seeing Mr Kasyapa with patients and, not only that, she has recent and regular experience of seeing him with patients – agreed?'

'Yes.'

Should not her evidence have been given particular weight, in consequence?'

'I do not think that it should necessarily have been given particular weight. I do not think anyone is arguing, or we are not arguing that Mr Kasyapa cannot be a good communicator, is pleasant, and talks to patients, and I think the evidence from the test of competence shows that. It is appropriate for me to say, that is based on the case-based discussion. No matter what Mrs Slattery said – and she was very positive about communication in general –. No matter how positive Mrs Slattery would have been, that still, if you like, was evidence from Mr Kasyapa himself that we felt was significant; but, as I state that did not make his performance unacceptable, but it did give us concerns that in the case-based discussion two of the patients that we discussed were given the wrong information.' Dawkins again trying to divert attention from the evidence in front of him.

'We will come to those two patients in a moment. Let us just press on with the acceptable comments: 'JF stated that communication with both him and his mother had been very good.' JF is Mr Fitzgerald, is it not?'

'Yes.'

'Mr Fitzgerald's mother had been treated by Mr Kasyapa on a number of occasions, and he, Mr Fitzgerald, was very supportive of Mr Kasyapa's communication with his mother on all occasions. Is that right?'

'Yes.'

'Mr Fitzgerald's father had also been treated by Mr Kasyapa; it appears from the third party interviews. Is that right?'

'I think his mother.'

'His mother and his father?'

'I cannot remember whether it was his father as well.' There was no way Dawkins would budge an inch.

'I will not trouble to turn it up, but I can assure you that it is there. Miss Helen Summerfield is HS. She had actually been a patient herself, had she not, of Mr Kasyapa?'

'Yes, I think she had.'

'She spoke very highly of his communications with her as a patient?'

'Yes.'

'Let us turn to the matters recorded as giving cause for concern:

> 'In a third party interview, CS (Mr Serpe) said that he had treated patients who had not been given information by Mr Kasyapa. Patients had not been given a choice of prosthesis.'

Is that evidence to which you gave less weight for the reasons that we discussed yesterday?'

'It is the evidence that we had and is to be considered.'

'The allegation that Mr Kasyapa had treated patients who had not been given information by him is something about which Mr Serpe brought no evidence whatsoever, did he?'

'He did not bring... I was not the person interviewing Mr Serpe but, as far as I am aware, he did not bring actual evidence.'

'Neither did the assessment panel seek any evidence from Serpe to back up that allegation?'

'We are not in a position to. If he has not brought it along, we cannot. We only have that time slot with Mr Serpe.'

'Then why bother to write it down at all? If it is an allegation from someone who has animus against Mr Kasyapa, who you regard sceptically, who makes an allegation with no supporting evidence at all, why ..'

Dawkins interrupted at that point, 'Because it is something that he said; it is something there. Again, as I think I tried to explain, if you followed that up, if anybody said anything positive about Mr Kasyapa without producing information, would we ignore that. It is there, it is said in a third party interview and, as I think I tried to say yesterday, I think we gave appropriate weight to what Mr Serpe said. If you read the report, I do not think we gave a lot of weight to what Mr Serpe said.'

'You certainly based this conclusion on Mr Serpe's allegation, did you not?'

'It was mentioned.'

'Bear with me, Dr Dawkins. Just look at page 41 and the next sentence for CS (Serpe), which reads, 'Patients had not been given a choice of prosthesis.' Once again, we can confirm – let us put it in short form – that he brought no evidence of that and you sought none from him. Do you agree?'

'He brought no evidence and we are not in a position to be able to seek evidence from him. We cannot tell him to go away and bring back the case notes or whatever.'

'Furthermore, this allegation was never put to Mr Kasyapa, was it, to hear what he had to say about it?'

'As I said before, it is impossible to put all the allegations made in third party interviews together because…'

'Yes, you have said that, Dr Dawkins, and ..'

'…most of us do not ..'

'Dr Dawkins, forgive me ..'

'Most of us do not know that allegation ..'

It was rapidly deteriorating into a farce when the chairman interrupted and asked Dawkins to answer the question.

'Most of us do not know that that allegation, if you like, has been made until it is tied together in the report, and it is in the report, it is an allegation that has been made, it is only an allegation, but it was made, but it does not take away from the fact that it was made.' Dawkins finished.

Dr Dawkins, if you would just listen to my questions, I am not going to stop you from giving any explanation that you wish to give about any answer that my question provokes, but I want an answer to the question first of all. The question was a simple one and, as I understand it, you are confirming that this allegation was never put to Mr. Kasyapa to get his side of the story?'

'No, for the reasons I have given, it was not.'

'Right, for the reasons that you have given. Now that allegation that patients had not been given a choice of prosthesis is, in fact, wrongly recorded. The allegation was that a patient had not been given a choice of prosthesis. Do you agree?'

'I would have to check, but I am sure you are right.' Dawkins sounded as if he had given up.

'You do not have to look very far, because the same allegation is recorded as unacceptable on the same page. If you look right at the end of the first bullet point ..' Again Dawkins interrupted.

'Yes, I have just looked at the thing. It says, '*The* patient had not been given a choice of prosthesis.'

'So we have yet another typographical error, have we, expanding 'a patient' to 'patients'?' It is so convenient for the assessors to get away with a 'typographical error' to give a wrong judgement.

'Well, as I said, it was not used, but ..'

'You say that it was not used but look over the page at page 42. In the first paragraph on the page and the last sentence, it says, 'Patients were not given management options.' That is exactly what Mr Serpe was saying, which you have accepted, is it not?'

'Yes, I have used it, we have been told it' It took an enormous effort to get an admission of mistake from Dawkins.

'Dr Dawkins that simply will not do. This section at the bottom of page 41 and the top of page 42 is your conclusion section and you have accepted Mr Serpe' allegation that not merely one patient but patients were not given management options?'

'I have not accepted anything, or the team has not accepted anything. I would agree that there is a typographical error, and that is down to me collating it, that 'patients' should read 'patient."

'Let us just take this in stages and see whether we can make some progress here. We have an allegation from Serpe that a patient had not been given a choice of prosthesis. One of your colleagues thought that that gave cause for concern, the other thought that it was unacceptable – right?'

'Yes.'

'The panel as a whole then drew conclusions in relation to that and accepted that allegation as the truth, did it not?'

'No. It accepted the evidence in this section as limited.'

'No, forgive me, Dr Dawkins, it does not say that. If you look at the top of page 42, it begins by saying that there is evidence from both colleagues and the case-based discussion that full information was not always given, and so on, and then it says as a fact, 'Patients were not given management options.' That is your finding?'

'No. I am sorry, I think you… Well, it may be that we are just going down the line of semantics. There is evidence, whether it is good or bad evidence, but there is evidence from the colleagues, and not only from Mr Serpe but one of the current colleagues as well, that ..'

'So are you inviting the panel to ..'

'No, I am sorry, can I just ..'

The chairman was again quick to interrupt asking Fred to let Dawkins finish his answer.

'All I am saying – and I do not profess to be great at English grammar – is what I am trying to express there and what I am saying to the Panel is that there is evidence.' There he goes again claiming his English was not very good. It was quite appalling that someone who claimed his grasp of English was not very good has been allowed not only to be an assessor, but also to be a lead assessor.

'So is it the assessors position before this fitness to practise panel that your report contains both good and bad evidence and that you have not distinguished between one and the other?' Fred did not attempt at hiding his incredulity at Dawkins's statement. Swayambhu was looking flabbergasted. I am sure he could not believe what he was hearing.

'It is probably, if you like, coming down to semantics. Maybe 'good' and 'bad' were the wrong words to use, but the report contains evidence that is... I mean some evidence is obviously stronger.' Dawkins stuttered in a hurry.

'In the case-based discussion it is recorded as having given concern by one doctor that Kasyapa said that he would tell a patient with gout that there was no risk of flare up after joint surgery, and that apparently was regarded by the other of your colleagues as unacceptable, because the same allegation is made in the second bullet point under the heading 'unacceptable' – Presumably, you want me to explore with your colleagues the details of that patient and whether the advice given by Mr Kasyapa was appropriate or not?' Fred continued.

'Yes.'

'I will ask them about that. The second allegation from the case-based discussion for cause for concern is that patients having arthroscopy were told about complications by the nurse practitioner but the risk of deep vein thrombosis was not mentioned because he felt that it was so rare, and one colleague regarded that as cause for concern and then it is repeated as unacceptable by the other. Is that right?'

'Yes.'

'Your evidence to this panel is that the conclusion of cause for concern is based exclusively on those two cases?'

'Mainly on those two cases, yes.'

'What else is it based on?' Fred challenged.

'I mention that we have evidence from colleagues about what I state in the conclusion but then go on to say that evidence from the case-based discussion, which is largely what I base that on, or exclusively if you like – I am quite happy with that – is what gave us cause for concern; those two cases, yes.' That was appalling even from him.

'You tell us – I do not want there to be an ambiguity about it – the way you say at the top of page 42 'There is evidence from both colleagues and the case-based discussion,' the colleagues being referred to are Serpe and Pakshar?' Fred persisted and he was again trying to bring out the fact that, large proportion of GMC case was based on statements from these two individuals.

'Yes, but I am saying that the cause for concern in that – and I am sorry if it is not clear for my use of English is not very good – from the middle paragraph on page 41, is that it is on current evidence from the case-based discussion would suggest that on occasion patients are not given full or correct information, so I am trying to say that that is what that conclusion is based on, and I apologise to the panel if that is not clear.' There he goes again about his poor knowledge of English. This time even the dozing reverend looked up in shock. It looked like he was trying his hardest cover up his mistakes for 'poor knowledge of English.'

'The next entry is that John Fitzgerald said that when juniors were in clinic Mr Kasyapa might be elsewhere in the hospital. That was not quite all he said though, was it?'

'No, he does expand more. That is all that was written down.'

'Shall we just see what he actually said? We have it in the third party interviews, D6. It is right at the end. It is the second section and page 32. You asked the question, a third of the way down the page.' Fred read out for nearly a minute what John Fitzgerald had actually said and finishes by 'I appreciate that you have to be very short in writing your report but, on reflection, the entry there that when juniors are in clinic Mr Kasyapa might be elsewhere in the hospital really does not do justice to what Mr Fitzgerald was saying, does it?'

'I agree that it is a brief summary because there is only so much that we can handwrite and do at the time.'

'But, to be fair, do you not have to add his words, 'He certainly does not leave the juniors unsupervised'?'

'Probably, if we were quick enough to get it down.' I thought Dawkins was smiling when he said that.

'Let us look at the next entry, which is PJ, who said that sometimes middle grades were given too much responsibility, e.g. fractures in children. That reference is also at the top of the page as well. If you look at the top of page 49 of your report, the first complete sentence reads:

'Occasionally it was possible that delegation to middle grades was inappropriate – for example, supracondylar fractures in children.'

'Yes?'

'That again is erroneous, is it not? He spoke of one case. Do you want to see it?' Fred went on to describe what Peter was describing about one child whose care was handled by one of the senior Middle Grades – who in fact acted up as consultant when one of us went on leave.

'So we can now make that correction, can we not, that the allegation that he allowed middle grades to look after fractures in children is wrong and must be corrected in both places at page 49? It is simply one specific case?'

'Yes, it is one specific case that he gave. It is just that if you look at judgment 460, if I have put it in the plural and it should be singular, that is my fault; I wrote the report' Dawkins was again trying really hard to justify the litany of mistakes in the report. By the time Fred went through a couple more of the issues where Dawkins had made repeated assumptions about what could have been said or what was said and what was in his mind, it was getting close to 12 noon. I could see the reverend was getting fidgety and the chairman had looked at the clock a few times pointedly. We broke for lunch just after 12.

As we walked out of the hearing room to the waiting room, Swayambhu wanted to know where we were going for lunch. In the waiting room, he tried to engage Fred in some discussion about the case, but Fred was too engrossed in his own thoughts and did not appear too keen in any discussion at that time. I gently steered him away and we went down to our regular spot at the Philpots at the corner of Portland Street and Oxford Road. I think Swayambhu was not enamoured by the sandwich shop. He would rather have an Italian with a glass of wine. Unfortunately, both Lopa and I were not in a mood to 'socialise' at that time and we wanted to get back as soon as possible. As we stood in the queue, we saw a number of solicitors and probably some witnesses to the numerous hearings. It was easy to distinguish who was who by the look on their face and their general demeanour. The guy looking depressed, haggard and with deep circles under the eyes must be another doctor being screwed by the GMC. That one in the corner with a dark suit and a gleam in his eyes and an air of arrogance must be a GMC barrister and talking earnestly in hushed tones and looking around furtively all the time to see if anyone was watching must be one of the GMC's witnesses or could be an assessor. That one at the back of the queue with a trolley and looking completely stressed who kept looking at her watch every couple of minutes and sighing must be a solicitor for one of the defendants. In such a small room, it was amazing to see such a variety of expressions and humanity that varied from happy go lucky to arrogance to desperation and sheer depression.

When we finally came to the front of the queue, Lopa took her own time to decide what she wanted as she always does and after what appeared to be ages we were on our way back with our sandwiches and drinks to the GMC. We decided to sit in the room set aside for witnesses, as it was empty so that it would give some privacy for Fred and co to do their work. I wanted our discussions to be private as well. We decided to get back to the waiting room around two to see if we were being called in. There was no sign of that happening. The corridor was empty and we could hear the tinkle of glasses from the secure dining room where, the panelists were having their lunch and customary glass of wine no doubt. It was not until 2.30 that we were called back in. I spoke to Nancy during the break and updated her about what we had learnt about Amoshin.

'Thanks Upaas. That is very useful. It is shocking that he has produced such a CV. I wonder what he is going to say under oath.' Nancy surmised.

'Can he be discredited for lying under oath or misleading information on his CV?'

'Can you get any data from the theatres where he had worked to see what the kind of work he had actually done was?'

'I am afraid that may not be possible as we would have to go through Freedom of Information act as Serpe did to get the data from our theatres,' I said with some disappointment.

'We could really discredit his testimony and his assessment report if we can show that he has been lying' Nancy looked at Swayambhu and me hopefully.

I said, 'I will see what I can do. However, it is going to be difficult. The hospitals are loath to part with any information as you know.'

As we neared the hearing room, we were asked to wait outside, as the panel had not reached the room yet. It was only an hour forty-five minutes for lunch break. Eventually we were ushered in and Fred started again with Dawkins.

'Dr Dawkins, at page 13 there are notes of the introduction remarks by the lead assessor. Were those notes made by you or by one of your colleagues listening to you?'

'I think they have been made by one of... well, they are not made by me; it is not my handwriting.'

'It begins: 'Object is to assess current performance. We hope to make it as stress free as possible. Do you have any questions about the process?' Presumably, that is accurate, that is what you said?'

'Yes. I could not quote it verbatim, but that sounds like what I would say, yes.'

'That is what the panel presumably was attempting to do, to assess Mr Kasyapa's current performance?' I could see Fred was stressing on the word current for obvious reasons. I wonder if it's significance was last on the panel. There was no visible reaction from any one of them.

'Yes.'

'We can now put that away. Let me ask you some questions about the tests. First of all, during the course of the first part of the process, Mr Kasyapa asked several times about the nature of the tests that were to come, did he not?'

'I cannot remember whether he asked several times. He certainly asked and I told him about them at the final interview at the first part of the assessment.' Dawkins replied with some urgency in his voice.

'He was also told that the tests would be explained to him nearer the time – yes?'

'Yes.'

'He was also told that he did not need to read any books for preparation?'

'He was told that the tests were not like a Royal College exam, not academically high flying tests, but that they were looking at a basic knowledge level to be expected of a consultant orthopaedic surgeon. I cannot remember what he was told about going out and reading books, but I would say that the tests are not the sort of things that you would revise for. They are the sorts of everyday things that you would expect someone to cope with.' I could see that he was not comfortable as he answered.

'When you say that he was told that they were tests for an orthopaedic consultant surgeon, was he also told to write about his normal practice at work?'

'Sorry, I do not quite understand what you...?' Dawkins was up to his old tricks of 'not understanding.' He knew perfectly what Fred meant.

'His recollection is that at the start of the written test he was told to write his normal practice at work, which appears to me to be consistent with what you have just said. Is that right?'

'To be honest, I am not quite sure what you mean by that. He was asked to answer the questions.' Dawkins was beginning to fidget. It would not be long before he would say his knowledge of English was poor.

'His recollection is that he was asked to write his normal practice at work, but you do not recall that?'

'I do not recall using those words. I think I would have to check with the lay assessor's record of the day.' He paused there for minute riffling through the papers looking rather uncomfortable 'Yes that just records that I explained the core test of knowledge and that if the doctor had any queries, we were next door.'

There was no way he would admit to what he said to me in public now, as it would undermine his testimony significantly.

'At any rate, you have a clear recollection that he was told that this was not like the FRCS exams and there were going to be questions – I am paraphrasing your words – appropriate for an orthopaedic consultant surgeon?' Fred continued.

'Yes.'

'The questions from the surgery core knowledge test, of course, were taken from the FRCS bank of questions of the Royal College of Surgeons, were they not?'

'Yes, they are questions that are derived from those, yes.' Dawkins was looking a bit confused now. He was not sure where the questions were heading.

'So it would have been possible for somebody who had been told that that was the sort of question that he was going to get to be able to prepare himself or herself for such a test?'

'I really do not know' Dawkins replied. I was sorely tempted to shout out, what do you know?

'What is clear from what you have said so far is that Mr. Kasyapa was not given a true idea of the level of questions that he was going to expect, was he?'

'I think he was' Dawkins's reply was very brief with no explanations.

'In the skills section this was an entirely artificial situation, was it not?'

'Yes, in terms of not using real patients.'

'It was extremely stressful for the doctor?'

'I think any test of any established doctor is stressful, yes.' The only admission from Dawkins for the day I thought.

'The facilities were poor?' Fred queried looking at the chairman this time.

'I would disagree with that. They are new and modern, and I have not come across any problems with the facilities at the Obs Centre.' Dawkins was trying very hard to defend the GMC now and was making every attempt to look sincere.

'We know, for example, because it is recorded at page 66, that there was no kidney dish available for the suturing part of the work?'

'I do not think you can say that the facilities are inadequate. It was pointed out by the assessors that there was a kidney dish missing, yes.'

'Well then what about this? The laparascopy was set up wrongly and it took five minutes before the technician realised that and it had to be set up again?'

'Yes, I know that there were problems with the laparascopy.'

'Arthroscopy equipment was faulty as well and there was no camera for the arthroscope, was there?'

'I do not know. You would have to ask the technical questions of the people up there.' Dawkins would not elaborate on who these 'people up there' were.

'The tendons Mr Kasyapa was asked to suture were completely dried up. Had they not?'

'I am not sure what you mean' Dawkins would not budge.

'Coming to instruments, did Mr Kasyapa not point out that they were inadequate and hence he had to handle the needles?'

'You will have to ask the orthopaedic experts' Dawkins was looking distinctly uncomfortable.

'I will do that. We have so far shown faulty equipment in a significant number of stations and yet you say the facilities were adequate' Fred would not let go.

'Yes. You will have to ask the orthopaedic experts' I thought we were beating a dead horse. Dawkins was not going to admit to any faults with the GMC's assessment process.

'Now let's look at your conclusion on Mr Kasyapa's audit. You have concluded, 'Mr K's own audit records may be inaccurate and there is uncertainty as to the outcome he records as an endpoint.' But you did not have Mr Kasyapa's audit records, did you?'

'No, but it was discussed with him what his defined endpoint was in the audit. We did not actually see the complete records.'

'You did not see any records, did you?' Fred persisted.

'No, we did not see the... we asked him about the defined endpoint.'

'But you had no audit to ask about?'

'This is where under 'Audit', which overall we found acceptable – this is on page 35 of the assessment report – we are not saying that they are inaccurate, but there is some concern. On page 35, under 'Judgments giving cause for concern', the bullet point for case-based discussion says: 'In the case-based discussion Mr K stated that his audit figures did not correlate with the department's. He liked to think that his were better and did not consider the department figures to be accurate.' It was clear to everyone in the room, except probably the panelists that Dawkins was waffling.

'But you did not see either his audit figures or the department's did you?'

'No, we were unable to see the department's, and without being able to compare the department's with his, we would not be able to say for definite about accuracies, but we were told by Mr. Kasyapa himself that his audit figures did correlate with the department's.'

'Yet you say on page 36, in the second from last entry, 'Mr K's own audit figures may not be as accurate as he perceives'?'

'Yes. It would come down to whose audit figures you believed. He says that they do not correlate with the department's, so there is a possibility that if the department's figures were accurate – and we would have had no way of going through both sets of audits and doing a proper audit and deciding whose figures were accurate. I mean it may well be that the department's audit figures are inaccurate, but there is a possibility of the inaccuracy because it is admitted to us that the audit figures do not correlate together.'

'So, going back to page 84, the foundation of the statement that we are looking at in the top quarter of the page, 'Mr K's own audit records may be inaccurate', is founded on the fact that he simply told you that his audit did not correlate with the department's and therefore it must be a possibility that his record is inaccurate?'

'Yes.'

'Do you seriously think that that is a proper basis on which to write a report on which a doctor's registration might be erased?'

'I think that it is a proper basis on which to put the information in, yes.' Dawkins insisted. He had been well and truly schooled by Sykes on this one.

'Is it not true that the allegation that the audit records were inaccurate came from Mr Serpe, did it not? And it had coloured your judgement?'

'I think he does allege that somewhere. But that would not affect our judgement in any way.'

Fred continued in the same vein for another ten minutes before giving up. There was no way Dawkins would budge from his stance that the GMC and the assessors have done nothing wrong. Sykes took Dawkins through few more questions very briefly and tried to bring in yet another argument into question – of the new report produced excluding all third party interviews, Fred resisted that very well and Sykes was stopped. That was probably the only time a discussion between

Barristers took place where a reasonable argument was seen and agreed throughout the whole process. Eventually, the chairperson wanted to have a break again and they went into 'camera.' Swayambhu was fascinated by this business of going into 'camera' and wanted to know the details of the process. He looked a bit disappointed when he was told all it means is that they are going to be talking behind closed doors. We trooped back to waiting room for more coffees from the vending machine in the corridor. During the break, Fred wanted to know if there is anything else that we need to ask Dawkins. I could not think of anything. My brain was overloaded with information and I firmly believed that Dawkins would not budge at any cost.

I said 'It is pointless asking this man any more questions as he either avoids answering them completely or tells you lies.' I was rather bitter by that stage. Fred and Nancy agreed. The consensus was that we would have to concentrate on the two orthopaedic assessors. Nancy explained to me that the panel members would ask some questions before going on to Amoshin. It was well into the afternoon when the panel members started to ask questions.

The chairman as usual made a big deal of introducing O'Neil as 'the only medical member' of the team. He appeared to stress that fact as if to emphasise that the team is quorate as they have an 'expert in the medical field' on the team. O'Neil started with Dawkins with questions about the number of joint replacements I was doing per day. His questions appeared to be rather random as he jumped from workload to questions in the test to physiotherapy referral. It was only later when I was actually reading the transcript that I realised that it was a clever way of consolidating all the negative points and probably justifying the mistakes made by the assessors or the GMC. He made an issue of the workload on several occasions and showed surprise that I was working from eight thirty in the morning until six in the evenings and some days doing evening clinics. It just demonstrated how far removed he was from the standard NHS practice, as it existed all over the country. Most of us were expected to work up to twelve hours a day and often five days a week followed by some weekends. How did he think the waiting lists had been reduced across the country to meet the government targets? The Government had made a promise to the nation that everyone will be seen and treated within eighteen weeks of referral without increasing the resources anywhere. When this was decided and decreed by the NHS Executive, the time for this spanned anywhere from six months to two years. If we had not worked the hours we did and continue to work at the same pace in the near future the whole system would collapse around our ears. The team of assessors and the

GMC in general were completely oblivious of the safe guards that were built into the system to protect the patients from harm during this process of expediency.

O'Neil made a big issue of 'unmet educational needs of junior staff' and how it is important to train the junior staff in 'record keeping'.

O'Neil started by saying 'Mr Kasyapa, when asked by one of your colleagues, did say that they had a teaching programme for juniors and what happened when he picked up errors, and he said 'By educating them or when I see a patient in the clinic.' Are such unmet educational needs of junior staff, or of any staff, important to informing their education?'

'I mean in any speciality, I would say, and this would include general practice, I would expect that the trainees would be taught how to keep proper records, record keeping, use of investigations, so it would be an important part of their education, yes.'

'From your own experience, how would you know that that was happening?'

'Usually, from my own experience, it would be by fairly regular audits of what his junior staff were doing in terms of note keeping or if they had made the entries in a clinic, maybe a random audit of a few cases. Well, when I say 'audit', probably a random review of a few cases to see what had been filled in.' Dawkins' reply was as expected. It would be interesting to see his 'audit'.

'Did you see any evidence of such educational type audits of the educational needs of Mr Kasyapa's junior staff?' O'Neil continued.

'We did not see any, no.' I do not remember him or anyone else asking me to show any audit data for such or any other activity for that matter during the entire process. I wished Fred would object and raise this issue.

'Did you see any evidence of any needs-based teaching organised or done by Mr Kasyapa?'

'We did not see that, no.' Dawkins lied through his teeth. He or anyone else for that matter had never seen our teaching programme and he did not have a clue as to the content of our teaching programme. The assessors never raised this question. Again, I was disappointed that

Fred did not pick this up and challenge them. I suppose he really could not as he was probably unaware of this omission by the assessors.

Dawkins was asked if he had seen any evidence of my own educational needs and personal development plan. He again lied saying that he had not seen any personal development plan. If he or any of the assessors had taken time to read the portfolio submitted to them before that assessment began, they would have seen my appraisal documentation, which contained my personal development plan. This travesty continued for a while. Dawkins denied that I had not had any training in 'teaching techniques.' If only he had read my portfolio properly, he would have seen that I had attended not one but several courses on teaching and training. I was getting more and more angry and frustrated by this litany of lies being put forward against me under oath.

There were questions being asked and statements being made which were way beyond either of their extent of knowledge of orthopaedics such as MRI and CT scans with metalwork in situ. The two of them together trashed the idea of work-based assessment against an 'objective test' and claimed that the Royal College of Surgeons was against it. This was news to me and as it was to the Royal College Advisor of the northern region when I brought this subject up. Perhaps they have no knowledge of NCAS (National Clinical Assessment Service) assessment or the Royal Colleges own assessment procedures, which are purely work based. Lastly, he was asked a question by O'Neil, which Fred was not allowed to ask – question about the conclusion drawn by the assessors. Dawkins tried to justify that there may have been 'mitigating circumstances' and that I 'was working too fast and let basic skills lapse' - a contradiction in terms if there was one. Yet again, I was being criticised roundly for working 'too hard.'

I was again disappointed that neither the chairman or Fred raised no objection at this obvious mockery of justice.

As O'Neil finished the chairman introduced the 'specialist performance advisor.' This grandiose title was given to a Miss Feras Mercia who turned out to be a consultant hand surgeon from London. It is a pity that we were not allowed to question her as to why she or the GMC thinks she is an expert in the field I was working in, which was purely lower limb orthopaedics. There was no curriculum vitae coming forth as to her expertise as the GMC had none. I had to look her up on the internet before the hearing started to find out who she was. When I raised the question of her suitability with my team, I was told we get either her or none at all. That would have meant a postponement of the hearing to God knows when.

The role of the specialist performance advisor is to 'facilitate' and 'advise' the panel with specialist questions during the hearing. Unfortunately, no one seem to have informed this to Miss Mercia. She was more prosecutorial than the GMC barrister! She started by accusing me of doing elective orthopaedics while I was on trauma call. This was based purely on what Serpe and Pakshar had said in their statements to the assessors. She appeared to concentrate on what Pakshar and Serpe had said about me to base all her questions to Dawkins. She practically accused me of not being in clinics, and junior doctors were taking consent for surgery and nurse and physiotherapists put the patients on the lists. She had in fact repeated allegations made by Serpe and Pakshar and she was allowed to get away with it. I sat there dumbfounded and shocked. I looked at Nancy and Fred in disbelief and I was hoping that Fred would put a stop to it. I was raging inside and had difficulty concentrating on the proceedings when the reverend started his questions.

I felt some of the questions being asked by the reverend were relevant. Particularly when he asked if the assessors were conducting an assessment and not an investigation. I thought he made a valid comment when he asked how one could do an assessment without an investigation. The question as to how or why no questions were asked to test the veracity of some of the statements made by Pakshar or Serpe was completely muddled by sudden verbal diarrhoea from Dawkins. Even after reading the transcript in cold light of day, I could not see the wood for the trees. Between the two of them, they concluded that the assessment team did no wrong by not asking for evidence to substantiate any of the claims by either Pakshar or Serpe. At this stage I was beginning to lose all faith in the justice system as they were getting away with sheer lies and fabrications. The reverend finished by asking Dawkins to define 'evidence' that brought a response you would not find in any dictionary. He finished off saying 'it would probably be more accurate to use 'information' or 'evidence/information.''

It was the chairman's turn to ask questions and I could see he was in no mood to ask too many questions. He had already looked at the clock a few times in the previous ten minutes. To justify his title as a 'Philosopher' he went off in a tangent into obtuse subjects and questioned about 'triangulation; in relation to judgements and assessment. Once he established that everyone was aware of him being a Philosopher he asked a couple of questions about the way the report was written and the way the assessors came to their judgement. It was all very esoteric and hid the fact that there were numerous deficiencies in their judgement and report.

When Fred said that he did have some questions to ask as part of re-examination, I could see the Chairman's eyes roll upwards is despair. I was glad that Fred brought up the question of the work-based assessment and made it clear that we do not accept Dawkins's statement that the Royal College of Surgeons had put a stop to it. He went on to question him about the teaching of juniors and audit.

'A number of issues have arisen and Dr O'Neil raised one – for example, that there was no evidence of audits of staff or needs-based teaching by Mr Kasyapa, but there was no problem about you asking him whether he had such things, was there, if you wished to?'

'I am not trying to say that his teaching and training is a problem. It is ..' Dawkins was trying to weasel out of it.

'No, forgive me, Dr Dawkins, I am not asking you about the merits of whether he was a good teacher or a bad teacher or not. All I am asking you is this: procedurally, there was no obstacle to your asking him what audits of staff or needs-based teaching he had been involved in, in particular in relation to the keeping of records by junior staff, was there?'

'No. We could have asked for that, yes'

'So. Without asking him that question, you cannot say that there were no audits of staff or such teachings. Can you?' Fred was looking directly at O'Neil at this time. Dawkins just nodded his head

The next question Fred asked I thought was probably the most relevant of the day. 'We have the third party interviews and we can see that everything that you asked them about was recorded, and you asked them about all the headings that appear in the report. You did not go through that exercise with Mr Kasyapa, and that is because that is not standard practice. Is that right?' I thought that was very relevant.

'Yes, it is not a part of the assessment to go through a third party interview with the doctor who is being assessed.' Dawkins replied. It is quite clear that the doctor who is being assessed is given no opportunity to defend against what was being said against him or her, as the assessors never raise the issue with the doctor. I cannot see this being a fair assessment.

'But there is no procedural reason why, having done the third party interviews and the case-based discussions and so on, you should not go through with the doctor and say, 'Look, let us go through the headings. This is what is said against you. What do you have to say for yourself?' Fred continued.

'But, we do not have an opportunity to talk to the doctor when all the information is present that we have gathered in a coherent form.' Dawkins was looking at the chairman and Sykes for help I thought.

'In that case, may I respectfully suggest that it is your procedure that is defective? It may be that the panel will think that it is both unfair to the doctor that the tentative conclusions that you might draw against him have not been put to him so that he has a chance to answer them, and to be undesirable that the first chance he has to meet that case is before them, whereas he might have convinced you?' Fred was looking pointedly at Sykes as well as the chairman. At this time of the day, when the panelists were trying to stay awake, the enormity of Fred's statement was not registered.

As a final matter, Fred did bring about the crucial question about 'deficiency.'

'The final matter is this: in answer to a question, you said, 'On the basis of the whole assessment, Mr Kasyapa's performance is deficient,' and I wondered whether you mean, '*was* deficient,' namely at the time that you carried out the assessment?'

'Yes. Not at this present time. I am talking about the time of the assessment, yes.' Dawkins's reply I thought was quite clear – in the past.

'With regard to the next question, I am going to pause just to see whether Mr Sykes objects to it, which is to ask you whether your view is that his performance is now deficient?' Fred was looking at Sykes and he replied.

'Yes, I do object to it.' I did not see the chairman saying anything about it. I still have not understood why O'Neil could ask that question and Fred cannot.

Sykes finished his re-examination by asking a couple of questions about my daily timetable and concluded. Fred wanted to know if the specialist performance advisor had been reading the transcripts of the previous days when she was absent. We were told that she had to our surprise.

It was not borne out by her questioning. I think by that time everyone had enough and finished just after five thirty in the evening. I for one was more than happy to get out of that room. I felt oppressed and was full of despair at the injustice of it all. I could see Swayambhu talking to Lopa under his breath and I could see the incredulity on his face.

As we walked into the waiting room, the first thing I asked Fred was, 'Are we going to let them get away with this? I cannot see how I am going to get a fair hearing. I cannot see even an ounce of fairness in what happened today. Dawkins was allowed to get away with murder and lying under oath.' I was really angry. Both Fred and Nancy tried to calm me down with 'you will get to speak when your turn comes.' and we can correct all these mistakes. I was not so sure. We all walked out of the building together agreeing to meet that next morning at nine for a briefing before the hearing resumes. Nancy wanted to know if we were successful in getting any documents from Amoshin's hospital. I promised to try again tonight and said our goodbyes.

All of us were quiet as we walked along Portland Road back to our rental apartment. It was Swayambhu who broke the silence with;

'I am rapidly losing faith in the British justice system. You know it, the panel knows it, and the barristers know it, that Dawkins is lying through his teeth and nothing is being done about it.'

I was too tired to answer. Lopa agreed with Swayambhu when my mobile phone rang. It was Gautam. I said hello and passed the phone to Swayambhu to give him the details of what happened on the day.

12.   Day Five; Friday 2 May, 2008.

Friday morning brought some drama into the proceedings. As we were waiting in the room for Nancy and others, Sykes knocked on the door and handed me some papers with a wry smile on his face.

'Good morning. Can you pass these papers to Mr. Barnard please?'

I said I would do, and I could see Swayambhu was particularly keen to get hold of the papers to see what was in it. The papers turned out to be 'more evidence' from the GMC. They had quoted details of three of the 'Review of records' by the assessment panel and Crouper had produced yet another 'Report'. I did not think much of it. It was further details of the assessor's findings, which I was sure Sykes had asked Crouper to elaborate on. After reading through, I gave it to Swayambhu to have a read. When Nancy and Fred came in a few minutes later, they were not pleased to see the new documents. I could see Fred lose his normal, good humour of the morning unusually quickly. As soon as he had read it, he rushed out looking for Sykes and did not come back for quite a while.

Nancy tried to explain to me, that it was wholly improper to produce 'new evidence' at this stage, and it would not be allowed in a court of law. When Fred came back in, he was quite furious and said 'This is a Kangaroo Court. Anything goes as long as it is produced by the GMC.'

After that, he was quiet and kept going through the lever arch files and making numerous notes. We were called into the hearing room around 9.45 as we were on to our second cups of coffee.

The Chairman started with, 'Good morning, everyone.'

Sykes stood up and began the day's proceedings. 'Yes, good morning. Could I call, please, Mr. Carl Crouper?'

However, Fred would have none of it.

'Sir, just before Mr. Sykes does that, I think perhaps we ought to say something about the documents we have been handed this morning.'

Sykes looked up and said he would like to clarify.

'It will not take a second to deal with this. In the body of the report, there are three judgments that are referred to, which I noted did not seem to have patient notes with them, as it were, in the case based discussions. What I did was I identified which those were and I asked Mr. Crouper to produce the patient notes that are relevant to those judgments. He has produced a small clip of documentation which I have had copied and given to the defence. They were available at about 8.30 this morning. I handed a note to Mr. Kasyapa at nine. It is simply because that is the background to the three judgments that Mr. Crouper has incorporated in the report, and I have handed them over.'

'Sir, I have to say that I am truly unhappy about this. This is a report from Mr. Crouper dated 23 April. We were handed it this morning, nine days later. It is two pages dealing with three cases and attached to it are some extracts of notes. It is quite plain we are going to have to take time to go through these with my client and, indeed, look at the entirety of the notes. It just does not seem right to me that we are five days into a case and we should be handed yet further evidence that has to be dealt with by the defence. It just seems to me improper, particularly given that this report is dated 23 April.'

'I apologise that he has only had it this morning. I got the background paperwork last night and I have given it to him as quickly as I could have done. I do apologise obviously for that. Can we get on, as it were, with Mr. Crouper to the extent that we can?'

I was getting increasingly worried that the whole thing was going to be brushed under the carpet.

'No criticism of Mr. Sykes at all, but may we have an explanation as to why the GMC have waited so long to produce it?' Fred Barnard said looking at the Chairman for some intervention and he went short of saying this was totally unfair if not blatantly illegal.

'Are you in a position to give that explanation?' The Chairman asked Sykes hoping for some reprieve.

'No, I do not think I am at this stage.' Sykes's glib remark did not impress me or anyone else in the room.

'In that event ..' The Chairman was still looking for a way out.

'We received the report. The one and a half page report was received last week, but the actual documentation that supports it, as I say, I think it was yesterday afternoon that I got it.' Sykes was trying to justify an action, which cannot be considered anything but unfair whichever glasses you are wearing.

'Mr. Barnard, on the basis that Mr. Bill Sykes has suggested, are you willing to proceed?' The Chairman was desperate to get out of the situation one way or the other.

'I do not think I have any option. I will take the time when needed, hopefully outside normal sitting hours, but my protest I know has been heard.' To say I was disappointed was an understatement at that stage. We had the GMC by the balls I thought and we let it get away. I was losing whatever little faith I had in the fairness of it all very rapidly.

'Indeed. Good.' I could hear the sigh of relief by the Chairman. O'Neil was still looking smug and the expression on the face of Reverend was one of boredom. I could almost see that he had been in this kind of situation before and he could not see what the fuss was all about. I sat there looking pretty dejected at the turn of events. I do not know what I was hoping for, but definitely did not expect this blatant disregard for justice. The Chairman asked the usher to bring in Crouper at that stage. Crouper was called in and sworn in on the Bible to say the truth and nothing but the truth. What a waste of oath I thought as it did not have any value in this room.

Sykes introduced him to the room, distributed his CV to everyone in the room, and took him through his CV. As he went through his qualification and training, it turned out that he was a consultant for about 20 years and was a hand surgeon for the last ten years of his career before her retired two years previously. Sykes did not go into much detail, as it would have exposed Crouper's weakness – which he had not done or seen a lower limb surgery for over 15 years for which he had been asked to assess. Sykes continued with the bunch of papers handed out that morning. As he started his questioning, we, that is those on my side of the room soon realised that we did not have the papers Sykes was referring to.

'I have not seen these before. I am afraid I have not seen these before. We had a smaller clip of extracts from the patient notes, but it certainly did not run to 146 pages.' Fred was waving two bunches of papers in his hands, one with about 12 sheets and the other one with a large bundle. Sykes had not given me the large bundle this morning. It came as a surprise to all of us. I was getting angrier by the minute. Does this team stop at nothing?

'Sorry, I think the smaller clip was double sided copies and this has been copied one page at a time." Sykes tried to justify those 12 pages that he had given us that morning would equate to 146 pages if copied on both sides.

'Right. Do not worry anyway. We will cope.' I was shocked at Fred's response. I was beginning to wonder if he had given up hope of a fair hearing by then.

'I am obviously uncomfortable - these are the records of the case based discussions. I do not want to continue ..' Sykes was being contrite in his apology.

'Let us just take a moment Mr. Barnard, and make sure that you have seen these documents before.' The Chairman wanted to be seen as being fair!

'I think the answer is, sir that if Mr. Sykes presses on and then before I cross-examine I might need a bit of time just to put these in order, or transfer the markings from the other notes that I have.' I was again disappointed at Fred's response.

'I am sorry Mr. Barnard has not had them - I am sure he has had them but I am sorry if he has not had them in this format because I know what it is like trying to transfer - I did not know that they had not been handed over to the defence.' Moreover, he is the Barrister for the GMC.

'Can I also say that I have not had them.' The legal assessor piped in. I was never sure of the legal assessor's stance throughout the hearing.

'Do you have them now?' Sykes looked at the legal assessor.

'Yes, because they have just been handed out.' The only bit of honesty that I had heard all day.

'Right, my apologies. If Mr. Barnard is content for us to continue then perhaps we can continue,' Sykes said looking at Fred and Fred nodded his head and asked him to continue. There was silence in the room and Sykes continued, as there was no objection from the Chairman.

'This was a patient who was put on the waiting list for a right total hip replacement by a Middle Grade, who was working with Mr. Kasyapa. He had the operation done by Mr. Kasyapa in September 2001, which seems to have been very successful. Can you tell us about this please?'

'We asked in the case based discussion for the process whereby patients who were seen in the outpatient clinic by junior staff, placed on the waiting list and then operated, how that actually worked and at what point the patient would be assessed for that operation by the consultant, because there seemed to be nothing in the notes to indicate - on these particular notes - that the patient had been seen by the consultant before the operation. Mr. Kasyapa said, as you will see in 651, that he said that, 'No one is allowed to go on the waiting list unless I see them,' although it is not recorded here. I flagged that up as a cause for concern in that there was no clear demonstration that Mr. Kasyapa had seen the patient before operation, although I had no reason to believe that they had not and the operation had gone forward quite smoothly and been appropriate and the patient had done well afterwards.' Crouper explained the statement looking at the Chairman. Here is a professional witness if there was one. He knew exactly what to say and who to say it to. Either he is very experienced in this scenario or he had been coached extremely well.

'So was it the lack of the notes ..' Sykes tried to intervene.

'It was a lack of a clear note, 'I have seen this patient,' confirmed the junior staff person's decision that it was appropriate and that the operation should go ahead on that basis.' Crouper continued without stopping.

There you have it, the GMC's version of how a patient should be managed. Successful management of a patient depends only on what is written in the notes and not the outcome of treatment. Nothing to do with clinical governance, the treatment, or the results. The fact that this episode had occurred 7 years prior to the assessment also was conveniently overlooked.

Sykes continued to question Crouper over the next half an hour and he showed his mettle as a clever Barrister by jumping from different aspect of assessment so that we had difficulty linking his questioning to reasoning. He pointed out to all the 'unacceptable' judgements by Crouper in his assessment and tried to justify the decisions. Crouper turned out to be an excellent witness of the GMC. He did not falter anywhere and he was almost believable when he tried to explain the operative procedure for a complex hip revision surgery. To everyone sitting in that room he came as a competent and extremely knowledgeable surgeon with wide experience of hip surgery. The fact that he had not seen one of these procedures for over thirty years did not get a mention and the fact that what he was saying was at least twenty-year-old practice also was not evident.

One of the cases discussed made the situation quite clear that not all was right with the assessment. Sykes asked Crouper –

'We are on judgment 766, Patient 6. Could you just help us please, by telling us what your cause for concern was in this case?'

'Yes, this was a patient who had had a left total hip replacement in 1995 and I have recorded later revised twice, so two further operations, and had a history of getting a clot in the leg veins after that surgery. The cause for concern is related to the right total hip replacement when he or she was put on the waiting list for a right total hip replacement. The records, as far as I could see, did not mention anything about a strategy for preventing a further deep vein thrombosis clot in the leg in relation to that surgery. In other words, we have a high-risk patient, demonstrably so, who is at increased risk of getting a clot in the leg. I was not able to be sure from reviewing the records whether there was a strategy in place for preventing that.' At this I nearly stood up to tell them that this patient never had a thrombosis and the assessors had made a serious mistake without looking through the records to see that she had tests done for thrombosis with negative results. However, I would have been shot down I am sure. Anyway, by this time, the panel had had enough and we all broke up for a tea break. The Chairman asked Fred Barnard to take a 'long break' so that he can go through the papers produced by the GMC during the hearing that morning. As we walked back to the room, I was angry and thoroughly dejected, Fred was in deep thought, and Swayambhu and Lopa were looking at each other. No one spoke as we entered the waiting room. I said to myself to calm down and after a few minutes, I said to Nancy;

'I don't like this. This is a gross injustice. This panel is as crooked as they come.; I could feel my ears getting hot as I spoke. Nancy tried to calm me down and said Fred will try to demonstrate the irregularities during his questioning. I walked out into the corridor with Swayambhu and Lopa.

Swayambhu started with; 'It is not looking good'

'It definitely is not.'

'You should ask Fred to object strongly and point out that the GMC is lying.' Lopa was clearly angry

'You should ask Fred to go for Mistrial.' Swayambhu had been watching too many Perry Mason episodes obviously.

'Well. I am not so sure we can do that. I'll ask Nancy about it.' We were clutching at straws. Moreover, the hearing is not even past the initial stages. There was still a lot to come. As we continued our discussion, the usher called us back into the hearing room. I looked at the clock in the corridor. It was nearly 12 noon. We had been out for nearly 40 minutes. We walked back in silence. I thought I should ask Nancy if we could ask for a Mis-trial later at lunchtime.

Sykes spent the next half an hour going through 'missing' operation notes, pre-assessment record, and record of patient going on the waiting list. The fact that the case that they looked at, had voluminous records going into an average of five sets each with large gaps in the records to show the state of notes did not seem to make any impression. That was conveniently over looked by Sykes and Crouper. They then spent the next half an hour discussing how much time all this is taking and that the trial may not finish by the end of next week.

'I was hoping very much to finish Mr Crouper today, even perhaps for Mr Barnard to start his cross-examination, but I am afraid at the rate that we are going - and I cannot go any faster because we have to find the paperwork - that may not happen. Then we have Mr. Amoshin. He is only available Tuesday and Wednesday of next week. We may be able to take Mr Amoshin much quicker in fact, and I think I am going to attempt to do so because I think the panel have the point, as it were. That really means that we will not be finishing the GMC's case until Wednesday. It is quite obvious from that, whatever happens thereafter, that we are not going to finish this case by Friday of next week. I wonder if it would be sensible over this short adjournment whether the Panel Secretary were to begin - perhaps she has already started to do so - to formulate some dates. I can see that we would certainly need another three or four days.' Sykes appears to be soliloquing.

'Let me just add to that - I hope this does not sound like special pleading - I am aware that I have been keeping people well past 5.30 for most of the week. I was hoping, bearing in mind that people have travel plans for the weekend, holiday weekend and so on, not to keep us sitting very, very late tonight if I could avoid it.' The chairman and I could see that the reverend had suddenly woken up.

'I think you will have the support of everybody on every side of the room for that. We will have to see where we go, but obviously if we find a convenient point somewhere between four and 4.30 I was hoping we can pull stumps then.' Sykes continued his soliloquy, which had been interrupted by the chairman.

'Fourish was the number that was in the front of mind, I confess. Clearly, our convenience is not the main factor here. I take your points entirely. It has been a concern of mine and the Legal Assessor's for some days now. As to whether - and there is certainly no objection - indeed, it would be prudent for the panel secretary to investigate the position. My concern is that panelists may not have come prepared to make this decision this week and may not be in possession of full diaries and so on. We could see how far we could get. Bear with me.' He then turned to the panel secretary who was sitting next to him looking rather dazed at the rapid turn of events. 'We have a plan, which is this: the panelists of course do not need a particularly long lunch break. I think what I will do is ask the panelists to be back with their diaries, if this is possible, at ten minutes to two. Bear with me.'

He then turned to the legal assessor who was sitting on the other side of him and had what appeared to be a furious two minutes of whispering. He looked up when he finished the discussion and said, 'Let us say we would not resume until not before ten-past two, that would give Mr Barnard an extra 20 minutes thereabouts. Is that about the kind of time you need or am I being overly optimistic?'

My heart sank at the thought of waiting for several more months of agony to come back to finish that hearing. I looked at Fred who was rather impassive and at Nancy who was looking increasingly worried at the turn of events that was taking place. As I was getting increasingly fidgety and finding the whole atmosphere rather oppressive, the Chairman called for a lunch break. For the first time I was glad that he did. I wanted to get out of the room and had thousands of things I wanted to ask Nancy and Fred. As soon as we reached the waiting room, I turned to Fred Barnard and asked him.

'What do they mean? It does not look like they do not want to finish the hearing before the end of next week. We have only Amoshin and then me to go through. How long will they need to make a decision?' I could not hide the anguish and the deep disappointment in my voice.

'This panel is deeply corrupt. I have not seen such corruption in all my life. This would not have been tolerated in a court of law.' I could see Fred was quietly furious. 'The amount of time this panel has wasted in the last five days, any judge would have finished the entire hearing.'

'It is a well known fact that these panels never give a decision quickly. For example it has never been known to give a verdict before two in the afternoon even if the case finishes in the morning.' Nancy joined in.

Both Swayambhu and Lopa were getting increasingly agitated at the turn of events.

'Why is that Nancy?' Swayambhu asked.

'If they sit after one in the afternoon they get paid for the full day and if they sit after five in the evening, they get paid extra. Some of the panels love sitting on weekends as they get paid double,' Nancy explained. I found this very hard to believe. Lopa was furious and wanted to know if the panel can be reported to someone for their behaviour.

'That is the beauty of their job. They are not accountable to anyone. They can do what they please with impunity. At worst, the chairman gets what we call as a slap on the wrist if the decision goes against them. The last case this chairman was involved in has just been through a court of appeal where his decision was severely criticised by the Judge and the decision overturned. However, it has had no effect and he continues to be chairman of FTP panels' Nancy continued. It was much later that I found out that during this hearing, the chairman's previous case had been overturned by a judge and the doctor in question was paid an undisclosed sum of money as compensation. Swayambhu wanted to know what happens in those cases.

'The panel chairman gets called into the chambers of the president of GMC and gets a slap on the wrist.' Nancy was smiling. I was disgusted at this.

'If that is the case, why would any panel give a decision against the GMC as they are the pay masters?' Swayambhu continued.

'You are right. They have no incentive to give a decision against the GMC. In fact, it is in their own interest to give a decision against the doctors. They just have to make sure that they go through the motion and find enough evidence; whether right or wrong against the doctor to make sure that the decision does not get overturned later in a court of law. They are supposed to be an 'independent panel' and not to be swayed by the fact that they are paid by the GMC. This is where every other regulatory body in this country differs from medicine.

'Every other field, be it the bar, solicitors or police, the investigation is conducted by an independent body and the case goes to a court of law where a Judge makes a decision.' Fred tried to explain. I could hear the exasperation in his voice.

We went to lunch with a heavy heart. I had this sinking feeling about the whole situation. I was certain that we were just wasting our time in this hearing. The panel had made their minds up and they are just fishing to find evidence to hang me. Swayambhu and Lopa unfortunately agreed with me on that score. We had our sandwiches in silence and walked back the GMC.

After lunch break, Sykes took Crouper until tea break about an hour later going through the test of competence. The questions were structured so that the answers would show that I was wrong and the assessors were right in coming to their conclusion. Crouper stressed on the panel that it is the duty of a consultant to know every minutiae of micro-management of every aspect of patient management. He essentially reiterated that an orthopaedic consultant should be a specialist physician capable of managing diabetes, cardiologist to manage heart problems, anaesthetist to manage pain, general surgeon to manage urinary problems, and a vascular surgeon to manage bleeding problems.

During the tea break Swayambhu looked rather defeated and was looking bewildered.

'It is absolutely amazing. The GMC expects every doctor to be a specialist in every field of medicine. By their yardstick every orthopaedic surgeon in this country should be struck off.'

Fred had been given extra time during tea break to prepare for his questioning. I could see him working away with numerous sheets of paper lying all over the desk. Natalie was running between the waiting room and the inner office photocopying documents furiously. We were called back into the hearing room about half an hour later.

Fred started his cross-examination of Crouper with the final conclusion of the assessors.

'Towards the top of page 86 of the report, question (a) is: 'Has the standard of the practitioner's professional performance been deficient?' You and your colleagues answer yes. Do you believe that his performance is *currently* deficient?'

Sykes immediately jumped up and objected.

'I object. We are not at that stage of the proceedings yet.' He was looking at the Chairman and he nodded his head in agreement.

'Top half of page 84, you were asked about the last sentence of the second principal paragraph, the last sentence reads: 'As far as we could ascertain a departmental audit data cannot differentiate between the performance of the different consultants.' The position is, as Dr Dawkins told us, that in fact you never saw the departmental audit data, so you were not in fact in a position to say?' Fred continued.

'No, we cannot say for sure. There were several audit data that were mentioned but we never saw any of them.' Crouper replied.

'You never saw Mr. Kasyapa's own personal data either?'

'No.'

'If that is the case, how can you say that the audit data is inaccurate?'

'I am sorry, I have lost you. Where is the statement?' Crouper was using the same tactic as Dawkins to avoid answering questions. When Fred pointed out the page reference, Crouper continued with

'All we said was that the data may be inaccurate.'

'That won't do Mr Crouper. You have clearly said that in your statement and reinforced to Mr. Sykes this morning.' Fred was looking at the Chairman this time. However, I do not think it had any effect on the Chairman.

'Can I just ask you about a series of propositions before I get to the end point of this line of questions? First of all, do you agree - and I think Dr Dawkins agreed - that Mr Kasyapa's skills as an orthopaedic surgeon were attested to by all the colleagues who had a third party interview with you and your team, save for Mr Serpe?'

'That is my recollection. I did not take part in all the third party interviews, of course.'

'The second proposition is that in this case, as far as you are aware, apart from Mr Serpe, no one alleged lack of basic surgical skills or competence on the part of Mr Kasyapa?'

'That is correct.'

'As far as you know - I appreciate you were not doing a full investigation - no such allegations of lack of basic surgical skills and competence had been made against

Mr Kasyapa?'

'Not as far as I am aware, no.'

'The next proposition is this: you and Mr Amoshin, having reviewed 42 sets of notes, selected apparently at random, did not find in those cases any evidence of lack of basic surgical skills or competence?'

'Not in relation to anything that was tested in terms of the tests of competence.'

'Certainly, can you confirm this, that in the 42 sets of notes that you reviewed there was no evidence that any lack of basic skills and competence on the part of Mr Kasyapa caused any harm or posed any risk to any patient?'

'I am speaking from recollection, but I think that is correct.' As Crouper replied, I could see reverend appeared to have suddenly woken up and taking some notice of what was happening for the first time that day.

'I think you know that within a few months of your recommendation he undertook the basic skills course, in accordance with your recommendation, and passed satisfactorily?'

'Yes.'

'It does seem curious, does it not, that given those propositions this chap appeared to score so badly on these basic skills and competence tests? Also, I suppose, we can factor into that the fact that he had done, what, 2,000 total hip replacements or revisions?'

'The two are not connected.' Crouper said and went on to explain what he meant in an obscure tangent. I was flabbergasted at his explanation and I could see looking at Swayambhu, he could not understand it either.

'But here is a chap who has been a consultant for quite a few years, with a very heavy caseload - indeed one of the complaints or one of the criticisms is that his workload was too heavy. He is doing many, many operations over the course of many, many years. It does seem curious, does it not, would you agree, that he appears to fail on these basic surgical skills and competence tests? Do you not find that curious?'

'No, we only looked at the tests of competence that we were there to deal with. I would regard that as a separate issue to the record of clinical practice, which we only looked at 42 or 43 cases. The tests of competence were related to the fundamental skills and knowledge of a surgeon. That is what we looked at and you have our findings there.'

'No, I appreciate that we have your findings. You found what you found. There it is and conclusions will have to be drawn. I just wonder though, when you found that his scores were low in the way that you described, you did not think to yourself, 'Well, this is very odd.' How can a successful, internationally known orthopaedic surgeon with a big workload have reached this point, with no apparent criticisms of his basic skills and competences previously and all his colleagues saying that he is highly skilled and that they trust their own relatives with him and so on? Did that not strike you as a bit odd?'

'It is odd, I have to agree, that somebody in that position should score so badly in a simple test of fundamental surgical skills and knowledge. I agree.' Crouper's reply was small consolation for a day full of negative happenings. Fred continued with his questioning.

'At page 84, we have, at the top of the page, the second sentence on the page: "The assessment team does not consider that Mr. K performs sufficient hip revisions to enable him to maintain an adequate competency.' You say that that is wrongly phrased. What it should say is that you do not consider that he performed sufficient hip revisions of fused hips?'

'Yes, that is correct. That would be my view of that and just to expand it to make it accurate.'

'Can you just explain to the panel how it is that that sentence, which means something so completely different as you have explained it, passed into the report and was not detected by you or Mr Dawkins or Mr Amoshin?'

'No, I cannot. I have to apologise for that. I should have spotted it. There is no question about that.' Crouper's reply meant that the assessors could make blunders in their assessment, which would probably end an orthopaedic surgeon's career without any problem.

'Let's now go to page 65, the second question, 2(c). We know the question was in relation to the matter of preparing for a total hip replacement. All three of the assessors have given cause for concern for the reason that Mr. Kasyapa did not check the identity of the patient, did not undertake pre-operative checks, did not know that the patient had a hip replacement on the other side, and did not check the notes. You were asked what the question was by Mr. Sykes and you could not remember, but you did recall that there was another question, positioning and draping for total hip replacement. Is that a question that appears on a list of questions from which you selected the questions that we see at page 65, or the issues at page 65?'

'We did not select those questions. They were given to us and we approved them. Mr Kasyapa confirms that there was a live actor at that stage. What he also says is that what he was asked to do was exactly the words that you used: to position and drape a patient for posterior access.'

'Yes, that may well be the case. It is just listed here as simply preparing for a total hip replacement.'

'It sounds as if you are prepared to accept that Mr Kasyapa's recollection is correct, that he was in fact asked to position and drape the actor patient for posterior access?'

'Yes, I have no reason to doubt that at all.'

'It does rather make a difference to the conclusion of cause for concern, does it not? If he is asked only to position and to drape, then he is not being asked to confirm identity, undertake pre-operative checks, or check the notes?'

'No, he was to prepare the patient' I was getting confused. Is he agreeing that they made a mistake or not?

'Absolutely. I understand what it is that you wanted Kasyapa to do or wanted to test him on, but if the message that got through to him, as you have confirmed - position and drape for posterior access - how is he to know that he is meant to do more than that?'

'I only have what is in front of me here.'

'Let us go to the exact wording in a moment. It is plain, is it not, from the reasons for your findings in item two here, that all that Kasyapa in fact did was to position and to drape?'

'No, because in section 2(c), the third part, there was the actual mention of checking the consent and checking patient notes, but that was not done. I would take it from that that was part of the station.'

'You are not hearing me, Mr Crouper. What I am saying to you is that what Mr Kasyapa actually did was simply to position and drape. When you look at your reasons for 2, it is quite clear that that is all he did because he did not do any of the other things.'

'I go back to my previous answer, which was that checking consent was mentioned. It is on this page.'

'I am sure it is me being obtuse, but let us just take it in stages. He did position and drape, did he not, from your recollection?'

'As I have said earlier, I am not clear in my recollection of this exact station because I only have what is in front of me here.'

'You have no independent recollection of that?'

'Only the notes that were taken at the time, which I do not have in front of me. Obviously if they are made available to me I could expand on this.'

'Could we approach it in this way: had he failed to put the patient in the right position and failed to drape the patient appropriately, you would have recorded it here, would you not?'

'Oh yes.'

'Let us proceed on the assumption that he did position and drape. We know that he did not check the identity of the patient because that is recorded?'

'Yes.'

'We know that he did not undertake any pre-operative checks at all?'

'Yes.'

'Finally, if you look at page 70, this item is dealt with on that page and it shows

The heading is 'Positioning for operation.'

'Yes, I would agree.'

'One thing that is absolutely clear is that if you ask a man who has done 2,000 total hip replacements over many, many years to carry out a total hip replacement, he is going to do all the things that you record him having failed to do on this occasion, is he not?'

'Yes, I agree entirely that is what he would be expected to do and should do.'

'It would be quite extraordinary, just wholly inexplicable, if this doctor did not know that he had to check the identity of the patient, carry out pre-operative checks, and read the notes before proceeding to a total hip replacement. It is just beyond belief.'

'If that is the situation, that the station was not clearly worded, again, I come back to the fact that I would really have to have a look at that and see what the wording was.'

'Let me ask you about that. We have not got the questions that were posed or the instructions or whatever form they took. Are they available?'

'Not to me here, no' Crouper replied. It will not be long before it is established that there was no record kept of the Test of Competence apart from the assessors' comments. With that, Fred finished for the day. It was just before five in the evening when we finished. Crouper was reminded that he was still under oath and was asked to return on the following Tuesday for a 9.30 start as the Monday was a bank holiday. I was by then past caring. I just wanted to get home and put my feet up. I felt as if I had been doing manual labour for the whole week. The mental stress was at times taking over my senses and I felt like giving everything up. Nancy reminded me again to see if I could get any details from Amoshin's hospital records before I set off.

As we walked back to the car, we were all pretty silent. Swayambhu started with, 'I am not sure what the panel is thinking right now. Do you think they have made their mind up?'

'I am sure they have.' Lopa was being her negative self. 'They are just going through the motion. I don't think they are paying any attention to what is happening.'

'What do you think Upaas?' Swayambhu wanted to know.

'I don't really know. Sometimes I feel we are wasting our time. Judging from the first decision they have given, I do not have much hope. Their decision was so warped that we seem to have heard completely different evidence to what they have.' I was trying to hide my disappointment and sheer frustration. As I drove my trusty Grand Voyager home, Gautam was on the phone. I let Swayambhu take the call and go through the events of the day. The biggest question on everyone's mind was 'have the panel made their mind up?' I could not answer that question and no one could. As we headed out of Manchester, we were stuck in yet another traffic jam and to make the matters worse, it was unusually hot for that time of May. We did not reach home in Seaport until very late that night. Pavaki had cooked dinner for all of us and the whole gang had gathered in Swayambhu's house for a debriefing.

That was a long bank holiday weekend and it was one of the longest weekends in my life. I tried to relax and get myself immersed in my woodwork. It did not work. My heart was not in it. There was a general feeling of doom and gloom and I could not get out of it despite all my friends efforts. I had a call from Helen who was trying to cheer me up and said that everyone in the hospital was rooting for me. She had started a Petition to be produced before the panel and there were already over 100 signatures on it. We set off again on Monday afternoon yet again on the now familiar road to Manchester. This time there was no rush to meet Nancy or Fred for a meeting before the hearing. I did not have any news for them. I was not successful in getting any documented information from Amoshin's hospital. We took our time and reached the rented flat late that evening. As before, we had the wishes of all our friends to take with us. As I was nearing Manchester, Nancy called. She sounded rather cheerful and very positive. She firmly believed that everything was going our way and she could not see how this panel could take a decision against me as rational human beings.

13. Day six; Tuesday 6th May, 2008.

The morning was bright and sunny as we walked down the Portland Street. There were the usual sights of people queuing up at the 'Home made sandwich' shop, for their lunch box. There were young men in dark suits dragging their pilot cases bulging with documents, women in dark suits, and high heels struggling with their bags and young men trying to look smart in the Primark suits dragging their suitcases full of documents. I could see 'lawyers' written all over their faces. The place was full of legal eagles from a go-for to Para-legal's to a full-fledged QC. The only people who were not in the legal profession were getting off the train in Piccadilly and catching the bus to Deans Gate and beyond. No one paid any attention to Lopa or me, even though both of us felt as if the whole world was watching us. I often felt as I walked down that busy Portland Street that the world was watching a convicted felon walking to his destiny. I only had to look up to see no one was taking a blind bit of notice of either of us. Everyone was engrossed in his or her own thoughts and problems. We had been there only for a week and already it felt as if we had been there forever. The city looked more and more depressing by the day. Despite the fact that there was bright sunshine that morning, there was no lift in my step or joy in the heart.

We walked past the numerous eateries along the street, a large hotel which was spewing out its guests who were mainly lawyers and barristers, a music shop which was selling all kinds of guitars and inevitable 'sandwich' shop with a queue of office goers waiting for their 'packed lunch'. Despite the fact that the breakfast was barely over, we could smell the Chinese cooking wafting over the crowd, from the little China Town across the street. We crossed the building works where they were ostensibly updating the age-old tram system, which had made Manchester so famous in the past. It was beginning to show its age with dated carriages rattling along most of the time. The street was bustling as everyone tried to get to their work on time, but the only noise you could hear was that of the incessant traffic. No one spoke to anyone, and there did not seem to be any human contact through the entire journey from the apartment to the GMC's office in Oxford Street, even though we passed hundreds of people on the way. It was as if we were passing through a science fiction fantasy full of robots going about their business.

As we entered the St James's building, Nancy was already there near the central reception waiting for the lift. Nancy looked bright and fresh after the long bank holiday weekend. We could not discuss anything in the lift. It was full of people going to work in different floors, in the building. I could see Nancy was bursting with questions and information. The minute we entered the waiting room –

'Did you get anything on Amoshin?' Nancy burst out.

'I am sorry. It is going to take time. The hospital has long bureaucratic procedures to follow, and won't be hurried'. We had tried over the weekend through Vishwa, and the only thing we could get out was his personal view, which was not of any use to us. According to Vishwa, the only thing Amoshin was allowed to do was bunions and minor procedures, during his period as a clinical assistant, and when he was appointed a consultant for the last couple of years before he retired, he spent doing the same trying to help bring the waiting lists of other consultants in the hospital.

Nancy was clearly disappointed at this as was Fred when he found out later that morning. As Fred walked in, he was deep in thought. He obviously had spent a fair amount of his weekend on the case looking at all the red marked sheets he was holding in his hand. He spent most of the morning waiting to be called, reading and re-reading what he had written down and marked in the folders. It was nearly ten in the morning when we were called into the hearing room.

Sykes had produced a schedule charting out various questions, and determinations of the assessment, and he wanted to use it. When it was shown that morning, I was not particularly happy about it as the schedule made assumptions on the determinations and had clearly left out all the faults of the assessment. Unfortunately, there was extremely little I could do about it as Fred felt he could negotiate around the schedule and make it work for him. I did not want to argue with my Barrister just as he was getting ready to cross-examine on one's behalf.

I did walk into the room with some trepidation and a sense of foreboding. I did not know what to expect of the new developments and I do not like uncertainty, especially going into a battle as it were. The day started off, rather innocuously I thought with Crouper being brought in and reminded of being under oath still. Fred started his cross-examination again taking each of the patient's records that had been criticised. There was one patient who was put on the waiting list by an Associate Specialist, and he had forgotten to add that it was discussed with me, as it was the normal practice. The patient had been pre-assessed by the pre-assessment team as it is done by every hospital in the country and not by me. The criticism was that my name did not appear in the records! In the same token, when Fred pointed out a mistake in the assessment panel's mistake in record keeping with the same patient

'There is an obvious mistake there. It should be - well, I do not know. Perhaps there is not. It is a reference to Mr Dawkin's question, is it not?'

Crouper looked a bit disconcerted

'Yes, it would appear - there is a misspelling in the original part of this. There was a suspicion that this patient had a dint. I am quite sure that is a DVT, a deep vein thrombosis, in the left leg so that puts the context of the question.   Dr Dawkins has asked a question about writing and Mr Amoshin, has made the judgment on that particular point there.'

I could not see Crouper backing out of this one. Fred carried on.

'The patient going on the waiting list, it is clear, is it not, that Mr Mustaf put him on the waiting list in 2001, and we can see page 6 of the notes that illustrate that?'

'Yes, that is correct, second note on page 6.'

'Did you ascertain that Mr Mustaf was a senior middle grade doctor?'

'Yes, that was my understanding.'

'The criticism here is that it is not noted that Mr Kasyapa, I should say, has authorised Mr Mustaf to put the patient on the waiting list. Is that it?'

'Yes. Not so much authorised, but checked that was what was done and the reasons for it. There does not seem to be any contact with Mr Kasyapa at that particular point.'

'A criticism is essentially that Mr Mustaf is not recorded that he has discussed it with Mr Kasyapa, something of that kind?'

'Not quite. It is whether the whole thing has been okayed at some point by Mr Kasyapa.

'Is there any reason to doubt that Mr Kasyapa did okay this patient going on the waiting list?'

'I do not have the information to answer that question, I am afraid. It is not in the notes.'

'Do you know when Mr Kasyapa began as a consultant at that hospital?'

'I do not know. I would have to refer back to ..' I could see Fred was getting rather frustrated at not getting Crouper to have made a mistake.

'Did Mr Kasyapa say whether he had authorised the patient to go on the waiting list?'

'I would have to refer back to - no. The questions that we have just looked at were about the process for checking when people had gone on the waiting list.'

'I think Mr Kasyapa told you that nobody went on the waiting list without him authorising it. Is that not right?'

'Again, I would have to refer back. My recollection was that it was the process that he had in place, but in this particular patient, he could not say whether that had been done or not. Again, I would have to refer back to those specific questions.'

'So simply the absence of a note from anybody recording that authorisation from Mr Kasyapa?' I was sure everyone in the room could hear the anger and annoyance in Fred's voice.

'The authorisation and the pre-operative assessment.' Crouper insisted. It looked like he had been well tutored by Sykes or the functionaries in the back office.

Fred decided to change his tack a bit and said

'If we look, please, at the entry for criticism 720, which is at page 270, Mr Amoshin has recorded to the question: Take us through your pre-op assessment. Mr Kasyapa appears to have been noted as saying:

> 'Seen by staff grade, though notes do not say spoken to me. Discussed the risk, go to Nurse practitioner for pre-operative assessment, they are given a leaflet. Brought in 1 or 2 weeks pre-op assessment.'

- presumably before. One or two weeks before the operation for a pre-operative assessment, I think that must mean, must it not?'

'Yes.' Crouper admitted rather begrudgingly.

'If they have Deep Vein Thrombosis, I would see them the day before surgery.' You have got no reason to doubt that that did occur. It is simply that it does not appear in the notes that we have got here that there is confirmation of that?'

'Yes.' Crouper finally admitted to that. However, I was not sure how much of this was being registered by anyone in the panel, as there did not appear to be any activity at the top table. It was as if they were mere spectators of a game.

Fred continued with 'A further criticism that is made in this case is a criticism which one finds at page 294. It is criticism 807, if you could just turn that up. It begins at 293. We can read what it says. The points are:

> 'Past history left deep vein thrombosis. [Post-operative] risk of deep vein thrombosis, no evidence to say discussed.'

In relation to that, can we go please to page 10? This is the nurse practitioner's pre-operative assessment. You see there is under 'Past Medical History' it is recorded on the right-hand side of that box, in the second entry, '[Left] DVT following [total hip replacement] (1995).' Over the page, we can see that in the questions put to the patient, question D has got added underneath it, 'DVT [left] leg 1995.' Yes?'

'Yes. Sorry, I was just trying to find D, but it is hidden there. Yes, so the risk has been noted.' Crouper replied.

'Then we go to page 12, the note from medical and nursing staff record, 'Informed about risks associated with surgery. Dislocation.' Then just under the hole punch, 'PE/DVT.' That is pulmonary embolism/deep vein thrombosis?'

'Yes.'

'It looks as though the patient was informed of those risks on the pre-operative assessment, does it not?'

'Yes. Certainly the nurse practitioners highlighted the risks and described them to the patient.' Crouper reluctantly agreed.

'Well if we go back to page 807 again, 'No evidence to say discussed' is untenable, is it not?' Fred was looking at Sykes at this stage to see if he was going to intervene. But, Crouper was not going to give in;

'The discussion was about, as we have established, what Mr. Kasyapa had said to the patient about risks and benefits of the operation before surgery.'

Fred was trying to stall with inane questions waiting for Nancy to come back from her photocopying trips. We had spent some time looking through the records to find substance in the GMC's accusations during our several interminable breaks. We had found numerous examples of where the assessors had conveniently 'forgotten' to look at the full records or show me the full set of records during the records review. I could see Fred visually lighten up when he saw Nancy come through the door.

'Miss Charlton is now back. I wonder whether we could produce the additional patient records. If I could just take a moment to sort this out?' Trusty Natalie handed several sets of papers to the Chairman and distributed copies to everyone else. Unfortunately this created no end of confusion among all the three panelists and I could see O'Neil's smile was absent. It took another fifteen minutes before Fred could explain what it all meant. Finally he came down to the particular patient that was being discussed and produced the copies of records that was missing from the GMC bundle.

Fred was waving one set of papers as he said, 'Now the first three pages are, in fact, a duplication of something that is already in the bundle, so we can ignore those and so is page 5 and we can ignore that, but what I would like to take Mr Crouper to is page 6 and there we see on 19 September 2001 a series of drugs were administered to this patient, including for his eyes and the last drug is Tinzaparin. You have probably a better pronunciation of that than I have, but is that not a prophylactic against deep vein thrombosis?'
'It is indeed.' Crouper replied.
'Does that not lead to the conclusion that this patient was administered a prophylactic for deep vein thrombosis?'
'Yes, we were aware of that.' I wonder if Crouper was feeling a tad uncomfortable when he said that. However, he was too experienced with this sort of hearings to show any emotions.
'This page was not included in the records.' Fred continued.
'No, because the case-based discussion was about informing the patient and what Mr Kasyapa had personally said to the patient during his pre-operative assessment.'

I was very disappointed to see Fred not pursuing this further to find out why I was not shown these pages during my interview.

'This is unreal' Fred commented looking at the chairman. Not a whimper from the Chairman.

'Yes, it is purely in relationship to what is recorded in the discussion with the patient who is at high risk of a DVT given their previous history.' Crouper continued as if nothing had happened.

'You say that the patient is at high risk, if you go please, to page 4 of D9, there is a record there in relation to this patient on 31 August 1995 where the patient's left leg was subjected to Doppler ultrasound. We can see what is written there and the conclusion is that, 'No evidence of significant clot,' is recorded. Is that not indicative that there was, in fact, no deep vein thrombosis in 1995 contrary to what was thought six years later?' Fred was trying to pin him down.

'I only have the one isolated note in relation to the Doppler ultrasound at that stage. That is negative, as has been recorded. There are other ways of looking for a DVT that might have been done.' Crouper was not going to back down and admit they have made a mistake in their assessment.

I was again disappointed that Fred did not pursue this matter further. This patient, as far as one could see, never had a DVT in the past, the risks of DVT was discussed and prophylactic treatment was given and I was still found at fault. The assessors had deliberately hidden the documents showing the prophylactic treatment, the ultrasound scan report showing absence of DVT and tricked me and came to an erroneous conclusion that this patient had a previous DVT, DVT risk was not discussed and that no prophylactic treatment was given.

What happened next was even more incredulous. Fred was onto missing dictation in notes. We had found a quite a few of these 'missing record' by now.

'Of course, it is unfortunate if a dictated tape is either mislaid or if it is present and it is not found or whatever sounds are on it cannot be detected by the secretary, but is this not just one of those things that happens from time to time?' Fred asked.

'It certainly does happen from time to time, although it should be a rare occurrence and there is, in my experience, almost invariably a policy whereby this is chased up.' Crouper responded.

'When you say it is chased up, if the secretary does not type it up that day or the next the surgeon's memory is going to get fainter and fainter to dictate it again, is it not? Is that not the case?'

'Yes. What does happen in this case, if there is no clinic typed because the tape has been lost. The notes are there and one has to go through them and dictate from memory and I would agree entirely with Mr Barnard that this becomes more difficult the further down the line the dictation has to be done. Normally it is brought to one's attention within a few hours of the clinic if the tape has gone missing or it is faulty.'

I could see the incredulity in Nancy's face at this statement. I need to find out which hospital did have enough secretaries to type out a letter within a few hours of the clinic.

Fred produced some more "missing records" and went on to question Crouper about 'planning for surgery.'

'On the second page of this, Mr Crouper is the note by Mr Kasyapa of his operation, is it not?

Fred invited everyone to read the notes on the page.

'Is that not indicative of a properly planned and, as it turned out, successful operation?' Fred continued when the chairperson nodded his head saying he had finished reading it.

'Well, there is not - the question in the case-based discussion was about the planning and anticipation of problems. That is all. There was not any criticism about the actual operation itself.'

'I have to say, Mr Crouper, I am not understanding what absence or lack of planning you have in mind in here. Where is the evidence for it?'

'This was simply the case-based discussion about these types of cases in general, how Mr Kasyapa would approach them, what particular problems he would be on the lookout for, and how he would cope with them.'

As we walked back to our waiting room, there was not much talking as none of us could make out how the case was going. I was rather disappointed that Fred had not pursued some of the issues that I thought were important and showed the blunders of the assessment panel. There was not much time to think, as we had to go through some more sets of notes that the GMC had made available to us. I had a quick cup of hot chocolate and sat down with the bulky tatty sets of notes.

'Did you have this note of operation, because it certainly was not in the clip of documents that was provided to Mr Kasyapa?'

'Yes, because we had seen this and, once again, it was - the pre-operative planning was the point that we were discussing and we - obviously the notes are very extensive, as we have said, and we chose pages from the notes that were relevant to the question asked in the case-based discussion.'

'So you were going to ask him about planning this surgery, but omitting the note that he had made of the surgery?'

'Yes' Crouper retorted without batting an eyelid.

'Can we look at D10, this time at page 1? If you look at the second entry, which is 22 December 2000, Mr Mustaf writes - we can see what he says in the first paragraph, and then he says:

> 'I discussed with Mr Kasyapa who also examined her and explained the possible complications including high risk of dislocation, infection, DVT, and earlier failure. She understands the complications very well and even then, she would like to proceed for operation. I have put her name on the waiting list for undo of arthrodesis of the right hip and then right total hip replacement.'

Then that is put in bold:

> 'Undo arthrodesis of right hip and then right total hip replacement.'

Somebody has written - I think Mr Kasyapa - left rather than right. Indeed, it was the left hip that was being dealt with. Does that not indicate quite clearly what the plan was exactly as carried out; undo the arthrodesis first and then subsequently do a total hip replacement?'

'Yes, the point is subsequently. I was just simply seeking clarification as to whether that was going to be done at the same time or at a later date.'

'Do you not think you might have got a better answer if you had given him sheets one and two of D10 so that he could have seen what the plan was and what he actually did ..?' Fred continued.
'Yes.' Crouper answered before Fred could finish his sentence.
'.. given that this operation was five years earlier and the plan was

six years earlier?'

'Yes. It was in 2001' Crouper did not actually look sheepish.

'Would you agree with me that it would have been fairer to have given him what we now have as D10, pages 1 and 2, so he could see what the plan was six years earlier and what he had actually done more than five years earlier?' Fred was trying to drive the point home.

'Well we certainly did not want to be unfair and I would agree entirely the more information the better, but we had to select some notes that would allow a discussion on the points of management of the various cases in relation to the headings of Good Medical Practice.'

'What was the basis of the allegation that you make in 656 that he had changed his mind?' Fred was now looking at the chairperson to see if he was getting the gist of his questioning.

'It was the .. sorry, if you will excuse me a moment I will just go back to these notes. .... Yes, I have to agree that the case-based discussion notes do not indicate anything in them about a change of mind and I accept responsibility for that because, as I say, I was quite clear that I was seeking some clarification about the comment of Mr Mustaf about 'Undo Arthrodesis' and then 'Total Hip Replacement.' It was simply that matter and that was not in the notes, the notes that we discussed, as I fully accept.' That would be the first time Crouper had accepted that they have made a mistake.

'So the question you put to him is why he changed his mind. You find that he is unable to answer that question because, as you now accept, the basis for it was unjustified.'

'Yes, I agree it could have been .. the matter would have been clearer had we had Mr Mustaf's note which does not appear to be there.'

'The judgment of unacceptable in the light of this simply cannot stand, can it?'

'No, I would have to agree with that.' I think Crouper was getting a bit tired of it by now.

I think Fred had enough of non-committal responses for the day and said this might be an opportune moment for a break. I could see the reverend's eyes light up and nodded vigorously in agreement. We spent the break again going through more clinical records to find those 'missing records.'

After the break, Fred tried to question Crouper about consequences of the serious error of judgement by the assessment panel. However, he was stopped and Crouper was asked to leave the room while the discussion of questioning took place.

'Sir, I had not appreciated on Friday just how serious this error, for which this witness apologised, was, it is my fault, but the consequence of the error for which he apologised was that the Interim Orders Panel barred the doctor from undertaking any hip revisions at all and I would like to explore with the witness whether he appreciated or ought to have appreciated that that was a possible outcome.'

Sykes would have none of it. 'What actually happened thereafter is not, frankly, relevant to whether he got it right or not and I do not see how it helps this panel in deciding head of charge 8 to have a review, as it were, of what actually happened as a consequence of what may or may not have been an error.'

Moreover, the Chairman did not agree with Fred to continue his questioning. I was quite devastated to find that the panel of assessors can make as many blunders as they want to, and they cannot be questioned and as far as they are concerned, it is 'irrelevant.'

Crouper was asked to come back in again for more questioning. Fred went to ask him about missing records. There was one patient who had not attended a clinic. As was the practice at the time he was sent a further appointment, which the patient did attend and the clinic letter was not shown to me at the time of my interview.

'Can I show you this page where it is recorded, as I will read out:

> 'At the end of the clinic I look at all the DNA's & give one more appointment. If child/older patient the clinic staff follow up with a phone call. Some I would not give a further appointment & mark 'NFA'. In this case I send a letter to GP. I don't if they are going to get a further appointment.'

What is wrong in that?' Fred wanted to know.

'Yes and as I say, I agreed that that would be a perfectly reasonable way of going about dealing with DNAs at a clinic.'

'So the absence of a letter to a GP is not a matter of criticism if the patient has been offered another appointment. Agreed?'

'That was my query as to whether there was a communication with a GP in these circumstances.'

'Then you had your answer, that there would be no letter to the GP because the patient was offered one more appointment and he did not write to the GP if that was the case. Agreed?'

'Yes.' Crouper was thinking fast.

'So the basis of your criticism goes, does it not?' Fred drove the point home.

'Again, I really come back to what is written on the response to this particular point, that we will now let the GP know of all DNAs.' Crouper would not oblige. He still insisted that it was not good enough.

Crouper tried his best to avoid admitting to any other mistakes throughout that morning. After the lunch break, Fred continued to try to get some more admissions of mistake out of Crouper. He tried to show that the assessors had made several wrong entries and wrong conclusions during the report writing.

He asked Crouper to explain one discrepancy where I was asked by the panel as to the system of allocating patients to be seen by the physiotherapist in the clinic.

It is certainly my handwriting and the response .. well let me say the question: 'You said you did not do debridement for OA yet you did so here. What was the rationale?'
  And if the response to that is:
          'It was a younger patient the knee might have been locking.'
It is not really an answer to the question that was put there which is as much as I can say about those two notes here and that is where it has been put down as 'C', cause for concern. But, the reason I hesitate and slightly puzzled by this was that in the recording of the case-based discussion this has been recorded about it being a younger patient and the knee might have been locking as an answer to:
          'Tell us about the system whereby patients referred .. are
          allocated to the clinical physiotherapy specialist'
That is my reason for puzzlement in relation to this.' Crouper tried to explain but he would not admit to making a mistake. There were several instances where the assessors had made similar mistakes. I was hoping that the panel would make note of these mistakes. That afternoon was spent on going through these mistakes and again Fred could not get Crouper to accept any of the mistakes. He came through as a seasoned witness and avoided all the questioning with evasive answers. When Fred showed some of the 'missing records,' Sykes was quite upset and rather annoyed.
'The next case is case 37, which is patient number 50443. Here we have your criticism at 795, which is page 291. It says, 'Right total knee replacement [21 September 2006]. Handwritten operation note with no

details.' Your judgment is unacceptable. That is based, presumably, on the fact there is no operation note.'

'Yes, that is purely on that point.' Crouper replied.

'Can we hand in what will become, I think, D14.' Natalie got up and distributed a single page to everyone.

'D14 is the document with patient 50443 in the upper right-hand corner.' The chairman wanted to keep the records straight after all the mistakes shown by Fred that day.

'Mr Kasyapa has found this in the full set of notes. This would appear to be, would it not, the operation note for 21 September 2006?' Fred asked Crouper.

'It is, yes.'

'The criticism in relation to this patient must necessarily fall, must it not?'

'Yes. I could not find it in the notes, I have to say, but that is what the criticism was, that there was not any typewritten note.'

'Can we just ask: when was this found?' Sykes was definitely suspicious. Perhaps he thought we had been typing these notes up during our spare time!

'Friday. The panel will appreciate we are trying to look at the notes in the breaks between the hearing, which is the reason why we have had difficulty. Understandably, the records have to be kept secure, so they can only be looked at in this room or with the permission of the secretary in our room, but only in the presence of our solicitors, so we have to view them on the premises.' Fred explained. However, there was not an ounce of response from any of the panel. It was as if nothing untoward had happened.

Finally, Sykes started his 'Re-examination' where he tried to undo some of Fred's work on Crouper's admission of mistakes. He was partly successful in getting the words so complex that it would take Sir Humphrey Appleby to unravel them. The panel had their own question, which I thought were so inconsequential that they need not have bothered. O'Neil brought his own experience of having had five arthroscopies on his knees with complications of DVT and pulmonary embolism. He had also brought his own literature search – an obscure

Dutch paper – which had shown a high incidence of DVT after arthroscopy of knees. Swayambhu's comment later that evening to that was that, he should change his surgeon. The reverend tried to make some sense what I should be doing for 'missing dictation,' did not get anywhere, and gave up after repeated evasive answers from Crouper. The Chairman did not have any questions for Crouper and he was excused at the end of the evening.

We were all drained at the end of that day. Nancy asked me to try again to see if we can dig up some details of Amoshin's work through that evening and we were asked to return the next morning by 9.30. We walked back to the flat in silence. Swayambhu and Lopa had decided that we were going to stay in the flat that evening instead of going out. We popped into the local Tesco's and Lopa picked up a few things for the cooking that evening. We also picked up a bottle of red wine as we could do with a bit of unwinding. As Lopa got busy with her cooking, we opened the wine and some olives. Swayambhu was on the phone to Gautam trying to explain what happened through the day. There were several phone calls from friends and well-wishers wanting to know how things were progressing. When Helen told me that Joan was lighting a candle for me in the church every Sunday, tears welled up in my eyes. There were friends and people, who were the salt of the Earth and they mean you well. This makes it all the worthwhile fighting a battle and gets your faith back in the humanity.

Swayambhu was quite proud of his doodling through the day. He showed me the pencil sketches he had made of the panel members and the Chairman. It was quite good. He said, 'You should write up your experiences with this nightmare. It will not only purge you of the event, but also give you a satisfaction of telling the world your story. You can use these sketches for your book.'

'I have already started putting down events as they have occurred and eventually thinking of making it into a book' I replied thoughtfully. 'I may have to ask Nancy about the legal issues.'

'As long as you make it reasonably anonymous, that should not be a problem.' Swayambhu felt.

14. Day 7; Wednesday 7th May 2008

As we walked down the road towards the GMC offices, none of us said very much. Swayambhu had to go home that morning to get back to work again. It was just the two of us, Lopa and me that day. I am sure Swayambhu wanted to stay for the whole hearing, but work commitments could not be ignored any longer. We were fully aware that we had Amoshin to cope with, and I had made no secret of the fact that we should go to town with his evidence, as he had misrepresented my answers in his report. Fred had reassured me that he would do his best to discredit his evidence as much as he could do. There was always the fear that it might backfire with the panel getting sympathetic towards him.

The morning started again with us waiting in the room until about 10 in the morning. I had seen Amoshin going in and out of the toilet a few times during the last few days when he was hanging around to be called. I had pointed him out to Swayambhu and Lopa. Swayambhu's words were, 'He looks like a Baniya rather than an orthopaedic surgeon.'

For those of us not familiar with the north Indian slang, Baniya is a rather derogatory term, for an unscrupulous moneylender.

Fred started the morning with Amoshin. He tried making him look terribly impressive with his CV. Unfortunately, for him, it turned out he was no more this, that or the other as he had stopped working a while ago. Sykes asked him about two of his 'publications' which turned out to be, presentations by his registrar, over 10 yrs previously in local meetings, and not published in any journal. When he described his work in the last hospital he was employed, it gave me a shock.

'Can we turn to the last page, please? This deals with your specific practice. Your particular speciality? Sykes asked, looking through the typewritten CV, which was all of three pages long.
'I used to do mainly hip replacement for our Hospital until 2002, but then I had a quadruple bypass, so I stopped doing major surgery'. Amoshin replied.
'So, In the time from 1972 to 2002 you describe yourself, I think, as carrying out approximately 2000 ..' Amoshin did not let Sykes finish
'Approximately. There were about 18 per week approximately. I used to do about two or three per list.'

That meant he would be doing between six or nine lists a week! The standard for any consultant in this country is between three to four lists a week. I knew he was not telling the truth because one of the leading hip surgeons in the country who did nothing but hip replacements during his entire career of nearly 35 years had just retired and he had done just over 2500 hip replacements. In the United Kingdom, very few orthopaedic surgeons have done 2000 hip replacements in their entire career because everyone has to do other operative procedures as well as manage trauma. Amoshin, it turned out was not even a consultant at the time. He was made into a consultant in 2002 and was asked to do foot surgery. It was extremely unlikely that he had done any hip surgery for the last six years.

Sykes spent the entire morning with Amoshin going through the same subject as with Crouper trying to reinforce his case. Some of the statement made by Amoshin would cause uproar in the current orthopaedic circles.

'I personally would not do such complicated cases though when I was young I was able to do them, but things have changed a lot now. You need to usually refer these patients to hip centres, i.e. places like Wrightington, Professor Charnley's Unit, Exeter, etcetera, or the person who just does nothing but revision surgery, nothing but revision. That means replacing second joints. There are now these who just do revision surgery, will not even do primary surgery.'

Such a statement would be shot down, as no one would dream of doing just revision surgery without doing primary surgery. There are no units in the country where such a scenario exists. The revision surgery of the hip is within the armamentarium of any orthopaedic surgeon with special interest in hip surgery. Moreover, there are at least two to four of these in each District General Hospital. If everyone started sending all the revisions to 'specialist' units, the waiting list for such a procedure would be several years.

Amoshin kept on insisting that a pre-assessment should be done by the consultant and not the nurses throughout his interview. I do not know of any unit in this country or anywhere else where the patients are pre-assessed by the consultant. This statement would be an insult all those highly qualified and trained nurses performing pre-assessments throughout the country. It turns out that he was some sort of superman orthopaedic surgeon, as he was not only doing six to nine lists every week but also running outpatient clinics to see these patients and also did all the pre-assessments himself! It meant, on my calculation, he would be working 8 hours every day seven days a week to 12 hours a day 7 days a week. This was on top of being a teacher in the medical school and basic surgical skills course and sitting on panels such as this etc.

Fred went through all the 'Unacceptable' determinations with Amoshin, to a lesser detail than either Crouper or Dawkins and finished off with,

'Was it your view, first of all, as a team that the standard of Mr Kasyapa's professional performance was deficient?'

'Yes.'

'Did you agree with that view?'

'Yes.'

The whole process was rather short I thought. It was still quite effective despite Amoshin's ramblings during his answers. It was just after the regular coffee break in the morning when Sykes finished.

Fred started straight away with Amoshin's CV. We had spent a fair amount of time dissecting his very brief CV and Fred did have some ammunition to use.

It transpired that Amoshin had spent most of his career working as a 'Hospital Practitioner' and he was appointed to a consultant post in 1995. A Hospital Practitioner grade was a permanent post created for those who did not have enough training or qualifications to become a consultant and were rarely allowed to do any major independent surgery on their own. They always worked at the level of a registrar under the supervision of a consultant. He claimed that he was 'trained' by famous orthopaedic surgeons to do hip replacements and he was 'asked' by the hospital to do these hip replacements!

'When were you in fact appointed as a consultant?'

'1995-ish. I cannot remember exactly but 1994/95.' Amoshin replied looking through his own CV

'And you undertook hip surgery between 1995 and 2002?'

'1972. The reason was I was trained by George Arden in 1970 to 72, who was one of the pioneers of hip surgery in this country. Our hospital Trust wanted somebody to take over doing the hips so I was doing approximately two or sometimes three hips a week since 1972 but continued doing that and then in 95-ish, 94/95. I cannot remember. They asked me if I wanted a full-time job and I said yes.' Like most of the day, Amoshin continued name-dropping.

'So in the period between 1995 and 2002, as a consultant what was your rate of doing hips then?' Amoshin wanted more clarification about his claim of number of hip replacements he was doing.

'Three a week.' Amoshin insisted. So what happened to his statement that morning to Sykes of 18 hip replacements a week? Pity Fred did not pick that up as it amounted to perjury.

'Three a week?'

'Yes. I would not do three a week on that list, and before that, I was doing the same – two to three a week. So 1972, I think I started doing it.'

There were several inconsistencies as I could see. I found it hard to believe that an NHS hospital would allow a Hospital Practitioner to perform hip replacements in 1970's when it was in the realms of highly specialised units and done by a handful of senior consultants across the country. Secondly, there was a contradiction by Amoshin himself about the number of operations he was performing per week. That was a significant difference over a couple of hours.

His name-dropping got worse as the questioning continued and at one stage, this became so bad that he quoted four names as part of an answer to one question.

'My question is, one appreciates you say you gave up hip surgery in 2002 but did you in fact develop a particular interest in foot surgery prior to that?' Fred asked.

'Yes. Can I explain to you? Professor Charnley used to have Professor Mike Wroblewski. He was our senior registrar for one year and I assisted him personally in most of the cases. John Bulmer was very keen on foot surgery and we were doing reconstruction surgery of the foot, he was doing them, and I used to help him. When he retired, I continued his interest and the procedure we did, Mr. Stainsby from Seaport, he adopted the procedure, and I continued doing that and the registrars published this. None of these publications are mine, they are registrars. None of them are mine.' Amoshin was looking quite jubilant at using so many names all at once, I thought.

Fred continued his questioning regarding training for a while longer.

'I am trying to investigate something slightly different though and that is that your interest in foot surgery plainly developed late 90s, something like that?'

'No, I have always … In early years of orthopaedic development we were trained to do everything, so you did everything. When I started in the 60s when I was in Oban, I was doing caesarean sections, so we would do everything and gradually the orthopaedic surgery became separate. From '70 onwards I was still doing feet, I was still doing spinal surgery, but as the time passed on and more developments took place I stopped gradually but continued doing hip surgery and foot, but I continued doing general orthopaedics like simple things, not complicated things, very simple things I would do which are common.'

Amoshin's reply made me think. Here we have a surgeon who not only did general orthopaedic surgery, but also obstetric surgery during his career and yet managed to perform more than 2000 hip replacements. I cannot reconcile to this fact, as it was unlikely to have been repeated by any other surgeon, not only in this country but also in anywhere else in the world. However, Fred could not impress on the panel about the false statements Amoshin continued to make throughout his testimony.

Anyway, Amoshin admitted that he had stopped doing any hip surgery in 2002, four years before the assessment. At this stage, Fred went on to question him about his assessment. I was disappointed that he did not pursue Amoshin's work a little further to show the fallacies in his statements. I thought that it was a missed opportunity to discredit Amoshin not only as a witness but also as an Assessor. How could someone who had not done any hip surgery for four years could be allowed to assess a hip surgeon?

Amoshin's inconsistencies continued throughout the day. Fred was asking him about pre-operative assessment.

'The central question here is what the pre-operative assessment was and what Mr. Kasyapa was saying to you is this, that the patient is seen by the staff grade, the notes do not record that, but the risk was discussed. Then the patient goes to the nurse practitioner for a pre-operative assessment. They are given a leaflet at that stage. They are brought in one or two weeks before the operation for a pre-operative assessment and then you have written:

'If they have Deep Vein Thrombosis, I would see
day before surgery.'

In fact, Mr. Amoshin, that is not quite correct, is it, because what Mr.
Kasyapa said to you was that he saw all his patients the day before
surgery. Do you remember that?' Fred asked.

'No, I do not.' Amoshin would not admit to that.

'If I could invite you to be given D12 which are the case based discussion
case sheets if you look on the first page these are the notes of Wendy
Mildred who was one of the four assessors. You all sat together, did you
not?'

'Yes.'

'Well, if you look at the first response that she gives on that page it is
very similar to your own, but it is slightly fuller. She says:

'Seen by staff grade – no one can go on list unless I see them. I go
through the procedure. If they want to go ahead, attend nurse
practitioner clinic to be assessed. Given a leaflet. 2 weeks before
surgery, they are brought in to check drugs, problems. I see all the day
before surgery.'

Has she not recorded that right?'

'Yes, but I had no evidence from the notes that he has seen them.'

'Let us come to the notes in a moment. That process that he is
describing there, that procedure, is an entirely proper and appropriate
procedure for a consultant orthopaedic surgeon to adopt, is it not?'

'I still do not understand your question, sir, I am sorry.' That was
Amoshin's tactic of avoiding the truth. He would not admit to writing
the wrong thing in his assessment and that is not the only time. As we
went through the day, we would come across several places where he
had recorded wrong statements. He insisted that a consultant should go
around checking every record every time a junior doctor sees a patient
and write a duplicate record for every patient. Otherwise, he would not
know how to treat the patient if he were to take over.

'Let us just examine the proposition then. You would agree that if
a junior doctor is instructed to write in the notes and does so there is no
need for the consultant to do so. That would be duplication. Agreed?'

'No, if he has not written then it is not a duplication.'

'No, just listen to the question, Mr Amoshin.' I could hear the annoyance in Fred's voice.

'Yes.'

'If the junior doctor has written in the notes to record a pre-operative assessment or an operation or whatever it may be ..'

'Yes.'

'.. then there is no need for the consultant to do so because it would be duplication?'

'Yes, but he still needs to write in ..' Amoshin had started to blabber.

'Are you suggesting that the consultant should on every occasion check to ensure that the junior has carried out his instruction to write in the notes?'

'Yes. That is the duty of a consultant. The patient is under care of the consultant, not the junior doctor.'

I could not believe what I was hearing.

Then we came to the question of preoperative planning for which I was roundly criticised for the absence of such planning.

'We can see what Mr Kasyapa is saying there. He says in the third paragraph:

'I am going to request a Bone Scan to see if there is anything going on in the trochanteric region of the left hip and we will see her again after the Scan to decide whether we should be embarking on revision surgery for this hip. After discussion with Dr Spalding, the request has been changed from a Bone Scan to a Tomogram. I will see her again after the Tomogram ..'

The next entry on that page is 21 December 2000.

'The lady had fusion of the right hip long time ago after an intertrochanteric osteotomy .. her X-rays are missing today. She is having a lot of pain in the right hip region ... asking for a hip replacement.

I discussed with Mr Kasyapa who also examined her and explained the possible complications including high risk of dislocation, infection, DVT, and earlier failure. She understands the complications very well and even then, she would like to proceed for operation. I have put her on the waiting list for undo of arthrodesis of the right hip and then right total hip replacement.'

Done by Mr Mustaf. Then he sets it out what it is. Somebody has corrected his right to his left and we do not need to trouble with that. If we go over to the next page we have got the operation notes on 31 October 2001.' Fred looked up to see if Amoshin was following his reading.

'Yes.'

'It is quite clear, is it not, that there was adequate planning for this operation.'

'Yes, he had investigated looking at that now, yes. Investigated, yes.'

'So that criticism falls, does it not?'

'Falls without planning.' Amoshin mumbled. The Chairman had asked him to repeat his answer.

The discussion about 'missing notes' was rather amusing, as he appeared to be completely lost. One of them went like this –

'Let us go on to the next one. Patient 37. We have three criticisms there. Do you have that page?' Fred asked Amoshin.

'Yes.'

'You have recorded -

'Operation notes missing total knee replacement right MIS operation notes blank sheet.'

You say if there is a typed note the criticism falls away.'

'That is right.' I thought I could see beads of sweat on his forehead.

'We have now got D14. I think you ought to look at it. That is a single sheet. That is the typed operation note, is it not?'

'Yes. We could not trace it, so it is there.' Amoshin was looking rather uncomfortable and started to fidget with the sheets of paper in front of him. He was not looking up.

'So that criticism does fall away.'

'Yes.' It was barely audible.

'Why was it that the assessors found the absence of this note unacceptable and were unable to find it or failed to add it to the clip of documentation themselves?' For the first time Fred raised his voice slightly looking a bit annoyed.

'What did you ask?' Amoshin was obviously taken aback at the tone.

'How did you miss it?'

'How did I miss it?' He was looking rather sheepishly at Fred.

'Yes.'

'I do not know if it was there or not. I cannot answer you why we missed it.'

'It was there because we found it there.'

'You are cleverer than me then, that is all. I cannot answer the question. I did not see it and not only did I not see it, the other person also..' Amoshin started to ramble before Fred stopped him again.

'How seriously were you taking this exercise?' Fred was looking at the Chairman this time and had his Head Master's voice.

'Very, very seriously. We were taking it very seriously.' Amoshin grinned sheepishly.

'Because this doctor could be erased from the Register because of your mistakes, could he not?'

'Yes. We did not make any mistakes. We were taking it very seriously.'

'Yet you missed this note.'

'Yes.' Amoshin mumbled again and Fred let it go. I wished he had continued a bit longer and stressed the blunders of the assessment panel.

The rest of Fred's examination went in a similar vein where Amoshin would not agree to facts of his and his colleagues serious mistakes in the assessment process. During the examination he claimed the new Treatment centre which was being hailed as a model of excellence by everyone in the country as a 'factory' where patients were treated on an 'assembly line.' He claimed that the pre-assessment was done in the centre on the day of surgery and was 'conveyor belt surgery.' Fred finished late afternoon and Sykes did his very short re-examination as Amoshin had said he could not come back the next day for further examination.

When the panelists started asking questions the whole place livened up. Most people were tired and lethargic by that time of the day when the 'Specialist Performance Advisor' started asking her questions. This was when fun started and woke people up from the afternoon slumber.

It was like watching a Monty Python show. First, it was very difficult to understand what she was saying because of her broad Spanish accent and secondly she mumbled the same way as Amoshin. She asked about the patient with a fracture clavicle and suspected Sudeck's dystrophy.

'There is another case it was a little confused for me. Case number 8, in page 90, page 88' Mercia asked Amoshin.

'88?' Amoshin looked at her confused.

'This lady with the sudeck's dystrophy.'

'The lady with shoulder pain, you mean?'

'Yes.'

'Fractured clavicle? Yes.'

'In the hospital of the surgeon it seems that they have a week trauma on-call, is it not?' Mercia asked looking at Amoshin.

'Pardon?' Amoshin was looking lost.

'They were on-call in a week for trauma?'

'Okay.' Amoshin did not have a clue what she was saying.

'Yes, agree? You remember that in the hospital?'

'No, I do not.' That bewildered Amoshin and he would not accept to anything.

'In few places they say that it was doing a week on-call on trauma.' Mercia was now getting irate and her Spanish accent got worse angrier she became.

'On trauma, okay.' Now everyone else was confused.

'Yes. So that means that the surgeon on-call is supposed to be on-call for trauma for the whole week?' Mercia tried to explain. Even the reverend had woken up now and started taking interest.

'Yes.'

'And only doing trauma. Right, this patient was admitted on 29 May, page 90. It is a young lady of middle age involved in a road traffic accident.'

'Yes.' Amoshin was finding it easy to say yes rather than argue.

'Right, you find that?'

'Yes.'

'In this road traffic accident it was ..' Mercia continued

Amoshin interrupted with something no one could hear. I think the Chairman had given up trying to follow what was happening by then.

'Do you think that this patient is a dangerous case is a simple case?' She appeared to be accusing Amoshin of something.

'No, no, no. I never said it was a simple case' Amoshin was quick to answer and he was looking at the Chairman for help.

'No, no, no. I did not say you did. So you, as a surgeon, was an orthopaedic you will expect him to see the patient straight away after admission?'

'I think I am not able to understand why I am being questioned.' Amoshin was decidedly worried now. He looked like a rabbit in the headlights.

Then all hell broke loose. Both of them started to talk together. It was hilarious to watch if it was not such a serious situation. No one could understand what was happening. The short hand writer threw her hands in the air and looked at the Chairman for help in despair.

'No, no. I just in general. No, no. I just want you to..' Mercia

'Well I was not in charge of the surgeon, so ...' Amoshin

'I just want you ..' Mercia

'... I cannot answer the question.' Amoshin

'I just want your opinion.' Mercia.

The short hand writer who was trying to follow all this had given up half an hour ago. She put her pencil down and looked at the Chairman in desperation.

'Can you just do one at a time, please?'

It did not make any difference to them. The verbal wrangling went on. It was extremely hard to make out what each other were saying. Mercia's English sounded more and more Spanish and Amoshin's language was becoming increasingly indecipherable.

'I just want your opinion as an orthopaedic surgeon what is ..' Mercia continued unabated.

'Okay, you want to know my ..' Amoshin started before she could finish and Mercia cut him down half way again.

'... said people things to do.'

'No, no, obviously it is a serious road traffic accident.'

'It is a serious traffic accident.'

'Yes.'

'If you are going to ..' Mercia did not seem to take any notice of what Amoshin was saying and continued regardless. None of us knew where this conversation was going as each of them was talking at odds. chairman finally intervened.

'Sorry, just pause for a moment. This is making life very difficult for the shorthand writer.'

'What?' Mercia looked at him questioningly. I almost expected her to say 'Che'

'Yes?' Amoshin also looked at him

'Can you slow down and speak a bit more clearly please?' The chairman could not hide his exasperation. The reverend was smiling and O'Neil's cheshire cat grin was back on his face

'Slow down?' Mercia still could not understand.

'Yes, can we just slow it down a bit, please?' The chairman continued.

'I am sorry sir' Amoshin said sheepishly.

Mercia then went on to throw some new accusations, which she created out of the records she had and started to ask Amoshin questions. He in turn became completely entangled and started to mutter and nobody could follow where her questioning was leading. In the end, Fred put a stop to it with

'With the greatest respect to the Specialist Adviser, I have to say that I am now dubious that she is in a position to offer you independent, impartial, and unbiased advice.'

Moreover, to my greatest surprise Sykes agreed with Fred's objection. The chairman went into a huddle with the legal assessor, turned to Mercia, and said, 'Dr Mercia, the panel is minded to accept the legal Assessor's advice on this matter. So what I am going to ask you to do is confine your questions to the matters that have arisen in the performance assessment that have been the subject of both the examination and the cross-examination.'

I do not think Mercia really understood what was being asked of her and she just nodded her head. The intervention did not make any difference to her. The chairman might have been talking to a wall. She just looked at him and continued in the same vein. It was as if she could not care less what the chairman had said. Once she had finished, O'Neil asked a few questions again on DVT after arthroscopy and drug's dosage for gout. The Reverend did not have any questions and the Chairman had only one question. He wanted to know if there were video cameras recording the assessment in GMC.

After excusing Amoshin, discussion started on the progress of the case and Fred wanted time for him to prepare his submission. He also indicated that he would be requesting the 'Specialist Adviser' to be recused the next day. When the realisation that this case was going to go on longer than I had hoped for and probably longer than the time limit set aside for this case, my heart sank. There was nothing I could do, as the matter was out of my hands and no one was taking any notice of me there anyway. Finally, they agreed that the hearing would reconvene the next afternoon after lunchtime.

As we came out of the GMC building, I was walking with my head down and Nancy tried to cheer me up.

'I think we have got them now. Fred has got so much ammunition; I can't see how we can lose at this stage.'

That did help me lift my spirits up a little. As we walked back to the flat, it was getting cloudy and damp with a slow drizzle. It just reflected my mood. Neither of us was in a great mood to do anything. After the usual phone calls to Gautam and Swayambhu to update them of the day's proceedings, we sat down to watch the TV with cups of coffee. Both of us felt that there was nothing we could do now but wait for Fred's submission. I was hoping against hope that we might get some justice if the Panel members have heard what we had heard over the last few days.

15. Day Eight; Thursday 8th May, 2008.

I was facing today with anticipation mixed with trepidation. We had been asked to come back at lunchtime and had the morning for ourselves. Swayambhu had come back down for the final sessions, as he wanted to be there for Fred's submission. We spent the morning wandering around the city centre and sauntered down to the Philpots, the sandwich place for our customary lunchtime sandwich and Lopa's soup. As we reached the Council rooms, there were quite a few developments. Fred had nearly completed his drafting of submission and needed some help from me to complete the draft. He handed me the skeleton submission to look through. I was quite impressed by his submission and could not understand how Sykes could oppose this submission. Part of the submission was our application to have the specialist performance advisor to be recused. As we entered the room, the first thing we noticed was the presence of Mercia. We all wondered if she knew that she was going to be removed from the panel.

Fred started with his submission after the usual pleasantries. He submitted the skeleton submission as D20, which was distributed to everyone. He started saying that before he does the main submission he has an application to make. I am sure the panel understood what the application was going to be. He started apologising to the panel chairman for the application and said that he did not mean any disrespect to the 'Specialist Performance advisor.'

He went on to say, 'The specialist adviser has misunderstood her role and adopted that of a junior prosecutor.' This produced the desired effect and the silence in the room was thick and could be cut with a knife. Fred was in his element when he said, 'Every question was plainly intended to produce an answer critical of the doctor. Even after my protests and the chair's intervention the specialist adviser continued to try to elicit criticism of the doctor.'

He was in full flow now, and nothing could stop him

'Regrettable, but with good reason, Mr Kasyapa has lost confidence in the Specialist Adviser to give independent and impartial advice to the panel.'

He further criticised the specialist adviser with

'Furthermore, it is not evident, and understandably given the blizzard of paper in this case, that the Specialist Adviser is sufficiently on top of the documents to fully understand the case as it develops.'

Fred highlighted the fact that she could not, and did not attend all the days of the hearing, and he pointed to the possibility that she was probably not into the intricacies of the case. I looked at Mercia while she was being crucified but did not see any response whatsoever. She probably did not understand most of Fred's submission.

'There is a question, and it cannot be put higher than that, as to the assiduity with which the specialist adviser has read the transcript of days on which she has not attended.'

Fred was quite ruthless and factual, and he was not taking any prisoners at this stage. The fact that the questions she was posing the witness were irrelevant and were already discussed the day before and discounted was gently but albeit firmly pointed out to the panel. Fred quoted a few court cases and earlier tribunal cases as references. He paid reference to the test, in determining whether a decision should be set aside, on the ground of bias is an objective one.

'The question is whether the fair minded and informed observer, having considered the facts, would conclude that there was a real possibility that the tribunal was biased.'

He went on to quote a few more references to reinforce the fact that the Specialist Adviser was probably biased, and 'cannot be seen as impartial'. The fact that we had lost complete confidence in her ability to give good, balanced advice was well established.

Sykes started his submission in defence and he was good. He registered his protest saying that, she had not given any advice to the panel yet, and she probably 'may not be seen as biased based on the questions she had asked,' which he considered relevant to the case. The argument that she was going beyond her remit did not appear in his rebuttal. However, he concluded saying, that he was not opposing Fred's application. The chairman appeared slightly flustered and asked for the legal adviser's opinion. The legal adviser had a grave face when she recounted the passage from the Guide to Specialist adviser, which to me appeared quite clear. It was also quite clear to everyone present, that Mercia had totally flouted the regulations, and she either had not read the guide, or did not understand the guide. Judging from the display of her grasp of English language, I would put a bet on the latter. When it came to the advice from the legal assessor, she made it quite clear, that the remit of the specialist adviser, is 'not only to be giving impartial advice but also should be seen to be doing so'. She also went on to reinforce the same to the function of the panel, as being 'not only impartial but also should be seen to be impartial.'

There was an audible silence after this statement from the legal assessor. The Cheshire grin was wiped of the face of O'Neil, and I could see Mercia rummaging through her notebook appearing to look busy. Everyone else's eyes were on the chairman, who had a rather grave worried look on his face. Obviously the panel needed to discuss this issue 'in-camera' and hence we had to go out again for a while, as they deliberated on the application of recusal. The panel took an awful long time over this – over 45 minutes. The assistant to the panel finally called us back in. We all hurried back in like a pack of school kids awaiting results. As we were going in, we noticed Mercia packed and ready to go and avoided any eye contact! The panel chairman had quite a severe face on when he made the announcement of determination. Like all decisions of the council, it was long winded – repeated almost everything Fred had said before coming to the actual decision. The short of it was that the panel agreed that the specialist adviser was biased, but did not agree that she had not read the transcripts of the days she had not attended and that she was not on top of the proceedings of the hearing. We were extremely glad to see the back of her. I was getting more and more worried about the tone of her questioning, and inherently obvious bias demonstrated during her questioning. It appeared as if she had already made her mind up that I was guilty and trying to fit the findings around that conclusion. Now the question of whether we need a specialist performance adviser came up, and our worries of postponement of the hearing were unfounded. The chairman said that the hearing will go on without an adviser and will appoint one if found necessary after the final submission. That was a relief.

By now, the time was getting on, and there was not enough time for Fred to make his final submission. I was extremely disappointed at that as I was hoping to get the submission out of the way and get a decision on Friday, which was the last day of the scheduled hearing. As they started to discuss the options available for future dates, my heart sank at the prospect of the whole process prolonging forever. The fact that they were discussing reconvening for two days for decision making, and looking at dates for second stage of the hearing if necessary at a later date, reassured me somewhat. I was hoping in my heart of hearts that it means that they have probably half decided that the hearing will not go into the second stage. I will just have to wait and see. The tentative date given was Sunday 1st June. I found the whole discussion of the future dates quite eerie and rather unnerving. It was as if I did not exist. Nobody asked me about my availability for reconvening or what I felt about the progress.

The General Medical Council's reason for removing its previous slogan of 'working for doctors, protecting patients' was becoming painfully clear to me at this stage. It felt as if it did not matter whether you are successful after the hearing or not. The process made sure that you are ignored, humiliated, trodden on, and generally treated like a low life of society. By the time the hearing is finished you are so badly demoralised that whether you win or lose you are not the same person again. One's self confidence takes such a beating that it will never recover again. If you are not either an exceptionally strong willed person or one with no insight, there is no way of getting out of this unscathed. The fact that they were discussing the dates for your case without any regard for you in your presence was not only odd but also rather insulting.

Both Fred and Nancy were extremely reassuring and said they felt the panel probably want to finish this case off one way or the other as quickly as possible. Nancy was quite elated at the outcome, as she had never come across a specialist adviser thrown out of a hearing before in her 15 years of service. Fred also said he had never asked anyone to be recused in his entire career. Therefore, it was a 'First' in this case! I was not sure whether that was a good thing or bad thing. Only time will tell.

We were discussing the happenings of the day and we started to do an analysis on the way back to the flat, as it had become a routine by then. Swayambhu and Lopa felt quite positive. All three of us felt that it was a minor victory for us, by getting rid of the specialist performance adviser, who was becoming a real worry and thorn in our side. Obviously, we were all disappointed at the prospect of going home without an outcome the next day.

Swayambhu, as usual was philosophizing about the different aspects of that day, and felt that we could have probably saved half a day, if we had made the application for recusal in the morning. He found it difficult to understand, why Fred had to have the whole submission prepared and ready in case the application was refused. After two attempts, I gave up. He had drawn caricatures of everyone on the panel except Fred Barnard. He appeared to be having some trouble drawing him. Again, that evening we found ourselves at loose ends, but did not feel like doing anything strenuous. We ended up going to an Indian

Restaurant to eat what probably was the worst Indian food I have had all my life. I do not think we will ever learn – the best Indian cooking is at home.

16.   Day Nine; Friday 9th May. 2008.

We were both exited and apprehensive. We had reached a stage where there was remarkably little we could do but wait and watch. We made our way back to the infamous St James' Building where Fred Barnard was already waiting for us. Poor Nancy was stuck in a lift, in her hotel, and was late arriving. We all trooped in when called into the hearing room 4. The Chairman did the usual pleasantries and invited Fred Barnard for his submission.

Fred started slowly and went through the submission in three parts. He said that the submission has three limbs as it were, and should be read in a sequence even though they are separate issues. The first proposition was that there is insufficient evidence for the panel to find the facts proved. In this, he brought up the problem that the panel faced at the start of the hearing, which was inadequate drawing up of the charges against me. The panel had to amend the charges and add a further charge that all the charges *were warranted*. He took up the test of competence as the first one to attack. The fact that I had scored low in the surgical knowledge was accepted with reservation, as we had not been shown either the questions or my answers. He went on to say, ' . that failure did not and cannot warrant a finding that Mr. Kasyapa's performance was deficient ..'

This was reinforced by the fact the one of the orthopaedic assessors accepted that 'it was inconceivable Mr. Kasyapa did not know and do these things in his practice.' He also pointed out that no one, both present and past colleagues, had suggested in the third party interviews or the assessors have found in the case based discussions that I 'did not know what to do in these respects or that he did not do these things.'

He concluded on this basis; 'The GMC cannot therefore say that because Mr. Kasyapa's performance in the knowledge and skills tests was poor his practice was therefore poor.'

He quoted the case of Krippendorf v GMC as the basis of his argument where the question of reliability of the test of competence and highlighted its relevance to the practitioner's specialty. He further attacked the skills test as being irrelevant and said it did not reflect in practice. He quoted my experience of over 2000 joint replacements over a period of 11 years as a consultant at the time of assessment without any demonstrable excessive complications as evidence of my surgical skills. This was borne out by the audit figures published by the Hospital Trust.

Fred was in full flow now and no one could stop him. The drinks break had to be postponed. He attacked the assessors' presumption that my workload was still excessively high as there was ample evidence to the contrary. As it appeared to be the case with every other allegation, the assessors had conveniently ignored the evidence presented to them by the seven current colleagues and taken the words of two disgruntled individuals who had left the Trust three years previously. The question of revision hip surgery came up next – 'The assessment team do not consider that Mr. K performs sufficient hip revisions to enable him to maintain adequate competency.' The statement is acknowledged to be 'fallacious ..' He went on to record keeping next and said the assessor's statement record keeping 'may be at time inaccurate and some operation notes are missing' was essentially wrong and cannot reasonably be supposed to be greater than other busy consultant orthopaedic surgeons. He demonstrated the so called 'missing operation notes' were actually never 'missing' but in fact had not been found by the assessors. These missing operation notes had been picked up by our team and shown to the panel.

Fred's second limb of the proposition was that there was 'insufficient evidence to support a finding of impairment.' Now we are getting into legal language and I hope I can decipher and make it readable and understandable. The proposition mainly states that 'if the panel finds all the evidence submitted by the GMC is found by the panel to be sustainable, there is still insufficient evidence to support a finding of impairment.' He further quoted the GMC's Fitness to Practice guide Rule 17(2)(k) which states the panel has to consider fitness at the time of hearing and not nearly 18 months before the hearing. The panel is not required to consider past impairment and only have regard to present impairment. In short, Fred said the GMC does not have a *prima facie* case against me at this stage. Well, I must say this took me by some surprise. I have a suspicion this will be soundly refuted by the GMC barrister and unlikely to get much further. He then quoted a report by the Judge in the Shipman case supporting evidence for his claim. He said that the GMC has failed to raise even a *prima facie* case that the alleged deficiencies persist. On the contrary, he went on to say that, I have taken steps to remedy the potential or perceived deficiencies by attending the basic surgical skills course and also going away for sabbatical.

The third limb of his proposition was 'if some disputed facts are proved, they are insufficient to support a finding of impairment by the panel.' This again is a legal argument, if anything slightly more confusing. This is on the assumption that the second submission fails in total, but the first submission succeeds only to the extent of knocking out part of the assessors' conclusion of deficient performance. 'This submission proposes that such alleged deficiencies are not sufficient to support a finding that the charges are warranted.' He continued.

With this three-pronged submission, Fred Barnard completed his submission and asked for 'no case to answer.' The submission was done in a very calm and calculated manner without any histrionics and drama. I was watching the faces of the three panel members through the submission to gauge their reaction. The Chairman appeared very interested and the Vicar was furiously writing away many things. The grin on O'Neil's face had stayed permanently off during the submission and he also appeared to make some notes. We saw the legal assessor nodding in agreement at several points during the submission. Once the submission was complete, which was around lunchtime, the GMC barrister said he wanted to start his submission before breaking for lunch as he had a document to be produced which would hopefully make it simpler for the panel to follow the GMC's case. This again filled me with dread, as I was getting very wary of the GMC producing new documents at the last minute. It just turned out to be a spreadsheet identifying case notes, criticisms and the author of the criticism all in one place. It was quite a formidable document and did help in speeding up the process. He produced the document and asked everyone to familiarise with the document and we broke for lunch.

We went down to the customary sandwich, at the Philpots and came back up to face the GMC barrister's assault. He started in his usual rather dry and by now a predictable fashion with his rebuttal using the criticisms, some of which had already been shown to be either false or unwarranted by Fred Barnard. However, I could see both Lopa and Swayambhu were getting more and more worried as the day went on, with increasing numbers of criticisms. In spite of Swayambhu's protestations, we knew he had nodded off in the middle of the rebuttal. It could not have been that interesting. His rather monotonous soliloquy was interspersed with a few smirks and sniggers every now and then as if to make a point. I do not think this was lost on anyone. His statement was essentially the repeat of the criticisms by the three assessors that he had been upholding over the past two weeks. I also could see Fred Barnard shaking his head quite firmly during the submission at several points. I must say that I was slightly disappointed at the rebuttal. I was expecting a much more powerful rebuttal from someone who had shown himself to be a quite a clever and shrewd man. When he finished his rebuttal, we took a drinks break and our camp was rather quiet. Both Lopa and Swayambhu looked rather worried. Swayambhu's comment was that the GMC barrister was very scathing and it appeared bad for us. I had taken notes during Sykes's submission and wanted to discuss with Fred Barnard for the final rebuttal. Nevertheless, Fred Barnard was not worried and said that he can manage the criticisms, as they did not seem to have much substance in Sykes's submission. Nancy said he could not produce a good submission because 'you cannot stitch a silk purse with a sow's ear.' I had not heard of this saying before and it took me a little time to understand the meaning. This seemed to calm Lopa and Swayambhu's nerves down to some extent.

After the tea break, we went back into the hearing room for the final submission of Fred Barnard. The Chairman asked if Fred had anything else to say. Fred said he certainly does and started with Sykes's dismissal of the legal issue within Fred's initial submission. He was quite passionate during the last submission and I felt that he blew Sykes's rebuttal out of the water. He took each of the headings in the assessors report and tore them apart bit by bit. I was quite fascinated by the clinical annihilation of Sykes's work in thirty minutes. I could see the Chairman nodding his head a couple of times through this. I felt much more reassured after this than at any time during the afternoon. After this, there was a lot of moving us out of the room and getting back while they discussed the possible dates for reconvening. I failed to understand the secrecy behind this discussion. At the end the chairman addressed me for the first time since the hearing began nine days ago saying that I'll have to come back on Sunday 1st of June to hear the decision and that the panel will reconvene on Saturday 31st May to deliberate the case. Sykes interjected with his suggestion of getting a specialist performance adviser for the second stage of the hearing. Fred objected saying that we do not really need a specialist performance adviser, especially after the previous one's fiasco. It did not fill us with enormous amount of enthusiasm about the quality of such an adviser appointed by the GMC. There was further discussions 'in-camera' and Sykes was firmly told that the panel will decide on that if the case goes on to the second stage.

As we walked back to the car, there was an audible silence in the group. I suppose we were all mulling over the events of the day with different feelings. I was filled with mixed feelings – one of disappointment as well as that of, oddly a sense of relief! I was very disappointed that we were going back home with no result and at the same time I was relieved that I did not have an 'unfavourable result.' My mind went back to the day we drove to Manchester and the meeting with Fred and Nancy at the Hilton. I was quite convinced on that day that I would be going home triumphant a couple of days later. Here we are two weeks later no further forward and the hearing had taken several twists and turns. I was going home with the slur on my professional performance still hanging over my head. This is not what I expected. I was hoping against hope that the nightmare would be finished by the end of the week and was quite looking forward to the end. I had prayed to all the known Gods and some unknown as well, to get to the end of this bad dream. It was not going to be and I was getting increasingly tired and despondent. Lopa and Swayambhu were trying to analyse the events in their own fashion but I could not take part in it, as my mind was full of self-doubt and recriminations over the past events. The drive back home was slower than before and the conversation was sparse with Swayambhu asking me to 'analyse the submissions closely and dissect it out' several times. He firmly believed that if we analyse the submissions by both the barristers, we could probably get an idea of the outcome. He always believed in the fairness of the British justice system. Only time will tell if he was right.

As we reached home, there were a thousand questions from Gautam and others. There was a very long debriefing session in his house. Eternal optimist that he was and declared that there was no way the council can continue after this submission, which had clearly showed that the assessors were incompetent, and the process itself was deeply flawed. By that time we had all convinced ourselves that there can only be one outcome at this stage and we were not even thinking of November or let alone next February. The human mind is such that if you keep saying the same thing repeatedly with enough conviction, you will believe in what you have heard. No wonder we buy so much rubbish that we neither need nor want, but have to have! The power of suggestion is used by the advertisers to the full extent at the gullible public. I was particularly vulnerable at that stage for any suggestions that I wanted to hear that it would have been quite easy to convince me that I was invincible! History has shown that dictators both past and present have used this power to convince their subjects of their invincibility. I was quite buoyed by all the talk of success and how we are going to attack the council after the decision and what actions can we take to teach the perpetrators a lesson they will never forget in their life. There was no end to the rate at which this imaginary horse was bounding. No one can stop me now.

That weekend there was a confluence of all of my close friends at home. We sat in the living room and went through the transcripts we had so far and started to dissect the barrister's submissions. After a lengthy discussion lasting several hours and a few bottles of red wine, we were no way forward. Swayambhu was fast asleep on the sofa, the girls got busy chatting among themselves, and Gautam got busy on the laptop. I was left to ruminate the events of the previous two weeks and got even more depressed.

17.   The Period Of Tranquility..

The sense of 'invincibility' did not last particularly long. The three weeks wait for the decision went extremely fast as I again became deeply immersed in my work. I had to try to finish writing papers, and respond to a couple of publisher's queries, which were outstanding for a while. It was ironic that, during this period of wait, I had visitors from Italy who had come to learn some tricks of the trade during hip replacement. One of them was a full Professor in orthopaedics from the University of Florence, and another was a busy consultant from the east coast of Italy – Lucca to be exact. Here, I was being questioned, and labeled as someone who did not know orthopaedics and lacked basic surgical skills, and at the same time, senior orthopaedic surgeons were from across the world coming to learn highly specialised surgery from me. Alessandro from Lucca had singularly little knowledge of English and Roberto's English was slightly better than my Italian was. Between us, we managed to get the message across with some difficulty and obviously a lot of hilarity.   The Italians generally tend to be gregarious, and Roberto was an archetypal Italian with lots of expansive gestures and expressive language. When I found out that Alessandro turned out to be a Sicilian living in the northeast of Italy, I half expected him to be carrying a violin case. Fortunately, he did not make any offers that I could not refuse! It took extreme skill and diplomacy on the part of Helen to pass off the National Health Service coffee in a plastic cup as 'espresso'. They were bemused, to say the least. Alessandro was extremely curious and full of questions despite the fact that this was his second visit to my unit. He could not understand the eccentric behaviour, of our Geordie youngsters cavorting in remarkably little clothing on a wild mechanical bull, in one of the local hostelries they had visited the night before. Some of the girls around me tried to explain the idiosyncrasies of the hardy Geordie with singularly little success I noted.

The visit went off extremely well and they invited me to visit their local hospitals for demonstration surgery. During the visit, I felt I was going back to my old self - supremely confident of my abilities and at the same time wanting to share my knowledge with others. The kudos I got from the Italian surgeons lifted my spirits and made me forget the entire Council nightmare. I immersed myself in my work both in the hospital and with the University. I had developed a close relationship with Deakin, the senior lecturer in Biomechanics and Professor of Sports

Medicine, Jan. We were busy recruiting a PhD student for doing research into total hip and knee replacement. Developing the protocols and literature search occupied a lot of my time. I thoroughly enjoyed this period when I was working every night late and spending several hours every day outside work time doing research. It was extremely tiring but at the same time extraordinarily satisfying. I could see myself to be taking this to a much higher level than before, and visions of developing a large research unit in the region. There were several meetings, both at the hospital, as well as at the university, to write the protocol, and decide a name for the group. Several names were presented each more bizarre and long-winded than the other. Even after several sittings, the name did not occur to anyone.

I did not know what to expect when I came back to work on the following Monday after the eventful three weeks at the Council. It was with a certain amount of trepidation that I went in to work that Monday morning. I was not without a lot of apprehension and misgivings. I did not know how my colleagues would react to this situation of no decision. Would they look at it as someone left in limbo? Would their mental domination over me change or would their behaviour change? For a few weeks before the hearing, there was a perceptible change in their behaviour was such that I was being asked for opinions and advice. This was conspicuous by its absence over the previous couple of years. I did not know how everyone else would react.

Whereas everyone knew that I was away for the hearing, remarkably few people knew about the outcome of the hearing. I am sure there would be awkward glances and whispered discussions as I walked into the hospital. I will have to face hundreds of probing eyes and try to answer them without making it too obvious. The next few days were going to be hard, to say the least. I wish I could have come home with an outcome.

It did not take terribly long to bring me down to earth. Every hill has a corresponding valley to contend with, but I did not expect I would face the valley so quickly and suddenly. It came in the form of a visit by Gautam one evening just a few days after our return. It was another evening visit, which had become routine by now. I expected Gautam to be at home almost every evening to discuss the issues and strategies. It gave me a sense of encouragement and a sense of momentum of the fight being kept up. He did not go straight into it. He started to discuss how things were going, and if there is anything new on the horizon. After one or two repetitions, I started to feel that he was fishing and started to feel uneasy about what was to come. When he finally asked me if anyone had asked me about a newspaper article in the hospital, my heart sank, and I had to sit down. It came out slowly – how the article was seen, by whom and how it was perceived by those who had seen it. He had a copy of the article in the car, which was brought in. I glanced through the article and quite shocked at the detail that the reporter had gone into. It gave the full extent of the allegations by the council and minutiae of the "deficiencies" that was aimed against me. It mentioned the allegations started by ex-colleagues in the hospital, but conveniently forgot to mention their names.

My mind went into a shell and refused to come out. I could not think of anything to say, and was extremely quiet for a long time. I could hear people speaking to me, but could not make any sense. Gautam was trying to tell me that the newspaper was an inconsequential little rag, which no one read. 'It is not your dirty linen being washed in the newspaper' I retorted in my own mind. I could see whatever little reputation I had left shattered into a million pieces and trampled into dust. I did not know how I was going to face my patients the next morning. I was firmly convinced that everyone would have read the article and would refuse to be treated by me. I could not believe how anyone would want to be treated by someone who has been maligned to such an extent by the newspaper. The adage "no smoke without fire" came to mind. Everyone will believe that there must be something wrong with me if the council was saying such derogatory things about me. Again, those little demons of self-doubt and self-recriminations start to dance within myself. Am I really that bad? Can there be any truth in all these allegations? Am I a bad surgeon? Am I incompetent?

It took me a long time to come around and try to understand what Gautam was saying. I had read the article twice again and was quite taken aback by the photograph, which was reinforcing the story. I was slightly relieved to see my chief executive trying to defend me in his own understated way. By then Gautam had started to analyse the situation and was trying to tell me that there must be someone's hand behind this story. I could not think of anyone other than the two people who had done everything in their power to ruin my life so far. It transpired that he knew someone who was a friend of the reporter. We would ask this someone to try to get to the source of the story. All of us knew that it was extremely unlikely that a reporter would divulge his or her sources to anyone. The fact that the story has surfaced in the press after all this time – nearly 18 months after the events – befuddled all of us. We could not understand why or how it surfaced now when we were nearly at the end of the episode as it were.

18. 'No Case To Answer?

It was not too long after the newspaper article that the decision time came around. The publicity had utterly demoralised me, and I was not looking forward to the trip down to Manchester to hear the decision. The panel was going to sit on a Saturday, to deliberate the submission, and let us know the decision on Sunday. Nancy called me on Friday night. She was on her way to Manchester.

'It is going to be fine. I cannot imagine how this panel can decide to continue with the case after what they have seen and heard. It would be obvious to the densest among them, that the assessment team had been quite incompetent, and they had come out with a warped decision'. Nancy said.

I had to give it to Nancy. She was an eternal optimist. After the battering I had taken in the media, I was not as sure as before. I brought up the subject with Nancy and said, 'What the Newspapers have said is diabolical. There is no truth in what they are saying. They are using the unproven allegations to sell their papers. Can we take any legal action against them?'

'Not really. The minutes of the hearing are open to public, and anyone can access them. I can ask them for an explanation of what they have said and why. I do not think we can do much more than not. Taking on the newspapers at this stage is not good idea.' Nancy tried to pacify me. It just made me even angrier. How can we let everyone get away with murder? It looked as if everyone was out to get me, and I had no defence. Nancy did her best to pacify me, saying that I will get my say in time.

'This panel as Fred said, is corrupt and not after reaching the truth. They will do whatever they can do to prolong the hearing. Have you wondered why the panel is sitting on the weekend? None of the panelists was working, and there is no need to sit on a weekend! You do not need to rush on Sunday either. They won't give a decision till after 2 in the afternoon.'

Nancy was just reinforcing what Fred Barnard had said a while ago. Lopa was listening in as I spoke and said she wanted to come with me on Sunday. I did not see the point of dragging everyone to hear what I had already assumed would happen. Just as I put the phone down Gautam walked in. He saw my face and tried to be upbeat.

'I would not worry about this weekend. It will all be over by Sunday afternoon. You have to start planning on how you are going to take this forward. You cannot let these people off the hook.' He said.

'I am not so sure now. Things are not going very well. I can just see the chairman hiding behind some obscure explanation and let the case continue.' I said.

Gautam was not quite surprised by my pessimism. He was quiet for a while and said we should all go for a movie. That will take my mind off this the weekend. I looked at Lopa, and she agreed.

'We'll have something to eat in Nando's and go and watch something at the Cinema. I am sure there must be something which can take your mind off this depression.' Gautam said. 'Best is to call the girls and they will tell us what to watch.'

After several phone calls to Sanvi and Shuchi, we decided on a Steve Martin comedy.

Next morning the drive was rather uneventful and a quite Sunday morning drive. We reached Manchester around nine and by the time we parked the car and walked down to Oxford Road, it was about 9.30. The place looked totally deserted, even the rotunda at the entrance, which was usually busy, was empty. We made our way up to the seventh floor, to find the GMC offices was like Mary Celeste, apart from a half asleep receptionist, who would have been anywhere but there. She opened the door for us, and as we walked in Nancy breezed in with her usual bright smile. She was oozing with confidence – a complete contrast to my feelings.

'Good morning everyone. How was the drive? Fred should be here in by about ten. We spent most of yesterday waiting around. No news so far.'

I did not see any activity in the corridor at all. I looked at Nancy questioningly and said, 'There does not seem to be anyone around? Are the Panel members here?'

'They were sitting till about five yesterday. They are due about ten again. I would be surprised if we heard anything before lunch time'. Nancy answered.

By this time, Fred wandered in. He had a look of resignation over him.

'Morning all! How is everyone?' He said with that wry smile on his face,

All of us chorused 'Good morning Fred.'

Just as we were settling down to idle chatter, one of the clerks of the GMC walked in with her ubiquitous clipboard under her arm. 'Good morning. You have been excused till one.' she said.

Nancy just looked at me and smiled as if to say, 'I told you so.' Fred said, 'I am going to stay back and get some work done. You guys might as well stretch your legs.'

He was politely telling us to get lost so that he could work with some peace, Nancy stayed back as well, and we made our way out and down the lift to Oxford Road again. I wanted to have a drink and we decided to go to the Nero's cafe we had seen on the way from the car park. After a snack and coffee, we wandered around Portland Street peered through windows of shops and wandered into an interesting bookshop. I picked up an architectural book that I thought Akshaj might be interested in.

As we walked into the GMC, again by lunchtime, there was a little more activity than this morning. I could see the reverend walking out of the toilet back into their dining room. I knew we would not be called in for a while, as they appeared to be settling down for a leisurely lunch. No one came to tell us what was happening. As usual, we were just left there in the waiting room to stew wondering when we would be called in; it was so humiliating to be left sitting in the dark waiting. I could not understand why someone could not tell us some indication when the panel was likely to restart again. But then again, that was the tactic to belittle the doctors we had come accustomed to over the past few weeks and months.

It was over two hours later, when everyone's patience was wearing thin, and getting on one another's nerves, the same clerk from the morning came around with her clipboard. 'The panel is ready for you' and turned around and started to walk down the corridor. We all rushed after her, and went through all those locked doors, to reach the hearing room. We were again made to wait outside in the corridor for yet another ten minutes. As we walked in, the panel were obviously sharing a joke and laughing. That was the first time I had seen any life in the reverend's face. There was not a word of apology or acceptance of delay by anyone.

They did not even appear to acknowledge our presence. I was convinced by then, that the entire thing was aimed at humiliating and beating down the doctor in the dock. The process I had seen so far would demoralise the strongest of us.

We all sat down in our nominated places as the Chairman started his soliloquy.

'The panel has reached a decision.'

He read for about 20 minutes. It essentially boiled down to the fact that Fred might have as well been talking to the walls of that room. They had not considered any of the arguments put forward by him. They had agreed everything Sykes had put forward and pooh, poohed the proof put forward by Fred. Then the discussion for the 'Next stage' of the hearing began with every one busy with their diaries. As they started to discuss September and November as possible dates, my heart sank. I have to endure this torture for yet another six months. I was again wholly ignored in the discussion. No one bothered to ask my availability. I sat there feeling like a turkey at a Thanks giving dinner. No decision was made about the dates, and it was decided that, the panel secretary would let everyone know eventually about the dates.

This was what I had expected, but was still extremely disappointed by the determination. It meant we had to keep going for a while. God only knows for how long. There did not appear to be any end in sight. Nancy tried to console me as much as she could do. She was probably more disappointed than I was. 'I just cannot believe this panel. They do not seem to have heard anything we said. This is not right.'

'Is there any way of redressing this?' I asked.

'We can go for a judicial review as we discussed earlier. But, that would mean the GMC process would be stopped here and if we lose in the courts, the process will re-start all again.' Fred said. I had visions of this carrying on for years. It reminded me of all those articles in Hospital Doctor journal about doctors suspended for five years and ten years while the process took place.

'How long will the Judicial Review take?' I wanted to know.

'Difficult to say. It is unlikely to be before next year.'

I was quite taken aback. I did not expect this to drag on for that long.

'Look. We have come this far. Now you have a chance to put your side of the story. I think we have a frightfully decent chance of winning from here.' Fred continued.

The discussion went on for a while. In the end, I decided that we should continue, as I was not prepared to risk losing in the JR and the case being dragged on for years. I also was rather worried how the GMC would react if we went for judicial review and lost and I had to come again before this panel.

'We will have to have a conference before the next stage. I will speak to Dr Smiths at the MPS and let you know when. I will call you sometime next week once I have had a discussion with MPS.' Nancy said. It was nearly five in the evening, by the time we started back again. There was the usual flurry of phone calls to Gautam and Swayambhu describing the day's events.

19. 'You have the patience of a saint; I would like to shake you by the hand, if I may.'

There is a twist in the functioning of the council, which I find difficult to understand to this day. While the FTP hearing was going on, there is another pathway, which everyone has to follow – that of the Interim Orders panel (IOP). This is another panel comprising of a similar complement of individuals as the FTP, which oversees the performance of the doctor. While the case is being investigated, discussed and argued, the IOP's function is to see if the Doctor is fit to continue practicing. That was the easy bit. The hard bit to understand is that the two panels are not allowed to talk to each other or discuss the case. The Barrister is not allowed to bring the findings of the IOP to the FTP. It is as if they are entirely two different organisations within the organisation of the council! The IOP is supposed to meet every six months or so and decide whether the Doctor should be allowed to continue practising. The maximum amount of time they are allowed to put any restriction on practice, is supposed to be eighteen months. I was due to attend the next IOP hearing to see if I should be allowed to continue practising with the restrictions placed on me. I wanted Fred to use some of the findings of the FTP so far and get the IOP to lift all the restrictions on my practice.

Nancy was quite firm when she said that I should be in London for the next IOP hearing. I was not sure if that would achieve anything. However, she felt that my presence would give more credence to Fred's argument to lift the restriction of revision hip surgery using the FTP transcripts. She had asked me to identify the sections where the bumbling assessors had admitted to making mistakes and apologising. Well, I did the usual booking of train tickets in advance – paying an extraordinary amount of money for a day return ticket to London! This must be the only country in the world where one pays premium rates for extremely poor service. I reluctantly shelled out an amount of money, which would have taken me at least twice the distance in much better luxury in any other country in Europe.

During the previous week, I sat down at my computer with all the transcripts from the FTP hearing opened to try to make some sense of the whole thing as it stood at the time. As I started to go through the maze of arguments and counter arguments, my blood started boil. As I went through Amoshin's answers, I could not believe that he had been allowed to pass judgement on any doctor let alone, a senior orthopaedic consultant. He came out as a bumbling fool, and particularly the section where there was some interaction, with the 'specialist performance advisor' was nothing but straight out of Monty Python's parody. I began marking out the pages and notations where they had apologised for making mistakes. I collated several pages of these and sent them off to Nancy along with a comment from myself. I was voicing my disappointment at letting these blatantly incompetent people get away with everything. I reminded Nancy about her and Fred's reassurance at the very start, that they 'could not see how this hearing can go ahead, with such overwhelming evidence'. It still carried on, and it was still proceeding like the juggernaut, with no one to stop it. I was quite scathing and sarcastic in my email, as I was pouring out my disappointment and anger, on the only one who could probably understand, what I was saying. It was not until the next morning, when I had calmed down that I realised that it was probably not appropriate to have sent that email to Nancy. Soon she was on the telephone and sounded decidedly defensive. She wanted to know if I wanted to change the team for my defence, and if so she would get in touch with the defence organisation, to make necessary arrangements. It took all my tact and patience to persuade her that I would not want any change at this stage. Finally she appeared to understand that I was just venting my anger on her and Fred at the frustration of my position. I said that these assessors would not get a locum middle grade job in our unit, let alone a consultant job, judging by their knowledge of orthopaedics. I wanted to know how such people are allowed to go around and judge doctors with impunity. I also told her clearly that I do not have any confidence in the FTP members giving me an impartial hearing and judgement. I wanted to know if we were ever going to take them to court. There must be some way of redressing the issue, as these people have been grossly negligent in their assessment. She did calm down and try to reassure me that I would get a fair hearing and that I would get a 'fair judgement.'

I left it at that and proceeded to get all the documents needed for the IOP hearing. I suddenly realised that I did not have a report from the 'Mentor' and who happened to be away on holiday. We had already been censured once, by the previous IOP, for not submitting all the documents on time, and it was not going particularly well this time either. I tracked him down returning from Spain and was luckily accessible on the email. He kindly did an impromptu report and sent it via email to be followed later by fax on his return. That should satisfy the bureaucrats in the council to some extent. It took me a fair amount of time to create an updated "Portfolio" to send out to the council. It had become a ritual now that I come home from work, have food, a nap, and sit in front of the computer sorting out the diary, logbook, and the portfolio. My social life and along with it my family life had gone out of the window a long time ago. It frustrated me every time the thought occurred in my mind. I decided to block it out of my mind. It is remarkable how one can block unwanted things out of one's mind and be oblivious of the pain such things are causing. I had become such an expert at it by now.

The day of the IOP came, and the temperature was as high as it could be. The sun had been out continuously for the previous few days with the pollen count extremely high. I was suffering badly with hay fever, runny nose and cough leading up to a chest infection. I managed to get up at three in the morning and got Sanvi up at four to drop me off at the station for the 4.20 train. Typical of our trains, it was late and slow and did not reach London until 8.40. The hearing was scheduled for nine in the morning, and I literally ran from Central Train Station to the council offices. I need not have bothered! The place was just waking up with people slowly filtering in. I had forgotten that the council works at a snail's pace and has its own standard time, which is quite different to the rest of the world. The council seems to work at a pace and view supremely oblivious to the suffering it may cause the populace or its members. Its mission statement of 'regulating doctors' takes an entirely new meaning to what you would find in the oxford dictionary. As I was rushing in to the council, I spoke to Nancy who was quite upbeat about the hearing and asked my expected time of arrival – 'five or ten minutes.'

We were all ushered into a waiting room, and we waited with no indication of what was happening. As far as the council was concerned you do not exist. Common courtesy of letting you know what is happening and how long you have to wait is not in their repertoire. Around ten in the morning, nearly an hour after the scheduled time, we were asked to come into the hearing room by this young girl, who promptly disappeared as we were collecting all our papers. We were left stranded in the waiting area looking like idiots. Eventually we found our way into the hearings room. It was again one of those nondescript rooms with tables arranged in the shape of a "U" with the panel sitting at the top of the table. The chairman of the panel asked me to say my name and number. There were no introductions as to who was sitting in the room, and who would be making the decisions. I had to read the little name labels kept on the desks in front of the people sitting there to guess who probably would be the panel for the IOP. It looked like all the three carried the title of a "Doctor", unless they were non-medical, I would have to assume that they were somehow related to medicine.

The chairman went on to ask the barrister representing the council to start his submission for the council. This time there was a rather suave looking barrister (possibly Greek, judging by his name) who started putting forward the council's case. I thought he was much less venomous than the barristers I had seen before in his statement. He even went so far to say that he understood that the defence would make a submission for varying a condition and the council would not object to that!

That statement took some wind out of Fred's sail to some extent. We were all prepared to go with all guns blazing, to show up the blunders the assessors had made in their assessment and ask the IOP to lift the restriction on revision hip replacement surgery. I had seen Fred going through the documents and transcript furiously marking many texts with red ink. He appeared to have rehearsed his speech a few times. There was an A-level student sitting in observing the proceedings with a hope of getting into the law profession. In addition, I am sure he wanted to impress. When it came to Fred's turn, he started off quite well and still carried on to put forward most of the arguments that he had prepared earlier, even though it appeared rather tedious and to me pointless argument as the council had already agreed for the lifting of the restriction. Once he finished his submission, no one had any questions, and the panel looked bored by this stage. The only little excitement during the proceedings was, when the legal assessor said that the IOP would have to ask the registrar to apply to court for an extension, of whatever restrictions the IOP might consider imposing. We were duly asked to leave the room as the panel wanted to 'go into camera'. This statement always amused me – what a strange thing to say, for a group to go into confidential discussion! It conjured up visions of little mice darting around inside one of my pinhole cameras that I used to make as a child. I used to take enormous delight in making these cameras and projected faint, yet exciting pictures on the wall of my parent's home back in Bangalore on most hot summer afternoons. I remember that by the time I went into High School, I had become so adept at it that all our neighbouring kids used to come and watch this during school holidays.

There was another long wait, not as bad as the previous ones – only 45 minutes. This young girl came back and said 'They are ready for you.'

This time she took us to the hearing room. Again, there were no formalities or pleasantries. The chairman got straight into his 'determination' statement. He droned for nearly 20 minutes. He was repeating what had been already said before in the previous IOP hearings with one change. The condition seven had been changed from 'You must not carry out any unsupervised hip revision surgery' to 'You must not carry out any unsupervised hip revision surgery on surgically fused hips'. This was as Fred would say 'unreal'. The panel still did not understand the intricacies of hip surgery despite Fred's detailed submission. It is just another demonstration of the competence of the council, to appoint people who would make a decision on aspects of a doctor's practice they had no understanding of whatsoever.

He finished his monologue with a dry 'that concludes the business for this morning' and closed his file indicating he had indeed finished. Not a single word was said after that as we all trooped out of the room back into the waiting area before Nancy said,

'That was a bit of an anticlimax, wasn't it?'

I said, 'They appeared to be in a hurry, didn't they?'

'Well, we got what we came for. That is the crucial thing. I want you to get stuck in and do as many of these blasted revision hips as possible before the November hearing' Fred added. Nancy gave me a copy of the determination – a poorly photocopied specimen as the council's photocopier had run out of ink.

They all started to pack their bags and were discussing the coming holidays. Fred was going away travelling down the length of France on his boat at a remarkably slow pace. He looked forward to time in his boat where one would do nothing but eat, drink and sleep. It turned out that he was a connoisseur in tea. I promised him that I'd send some unusual teas from some small plantations from the south of India. As we parted, he looked at me for a minute in silence, and he said,

'You have the patience of a saint; I would like to shake you by the hand, if I may.'

That statement kept repeating itself in my head all the way back home. To me, it was one of the most poignant things, anybody had ever said to me. It would stay with me for a long time. On the way back I sent a text to all the near and dear ones telling them of the outcome of the hearing. I had a couple of hours to kill before my train back home. As I was walking back to the station, I had to pass the British Library with a large hoarding advertising 'Exhibition of Ramayana.' Intrigued, I wandered in to be amazed by one of the most comprehensive exhibits about this immense epic as read and practiced around different parts of the world. There were even a few artefacts from different parts of the world depicting the life of King Rama. I had to prise myself away from the exhibition. It was getting late for my train.

The train journey was not particularly comfortable despite booking into a first class cabin. There were three other people at my table who talked incessantly over the din of the train through the entire journey. By the time I reached Seaport I had known everything about everyone in his or her office. Increasing the volume on my iPod did not make any difference to the noise level coming from these three. The three droned on totally ignorant of their surroundings. It is unbelievable how some people can continue irritating a whole cabin full of people with no compunction whatsoever. No number of 'dirty looks' from some of the less sensitive travellers made any difference to noise level. The first call I got as a response to my texts was from Daine –

'How are you? That was brilliant progress wasn't it?'

I tried to convey my annoyance over the phone "the decision was good, but I cannot speak now as I can barely hear you for the noise here. I'll call you later when I reach Seaport". This produced a bit of quiet for exactly ten minutes before they started again. I tried to concentrate on the book I had bought in Waterstones last week, William Zinser's 'Writing about your life'. I was into an interesting part of the book, where he was trying to tell me how I should write things down about the most engrossing that I could remember and how I should not pay much attention to the chronology of events in the initial stages. My brain tried to block off these extraneous noises, and concentrated on the book. I tried to get some sleep again to no avail. By the time I reached Seaport, I had a splitting headache. There were calls and texts from all my near and dear ones asking about the hearing during the journey.

Sanvi picked me up from the station and was quite pleased with the outcome of the hearing so far. I just wanted to get home and get some sleep. My head was pounding, and I was getting more and more irate by the minute. As I was nodding, off to sleep on the sofa after another wonderful meal, who walks in but Swayambhu. I had to go through the whole hearing episode again with him. I have a distinct impression that sometimes he asks questions, but does not always appear take in the answer. I had to repeat the episode at least twice. He appeared darned tired after yet another long day at work. By this time, the Paracetamol was beginning to work and I sat down with patience and explained to him as he was downing the second glass of a fine Italian red wine from Puglia along with spicy olives and cashew nuts. By this time Pavaki had read the determination and felt that 'we are getting somewhere with the whole nightmare.' As she read out the 'conditions' she said,

'I think you should ask your supervisor to check every patient's investigations and treatment. Because, that is what the council wants. You wash your hands off after every case and walk off.'

I can just see what George would say if asked him to do that. The entire clinical practice would come to a standstill, and the patients would be the sufferers at the end. Again, this does not seem to be in the council's equation even in the slightest. I can just see our business and service managers' faces, if two of the leading and busiest clinicians' time is occupied almost entirely in writing out and checking patient's notes and investigation etc with singularly little if any time to patient care. It will grind the unit to a halt, and the waiting list will shoot through the ceiling. Especially as the recently audited figures had showed that, I was bringing in the highest revenue among all the consultants in the hospital.

It was quite late when Swayambhu and Pavaki left. I went back to the computer to try to gather my thoughts and put them down in my diary. It had now become a regular habit, and I was thankful for that. It reduced the stress of a backlog, which I used to dread. It is remarkable how quickly the paperwork accumulates, if one do not 'keep at it' as, it was on a daily basis. I went to bed thoroughly shattered with Fred's voice ringing in my ears

'You have the patience of a saint; I would like to shake you by hand, if I may.' I was somewhat content after a long time.

20. The period of introspection;

The weeks and months passed by, and the memories of the hearing were beginning to fade when I had a letter from the GMC telling me about the next stage of the hearing. As usual, we had several discussions about how to progress with the case in the next stage. I spent an awful lot of time working on the statements of the assessor and the 'surgical skills test paper'. The more I read it, more I was convinced that this was a farce and wholly inappropriate way to assess a senior orthopaedic consultant.

I was sure that if I sent out this test paper to 100 orthopaedic consultants of my age group and seniority in the country, most of them would come back with similar answers as I did. Gautam thought that it would be a terrific idea and gave me a copy of the British Orthopaedic Association handbook, which gave details of all the orthopaedic consultants in the country. I sat down to work on a format that would get the best response from everyone. If, I sent out questions as a test paper, the chances are, no one will send it back. I wanted the opinion of the consultants as to the appropriateness of the questions. Finally, I decided that I should send out the test paper, as it was, and ask how they felt they would cope with answers, without any preparation in an exam situation. There was a lot of discussion with both Gautam and Swayambhu about this before a final version was produced. I trawled through hundreds of names in the British Orthopaedic Association Register, before coming up with a list of 100 orthopaedic consultants of my age group and seniority, with special interest in hip and knee surgery. I prepared a spreadsheet of the names and their email addresses. It took me a while to get the details of the questionnaire right. After probably the tenth edition, I was happy with the product and decided to pass it through Gautam before sending it to the MPS. I wanted the survey through MPS, as it would give legitimacy to the survey. Gautam went through the questionnaire and made some suggestions. I called up Nancy and discussed the idea with her. She wanted to pass it through Fred Barnard and Dr Smiths for approval. I sent the questionnaire and the associated notes to Nancy to have a look.

It was nearly a week before Nancy got back. I was just getting back home one evening after yet another long day in the theatre when my mobile rang. I could not pick up the call as I was driving and did not have one of those 'hands free' sets with me. I knew it was Nancy as the name came up on the screen. I knew it would be news about my survey and was desperate to find out what it was. As soon as I stopped the car in my drive, I called her back.

'Hi Nancy. What news? Did Dr Smiths agree with the proposal?'

'He agrees with it in principle, but he has to take it through some MPS committee before it can be done' Nancy replied. I knew what it meant. In legal speak, it meant 'No,' without being rude. I was rather disappointed at that and was quiet for a while. I am sure Nancy realised that this was not what I wanted to hear.

'His hands are tied. Off the record, he is very keen to get it done. Nevertheless, he wants it to be legally watertight as you can imagine. Another problem is that we may not be allowed to use the results of the survey as it would not be considered 'independent."

I did not want to argue with Nancy, regarding the legality of the issue. She went on to discuss the upcoming conference. I wanted Gautam to come with me.

'I will have to pass it through Dr Smiths. I don't see any problems though.' Nancy said.

'Can you let me know as soon as possible please? I need to book flights down to London.' I said.

'I will let you know by the end of the week.' Nancy said.

I mentioned this to Gautam that evening when we were in the Badminton club, in Garmond.

'Let me know, as soon as, you can. I'll have to change my clinics and theatre lists that day.' Gautam said.

It was wet October morning when we flew down to London with Gautam for our conference with Fred, Nancy, and Dr Smiths. By the time, we got off at Stansted and took the train to central London and then a taxi to Fred's offices in that leafy area of Kensington, it was getting nearer twelve. As I reached the office, I found out that Nancy could not be there, and we were going to have a video conference with her in Leeds. We were due to start at 12.30, and as we waited in the waiting room, I was impressed by the offices. It was in an exclusive part of London and obviously extremely well furnished with oak oozing out of every corner – cabinets, desks, drinks bar, library etc. We were just finishing an excellent hot chocolate when Fred came out to greet us.

'Good afternoon. Hope you had a pleasant flight down' he said shaking us each by hand. 'Hope I did not keep you waiting long. They are just linking up with Nancy in Leeds. It looks good.'

We were ushered into a sumptuous, and yet remarkably functional conference room with a large plasma screen on the wall, where I could see Nancy busy with her papers. She was saying something, but we could not hear anything, as there was some problem with sound. It was not long before that was fixed, and we got down to business. Dr Smiths was already there sifting through a pile of papers. I introduced Fred to Gautam, and we all sat down to this business. Fred started with

'I am, extremely disappointed with the Panel's determination. It beggars belief. I might as well have not been there at all for all the attention they paid to the proof that was produced to the contrary. I have been in this business for thirty years and presented cases to hundreds of panels of all ilk's –both medical and non-medical. This is the first time, where I have come across such blatant flouting of reasoning.' He went on for another five minutes in the same vein before finishing with 'There. I have vented my gripe. Now, shall we get down to the business we have come here for' with a smile.

We spent a considerable part of two hours dealing with primarily the assessment of the three stooges who came to Seaport and ended with the test paper.

'I am a bit disappointed that we cannot do my survey. It would have shown how far removed the council is from day to day health service, and how orthopaedic consultants work'. I said.

'I agree with Kasyapa on this. It would have given me a powerful tool to play with, in the next stage.' Fred added.

'The MPS feels that this is something that should be done, once the case is finished, as it might jeopardise the outcome of this case' Dr Smiths said. He went on to explain why, in a long-winded statement, which I could not understand then, and still cannot understand today. We finished at around four that afternoon. We had to rush out to the taxi to Central Station. We nearly missed our flight back home from Stansted. Not much was said in the taxi as we were mulling over what was said during the conference. As we settled down in our seats, on the train, back to Stansted, Gautam said,

'I think that was a useful meeting. I have a feeling that this is a chance to make public some of the cock-ups that have gone on during this fiasco. You have a chance to say your side of the case with Fred's help. So far we had to try and dig out things from the assessors and were quite diluted by Sykes for the Council.'

I was not as sure as before. Gautam was an eternal optimist. He always saw victory in the eye of adversity. I had mixed feelings about the next stage. First of all, I have to face gruelling from not only Fred, but also from Sykes. I was not looking forward to that.

It was not long after the conference that I got a confirmation date for the next stage of hearing from the Council. It was to be in November, and they had given two weeks for the next stage of the process. I was slightly concerned about the length of the next stage of the hearing. I called Nancy to find out if the hearing will go on for that long and if I had to book accommodation for two weeks. Nancy was not sure this time.

'Going by the speed at which this panel is going, it would not surprise me if they take all of the two weeks for their deliberations.'

I spent a couple of hours trawling through the net that night, looking for a flat, to stay in for two weeks that I could afford, and at the same time not too expensive. Then there was a discussion about who would come for the hearing. It looked like quite a few wanted to be there to show support. I was quite touched by the overwhelming support I got from my close friends. Finally, it was decided that Lopa would accompany me for the duration and others would join us for day's in turn.

There was some activity going on in the hospital. There was a suggestion that a group should go and meet the local MP and ask for his intervention and support. I could not take part in it due to obvious reasons. I arranged for some friends in the hospital, to join hands with Gautam and Swayambhu, to take it forward. I hired a room in a local restaurant for everyone to meet and discuss as to how to take it forward. It was well attended, and there was a lot of discussion as to how it should be done. It fell down, when it came to, who would take the lead. Like most of these protests, it needed a leader who had to sacrifice a lot and spend an awful lot of time and effort with often remarkably little to show at the end. The meeting ended with no firm decision being taken. It needed someone with plenty of time on their hands to be successful. Unfortunately, time was in short supply for most people. After a few more discussions, the whole thing frizzled out.

Then there was the discussion of going to the local and national press and even the BBC to get some coverage for what everyone felt to be a gross injustice. Again, the question came down to, who would bell-the-cat. There were many suggestions, but no one to take a lead to act on it. There was an awful lot of good people with an enormous amount of good intentions but no time or the know-how to carry them out. Like most protests, all these ideas, unfortunately, stayed on the drawing board without any progress. If all of the planned protests across the world came to be acted, there would be chaos in the world, with no work-taking place. There would be no progress and the civilisations would come to a standstill! In a way, it is a good thing the majority of planned protests stay on the drawing board.

It was during this lull in the proceedings that I got a call from my mum. She normally did not call me unless there was something wrong. Whenever the telephone rang early in the morning around six, I know it is from my mum or brother and it always made my heart skip a beat. It was one of those calls, which gave me the news of my dad's death and my sister's illness. An early morning call almost always brought some bad news. This time it was not so.

'How are you Upaas? You have not called home for a while.' and mum went on for a few minutes telling me off for not keeping in touch with her. I felt guilty, and she knew that I would feel guilty. It was only after another a few minutes of this, that I came to know the reason for the call.

'Is there a problem at work?' Mum wanted to know. For mum, like countless Indians, a 'problem at work' means you have 'lost your job.' I had kept the troubles with my colleagues and the council quiet from my mum, brothers, and sisters all these years. It brought a lump to my throat. I was very close to my mum and had never kept anything from her in the past. Since the death of my father, I had not told her of everything as there would be no one to explain to her the details and reasons behind the problems. My dad was very good with it. Both my mum and dad were particularly sincere people, and they lived in a world of black and white with no place for grey anywhere. She would have difficulty understanding that a fellow human being, particularly someone I had helped would harm me in any way. She just could not comprehend such a scenario. I still remember her explaining to me, the essence of the revered Hindu epics were written, with 'bad people' in it to teach the people the right, and bad ways of living one's life. Neither of them believed that there are real evil people in this world. I still remember my dad telling me that there must have been some goodness, even in Hitler. She always felt that one should aim to live like the heroes of those epics – always righteous and honest.

'Yes. There has been some problem at work. One of my colleagues did not like me and has caused problem with reporting to the council some false allegations against me and it is going through the tribunal'. That was the best I could do to let her understand what was happening. There was no way she would understand the ramifications of the council, its relationship to my work and the hospital etc. The call went on for a long time, and she promised many Gods, obeisance if we get through the case and she wanted me to visit all these holy places once the case was finished. I knew this would not end with her telephone call.

It was about an hour later, that I get a call from my elder brother.

'Hello Upaas. What is this I heard from mum? Are you OK?' He was always calm and balanced. I had never seen him lose his composure even in the worst of circumstances. I went through the process in some detail. Even he could not believe that someone who I had helped would do such a dastardly act.

'And this has been going on for over two years? Is that right?' He wanted to know. I could detect a scent of disappointment in his voice. As my dad spent most of my childhood away from home and he was essentially in charge of the family during most of my growing up phase. He was the one who bought my clothes, he was the one who took me to doctors when I was ill, he was the one who guided me into university, and he was the one instrumental in my progress after university. He was there for me with thick and thin. I felt guilty in a way that I had not told him or asked for advice. Maybe I thought that the situation would be alien to him, being six thousand miles away from me! I do not know. It still made me feel immensely guilty.

'I am sorry, but I did not want everyone in the family to be stressed out.' I said. It was not a complete lie, as I did not want my mum to be stressed out. I had never lied to my mum or my brother, and I was not going to start now. The phone call went on for nearly an hour, and I felt rather comfortable, and at the same time drained. I was late for the clinic that day and I did not particularly care.

'Look Upaas. If things do not work out or you do not want to fight the battle, come back home. We have managed before, and we will manage again. It is not the end of the world. The essential thing is that you and the family should be happy. Unfortunately, there are dishonest people in this world and only God can forgive them.'

'I want to fight this battle if it is the last thing I do. It is a question of my honour and name. I have not done anything wrong. I have always done good for people, and I have never meant any harm to anyone in my life. It is not fair that my name and work is besmirched this way.' and I went on to explain the newspaper articles.

'I can understand your pain. But, you have to remember that you are not alone in this. You have a family to think of. You cannot allow this to destroy you. It will destroy your family and that is not worth anything' he went on.

'I know it has implications on everyone. If it comes to a situation where I have to bail out, I have several options. I have worked on some bail out options'. I went on to explain the work I had done with jobs in the Middle Eastern countries, such as Dubai and Kuwait, and I told him of the job offers that I have had so far. He appeared to be content when I signed off. I felt as if some weight had been lifted off my shoulders, and for some strange reason felt contented. I had not gone any further with my case, and there was no sign of me winning the case. That day, after speaking to my mum and more so my brother, I felt a lot of relief and comfort. I felt that 'nothing was lost'. I still had my family, and my knowledge and my talent. I could earn a living anywhere in the world. With that, I set off to the dreary day of work in my clinics in Seaport.

There was a lot communication between Nancy and the council with comments from Fred as well as Dr Smiths. The council had suddenly decided that they have to have a 'specialist adviser'. After the shambles, we had from the last one I was not so sure as before. It was straight out of a Monty Python parody. This time the council had come up with someone called Mr Furzfield at the last minute. All our requests to get his CV were met with no response. When our solicitors threatened them with court action, they came up with an excuse that they do not have any CV for him! It was just unbelievable. Here, they have appointed someone as a 'specialist adviser' for orthopaedics without ever looking at a CV of the doctor. He could have been anyone. He need not have even been a doctor as far as the council was concerned. Moreover, they were going to let him decide on a senior orthopaedic consultant's fate. I looked in the British Orthopaedic Association book, only to find out that he did not practice in the NHS, and there was no record of when he was in practice. Trawling through Dr Foster's register did not produce much joy either. He was registered as working for a private organisation somewhere. There was remarkably little, about when or where if he ever did work in the NHS.

'This Mr. Furzfield does not appear to have worked in the NHS at all in the recent past. I am not comfortable with him, as a 'specialist adviser' as he would have remarkably little knowledge of day to day running of NHS work'. I said to Nancy.

'I will let Fred be aware of it. The council does not really have to produce a CV of a specialist adviser. But don't worry, if there is any chance of him being incompetent, Fred will have him recused, just like the last one'. Nancy replied. The memory of the charade that occurred with Mercia and her eventual dismissal came to mind and brought a smile to my face.

'I am still concerned that this guy might give wrong advice to the panel, whose power of grasp leaves a lot to be desired to start with.' I repeated.

'I will speak to Fred and get back to you. I would not worry about it though'. She said.

21. The Inquisition begins.

We were in Manchester as usual in one of those short stay apartments, which probably thrive on the council cases. We had reached there the night before and already figured out that we can walk to the council offices within ten minutes. It was just Lopa and me to start with to be joined later by Sanvi and Shuchi and Swayambhu for some days. Gautam had decided that he would come as well, for one of the days.

Monday morning was cold, drizzling, and dark as we set off to the council offices. As we reached the offices to be greeted by the same bored looking receptionist in the rotunda, and then followed by even more bored receptionist at the council office. Nancy was already there, and Fred came soon after. After the customary greetings, Fred said, 'I want to go through your CV in detail. Can we go through briefly now? I want you to stress on your international work and teaching and research.'

We sat there for about half an hour going through my CV before the usher from the council came and called us in. I did not have any chance to speak to him about the 'specialist adviser'. As we walked into the hearing room, the usual suspects were sitting in their places, and we had a new counsel for the council. She was a Miss Norsworth, a middle-aged spinster who obviously spent more time in her office than socialising. I had done some background work on her. She did not appear to be a terror at the first look. However, looks can be deceiving. We had a change in the Legal adviser as well, and it was someone called Mr. Stadeus, who looked like a shop steward in a factory, than a lawyer. The Chairman started with introductions and asked if Fred had an application to make.

'Good morning, sir. We do have a short application. There has been correspondence between my instructing solicitors and the administrative people at the GMC about the appointment of Mr. Furzfield, who obviously everyone is delighted to have here this morning. What we wanted to ask was to see his Curriculum Vitae. The GMC have said that they do not have a copy of Mr. Furzfield's CV, and they are not compelled to obtain, and provide a copy, and in short, they have not been tremendously helpful. We would like to ask, through you, whether Mr. Furzfield would be kind enough to supply such a CV.' Fred said.

The Chairman looked at Miss Norsworth, to see if she had any objections, and asked the Legal adviser for his advice. There was a short discussion and the panel went 'into camera' for discussion. One would have thought we had asked for some state secrets to be revealed! We had to wait outside for twenty minutes before being called in again. It turned out that Furzfield did not have any CV, and he would produce one the following day.

I sat there with some trepidation while all this was going on waiting to be called on to the witness stand. This short interlude was probably an opportune distraction, at the same time rather unnerving.

I was asked to take the witness stand, and I was sworn in on the Bhagavad Gita by the usher.

'Mr. Kasyapa, can you identify yourself, your registration number, and your full professional address, please?' Fred asked.

'My name is Upaashantha Kasyapa.' And I gave them my registration number. 'I work at St Edwards Hospital in Seaport'. I replied, and that was the end of my involvement for a while.

'As you know, I just make one point before I continue. As you know, there are two strands to Mr. Kasyapa's case. One is that whatever his fitness to practise was in the past, is not impaired now, and that requires an examination of what he has been doing since the assessment report, and the other strand of it is that his fitness to practise never was impaired and the assessors got it wrong. Unfortunately, the second strand will take us longer than the first strand, but I will begin with the first strand if that is convenient. As you recall, one of the conditions imposed on Mr. Kasyapa, by the Interim Orders Panel was that he should keep a portfolio, and I would now like to distribute that portfolio, and by reference to it, we can see what he has been doing'. Fred was addressing the Chairman, and as he finished, Natalie who had obviously spent a considerable amount of time copying my portfolio, distributed them to everyone in the room. I had started to collect everything I did, over the previous 18 months on a daily basis, and it had filled three large Lever arch files.

He took me through my CV, which was the first part of my portfolio.

'Mr. Kasyapa, can you take Volume One and go to divider 1, behind the first page, there is your Curriculum Vitae. Can we just run through that document and I will ask you some questions as we go along? We see you have got a BSc in 1972 in Bangalore University, followed by an MB BS in 1979 at the same university. You got a Fellowship of the Royal College of Surgeons in Edinburgh in 1985, and the Royal College in

247

Glasgow as well in the same year. When, in fact, did you come to Great Britain?'

'1982.'
'And a Masters in Orthopaedics from the University of Liverpool in 1989. We see your academic distinctions there. You have been on the Specialist Register, we see over the page, from June 1995, and we can cast an eye down the chronology of your work experience, as you progressed through SHO, Registrar, Orthopaedic Scholar and finally became a Consultant in 1995?'

'That is right.'

'At the Johnston's Hospital, at Seaport. After a short stint there, you became Consultant at the St Edwards Hospital in Seaport. And you were Clinical Director from 1999 to 2003, and you have been there ever since. So you are now in your thirteenth year, twelve and a half years?'

'Yes, since 1995, in my thirteenth year now.' I replied.

'We can see your list of publications there. Are there any particular of your publications, which have particular relevance to any of the cases raised by the assessors? Fred continued into my research as we had discussed that morning.

'The publications I have done on revision total hip replacements, like number 16: 'Dall-Miles plate and cables without bone graft in peri-prosthetic fractures of the hip,' and then on rapid recovery programmes, number 17: "Setting up of the programme in a District General Hospital". Again, a few on revision total hip replacements, and looked at the problems encountered in the less invasive total knee arthroplasty by high volume centres, number 22. Again, number 25: "Radial impaction bone grafting and collared long stem prosthesis'. There are quite a few papers that have been submitted, and still have not heard from the journals whether they have accepted them or not. For example, there is one paper actually not in here, it has been accepted by the BASK (British Association for Surgery of the Knee) meeting to be presented on the podium'. I was well into my rhythm when I was stopped by Fred with -

'What meeting is that?'

'BASK - British Association of Surgery for the Knee, in April, and the paper is on deep vein thrombosis after day case arthroscopy of knees..'

'I think, Mr. Kasyapa, you are going to have to speak up and speak slowly. I think it may be difficult for people to appreciate every word that you are saying. You were saying that paper was on deep vein thrombosis and I did not catch the rest?'

'After day case arthroscopy of knees.' I repeated. Fred asked me if I could produce a copy of the paper and I said that I would.

'Just going back for a moment to paper number 17, the Rapid Recovery Programme, setting up of the programme in a District General Hospital. Can you tell us something about the Rapid Recovery Programme?' Fred asked. This was one of my favourite topics and I had worked exceedingly hard at it to make it successful.

'I used to visit, like most orthopaedic surgeons, American centres to learn more about their way of operating on their knee replacement and hip replacements and one of the things that I noticed, was this programme called Rapid Recovery Programme. They were being pre-assessed thoroughly and they had a lot of information given so they were not stressed out. They knew exactly what they were going to go through in surgery and the post-operative period and also they knew what to expect from the surgery, pain-wise as well as mobility-wise afterwards. The team from the hospital visited the patients' homes to make sure that after surgery they can manage when they are discharged home early. There were one or two centres where the patients were being discharged on the same day of surgery after a major procedure, such as total knee replacement or total hip replacement. One of the reasons that impressed me was because of the patient being discharged home a lot earlier, the complications, such as infection and deep vein thrombosis were a lot less. I wanted to set up something similar, but the NHS, unfortunately, is slightly different to the American practice. I spoke to our hospital management and finally they agreed to set up a pilot project in 1999. We used 50 of my patients to run a pilot programme in which there were chosen patients. We followed the same protocol as the Americans did and we showed that using this kind of a protocol we can reduce the stress and anxiety of the patient and also reduce the complications for the patients, especially deep vein thrombosis and infection. The hospital was so impressed with the results of this pilot project they funded the whole programme completely and that is the start of the Rapid Recovery Programme in 2000. Since then, every patient goes through the protocol. Initially, it was only my patients and later on my colleagues were so impressed by the programme that they all took on the programme and everybody now goes through this protocol and we have produced information leaflets and a DVD to go with it. What happened was, one of my research fellows took up the pilot project and wrote a paper and Health Services General actually invited to us write up the paper and that was written and published in the Health Services Journal.' I stopped to take a breather.

'The Rapid Recovery Programme at your hospital, how has that been operating?'
'It has been extremely successful and we are one of the pioneers in the country. We are so successful we now get visitors from all over this country, but also from Europe to come and see us. Now they have gone back and started their own programme. I can quote two major centres where they have set up similar programmes successfully. One is in London, the Hillingdon Hospital, and the other one in Torbay. We have visitors from Denmark, Holland Germany, and Austria, coming to see how it is done and they have taken our project back and set up their own programmes, so we get visitors once every six weeks.'

Fred asked me about my other projects in relation to knee replacement surgery.

'I am on the faculty for the less invasive surgery programme for Total Knee Replacement in Vienna. I have chaired this programme on a few occasions. I this programme, we have 16 orthopaedic surgeons as delegates. It is only for senior orthopaedic surgeons, some of them are distinguished professors, who come to learn to do how to do minimally invasive surgery for total knee replacements and I demonstrate on cadavers the technique. They learn and go away to practice in their centres and we have had extremely good feedback and high satisfaction rate. We started this programme in 2005, and in the last three years, we have had over170 of these surgeons through the programme. We actually wrote up the proceedings of the project and now it had been used by other surgeons across Europe.' I kept watching O'Neil as well as the Chairman to see if any of this was having any impact on them. There was not even a flicker of a reaction from any of them.

'To the lay person, I obviously speak for myself, the idea that a total knee replacement can be done by minimally invasive surgery sounds like a contradiction in terms. Is it possible just to explain what the difference is between total knee replacement by the standard method and by minimally invasive surgery?' Fred continued. 'The total knee replacement done by a standard method, is usually requires quite a large incision and the muscles are quite badly damaged and they do have a lot of bleeding afterwards and post-operative recovery takes a long time and it is painful, and they never really regain full function. By using a much smaller incision and not damaging the muscles so much internally, obviously you have to use specialised equipment and we have shown that the blood loss is less and the post operative pain is less and the complications of infection is less and we have also shown that the recovery of the muscle function is a lot quicker, a lot faster. The only shortcoming is there is a learning curve; it does take a while to learn. Once it is learnt it can be done just like a standard total knee replacement. Nowadays some people are using computer navigation to do the same.'

'How did you become familiar with that technique?' Fred asked.

'Again, one of my visits to an American centre in Columbus, Ohio, one of the leading surgeons there, demonstrated this minimal invasive surgery and I was very impressed with the technique and the results they were getting. I spent some time, learned the technique and one of my colleagues from Holland, he came with me as well, and the two of us spent a week learning the technique and we did a lot of cadaver work before we started. Once we were happy that we could do them, and then we started a trial, with obviously ethics committee approval, et cetera.' I was looking at the Chairman to see if this produced any interest. Nothing! He was doodling something on some paper in front of him.

'You started a trial?' Fred continued.

'Yes. We started a trial and we found that it was very successful. We compared 25 of the knees which were done using minimally invasive technique to 25 done to the standard technique and obviously it was a randomised trial and we found significant differences, which, again, have been published in journals. In addition, we have been presented at international meetings, me, as well as Dr Ommeren from Holland. Therefore, after that gradually we increased the number of patients going through minimally invasive surgery technique and now 99% of knees done by myself is done through this technique. We are so successful that, I get surgeons, again senior consultant orthopaedic surgeons, from this country as well as Europe, coming to see me operate at my hospital and learn the technique. We have visitors almost every two months to view this.' I was quite enthusiastic. I might have as well been talking to myself for all the interest that was being shown by the panel.

Fred went through the book that we were writing at that time describing the development and technique of minimally invasive surgery for total knee replacements. Fred then took me through some more publications on revision hip replacements and knee replacements before moving on to presentations.

'We have got then your presentations. Just help us with, for example, the first one, which is a podium presentation at SICOT congress. What is that?' Fred continued,

'SICOT is International Society of Orthopaedic Surgery and Traumatology. It is an international organisation where orthopaedic surgeons from across the world come once every two years for a meeting. This time it was in Hong Kong and one of my registrars went and did the podium presentation. We set up a multi-centre trial comparing metal-on-metal total hip replacement, comparing with metal and polyethylene in total hip replacement. Just to explain to the lay people, standard total hip replacement developed by Professor Charnley was metal on polyethylene. High density polyethylene has a very low wear rate but still it wears out so you end up having to revise five to ten per cent of hips in ten years, probably more after 15 or 20 years, so people have come up with a hard wearing surface, which is a metal surface, cobalt chrome against cobalt chrome, where the wear is almost non-existent. It does have other problems but we wanted to see if the other problems exist or not and if they are as successful or more successful than metal on polyethylene implants, so we set up a randomised controlled trial using four different centres. One is my hospital, another one is Royal Hospital and University Hospital and South Side Hospital. We set this up in the year 2000, we have recruited 200 patients in each limb, and these patients are being followed up at the moment. Obviously, for something like a hip replacement, we need to be following them up for at least ten or 20 years before we know if there is a difference, if there is a problem, so we still do not know the final outcome yet.' I finished and looked at the Chairman. For the first time he responded,

'I am going to ask you, doctor, if you could speak a little more slowly, just for the benefit of the shorthand writer. I think it is a bit challenging.'

I was a bit taken aback by that. I did not think that I spoke fast! No one had told me that I did so far. I just wanted to get my message across to the listener before he or she loses interest in what I was saying.

'We see presentation number 2 was a presentation earlier this year at the International Primary and Revision Knee meeting in Rome. Was that presentation by you personally?' Fred continued.

'Yes, it is my personal invited lecture by the organisation, the organisers for the international meeting. The type of total knee replacement that I was invited to talk on was at the forefront of technology as far as total knee replacement is concerned. I have probably one of the largest experiences in this type of total knee replacements, so the organisers asked me to come and talk about my first one hundred cases of this particular type of knee implant.' I answered.

He went through few more of my presentations in detail paying particular attention to presentations with revision hip and knee surgery. He moved on to the courses I was involved in.

'Tell us about courses you run. Is that courses that you have been running with others?' Fred asked.

'Yes. These are courses that either I co-chair or one of the tutors on these courses, one of the instructors on these courses. The minimally invasive surgery I had previously mentioned, which is done in the University of Vienna once in six weeks and the Rapid Recovery Programme now has become a standard meeting which attracts Royal College of Surgeon CME (Continuous Medical Education) points. We also have the Centre of Excellence visit for which we have applied for CME points but still we have not got it yet. That is again by the surgeons from across this country as well as Europe coming to see me to learn how to do resurfacing and total hip replacement, minimal invasive surgery, revision total hip replacements and revision total knee replacements.' I was stopped by Fred at this stage.

'That is number 3 in your list of courses you run?'

'Yes, number 3. Number 4; regionally run training courses in joint replacement for their trainee registrars. The lectures are done in the region first and Oxford and then we take the registrars across to Lille in France where we show our trainees how to do total hip and total knee replacements using cadavers and I have been an instructor on that course.' I replied.

'These courses that you have been running, have they been affected by the fact that you have been, let me put it this way, under investigation by the GMC?' Fred was looking at the Chairman when he asked me that question. However, it did not seem to register any emotion on his face.

'Yes. I had to stop all the Centre of Excellence visits, obviously, because when this cloud is hanging over your head you are not as comfortable when other people are watching, you operate, so that has actually reduced the number. The last Centre of Excellence visit was probably about six months ago. I used to get a visit every two months; now in the last 18 months I only had about four visits, so the number of visits has reduced and I have stopped going to the SpR training programme because some of my faculty colleagues have heard about these investigations and I feel embarrassed to go and do these training programmes.' I replied with some emotion in my voice, as I did really feel rather aggrieved by the effect this council hearing has had on my reputation.

'Which training programmes? Number 4?' Fred persisted.

'Number 4, yes.'

'What about number 1?' Fred asked.

'Number 1, that again I had to reduce the number of visits that I was doing, mainly because of time constraint. This has taken an awful lot of my personal time.' I replied with some venom in my voice.

'When you say 'this', you mean the GMC proceedings?' Fred persisted.

'The GMC proceedings have taken an awful lot of my personal time and I cannot afford to go to these teaching programmes.' I replied.

'When was the last one that you went to, for example?' Fred wanted some details.

'June of this year.'

'So you have not been to any of the teaching programmes or had any visitors to your unit for nearly six months then?'

'Yes. At this rate, I'll have difficulty getting up to scratch with my skills at presentation and demonstration surgery which I had painstakingly developed over previous thirteen years.' I replied. Fred moved on to the research projects I was involved at the time.

'Then we see you have got some research projects in progress, if we can just cast an eye down. There is quite a lot of work there. Any updating that the Panel ought to know about on those projects?'

This again was one of my favourite topics and I went into it with gusto.

'Some of the things that I mentioned, because the revision hip surgery is one which has been criticised. I am one of the Faculty and one of the members of multi-centre trial for a pan-European group for radial impaction grafting and revision hip surgery under the auspices of Professor Malchau and Professor Herbert.

After that, we went through the projects set up in association with the University. I had appointed a PhD student to assess the biomechanical aspects of total hip and knee replacements using Gait analysis in their Gait lab. Both the studies have been passed through the regional ethics committees and the study was well under way recruiting patients into the study. He took me through the projects I was involved in cadaver research to develop a new technique of doing total hip replacements using minimally invasive surgery. We were hoping that it would revolutionise the hip replacements in that we could do such major joint replacement surgery as a day case surgery. This project was being developed in association with Danish orthopaedic surgeons in Copenhagen.'

Fred took me through the hip and knee meetings that I ran every year in our hospital. I used to invite internationally known surgeons from Europe and USA to do a live demonstration surgery of new and latest techniques. These meetings attracted large audience and were extremely popular. They were invariably oversubscribed.

We had decided before the start of the latest stage of the hearing that we would expand the pre-assessment protocol that I had set up in the hospital several years ago and which the assessors had completely ignored. Fred asked me searching questions about the protocol, which had been termed 'Joint care programme.' This involved every patient being admitted for a hip or a knee replacements going through a process of meeting the surgeon, the anaesthetist, physiotherapist, occupational therapist and the nurses involved in their care well before they are admitted for surgery. They were given a lecture demonstration of the procedure, an Information leaflet describing the entire pathway including possible benefits and complications of the joint replacement. I had produced a DVD, which would visually demonstrate previous patients' experiences with the surgery. It had proved extremely successful with all our patients. I took my time to stress the time and effort spent on the pre-assessment of patients as it was one of the criticisms of the assessors. Unfortunately, I was not sure if the discussion had any impact on the panel members. They looked as disinterested as before.

We then went on to the work I do with my charity foundation which I had set up a few years ago funded by the fees I earned from my lectures and teaching across the world. This charity was set up to help nurses attend courses and improve their knowledge. We spent some time discussing my arthroplasty register, which had information on every patient I had operated over the previous thirteen years. All the patients with joint replacements were followed up in a special clinic run by nurses and the progress was recorded every year. Fred took me through the data of the over 3000 joint replacements that I had done over the years just to try and impress the panelists about the amount of work I had done over the years. He took me through the complications recorded in the register to show my complications being less than the national average.

By this time, we could see that the attention of the panelists was wavering and the reverend was half-asleep. The chairman promptly asked for a 'short break.' We had spent nearly two hours just going through my CV. The panelists were going to watch my DVD during the break. I was not allowed to speak to Fred or Nancy during the break as I was under oath.

The first thing the chairman said on our return was

'Doctor, I should have reminded you and did not but I believe with you were told that while you are giving your evidence you must not discuss the case during the breaks. Thank you. Mr. Barnard.'

The next hour and a half was spent on my portfolio going through the effects of restrictions imposed by interim orders panel.

'We know that there was a constraint imposed by the Interim Orders Panel but how does this log of daily operations compare to the numbers of operations that you were doing back in 2006 when the assessors were meant to be looking at your practice?' Fred asked.

'The very first action plan meeting, I was advised by Medical Director that we need to reduce it by at least about 25%, so at the time of doing six joint replacements on a full day list, it was reduced to four joints plus, if necessary, a small case.' I replied.

'Then at the end of this section we have got operation notes. These as I understand it, are simply examples of operations notes?' Fred was trying to let the panel understand that the record keeping is as robust as can be'

'Yes. I had decided a couple of years ago, because of the tapes getting faulty and missing notes, etcetera, I decided to get our hospital, the Trust, to arrange a system so I can put the operation notes directly into the computer right there in the theatre and get it printed out and put it in the notes. A template of all operations notes is stored in the theatre computer and I fill in what I need to fill in and the postoperative instructions. It gets printed out and copies are kept in the patient's notes.' I stopped to see if everybody understood what I was getting at.

'I think this is relevant to the issue facing the Panel at this stage. Just explain to us how the operation note is constructed. You have conducted the operation, you are still in theatre?' Fred obviously wanted to make sure the panel members understood the details.

'Yes.'

'You still have your gown on?'

'As soon as the operation is finished, the dressings are on; the patient is being recovered by the anaesthetist, so I go to the computer. There is a terminal inside the theatre; I go to the computer terminal.' I continued.

'You have taken your gloves off?'

'Yes. I take my gloves off, my gown off and then type whatever I need to do. Because it is already templated, the amount of material that I need to put in takes about two or three minutes at the most, and then I get it printed out. There is a printer in the corridor; I go to the printer in the corridor. By the time I get the printout the patient is in recovery so I take the printed notes back and put it in the notes.' I finished.

'You take the printed out report?' Fred continued. It looked like Fred wanted to make sure they get every detail of the procedure. I was quite impressed. After that, he took me through the Informed Consent forms that I had designed based on the American Academy of Orthopaedic Surgeons model. This was again to impress on the panel the amount of information given to the patients before surgery. He took me through all the versions, which I had introduced and modified over the years.

'To whom is this sheet supplied?' Fred asked.

'This is given to every patient who goes on the waiting list for surgery, when either myself or colleagues, in the sense of middle grade doctors, put them on the waiting list, the patients get this information sheet to take home and they take it home and read it and sign it and bring it on the day of the surgery to show me yes, they have signed it, but it does not go into the patient notes.' I replied.

'When did you start using version 2?'

'Version 2 is from middle/end of 2006, I cannot remember the exact date.'

'Version 1?'

'2000.' I replied this time looking at the panel Chairman..

We spent the next half an hour discussing the characteristics of the hospital. We discussed the new development of the Surgery Centre which was hailed by everyone as a beacon of modern patient care and which was labeled as a 'car assembly line Factory' by the assessors. We spent some time describing the meticulous and highest standard of care everyone gets in the hospital. We also spent some time trying to impress upon the panelists how popular the place was among the people of north east of England.

We spent another half an hour discussing the preoperative planning of every operative procedure that I perform in the hospital. We spent some time discussing how patients go on the waiting list and how they are prepared for surgery.

He then went on to the complaint and Serpe.

'We know that the complaint that triggered ultimately the assessment report was made by Mr. Serpe. Can you tell us something about him?'

'Mr. Serpe is a retired consultant from the Royal Hospital. After he retired from there, he went to work in the South Side General Hospital, where he was asked to leave for reasons that were not made very clear to us. We were running short of consultants at the time, so we were looking for locums, and a couple of the appointees at the time to consultant, Mr.

Pakshar and Mr. Foster were Mr. Serpe's registrars. They suggested that we should appoint Mr. Serpe as a locum, and I agreed because I did not know the background of him leaving the Royal Hospital or South Side Hospital and that he had left both places under a cloud. Very soon after the appointment, we started to realise that there were problems. We tried to help him as much as we could but unfortunately he did not take that very well and he started to complain, and he complained against me to the Trust twice, and I was investigated twice and cleared. Then he went beyond the Trust and he complained to the regional adviser. Then further investigations were instigated and the third investigation also did not prove that there were any problems with my clinical practice. At this stage when the third investigation was taking place, the trust decided to investigate all consultants, and the Trust found there were significant problems with the Mr. Serpe's practice. The chief executive at the time decided to end his locum contract, which he did not take very well. And he decided after a lengthy period of absence to take revenge as it were. I think he firmly believed that I was the cause of him losing his job.' I finished.

'We probably do not need to go deeper into that, because the Panel have a document, D5, which is the letter effectively terminating Mr. Serpe's employment with the Trust, the letter is dated 23 February 2004. He was terminated one month later on 23 March 2004 but not required to work during that month.'

Fred then went on to the Assessment report.

'In the hearing bundle, I will invite you to go to page 82, which is page 81 of the internal pagination of the report itself. The Assessors' Report. There they set out a summary of findings beginning with the acceptable judgements and their causes for concern, and their unacceptable judgements. Then at the bottom of the page, they say that the position can be summarised as follows. Then they say why you were required to undergo an assessment, and the team undertook a wide ranging assessment; your qualifications were acceptable; your context of practice was acceptable; you cooperated completely; you were a hard working surgeon in a busy unit; that you were capable of appropriately assessing your patients and following them up; you have made appropriate use of your investigations; and your peers consider that you have appropriate surgical skills; you are willing to ask for advice and help; you have a good relationship with your colleagues; a good team member; popular with everyone; capable of keeping adequate medical resources; works well with the resources available; instrumental in developing the present surgical centre; capable of handling orthopaedic emergencies; keen to keep up-to-date; enjoys teaching; complies with laws and guidance; approachable; supportive; listens to constructive criticism; audit showed no problems; capable of acceptable communication with patients; polite; respectful; respects confidentiality, privacy and dignity; always accessible and available.'

Fred continued.

'However they had pointed out a few faults. They go on in that sentence to say that this may be the cause of an apparent lack of basic surgical technique and knowledge. We all appreciate that you challenged the assessors over the basis of that assertion, but let us begin with asking you the general question of what your comment is as to whether you did, in 2006, lack basic surgical techniques and knowledge.' I could feel my ears warming up and my heart pounding as I heard the question. I said to myself that I should calm down and answer as clearly as possible.

'They were basing their opinion; I think a lot of this on what I could only say as misconception. Basic surgical skills course was developed probably in the late 1990s. This was of course developed for very junior people who are starting their surgical training. It is one way of dealing with the suturing techniques, or dissecting techniques, handling soft tissues and surgical instruments his, etcetera. It is very similar to what we call an ATLS, advanced trauma life support systems; it is one way of dealing with this particular problem. When I was training, there was no such course available in the country, we developed our own techniques taught by our consultants and teachers, which was successful in their hands, and it is successful in my hands. My challenge is, if I did not have basic surgical skills, there is no way I could have done thousands of hips and knee replacements or major complex revision procedures and there is no way would hundreds of senior orthopaedic consultants come to see me operate and learn from me. I have done demonstration surgery in this country and across the world in front of very distinguished, very senior professors of orthopaedic surgery. I am sure somebody would have picked up, 'Look, this man does not know how to operate; he should not be called back.' Why do they keep calling me back again and again to come and show them how to do this procedure or that procedure? If I lacked basic surgical skills that is not possible. The assessors have not been honest with me. At the start of this process they did not tell me they are taking all these questions from a bank of questions meant for junior surgical trainees.' Despite my best effort, I was getting rather emotional. Fred tried to intervene to give me some time to calm down. It did not work.

'I am going to stop you there, Mr. Kasyapa, because I am going to come to those particular tests. I just wanted your general observations on this general allegation?' I looked at the panelists who all had their heads down looking at something on their desks with a lot of interest.

'They did not tell me that they were going to test me on the basic surgical skills course. If they had told me, I would have taken my time to look at what exactly they do and the technique they use and reproduced them. Three or four months after the so-called assessment process, I attended the Royal College of Surgeons recognised basic surgical skills course in Basildon. To my surprise, the Chairman felt that I should not be coming there as a candidate, I should be there as an instructor and I scored very highly in almost all the segments of that skills course. Basically, the assessors were testing me on something, which I did not normally do before, and I used the techniques that I have done all my life and I have been doing surgery since 1982. I have learned my skills with leading orthopaedic surgeons and they would not be teaching me a wrong technique. If I have been doing wrong technique, I would not have been a successful orthopaedic surgeon. Let me tell you, I am not just a 'successful orthopaedic surgeon,' I am internationally known. People come from all over the world to see me operate and learn from me.' By this time, my face was red and I was sweating under the collar.

'Let us go on to the next paragraph on that page:

> 'Mr. K is hardworking but the assessment team
> considers that his operative workload is too high.'

Let us pause there. Was your operative workload too high in the latter part of 2006?' Fred continued.

'I do not think so. I was doing what I thought was comfortable in my own capacity. Different people have different capacities and I have two or three colleagues of mine who can only do two joint replacements in a whole day list. I cannot see that as at an acceptable level. I know a lot of surgeons in this country, not just United States of America, not very far from here, in Birmingham, in Manchester, in Oswestry, in Nottingham, where they do seven or eight joint replacements in one day but they are not being criticised by the Council.' I replied.

This line went on for another half an hour before Fred changed the tack to look at clinical records. One of the criticisms was that I do not keep good records.

'Let us have a look at the next criticism, shall we?

> 'There is evidence that his record keeping may be at times inaccurate and some operation notes are missing.'

Again, just talking generally rather than about specific cases, "record keeping at times inaccurate.' What do you say about that? We are looking at this at the end of 2006?' Fred asked.

'I do not accept that. When patients are seen in outpatients, I do a dictation and I make sure that it is recorded. However, we do live in an era where the tapes can be faulty, and you can have missing bits in the tape or the whole of the dictation can go missing. We also live in an era where the patients do come in again and again and some of these people had four, five, six volumes of notes and these volumes of notes are moved from one department to another department all the time and pages drop out, pages often go missing. I cannot be held responsible for pages of notes going missing. If you take a snapshot of any orthopaedic surgeon in this country, I can bet there will be bits of records missing. I can say that not just for the health service but also for other services.' I was getting rather heated by this stage.

'Let us move on to the next one, which is:

> 'Mr. K's own audit records may be inaccurate and there is uncertainty as to the outcome he records as an end point.'

'Mr. K's own audit may be inaccurate', I think the assessors told us that they never saw your audit records. Was there any reason that you can think of why they might have thought that they were inaccurate in the absence of actually seeing them?' Fred went on.

'I am not sure. You will have to ask them, but my guess is that it was based on two things. One is that I said that the department audit data may not be very accurate, because the department data could be filled in by anyone, a junior nurse, a healthcare assistant, or whoever is there in the theatre at the time fills that in on the computer. So for example, if you are doing a hip hemiarthroplasty, as you do for a fracture of the femur, often it gets filled in as total hip replacement and total hip replacement gets filled in as something else. There are a lot of inaccuracies in the departmental data. That is what I said. The second thing, these two individuals who have a grudge against me said that my data is inaccurate. Nobody apart from the Chief Executive and myself has seen my database and as they did not have access to my database. Only when the Chief Executive was investigating the complaints, I had to produce my database to him to have a look and the Medical Director, obviously, looked at it, and the person who was doing the investigation looked it. No one else has seen the database so I do not know how they came to this conclusion that my data is inaccurate. They did not see the database; they never asked me to show them.'

'Do you mean to say that they came to a conclusion that your database was inaccurate without setting their eyes on them? You said the two individuals had a grudge, who is that a reference to?' I could just hear the faint sarcasm in Fred's voice.

'Yes. They have concluded that my database was inaccurate without ever seeing them and based their judgement purely on the statement made by those two - Mr. Serpe and Mr. Pakshar.' I was equally sarcastic.

'The database that was checked, who was it checked by, did you say?' Fred continued.
'At the time, there were three investigations done. One was done by the Chief Executive personally and second one was done by the Medical Director and the third was done by our Service Manager, who was the Audit Facilitator for the trust.'

'OK, before we break for lunch let us just look at that last part of that sentence on page 84:

'There is uncertainty as to the outcome he records as an end point.'

What is that about?' Fred asked.

'Neither of the assessors understood the meaning of the arthroplasty register. Arthroplasty register does not have an end point. It is a data collection of patients who are having surgery and their outcomes on an annual basis and when you want to do any audit then you extract the data from this database and then do an audit. It is then you decide what your end point should be. It is generally agreed that the end point could be removal of an implant. I also said that I would use a system called Kaplan-Meir Survivorship Analysis which is...' I was interrupted by Fred at this point.

'What is Kaplan-Meir?' Fred wanted to know. I could see blank expressions on the face of the panelists. None of them knew what I was talking about.

'Yes, it is a Survivorship Analysis, which tells you exactly how your implant is performing and which is accepted world over as prime indicator of success or failure of any procedure. However, neither of them understood what I was trying to get at.' I was hoping to stress the level of ignorance of the assessors, but to no avail.

'What were you trying to get at?'

'I was trying to get at was that this is an arthroplasty register and not an audit database. One would use this register, as an audit database is when one wants to do an audit. You extract information from this register to do your audit, decide what should be the end point, and then do an audit. I was trying to make them understand that this was not an audit database but a pure register of data.' As I finished, I could see the Chairman looking at the clock a few times and Fred.

That is when my flow of thought was interrupted for a lunch break. The gist of the discussion was that anyone would work as hard as they want to and not everyone is the same. The lunch break was strange, as I had to go out with Lopa and sit separately. I was reminded again by the Chairman that I should not discuss the case with anyone.

After the lunch break, Fred started again on the assessment report. He went through the audit and pre-assessment once more in slightly more detail than before lunch break. He moved on to the comment by the assessors of 'conveyor belt surgery.'

'Then they say:

> 'The assessment team also considers that to some extent there is an institutional problem with 'conveyor belt surgery' being encouraged by management pressure. It is not entirely Mr. K's fault that he is in this situation. His deficiencies exaggerated by his work environment.'

Leave out the issue of whether you had deficiencies at all, but have we dealt with that issue? Is there anything you wanted to add to what you said this morning about that workload and so on?' Fred continued

'I take issue with the term "conveyor belt surgery" because we never treat our patients as machines to be produced on a conveyor belt. These are people, they have a great regard for me, and they specifically ask for me to operate on them. The large number of thank-you cards at the end of my portfolio is just a very small snapshot of examples to see how satisfied they are with how I manage my patients. I have a fantastic team with me, they are one of the best teams in the country, and because of the team effort, and we work very efficiently. If you call, working efficiently is wrong and you accuse them of doing conveyor belt surgery, then I am sorry but the assessors are wrong. I do not agree with that statement.' I hoped that the strength of my feeling came out in my statement.

Fred moved on to the criticisms the assessors had made regarding my record keeping. One of the records the assessors had picked up was someone who had been put on the waiting list for a total hip replacement over seven years ago. At the time of there was no mention of a deep vein thrombosis by whoever had seen the patient. The assessors had picked up a statement by a Nurse about nine years previously of 'gives history of deep vein thrombosis.' The criticism was that this patient should have been warned of high incidence of recurrence of the thrombosis.

'There the staff grade in orthopaedics, is saying at the end of the first paragraph, 'Wound has healed satisfactorily though within a fortnight he was admitted to the medical ward with query deep vein thrombosis, but the diagnosis investigation did not prove any evidence of deep vein thrombosis. Advised to see again in six months time.' What conclusions should the Panel draw about that?' Fred asked.

'It is very simple; this patient never had a deep vein thrombosis. There was a suspicion because of pain in his leg, which quite often occurs one month after major surgery, such as a hip replacement, the leg swells up, they get edema, a collection of fluid in the leg, it can be painful and when that does happen the first thing you need to rule out is deep vein thrombosis, which was done correctly. I ruled it out and they did not need any treatment for deep vein thrombosis. This patient never had a deep vein thrombosis in 1995.'

'Why do you think the assessors criticised you on this then?' Fred continued.

'At the time of the interview, they showed me only very few pages of this patient's notes which did not contain the relevant reports showing the Ultrasound scan result. They had obviously not seen this report.'

This was first of the several missing pieces we would unearth during the course of next few days.

We went through several of the assessors criticisms including a planning for surgery for a complex hip replacement. The assessors had conveniently "forgotten" to show me the records, which would have shown the pre-operative planning that was done for that patient. Of the twelve cases they discussed with me, they had shown me only about a dozen pages of each set of notes and expected me to answer their questions about management of the patient. Each of these patients had about two to three hundred pages in their set of notes and the management they were asking me had taken place a few years earlier. By the time we got through three of the twelve cases, it was getting towards one in the afternoon. That was probably the first time the hearing went on till so late before lunch break. I had been giving evidence for over an hour now and welcomed the break for the first time.

Most of the time after the lunch break was spent on the twelve cases they had discussed with me. What rankled me most was that they had shown me a very few pages of each set of notes and expected me to answer what happened to the patient. One example of trying to mislead me was again to do with pre-operative planning.

'I think Mr. Crouper suggested that you did not have a plan for this operation. What do you say about that?' Fred asked

'This makes me laugh because I spoke to the International Faculty of Orthopaedic Surgeons doing something similar and I spoke to colleagues. It is made very clear in this letter on 20 November and the plan was there and we discussed it not only with the patient and also with her husband and told her exactly what we are going to do and I also warned her that we may or may not be able – because she did have a quite serious arthritis in the knee so some of the pain would be coming from her knee so I told her that she may or may not get rid of all her symptoms so she knew exactly what she was going to face and the plan there was done on 20 November.' I answered.

'Then why did they criticise you?' Fred persisted.

'They did not show me this letter at the time of discussion and I could not answer their question without looking at this letter.'

'They did not show you this record?'

'No. They did not.' I was brief and firm.

He then went on to another case, which was even more obvious.

'Then there is a criticism, 656, that you were initially going to take out the spline and then do a total hip replacement, why did you change your mind?' Fred asked.

'If they do not show me the letter that was dictated, when she went on the waiting list what do they expect? They should have sent me the full set of notes. It is the only sensible way of doing things. They gave me half a dozen pages of notes and tell them what was probably in the full set of notes that was not there, how could I tell them? There was no change of mind; it is very clear in the letter by Mr. Mustaf that the patient put on the waiting list, so how can I explain to them if they do not give me the full set of notes?' I was getting rather angry by then. I could see Nancy signalling me to calm down.

'What are you saying about the allegation that there was no sufficient system for dealing with patients who did not attend for appointments?' Fred continued.

'I did tell them exactly what happens routinely at our unit. Whenever patient fails to attend an appointment, he or she is automatically sent a further appointment for the first absence. No further appointments are sent out for second DNA (did not attend) and a letter is sent out to the GP of the patient's non-attendance. I still do not understand what else one could do, apart from send a letter or another appointment. What else could I do? Go to the patient's house and bring him back?' I said with exasperation.

'Did the system work or fail in this case?'

'No. It worked very well in this case the system obviously worked because the patient did come back, and he was seen and he was dealt with appropriately.' I replied.

The discussion went on about the records until about three that afternoon when the Chairman decided he wants to have another break. We streamed off to our respective waiting areas. Lopa was allowed to come and sit with me in a separate room. The Chairman had made it a point to warn me not to discuss the case with anyone again during the break. These breaks were taking a toll on me. It was frustrating to sit there not knowing how I am performing as a witness, not being allowed to talk about it with anyone. The breaks were the longest 30 minutes that I had ever spent and there were many.

We were ushered into the hearing room again by the council assistant with an ever-present file in her hand. The discussion after the break moved on to complex hip surgery that they had found faults with. The first one was a complex primary hip replacement done for someone who had previous surgery done on her hip as a youngster. She had a procedure done during 1960's, which was redundant in modern times. Unfortunately, the assessors did not understand the procedure and termed it 'Revision Hip Replacement' which is a term normally used for changing a failed hip replacement. The fact that this patient did not have a hip replacement to start with did not make any difference to them. They had not shown me the pages of notes, which had recorded my discussions with colleagues about planning for surgery and blamed me 'no pre-operative planning done.' As the case was over 6 years old, I could not remember the discussions and the assessors were clever enough to hide the pages containing these detailed planning for the procedure.

We went on to the information given to the patients. The assessors had alleged that I do not give enough information to patients, particularly complications after an arthroscopy.

'What about the criticism that the risks have not been explained to this patient?' Fred asked.

'We discussed the most common complication of arthroscopy at the time and she was given the new arthroscopy information leaflet which fully explained all complications that can occur and the benefits and the risks. She has been given the full information about arthroscopy, what she can and cannot get out of it.'

'We saw in your portfolio this morning a leaflet about arthroscopy, would the patient have had the relevant addition of that note or not?' Fred continued.

'It is 2006, June 2006; she probably would have the first version. The second version came out about September/October 2006, the third version in the early part of this year.' I replied.

'Are there significant differences between the first and second version?' 'No, the format is slightly better, but the content is exactly the same.' I replied. Fred invited them to have a look at the information leaflet.

'What about the risk of deep vein thrombosis?' Fred continued.

'Well, the risk is extremely low. If you have a scan anyone after an operation, you probably find significant number will have evidence of thrombosis. We have recently done an audit, and it is still going on, and the first report of the audit is being presented at the BASK meeting in April. Just fewer than 500 cases have been looked at, none of them had symptomatic DVT, and we have now extended the audit to the entire unit, which will probably be over 2000 arthroscopies, and we suspect none of them will have symptomatic DVT. But if you go on to do ultrasound scan for all of these patients you will find between five and ten per cent of them will have evidence of deep vein thrombosis, but if you start to mention these theoretical risks of deep vein thrombosis the chances are the patients will get so scared and they will refuse to have surgery, and where will we end up?' I finished with a question looking at the Chairman.

'Just to save the Panel reaching for the relevant volume from your portfolio, does the leaflet mention that risk or not?'

'Yes, it does.'

The discussion went on till about five in the evening and mainly centred on the case based discussions. Fred tried to show the panel how many mistakes the assessors had done during the assessment. Towards the end, we found that all the medical records have been sent back to the hospital. Fred made a request that they should be made available to continue with the hearing. The council secretary was not very hopeful. The hearing broke up with Chairman asking everyone to be ready for 9.30 next morning and again his usual warning to me not discusses the case.

I was not looking forward to the next day. I was emotionally drained and felt sick most of the time. I wished the whole thing would end soon and go away. It did not matter what I did, the feeling of desolation and despair would not go. I felt that I was alone amidst all the friend and family around me. The feeling of fighting a lonely battle was overwhelming and there was many a time I wanted to drop everything and go away or end it all forever. I was sure no one would miss me and I would not even be a footnote in history.

The next day was the thirteenth day of the hearing and it started just like any other day. The whole procedure of getting up in the morning, trudging up to the council rooms, sit and listen to Fred's questions and answer them without losing my temper was all too familiar. It had taken over the need for existence for the day and had become extremely tedious. The questions from Fred were the same and I was trying to show how incompetent the assessors were throughout the day.

The only exciting thing that happened that day was what happened at lunch break. As I walked into the toilet, who should I find standing next to me. None other than the Specialist Performance Adviser. He turned around and smiled at me.

'Don't let the beggars get you down. Fight all the way.' and turned back.

'Thank you. I will.' I said looking at the wall.

I did not what to make of that brief interlude. Was he trying to tell me something? Will I get some help from him during his 'advise' to the panel? It lifted my spirits up a little, albeit temporarily. It just goes to show how desperate I was. He appeared to know his way around the council. Obviously, he has been around these offices for a while. His CV was handed out during the lunch break which showed that he had left health service and was practicing privately full time doing hip and knee replacements. Well, at least we had someone who was specialising in the same thing as I was. That day, we found several "missing records" that the assessors had blamed me for during the interview.

'Let us turn to case 37. The criticism there is that there was a handwritten operation note with no details and the criticisms are at 637, 795, and 837 and they are all to the same effect and in the extract produced by the assessors they start at page 104. It was a right total knee replacement. We can see that at 105 and at 108 do we see your handwritten note of the operation?' Fred asked. 'Yes. It is around that time when it would be my standard practice to give a handwritten note to say what the title of the operation was and at the bottom the instructions for the ward and then dictate the entire operation notes which should be typed by the secretary and put in the notes.'

'It was put to you by the assessors that there was no fuller note than that but we produced on the last occasion D14, if you could just look at that for a moment?'

Fred continued.

'That would be type written note, dictated notes which have been typed out.'

'Did the assessors show you this?'

'No, they did not show me this. They told me they could not find any typed operation notes.'

'Is the allegation that there was an inadequate operation note one that has any justification or not?'

'I think it is completely unjustified because they did not bother to look at it properly.' 'When you say they did not bother to look at *it*, what do you mean?'

'Look at the full set of notes properly. On the other hand, if they had given me the full set of notes I would have looked for them and showed them where it was. They did not take enough effort to look for the operation notes. If they had bothered to look for it properly they would have found it.' I had hoped the sarcasm in my voice had not escaped the panelists.

It was well after lunch break before we got on to the 'Surgical Performance Test.' I made it very clear that I was given no indication as to the nature of the 'test' and stressed the fact that the questions were directed to a junior surgeon in training and not a consultant of over a decade of experience. I tried to impress on the panel that it was twenty years since I had passed the fellowship exam and it was unfair to use the questions that are used in a fellowship exam to assess an established consultant. I cannot tell whether the assessment team was trying to mislead me or not.

'Give the Panel in your own words your recollection of those discussions?' Fred asked.

'I have to go back to the time when they came to see me in Seaport and I asked them what this test of competence is and what the test entails. At first, they said they would let you know nearer the time. At the final interview where

Mr. Jankoweicz was with me as the support they said, that it is nothing to do with reading any textbooks. It is everything to do with your daily practice in the hospital. They never told me it was going to be a practical skills test. They never told me the skills test was based basic surgical skills course. Even on that day, just before the test started, they did not tell me that. Even then they told me that this test is you have to answer on your hospital practice and my hospital practice is as a consultant orthopaedic surgeon, not as an SHO.' I replied

'Then let us turn to page 53 and we go to the surgery core knowledge test. They write: "This test comprised eight questions each with several parts to be answered as short notes. The questions were selected from a larger GMC bank derived from the FRCS bank of the Royal College of Surgeons, England. They are considered relevant to the clinical practice of all surgeons. They are marked using structured marking schedules from the FRCS bank, which were revised during test development by the surgical assessors. The standard applied by the assessors is the minimum standard for an established consultant surgeon. In addition to this, an independent volunteer group of nine practising surgeons determined a minimum acceptable score of 85% using Angoff's method with the Hofstee modification. The group consisted of five consultant surgeons and four specialist registrars from various specialties.' Did they tell you those things?" Fred asked.

'No. They never told me anything to do with the FRCS bank of questions. They never told me that method of evaluation or assessment. They never told me that you need to answer the standard of FRCS questions and to be honest I did my FRCS in 1985, that is 23 years ago, so if they asked me these questions in 1985, I would have answered to their satisfaction. Secondly, I have reservations about these nine volunteer surgeons. Were they given full information as to what the content of the test is going to be? Were they told that this is based on the FRCS's bank of questions? Did they go through a basic surgical skills course? Because I did not go through a basic surgical skills course in 1985. There was no such basic surgical skills course at the time of my training. Therefore, the whole scenario is made for a junior surgeon who is just coming out of or going through the training. If they had told me that it comes through the FRCS's bank of questions I would have made some attempt for preparing these questions, or if they told me that the I have to go through the basic surgical skills course, I would have tried to find out what the content of the basic surgical skills course was and tried to learn the techniques that is shown in the basic surgical skills course. I have been a orthopaedic surgeon for 20-odd years and you tend to develop your own way of doing things which is taught by one's teachers and which has stood me in good stead in all those years and has stood my teachers in good stead for lots of years before me and that is the system I followed.' I finished looking at Fred.

Fred then went on to the test questions themselves. He went through the questions as they were interpreted by the assessors and showed how the assessors got the answers wrong as well as the scoring badly wrong.

'If you look at the box below that each bullet point has been numbered and scores attached to it by Mr. Amoshin and Mr. Crouper and those scores, apart from one example, differ from each other and what has been done is that the mean between the scores of those two assessors has been taken in the third column. The scores, as we see, are calculated to two decimal places. Was the scoring system explained to you?' Fred asked.

'No.'

'Was it explained to you how Mr. Amoshin and Mr. Crouper arrived at different scores for the same answer that you had given?'

'It is not uncommon to have different opinions about the same answer but not such a wide difference.'

'I said there was one – in fact there are two that are identical, the answer to question 3 and the answer to question 8 are the same and all the rest differ. Let us turn over to page 53, Knowledge Test Percentage Scores. We have there got a grid in a standard form used to assess answers to a knowledge test. Was this methodology explained to you?'

'No.'

'Were these results shown to you?'

'No.'

'Were the results in the previous table shown to you?'

'No.'

'Did they tell you what scores they had given to your answers?'

'No.'

This went on for a while with monosyllabic answers from me. Then he went on to show where the assessors had got the answers completely wrong.

'Let's look at this question about pain relief. Mr. Amoshin said, 'On the whole has described common complications' – just reminding ourselves, the subject matter is post-operative pain relief – 'described common complications though not in an organised way and some of which don't occur, i.e. epidural does not cause respiratory depression.' Any comment?' Fred asked.

'Unfortunately he is completely wrong, is he not? One of the most serious complications of epidural anaesthesia is respiratory depression. This is why if the patient has an epidural catheter he or she has to go into a ward where the nurses are qualified or trained to look after respiratory depression. It is very common knowledge. I do not know where he got this from; epidural catheter does not cause respiratory depression. Speaking to the anaesthetists, they were shocked when I said the epidural does not cause respiratory depression. That is one of the complications that they are wary of after Epidural anaesthesia.' I replied.

Fred managed to bring out several instances where the assessors had got their answers dreadfully wrong. Then he moved on to the 'practical test' where I was assessed on suturing, knotting etc and scored me very badly. Fred showed that the equipment given was substandard and the tissues that were given were dried up tendons and pig's mesentery. They had asked me to dissect out a lymph node from a pig's mesentery – when I pointed out that it was over 25 years ago that I had done anything of the sort, I was told to 'just do it and let's see.' He then went on to show the scores that I had achieved in a Basic Surgical Skills course run by the Royal College of surgeons just a couple of months after the 'assessment' where I had scored very highly and I was invited to take part as an instructor for future courses. He pointed out the fact the Laparoscopy equipment was set up wrongly and it was over ten minutes into the procedure before the technician recognised the mistake and corrected it. The assessors who were supposed to be 'experts' had not noticed the blunder. When I pointed out the I had never seen a Laparoscopy on an abdomen before let alone do one the answer was the same – 'just do it and let's see.' They had asked me to 'drape a patient for posterior approach to the hip' and they scored me for 'preparing a patient for total hip.' The Catalogue of blunders goes on throughout the test.

The day finished with me on stand with Fred going through the Test of competence. I was again completely drained and felt like I had done a whole day of physical labour. I have to prepare myself for questioning by the council's Barrister and that will not be nice. At that stage, I was not sure if I was capable of going through the interrogation by the opposing lawyers. I could not even think about it without breaking into a sweat.

The next day 14th November 2008, was the fourteenth day of the hearing and my third day on the stand. It had now been well over six months since the hearing had started. The council's Barrister was Miss Norsworth who started in the morning. She started with

'Good morning, Mr. Kasyapa. I anticipate that I am not going to take much longer than half a day, if that gives anyone any relief.'

That did give me some relief and I hoped that she was right. She went on to my criticisms of the assessors and the whole assessment process. I suspect she had hoped that I would apologise and say it was a mistake. When I would not budge my position and reiterated quite vehemently, she started to pick holes wherever she could find. She tried to make the panel believe that I had changed my practice because of the criticisms from the assessors. When I pointed out that, the practice had evolved over the years, long before the assessors came to Seaport, she was not very impressed and tried to pick faults in exactly the same place as the assessors.

'You are making some assumptions there, as you have done at various points in your evidence, not just today but on previous days, that there must be notes and the fact that they cannot be found is not your fault, it is simply that someone is not looking hard enough. They must exist.' She suggested.

'Absolutely. I fail to understand, as I was trying to explain before, and we did see yesterday, that there were records the assessors had clearly missed. I know for a fact, I am not making assumptions here, that there are other notes and the assessors did not look carefully enough to find them.' I replied

'Sir, I am sorry to intervene at an early stage but I did say on Monday that we would like to have the patient records back again and here is a case where my learned friend is suggesting that in some way Mr. Kasyapa is at fault for not three years missing notes but four years, just one month short of four years of records. We would like to see the records, if we may.' Fred interrupted. I was glad as Miss Norsworth was yet again trying to blame me for missing records as 'no records.'

She tried to blame on the fact that she was not there for the earlier part of the hearing and hence she is making some assumptions. I was quite sure that it was nothing of the kind. She was just trying to reinforce all the negatives so that the panel will have these fresh in their minds when they come to pass judgement. She tried to trip me up a couple of times on statements I had made to Fred.

'You have told us yesterday that you are internationally known for your work in the area of knees and hips. Is there anything that is beyond your limits? Or do you think you are capable of dealing with anything?' 'Absolutely, I am not super human, I know my limitations. When I find that there is a case, more appropriately dealt with by any of my colleagues, or can be dealt with by somebody else who is much better than me I send them across. I have referred patients elsewhere, especially if they are fields which are definitely not mine like spinal surgery or podiatric surgery or paediatric surgery, or even hips and knees there are situations where I have asked for advice and if the advice they give me I feel that I am not able capable of performing I send the patient across to them. I cannot say that I can do everything. That would be foolish.' I replied.

She took patient by patient – of the twelve case discussed with the assessors and tried to blame me for mistakes in almost all of them. She would not accept any form of explanation and clarification in any of them. She refused to believe that if a junior doctor has not recorded something he or she had done, it is not really my fault and it should be taken up with that particular doctor. She again tried to blame me on 'missing notes' and said that it is my responsibility to make sure all the notes are there at all the time for all the patients. When I pointed out that I see something in the tune of 1000 patients a year and it would be an impossible task, all she had to say was "the buck stops with you and it is your responsibility.' I was hoping that Fred would come to my rescue on that point, but it was not forthcoming for some reason. As she kept on insisting that there were missing records, Fred finally demanded that the complete sets of notes be produced so that we can have a look and produce the missing records. Miss Norsworth said

'The council has requested the hospital to release the records. Unfortunately, I have been told that they have been sent from this office to London by mistake. They are being retrieved as we speak and we should have the notes by tomorrow.'

'That is no good enough, I am afraid. You are criticising the Doctor of not telling the truth and he cannot defend himself with evidence being withheld.' Fred retorted. He then turned to the Chairman and said;

'Sir, if the notes are available we would like a reasonable opportunity to go through them, which we attempted on the last occasion, as you recall, in the tea breaks and the lunch hours, but we would like a bit more now if the material is here. If the material is not here I am not suggesting that the case cannot go ahead but I will be making submissions on the basis that material is not here.'

Miss Norsworth reassured that the notes would be here tomorrow and should be ready before the hearing commences on Friday morning. The panel was not sitting on Thursday for some reason. The rest of the day was spent on Miss Norsworth trying to justify the assessors' judgements and tried her best to discredit all my statements made to Fred on the previous two days. She was very good at twisting my statement to suit her case. I was disappointed that Fred did not intervene more often as she was trying to trash his work of the previous two days.

I lost my temper at one point when she started questioning about the test paper.

'Let us start then with the first issue that you did not know in advance what this test would entail; that you were not aware that this was from the FRCS bank of questions. Help me, and it may be clear to everybody else but I struggle to understand what difference that would make to your performance in this if you knew from whence the questions had been derived?' She asked.

'Let me put it to you, that FRCS examinations are broken down into two parts, part one and part two. Part one had the basic sciences and the part two had the clinical sciences in those days and I did this in 1985. I would have read all these questions in detail and I would have been able to answer those questions in detail and what I was told at the time of the test was that, no, we do not want you to write anything in detail, we do not want to any didactic answers, we want what you practice in your hospital and does not need a preparation. Therefore, that is what I actually produced in the test. For example, intra-operative management of a diabetic patient is I ask the diabetic team to take over. In my part, I make sure that the patient knows of the increased risk of infection and DVT and I also make sure the patient is the first on the list and I also make sure that the anaesthetic team and the diabetic team know that the patient is coming for surgery and that is my role. If I do not micromanage the diabetes on a day-to-day basis, I do not know the doses of insulin, I do not know the GKI regime or whatever they do. I knew this 20 odd years ago because that is when I was training, I was doing my part one exam. If they had told me that this is the type of question that I am going to put to you then I would have made some attempt to go and refresh my memory to what I did 20 odd years ago but unfortunately to throw this at me without any notice is unfair. I had Mr. Cooley at the time as my supporter and he can vouch for that. I repeatedly asked them and at the final interview just before after they finished the initial questioning Mr. Jankoweicz was with me, even then I asked them at least two or three times and even then they were not coming forward with what the test is going to be. They said, oh, it is just about your hospital practice. You do not have to worry, you do not have to read any books.' I was getting hot under the collar by this time.

'You were given the opportunity to have as much time as you wanted to answer these questions?' She insisted.

'Yes, if you do not remember what you are going to write it does not matter if you have half an hour or three hours, you will not be able to write it.' I nearly said would you be able to give detailed answers for conveyance practice you learnt 20 years ago.

'You are saying you do not remember because you would have last had chance of questions such as this 20 odd years ago?' She continued.

'Yes.'

'If we look at page 93 of the report, we have as an appendix 3 demography of the volunteer group for the surgery core knowledge test using scores, grade, age, and specialty of the volunteer members. Some of them were consultants of comparable ages, I would suggest, some of them with you?' She asked.

'Yes. Absolutely, but what I want to know is, were they asked to come and sit in a PLAB centre and then given no notice and they were not told what their questions are going to be? Were they told that this is the based on the passes FRCS's bank of questioning? Nothing is here. I strongly suspect that, they had been told they were going to be asked questions on part one of the FRCS examinations before they answered these. If I were given the same opportunity, I would get very high marks as well. I passed my FRCS part one. I passed the FRCS part two and got my fellowship. Do you think the examiners have passed me because I did not know all this?' I threw the question back at her.

'The point might be made that if any of us are told what the questions are in advance we can work out what the answers are?' She answered back.

'That is an insult. I am sorry, Ms Norsworth, that is not what I meant. You know perfectly well that is not what I meant. Nobody expects to be told the questions. I want the subject matter. I did not want the questions. Nobody expects you to have the questions. I am sorry; I feel that I am being insulted.' I looked at the Chairman if he would intervene. No luck.

'The questions that you were asked were all questions which, so far as the assessors gave evidence to the Panel are concerned, are straightforward surgical problem issues that may arise in day-to-day surgery?' She continued.

'I have to repeat exactly what I said before. These things are dealt with by a

Multi-disciplinary team day in and day out. This has been the course of events for the last 20 years, so they do that all the time and so if am I am going managing a diabetic patient day-in-day out I would know what kind of drugs are being used and what are the dosages and what I have do and I will keep up with it but that is not my job. So if I am not doing it on a day-to-day basis you tend to forget after 20 odd years. 1985, for God's sake, is 23 years ago.' I retorted. I was really getting angry by this time.

'The point that was being made, as I understand it, by the assessors, Mr. Kasyapa, is not that you would have to have an in depth knowledge and micromanage these individual problems but you need to have a working knowledge, a basic knowledge of some of the issues that might arise. Do you agree with that?' She insisted

'No, because that is not what they scored me on. They scored me on detail. If you look at their comments I did not know the drugs, I did not know the dosage, I did not know this, I did not know that and they are looking at the micromanagement, they are looking at the details of these topics they have produced which you can only produce if you actually read the book, otherwise you cannot, or if you are doing it every day of your practice.' I was really losing my cool.

At lunch break, I sent a message again that we should insist on the Council to release the question and answer papers so that we can fight this battle on a more level playing field. Fred had made veiled threats of court injunction etc.

Miss Norsworth did come back after the lunch break saying that the GMC had refused out request before and they may be reconsidering the decision now.

'You also know there have been various applications for disclosure by the defence, which have hitherto been refused. I have received communication shortly before the lunchtime break, which appears on the face of it to suggest that the GMC may have reversed that decision and that material should be and could be made available. That would be, I have to say, something of a departure from their normal procedures in performance cases.'

I later found out that it was not just a simple 'departure from their normal procedure' but it would be the first time on record. There was a break in the proceedings for about an hour while waiting for the Councilperson to get back with a decision. She came back with no news as they had failed to contact the person who could make a decision. It was quite late that evening when she came back with a decision to say that the council had agreed to disclose the question and answer papers to everyone's surprise.

She continued for the rest of the day in the same vein trying to trash Fred's work of the previous days and discredit my statements. She went through the practical skills test and again tried to twist my words repeatedly. Finally, she finished by about five and when Fred said that it is time for questions for the panel to ask, they were not ready. When Fred protested that he could not discuss anything with me particularly with the Council finally agreeing to disclose material crucial to the case, they agreed to 'release' me from the witness box so that we can discuss the case.

The day ended with me being no further forward. Nancy was enthusing with the news that the Council had finally agreed to disclose the test papers. Fred said he had never seen this happen in thirty years of practice. He asked me to take it easy and have a bit of rest and will meet up on Friday morning and see where we go from there. The drive back home was rather quiet, as I felt totally drained emotionally and physically. I let Lopa answer all the inevitable phone calls from friends and drove in silence. I could not wait to get home and get to bed. Unfortunately, sleep was not something that still eluded me. There were so many things on my mind and battles going on inside my head that I had very fitful night.

It was probably one of the worst Thursdays for a long time. I could not concentrate on anything. I could not do anything. Finally, when Gautam came in the evening and dragged me out to a movie with Lopa, I was glad for the interruption. We drove back to Manchester on Friday morning and reached the council offices just as Nancy was going into the building. As I entered the waiting room, it was very quiet. Even Natalie was not saying very much. Nancy said, 'There have been some developments and Fred is looking into it. He would rather not discuss it at present.' That was odd I thought. Anyway, it was not long before we were called into the hearing room. The first thing I noticed was missing Specialist Performance Adviser.

As soon as we sat down, Fred started off;

'Sir, last night I got a telephone call from Ms Norsworth telling me that a note had been placed on her desk from Mr. Furzfield and this note I saw this morning has now been copied. I do not know if everybody has copies. Mr. Stadeus was making some copies.'

'Yes, we have copies.' The Chairman replied.

'Those note I should just read. They say: 'Six to seven cases on a day. A lot! Why? Waiting list monies? One recent case - £200,000 earned by one surgeon in one year extra on [waiting list] initiative. Does this give motive for corner cutting?'

Sir, my submission, regrettably and embarrassingly, is that I have to ask Mr. Furzfield to be recused from the case as a Specialist Medical Adviser. This is a case where what the lawyers call apparent bias, that is to say bias that might be perceived by a fair minded outsider knowing of these events, destroys the basis on which Mr. Furzfield can remain as the Specialist Medical Adviser.' Fred said looking rather serious. 'Clearly somebody who is meant to be impartial and independent and who, no doubt, is impartial and independent but providing notes to the prosecutor, so to speak, in the absence of the defence is not proper and appropriate. For those reasons, I make that application. I understand it is not opposed.'

'Thank you, Mr. Barnard. Miss Norsworth?' The Chairman looked at Miss Norsworth.

'The application is not opposed.' Miss Norsworth accepted.

'I will ask the Legal Assessor for his advice.' The Chairman asked the legal adviser. He went into a long spiel about the impartiality and bias and finally agreed.

'Sir, I am sorry, I omitted to mention one matter which does not touch on Mr. Stadeus's legal advice to you and that is just to make clear that there has never, ever been a suggestion in this case that Mr. Kasyapa earned a single penny from working hard at all and the implication that in some way what he did and what is at issue before you was done for financial gain is utterly repudiated" Fred said to my great relief. All these lists were done in my work time and were part of my work and not done as a 'waiting list initiative' as Furzfield was implying. I was very disappointed at the turn of events. I was hoping that Furzfield would be of use to advise this Panel which increasingly appeared to be completely ignorant of hospital practice, let alone hip and knee implant surgery. Next question was whether the hearing should continue without a specialist performance advisor to advise the panel. My heart sank at the thought of an adjournment of the hearing. God only knows when it can be resumed. Judging by the speed of the past performance of the council, there would be another break of six months. It was agreed that the hearing would continue without a medical adviser. This was in a way bad news for me, as I will have to depend on these three to make a decision on medical matters they are completely ignorant of. There was nothing I could do. I just to hope for the best. Things were not looking very good for me at that stage.

It turned out that the test papers had been delivered but the Council insisted that one of their officers have to be present when we are looking through the papers and we were not allowed to take the papers out of the hearing room. There were ten large cardboard boxes in the corner of the room, which turned out to be the clinical records of the cases discussed by the assessors. The x-rays were still missing and the council could not produce them. Fred wanted that day and probably Saturday as well to go through all the records and the test papers. There was a lot of discussion about the proceedings and Fred vented his gripe with a long-winded statement at the Council and thinly veiled one at the panel. There was a silence for a minute when he had finished, as it was quite a direct attack on the Council process.

'This is a case where the assessors chose to interview and base some of their criticisms on the evidence of Mr. Serpe and Mr. Pakshar. Leaving aside their motives, whatever else is clear is that they could not conceivably shed light on the current practice of Mr. Kasyapa in 2006 since they had left the employ of the Trust a couple of years earlier. This is a case where we know that gross errors have been made by the assessors, in particular, the most glaring one, that Mr. Kasyapa had insufficient experience at hip revision surgery when, we all know, and the assessors have now accepted, that that was a fundamental error, that what they were referring to were the very rare cases of revision of trochanteric osteotomies, followed by ankylosing, and so on. Now we have two medical assessors recused on the basis of apparent bias and now we are in a situation where we cannot have a medical assessor without prejudicing the timetable. Of course, the Panel is in a position to continue and will continue, but I have to say that Mr. Kasyapa feels very, very uncomfortable about these events, and he is losing confidence, not in you and your Panel, sir, and not in Ms Norsworth, but in the GMC process. When you read the three-volume portfolio, you will see that Mr. Kasyapa is supported here by his employer, by the chief executive, by the medical director, by the clinical director, by all his fellow orthopaedic consultants, by his nurses, by the managers and, of course, by the patients. He has satisfied all those who have instructed, supervised and mentored him in the steps that he has taken to satisfy the requirements of the IOP and the question, if we reach that stage, whether his performance is now impaired, when we come to it, in my submission will be it can only be answered in one way. Therefore, we reflect on, really, whether the cost of these proceedings to the GMC, to the MPS, who are supporting him, the burden on the Panel, and the agony to Mr. Kasyapa is really warranted.' He did go on for about ten minutes in the same vein before stopping to look up at the chairman.

The chairman concluded the day's hearing and we got to work straight away with the clinical records that were in the ten boxes. It was hard work going through those sets of notes. Each patient had an average of six sets of very large sets of notes and they were in a dreadful state with pages falling off all over the place.

Nancy said 'No wonder the pages go missing in these records.'

'We should use these records and show the panelists the state of these records to highlight why some of the records could be missing.' I asked Fred.

'Not to worry. I will make it a point in my submission.' Fred replied. It took us all of that afternoon to go through the records, but still left some to be picked up the next day. I went down to the offices again on Friday to sit with Nancy to look through the records. It was about one in the afternoon when someone arrived carrying a card board box into the hearing room accompanied two others and they would not let the box go out of their sight for even a minute. It was like watching one of those American movies with the FBI moving files. The only thing missing was armed guards. I half expected the doors to be flung open and half dozen heavily armed secret service men to rush in. We were told that I can look through the test papers in their presence and we cannot make any copies.

There were surprises as I went through the papers. Each question was made up of three segments – first was the question, second was my answer and the third was the Council's crib sheet explaining what was the expected answer for that question. What surprised me and Nancy who was sitting with me was that I had answered all the questions almost exactly as what the Council crib sheet had expected as answer. She furiously scribbled in her note books as much as she could.

'This is a bombshell!' Nancy was over the moon and so was I. I was not as bad as the assessors had made it out to be. I had answered all the questions correctly. There were only one or two points that I had missed. Our calculation showed that I should have scored at least 95% in the test where as I was given only 50%. Unfortunately we were not allowed to copy these and use as evidence.

We were allowed access to the test papers and the documents before being taken away and locked up. Nancy said that there was enough ammunition to sink a ship in those papers. I drove back home much happier than that morning. Finally something is happening which may be a light at the end of the tunnel.

When I finally got home and told Lopa and everyone else, it was as if I had won the case. Gautam felt that it only a matter of days before the case is thrown out. He took me through all the questions and my answers – part of which had been scribbled down by Nancy and copied. She could not write down everything as the council officer was breathing down on her neck.

We drove the next morning hoping we may be coming to the end of this nightmare at long last. Nancy was waiting for us at the front of the building and she looked very happy.

As the chairman wished everyone and asked Fred to start, it was the start of a different kind of battle.

'The position is that the doctor has now reviewed all the medical records. We found some pages, which need to be photocopied. We have got two more cases to look at, which means half a dozen sheets of paper. When that is done, those pages need copying and obviously, Ms Norsworth needs to look at them in advance. We have dealt with the question and answer records, which were made available to us yesterday and this morning. The position with that is – and I had not appreciated it until yesterday – that the GMC insist that we cannot take copies of that. Anyway, we have managed to take instructions on it but it seems to me an intolerable and inexcusable condition to impose. It makes it virtually impossible for the Panel and it makes it very difficult for me and, indeed, for Ms Norsworth because obviously the doctor is going to have this material in front of him in the witness box. Perhaps it is easier for me because I am just going to ask him to take us through it, which is not that difficult because we will have the assessors' report which says what their conclusions were on the questions and answers and then he can tell us what he wrote, but for Ms Norsworth that is not going to be possible. Anyway, that is a difficulty of the GMC's making, not of hers, of course. For the Panel I just cannot see how you can deal with this without a copy of the material.'

That was probably the longest of Fred's outbursts. The legal adviser said that the panel has powers to demand that copies of the documents to be made. Miss Norsworth did not agree.

'I am not sure that it is that simple, I am afraid. I entirely agree and accept the advice that has been given to you that you have inherent powers to make various orders, but it may well be, I do not know, that the GMC claim some kind of privilege over this material. They have a difficulty in that, legally, because having disclosed it in one form, they have effectively waived that and I will so advise them, but as of yesterday my instructions were quite firm that no copies were to be made. I explained to them the difficulties and it was something that I flagged up that it would be a possibility that we could have copies made, that you would all need to see it and that they could then be kept within this room and destroyed afterwards, but at present my instructions are no copies are to be made – something that I will have to go back and take further instructions on.'

I thought she was rambling. The Chairman was not pleased. The situation became so confused that the Chairman decided to take the Panel into "camera" again. That gave us some time to go through the rest of the patient records. We managed to find some more of the 'missing notes' that the assessors had claimed were not there – more operation notes, pre-assessment records and clinic notes.

When we came back, the first thing we all wanted to know was if the Council had given permission for the test papers and answers to be copied. I was made to wait outside in the corridor while the discussions were going on inside.

'The position as informally communicated, I think, to all parties is that I have been given permission to provide copies to everybody within this room of both the questions and marking sheets completed by the assessors for all of the Phase 2 tests and for Mr. Kasyapa's answer sheets for the two written tests that he undertook. They are to be kept, my instructions are, within this room and not removed and in order that details of the questions and answers do not find their way into the public domain, which was the overriding concern of those instructing me, we would ask that when we have any questions about those documents and about those tests that that be *in camera* so that it does not appear on a public transcript although, of course, another transcript will be prepared of it.' Miss Norsworth said.

We saw someone wheel in a large shredder and Miss Norsworth explained that the copies would be shredded in the room once the 'private hearing' was over. Fred wanted to take his copy to our waiting room and discuss the notes with me. He was flatly refused. Finally, it was agreed that he could discuss the notes within the hearing room. I was called in and sworn in again at the witness box.

Fred started with the papers we had found the day before which the assessors had claimed did not exist. The Chairman found it difficult to believe that we had found them the day before.

'May I ask you to pause just a moment so that we can be absolutely clear? Can we just be absolutely clear that the documents you are now taking us through are documents that have been produced by the search of the records yesterday and today?' He asked.

'That is absolutely right, sir.' Fred replied.

The discussion went on for another hour showing the panel all the papers we had found looking through the patient notes the day before. I do not think the panel somehow believed that we had found them.

After lunch, it was going to be the '*Private hearing in camera.*' Shuchi had come for the day, as she was free that weekend. The panel found out that she was a doctor and asked her to leave the room for that part of the hearing. Fred asked permission for Lopa to stay in the room and guaranteed that she was not a medical person.

Fred spent some time explaining to the panel that nature of the papers – Test paper, my answer sheet, and the Council's crib sheet. He went through each of the questions and showed how in each and every question I had answered all the points the Council expected as answers to the questions. I showed how the assessors got at least two of their answers badly wrong – one on local anaesthesia and one on epidural anaesthesia. I was just hoping that not all this was too technical and the panel would understand how wrong the assessors were.

'First thing to say is both of them have given unacceptable for call for help. If you look at flow chart, Mr. Chairman, if you come to the left column of the flow chart, if you look at the top it says clearly:

'Can you see a bleeder,'

and if it was, 'yes" come down:

'Apply clamp, vessel can be isolated'

That is the first thing you do before you call for help. Then if large artery:

'Ask for vascular surgeon's help for repair/ stent/ bypass.'

I do not know why they have not accepted that and said that I have not asked or called for help.' I said

'Mr. Crouper said in terms: "No mention of asking for vascular surgeon?' Fred continued.

'I am fairly sure they obviously have not really read the answer sheet properly.' I hoped my sarcasm was obvious.

The evidence went on in a similar vein throughout showing the Panel how the assessors had completely mis-interpreted my answers and marked them as wrong. Unfortunately, I cannot reveal the details of the rest in this book as the contents of that day is marked 'Private' and is not in public domain.

Miss Norsworth started her cross examination and tried to make holes in my statements using minor points of English used and tried to justify the assessor's marking. The questioning probably took about ten minutes, as she did not have much to go on. She followed that on to the rest of the cross examination she wanted to do. Again there were not many questions she could ask and the hearing was adjourned early that day – about four thirty in the afternoon. We were asked to come back on Monday morning for the Panel questions. The Chairman reminded me again that I was under oath and I should not discuss the case with anyone.

As we walked down to the car, both Nancy and Fred were quite hopeful and wished me a restful weekend. Neither of them was allowed to discuss anything with me. I desperately wanted to ask Fred what he thought of my evidence so far. He probably understood and said.

'You are doing extremely well. I wish I had more clients like you to work with.' and smiled as he left.

The drive back home was less painful being a Saturday evening. Shuchi came home, that made the drive much more pleasant, and we discussed all the issues that had been going on in the council and at work. We reached home quite early and Swayambhu had insisted that we go to his house for dinner that night. It was quite late by the time we had finished dissecting the entire goings on through the week.

I got a call from Nancy that weekend. She wanted me to get some literature on the surgical core knowledge questions. I trawled through the internet and medical search engines and came up with several excellent papers on Epidural Anaesthesia, which clearly showed the complications I had pointed out in my answers and which the assessors had got wrong. I managed to find the NICE guideline, which is the Bible for all doctors in the country, which again did not make any recommendation for thromboprophylaxis for arthroscopy procedures. This was one of the criticisms of the assessors. I also managed to get records from our hospital's Audit, which showed our discharge procedures, and data on my in-patient stay during the period of assessment.

Monday morning was cold, wet, and miserable as can be. It was the seventeenth day of the hearing. It started with Fred wanting to show the documents and discuss the relevance with me. I was again cross-examined by Miss Norsworth. As she did not have much to say, it appeared as if she was going through the motions. It was the turn of the

Panel members to ask me questions. O'Neil was given the exalted role of the only medical person on the panel as the two Specialist Performance Advisers who would have been able to advise the panel had been removed because of bias. This was worrying me significantly.

It was the Reverend who started asking me questions first. He appeared to concentrate on missing dictation and faulty tapes. The way the questioning went, I thought he was trying to help me. However, when he went on to question about the surgeon visits to my unit, I began to doubt that very much. I got the distinct impression that he was implying that I was teaching all these surgeons from this country as well as other countries in Europe for financial gain. For someone who started saying that he does not have much to ask, he went for over an hour, mostly going round in circles with his questions. I wonder if he was trying to trip me up. It was time for lunch break by the time he finished.

O'Neil started after lunch break. Some of his questioning left me worried about his qualifications to be on the panel and even made me wonder if he really knew anything about surgical training in this country. He started with my CV and tried to make out that my grasp of English may not be good as my first language was not English. The dialogue went something like this

'When we are talking about the tests of competence, could possibly suggest a difficulty with the English language, so I just wanted to ask about that to begin with. Is English your first language?' O'Neil asked.

'No, English is not my first language.' I answered.

'Obviously throughout your testimony you have spoken really well and I have been able to understand you really quite a lot, but do you use English at home?'

'With the children obviously because they were born and brought up in this country but with the wife and the rest of the family I use my own language.'

'Working backwards in time you did a Master of Orthopaedic Surgery. Was that work in English?'

'Yes.' There would not be a Master's degree course in Orthopaedics in Liverpool in any other language but English.

'How about your Surgical Fellowship exams?'

'All the qualifications are in English.' What I really wanted to say was that the spoken language as well as language of instruction in Great Britain was English.

'How about your medical degree because that was in Bangalore.'

'English.' I thought this was ridiculous.

'Were you taught medicine in English?' He obviously did not believe me the first time.

'Yes.' I replied.

He went on in a similar vein throughout the morning and well into that afternoon. He tried to imply that I had some sort of business links with one of the surgical companies until Fred intervened. I wish Fred had intervened more often. He implied that I had not really been doing any research and that all the work was done by someone else and I had put my name on the publications. It also turned out that he had two arthroscopies on his knees and had sustained deep vein thrombosis and a clot in his lung. I nearly told his that he should change his surgeon. It was quite late that afternoon when he finished his questioning. It left a bad taste in my mouth and got me severely depressed. It did not appear to be an impartial questioning by any means. It was distinctly antagonistic and I felt that he had already made a decision that I was guilty and trying to find excuses to fit his decision.

It was the turn of the Chairman to ask me questions once Fred had finished. He spent about ten minutes asking me questions mainly on the multidisciplinary nature of our work in hospitals. I did my best to explain this to someone who had probably never been in a hospital in his life except may be as a patient. It was quite late that evening by the time we finished that day. I felt like I had been dragged through a rough mill without an anaesthetic. I was totally drained emotionally and physically. My brain was numb with exhaustion and was beyond any powers of reasoning. The only good thing was the knowledge that the questioning was finished. Now it is up to Fred to collect everything and produce a strong submission.

As we came out to the waiting room, Fred was deep in thought. We sat down for a few minutes, as Fred wanted to clarify some doubts for the submission. I had to sit and answer the questions had even though my brain was completely dead. I had to drag out the information he wanted.

We were bright and early the next day to listen to Fred's submission. There was no one in the office when we reached the waiting room. Nancy and Fred soon joined us. Fred had his usual inimitable smile on his face and he was carrying a large folder with papers full of his remarks in bright red ink. He sat down at the only desk in the room and started to go through the papers and kept asking me many questions and writing some more in red ink. It was nearly half past ten when we were called into the hearing room saying they were ready.

It was only when I reached the room that I found out that the first submission would be from Miss Norsworth and Fred would do his submission afterwards. That deflated me a little for no good reason.

Miss Norsworth started with 'Sir, we have reached the end now, just about, of stage one. As you all know, the only issue that remains for you to decide on the Notice of Hearing is whether or not the conclusions reached by the assessors were warranted; whether their conclusions were valid on the information available to them at that time. I remind you that you are at the fact-finding stage only. You are not looking at what has been done or what may have been done since the time of the assessment, or speculating as to whether or not, were Mr. Kasyapa to be reassessed now, there would be a different outcome, but simply whether the conclusions reached by the assessors were warranted on the information before them.'

She picked out all the 'mistakes' that the assessors had 'identified', expanded, and stressed them as if they were facts. She had completely ignored that we had found the 'missing notes' and 'missing records' and she had completely ignored the blatant blunders done by the assessors while marking the test paper. She insisted that Fred was wrong in assuming that the assessors had got it wrong. They are the 'experts in the field' and if they say I am wrong, I must be wrong. She glossed over the fact that not one of the patients had come to any harm. She said that it was 'by chance' that none of the patients had come to harm. She completely trashed the country wide accepted practice of pre-assessment by Nurses. She insisted that the Assessors were right in that Nurse were not qualified enough to make such decisions and every patient had to be pre-assessed by the consultant. She was trying her best to make me look like a careless and cavalier type of surgeon with very poor surgical skills and knowledge. This went on for the entire morning and it was extremely distressing to listen to. Here she was trashing my character in public and there was nothing I could do to stop her. I was getting angrier and angrier listening to the tirade. She asked the panel to reject my evidence altogether as there were too many 'inconsistencies.'

She finished her submission with an indictment on everything I had done in my career and everything I had believed in;

'The conclusion of the assessors was that there is a deficiency in basic skills and knowledge combined with an environment of what they describe as "conveyor belt surgery", and you may feel that that combination has resulted in the cutting of corners. What is important is not as simple as whether the patient in fact came to any harm but the potential for that. Where that potential is demonstrated, the conclusions reached by the assessors that aspects of Mr. Kasyapa's practice give rise to cause for concern or were judged to be 'unacceptable' are conclusions that, we would submit, are entirely warranted. The conclusions that they came to and the grading that they reached were inevitable on the information that was presented before them. Accordingly, we would suggest that it is inevitable also that you would find that their conclusions on the information presented before you was inevitable and correct.'

I was simply flabbergasted. I could not believe what I was hearing. All that hard work over the previous fifteen years is being flushed down the toilet by this person who does not know her hip replacement from her knee.

Fred started after the coffee break. I wanted to ask Fred lots of questions about Miss Norsworth's submission during the break, but he was too busy with his papers.

He started with a statement to refute some of the allegations made by Miss Norsworth.

'I say it with the greatest respect to Ms Norsworth – there are some grave generalisations in the GMC case as it was put this morning and those generalisations need analysis in detail and I am going to have to do that. For example, in her submission this morning, her comment is "One of numerous examples of situations in which there are no notes. Whatever the reason, ultimately the responsibility lies with the doctor." There are not numerous examples of situations in which there are no notes. There are some examples, some cases where that is alleged and you will have to analyse that second part of the sentence, did the responsibility for the absence of notes lie with Mr. Kasyapa? Generalisations of that kind, in our respectful submission, simply will not help you.

The second thing, before I get to the text here, is to emphasise that there is no challenge to the credibility or probity of Mr. Kasyapa. It has not been said to him that he has been dishonest with the Panel or told lies.

True it is that Ms Norsworth has drawn attention to internal inconsistencies, between the evidence that he gave in relation, for example, to the questions and answers in chief and in cross-examination, but I remind the Panel that one of the reasons for that is that when he answered the questions the first time round he had not seen either the questions or the answers for over two years. When he came to deal with it the second time round we had the text of both the questions and the answers.

The third and final point by way of opening remark is to re-emphasise what Ms Norsworth mentioned I think just but once in the course of her submissions this morning. The burden of proof is on the GMC. It is they that have to satisfy you that the facts that they alleged are the truth. It is they that have to satisfy you that the assessment for the assessors was warranted. It is not for us to disprove it; it is for them to prove it. In our respectful submission, there are no significant discrepancies in the evidence that Mr. Kasyapa gave and, with the greatest respect, the Panel are not in a position to reject any of his evidence. You may reject his explanations, that is a different matter, but the credibility, the honesty with which he gave his answers has not been challenged, not been questioned and is not in doubt.'

With that, he went on to his submission. I am not sure if his rebuttal made any impact on the panel. We will just have to wait and see. He started with unjustified allegations made by Pakshar and Serpe due to pure malice and for which no proof was ever found. He went on to the nature of the assessment itself and said the assessors were assessing a performance in a test rather than assessing my performance as a doctor. He pointed out that the Council's documentation clearly demonstrated that I was never given any information about the nature of the test. He went on to quote an earlier case where the Judge had ruled that;

'to have regard to the track record of the practitioner in the work which he has actually been doing. It is not their function to conduct an examination equivalent to that of a student's examination board. Theoretical questions are relevant only insofar as the answers may throw light on the practitioner's professional performance in the specific areas of work which he has actually been doing.'

He quoted a couple of more similar cases before going on to evidence itself. He went through third party interviews with some of my colleagues who had vouched for me and one of them had said that he would ask for my help in difficult cases – 'When put on the spot he has been more thorough than probably I have been at times. I have asked him to look at a couple of cases that I was not sure about and he has picked up things I have missed. The cases I have operated with Mr. Kasyapa, I have had no concerns with his operating ability. He has got a good pair of hands, and if I had concerns, I would not ask him to help me. In fact, he has been very helpful. When I have struggled with a case he has come straight into theatre to help me ... He has got a good pair of hands. I would say he is probably above average.'

He then went through the investigations done by the trust as well as the regional adviser in surgery who had not found any truth in the allegations. He took them through the test papers and my answers and again pointed out the mistakes made by the assessors. He pointed out to the wide discrepancies in marking by the two assessors, which was often diametrically opposite to one another.

He pointed to the extensive experience I have had with major surgery and said 'Justified or not, the GMC have failed to prove that the assessment insofar as B78 is concerned is warranted in relation to his actual practice. There is no basis to conclude that he lacked basic skills or knowledge in practice. If he had lacked them, it is inconceivable that no evidence would have emerged to suggest it over eleven years and 3,000 major joint replacement surgeries or, indeed, before that.'

His submission was going on quite well I thought. First part of the submission went on up to lunchtime. He continued after lunch break.

He went through point by point of Miss Norsworth's allegations and the assessors assumptions, particularly the missing notes 'We have to say that the discovery of the operation notes in two cases, and indeed a discovery of many other notes that are relevant to issues in this case, shows that the assessors made their allegation on a false premise without taking care to ensure that they were right.'

He pointed out on more than one occasion the unhelpfulness of the Council. 'We have to say that the discovery of the operation notes in two cases, and indeed a discovery of many other notes that are relevant to issues in this case, shows that the assessors made their allegation on a false premise without taking care to ensure that they were right.'

He went on taking each of the cases that the assessors had found fault with and demonstrated how wrong they were in each and every one of them. There was a counter submission by Miss Norsworth. I was disappointed to find out that Fred will not have a chance for rebuttal. The day finished with the Legal Assessor giving out his long-winded, 'advise.' The day was adjourned with a statement from the Chairman saying that the panel secretary would be in touch on developments. That was the first time he actually said 'thank you' for my time.

Nancy said that they will probably take the whole of next day to go through the transcripts and papers before making a decision. She said it is unlikely that we will get a determination until Thursday afternoon, as it has never been known to have determination before lunchtime on any day.

We made our way back to the car park and drove back home weary and tired out of our minds. Despite Nancy trying to cheer us up with, "After that evidence, it is difficult to see how this panel can give a decision against you", I was not in any mood to speak to engage in conversation with anyone. Nancy had said that she would get in touch with me and keep me up to date with any developments. Both Nancy and Fred were going to stay back in Manchester awaiting developments.

Nancy called the next afternoon with some developments. The Council had the headings of the charges against me wrong. Nancy tried to explain the intricacies of the legal arguments that had taken place that morning in my absence. I could not make head or tail of it. I said, 'I will leave it to you and Fred to agree whatever is right and act on it. I will be guided by your advice.'

'Don't worry. It is just legal wording of the charges and the change of rules etc. It is going to be a couple of days before we get a determination. I would put it out of your mind and carry on with your life.' Nancy said. It is easier said than done. Every time the phone rang, my heart was missing a beat and I was stressed out tremendously. I was not sure how long I could cope with this pressure and enormous strain. It was Friday afternoon by the time I got the call from Nancy. 'We have been asked to be available tomorrow morning.' My heart was pounding as I took the call.

'What do you think Nancy? Do you have any idea how they are going to go?' I asked.

'I think we have an excellent case. I have never seen a more open and shut case before. Your evidence and Fred's demonstration of the assessors cock ups should swing the case for us.' Poor Nancy. I think she was trying to cheer me up.

We reached Manchester well on time, as the traffic was very quiet on Saturday morning. We even had time to go to the local Starbuck's to have a coffee before walking down to the Council offices. Only to find out that the panel was not ready. We were told that we were excused until noon. Nancy just looked at me and smiled as if to say, 'What did I tell you?' Both Lopa and I decided to take in the shopping delights of Manchester in Piccadilly and walked over. Lopa said she would get in touch if there were any developments. We had an early lunch and sauntered back to the Council offices by twelve only to be told that they were not ready yet. We hung around until about three in the afternoon before we were called back into the room. My heart was pounding and mouth was dry as I walked down those corridors to the hearing room.

There, I found that Miss Norsworth has been replaced by Sykes again. I also found a stranger in the room. I asked Nancy who it was. It turned out to be a reporter for a News Agency. This made matters worse. If I get a bad result today, it will be out in every newspaper tomorrow morning.

To say it was very disappointing listening to the determination would be an understatement. The panel agreed with everything that Miss Norsworth had said and said that the Assessors were right in every one of their criticisms. They said that they have relied on the 'expert assessors" and that 'The Panel notes that the defence has not called expert witnesses to challenge the experts' evidence on which the Panel has relied.' They looked at the test papers and said 'The Panel has looked behind the conclusions and supporting statements and is satisfied that the Assessment Team were correct in concluding that overall your performance in the surgery core knowledge test was unacceptable.' I could not believe what I was hearing. They upheld every allegation made by the Council and asked Sykes to make any submission on behalf of the Council and for Fred to make his submission.

Both of them said that the determination was very lengthy and they would need time to read it before making any submissions. As we walked out of the room, my hands were trembling and I was livid with rage. Fred calmed me down and said we will discuss in the room.

As soon as I entered the room, Fred said.

'I might as well have not been there at all. They have completely ignored my submission. They have not even bothered to acknowledge one part of my submission. This cannot be happening. I am very sorry Upaas. This is not what I was expecting.'

'I don't know what the hell happened there. I am disgusted. This is gross mis-carriage of justice. Fred, you cannot allow them get away with this. I think we have to call a halt and take the Council and these panelists to court.' It was an outburst that surprised even me.

'I know you are upset. We will not let them get away with it if I can help it. I think we will have to decide what we are going to next. The Panel obviously want to go on to the next stage now. I am not sure that is good idea with you being upset.' Fred said

'I think we need time to organise our defence and our witnesses. I don't want to start the next stage now.' Nancy agreed. 'We are not prepared.'

I was quite taken aback. I had not expected this. How can I go back and face hose three people in the room who I have no respect for now? I might say things to them, which might make it worse. I told Fred that there was no way I am going back into that room that day as I might say or do something which would not be politically correct.

'I agree with you. Leave it with me. I'll tackle them and we will come back to fight another day.' Fred said.

I just sat down in the chair. I could see tears welling up in Lopa's eyes. I was not going to show my despair to anyone. Nancy said that we should leave and get some rest and we will discuss the next course of action over the phone. I just gathered my papers and left along with Lopa. The trip back home must have been the longest one I have done of all the trips from Manchester. It was very quiet during the trip. Neither of us had much to say to each other. Thousands of things were going through my mind. Most of it was rage. Lopa called up Swayambhu and Gautam and updated them of the situation. Within minutes of coming home, Gautam was at the door with Yadavi. He spent a long time trying to console Lopa and me. Soon afterwards, Swayambhu came home with Pavaki. I had all my friends at home and still felt completely alone. We spent some time talking about who should be called as my witness. It was finally decided that I should concentrate on as many senior consultant Orthopaedic surgeons as possible and call on John Fitzgerald, the Chief executive of the trust as my witness.

It was not until Sunday afternoon when I found out what happened after we left. Apparently, the Panel was a bit surprised that I could not continue. They were quite happy when Fred suggested that they use the Sunday as a "Reading day", to go through an independent audit done on my work by John Worthing. This was an audit commissioned by the

Seaport Trust. The hearing was adjourned to a date to be decided later. That meant another wait for God knows how long.

It was the following Monday, when I got the call from Nancy.

'I am really disgusted at the outcome Upaas. I am really sorry. I have spoken to Dr Smiths and Fred and we have to prepare for the next stage. The panel have completely ignored our submission. I have never come across such a warped decision-making in my life. We have to produce our witnesses for the next stage.' She suggested that 'We should call John Fitzgerald, the Chief executive of the Trust who has been very supportive of you and also the Medical Director and George Cooley your supervisor at present. If you can think of any character witnesses, it would be very useful.'

I was quiet for a minute before speaking 'How can the panel say that we did not produce any expert witnesses to refute the Council's experts. I thought we were not allowed to produce any witnesses during the last stage?' I was referring to the Panel's statement that they are agreeing with the Council's experts, as we had not produced any of our own experts.

'I don't understand that. It is quite clear in the rules that we are not allowed to produce witnesses during the "fact finding stage.' Nancy replied.

'I really think we should take this panel to court. There has been a gross mis-carriage of justice.' I insisted.

'I don't think we can do that Upaas. No one has done that in the past. I will have to look into it. In the mean time, can you give me names and contact details of people you want to call as witnesses please?'

'I will do that. Let me think about it over the next few days.' I replied.

The decision on who to call as a witness was going to be a difficult one. I had a lot of friends and a lot of acquaintances. I wanted someone who would show me in a good light, both professionally and personally. At the same time, it would be embarrassing to say the least to ask my friends to come and give statements on my behalf. Lopa had some ideas as to who to call and suggested that we should discuss with Gautam before making a decision. That night we all got together over a bottle of wine and started to work out who best to call.

'I think you should get as many of senior respected orthopaedic surgeons as possible. I remember you helped out Howard Menzies some time ago with a case. He is a highly respected very senior surgeon and he does not mince his words. I know that he has high regard for you.' Gautam started off.

'That is a very good idea. I'll speak to him tomorrow at the clinic.' Swayambhu said.

'We have to get George Cooley and he is one of the senior most in the country. We will be asking John Worthing as he is the only one who has done an independent audit on my work and he is a senior high volume surgeon experienced in hip and knees.' I said.

'You need someone who can vouch for your training.' Gautam continued.

'I can ask Douglas Rayner who was my trainer when I was a registrar and he has worked with me in the recent past as well. We can ask Simon Bridge from Marsden on Sea where I spent my sabbatical with. You cannot get anyone senior than that. He is the advisor to the Royal College of Surgeons, advisor to the British orthopaedic Association and he is also the STC chairman for the London region.' I replied.

'You need someone from your theatres, outpatients, and wards to tell them about your work in those areas.' Pavaki said.

'I can call on the senior sisters to be witnesses.' I replied.

'Upaas, you have a vast base of support. People will queue to say good things about you. I think we should get a large delegation of your patients and supporters in the hospital to demonstrate in front of the Council.' Swayambhu was getting rather emotional I thought. I can just see the furore something like that would cause at the Council offices. I had my doubts about the efficacy of such a venture with the present panel.

We finally decided that I would approach as many people as possible for help. The thought of talking to many people with literally a begging bowl in my hand asking for help filled me with dread. However, I had no other option if I wanted to save my career. Already it appeared to be in tatters and was heading towards complete destruction. If I wanted to look after my family and support my children, I will have to suffer this humiliation in public. Sanvi and Akshaj were still at the university and they were still a long way from finishing their education. After that, I had to get all three of them married. That needed money and if I do not have a job, there is no way any of that would be possible. If I do not do this, I would be rapidly heading towards destitution.

I called Nancy next day to apprise her of the list of names I wanted to call.

'Upaas. I do not think they will let you call more than four or five people as witnesses. They are very fussy about it.' Nancy said. My heart sank at that and got quite angry.

'They tell me we have not called any witnesses and when we want call witnesses, they are putting restrictions on it. I have a good mind to call the newspapers and tell them of what I think of as an obstruction of justice.'

'I can understand your frustration. At the same time, we do not want to upset the panel. At the end of the day, they are the ones who will be making a decision on impairment.' She said. There you have it. The council holds all the cards. There is no way of winning the battle. It was utterly sickening. We are at the mercy of these three individuals who have shown themselves to be incompetent and incapable of understanding the workings of the health service and appeared to be downright unreasonable. They can do what they please with complete impunity. I had to decide on whittling down a list of about twenty people down to about six or seven people to tell the GMC about me.

22. The final stage or is it?

Unknown to me there was a groundswell of support from the hospital. My friends in the operating theatre, had taken upon themselves, to raise a petition, and they had already collected a couple of hundred signatures, before I found out. This was the time when I found out who were my real friends. Helen and Sinnie had taken the lead to collect the signatures. The process was not straight forward as there were elements within the hospital who were actively dissuading anyone signing the petition. There was also scaremongering going on with threats of losing their jobs. When they showed me the petition, and I read the names on the list, tears welled up in my eyes, and I had difficulty controlling myself. The entire episode was extremely moving and brought my faith in humanity back. Quite few of the people who had signed the petition were unknown to me personally. It ranged from Hospital porters to administrators, and there were nurses and doctors of wide specialties from my own to surgery, gynaecology, anaesthesia, out patients, physiotherapy, radiology, and the list goes on. They told me that they were going en masse to the Chief executive's office and submit the petition.

I called Nancy that night and told her about the petition. She was extremely enthusiastic about the petition.

'That is fantastic. Can you ask them to send a copy to the GMC or better still address it to the panel?' She asked.

'I could do that. My only worry was that it might get lost, in the GMC or the Panel might altogether ignore it. Can Fred not produce, the petition as evidence? I replied.

'I see your point. Let me speak to Fred and find out the best way to introduce the petition. It should be seen as independent and not instigated by you.'

'It is independent. I did not know about it till today, and they have been collecting signatures for over a while now'. I was rather indignant at the suggestion, that this petition was anything but independent.

'Don't get me wrong. You have seen the panel. So far they have not believed anything Fred has told them, and I would not be surprised, if they would find a way to ignore this, as well. We have to make sure that it is independent. I don't want you to have anything to do with it.'

Nancy was being defensive. 'I will speak to Fred about this and get back to you.'

Next day there was yet another surprise when I got to work. Helen came with a sheaf of papers in her hand neatly stored in a file.

'What is this?' I asked.

'These are statement made by your friends here on your behalf to the GMC. They have written to the Chief Executive of the hospital, and these are copies of the letters'. Helen said smiling.

There were 32 letters in the file. I did not what to say. This was overwhelming. I took the file gratefully and sat down to read them. I could not believe my eyes when I saw the names in those letters. It included senior figures such as the Clinical director of anaesthesia, Clinical director of the Cancer services and consultants from neighbouring hospitals. There were also several letters from some of my patients.

It was not long before the GMC sent me the date for the next stage. It would be December and in London. They were going to go sit from 20th to 24th December, 2008. It would be a delightful Christmas present I thought. If the decision goes against me, it would be my worst Christmas ever. December has not been my lucky month for the last few years. This nightmare had started in December 2003, 5 years ago.

There was another call from Nancy that night.

'Did you get the notification about the dates for the next stage of the hearing?'

'Yes. I have just this morning. How are we going to arrange for my witnesses, to attend the hearing?'

'Leave that to me. All you have to do is to speak to them and get their permission for me to write to them or speak to them. I will arrange the logistics of dates etc.' Nancy said.

'Will the MPS, pay for their travel and costs? I was rather anxious that my friends should not be out of pocket on my behalf. There was no way I could afford to pay for their travel.

'Yes. All the travel and expenses would be paid for by the MPS. I would not worry.' Nancy replied. I was grateful for that. I will never crib about the fees that I pay to the defence organisation again. It must have cost them a fortune by now.

It took me a lot of introspection and thinking before I plucked up enough courage to speak to all the people 'selected' to act as my witness. I decided to speak to some people over the phone, and some of them would be better off speaking to them personally rather than over the phone. It was a highly embarrassing and humiliating task. It took me the whole of that week and weekend before I could get everyone. All of them were more than willing to act as a witness, and they tried to make me feel at ease as much as they could do. That just made it worse. It was emotionally draining, and I was not sure how long I could put up with emotional stress. Some of my friends suggested that I should see my GP and get some help. For me, that would be accepting defeat – may not be in the fight with the GMC but with myself. After a fair bit of nagging from my friends, I did make an appointment to see my GP. That was a stressful visit with my extremely friendly doctor. He was obviously terribly sympathetic and went through the assessment in detail. He finally said that I was "depressed" and gave me a prescription of anti-depressants.

I had friends with me for every visit I made to the GMC during the hearing. This time Yadavi decided to accompany us to London. The trip to London was another ordeal. As we set off, I stopped at the petrol station for some fuel. I started to fill the tank in when I suddenly realised the mistake. I was filling in petrol into a Diesel tank. I stopped as soon as I realised the mistake. However, it was the last straw. I simply do not know how I did not break down at that point. Getting this sorted out would take some time and I was due to appear first thing next morning at the GMC. Yadavi called Gautam and explained the situation. He came immediately, and asked me to take his car, and he will get my car sorted out later. By the time, we got the car into the garage it was nearly ten at night, and I had to do a 300-mile drive to London. It was 3'O clock in the morning by the time we got to the rental apartment.

I could not sleep that night even though I was dead tired and exhausted. We took the tube to Euston and walked along to the GMC offices on Euston road. I called George Cooley to make sure he was on his way. He had already landed at Heathrow and was on his way in a taxi. He had to return that night as he had commitments for the rest of the week. I did not want to miss him, as he was one of my crucial witnesses. By the time we walked into the waiting room at the GMC, George was already there and was sitting sipping a cup of coffee.

'Hi George. I am extremely glad you could make it. I honestly appreciate your help.'

'Glad to Old boy. Anything to get you over this nightmare. Tell me, what is the drill?' George said with a smile on his face. Nancy had already introduced herself to George by then.

'We would like to get you on the stand first so that you can shoot off this afternoon. We will have to wait for Fred to come and discuss with the GMC counsel before we start.' Nancy said.

George saw Lopa sitting in the corner alone and went to speak to her.

'Hi Lopa. How are you? I would not worry about this thing. We will get Upaas through this. I have a suspicion that this is only a formality. He has so much support that the GMC cannot do anything but clear his name. It is all a big misunderstanding I am sure.' George was yet another eternal optimist, I thought. Lopa gave a faint smile and said.

'Thank you for those kind words. How are Jane and the children? She asked.

'They are fine. We were supposed to be flying off tomorrow on holiday to Sicily. It is a cycling holiday. I don't know how I am going to cope with all that.' he said with a laugh. Just then, Fred walked through the door. It turned out he had been in the GMC since early that morning. He did not have very far to travel as he had an apartment in London, as well. I introduced George to him.

'I am extremely grateful you could make it Mr. Cooley. Can we just have a couple of words before we start? I have had to take a special dispensation from the GMC to put you on stand first. They were insisting on getting Upaas first on the stand.' George said. He took him along to a neighbouring room to discuss the obvious strategies and questioning. George appeared to be lot more happy and at ease with himself after that discussion. It was nearly ten before we were called in.

The room in the London offices of GMC was remarkably similar to that in Manchester. The same rectangular shaped room with same drab furniture and set up. We might as well have been in Manchester. As we all settled down the discussion started and there was more drama. The Chairman asked for details of the position of the defence. George stood up to reply.

'Thank you, sir. The position is that today we have Mr. Kasyapa and Mr. Cooley. I propose to call Mr. Cooley first because he has come down from Seaport especially so he can go back. Tomorrow we have Mr. Gautam, Mr. Menzies and Mr. Rayner, and on Monday Mr. Fitzgerald, Mr. Worthing and Mr. Bridge, It would have been nice if we could have got them all in on Saturday, and the Sunday but the last weekend before Christmas with witnesses coming from Seaport has proved simply impossible. Nevertheless, the witnesses on each day are going to be relatively short, so I am optimistic, touch wood, that we will complete the evidence by lunch time on Monday.' Fred said.

The Chairman was not particularly happy. He wanted to know if those witnesses who could not come that weekend could be interviewed over the telephone. We had decided a long time ago that we have to resist interviews over the telephone, as it would not be as effective. The problem with getting everyone to London was only three-week's notice of the hearing was given to us. The GMC obviously is not aware of the way Health Service works, where everyone needs to give a minimum of six week's notice, to be away from work.

'I have to say that, I would have thought, that unless there is some really unforeseen difficulty, I cannot see how Mr. Fitzgerald, Mr. Worthing, and Mr. Bridge are going to take more than to lunch time on Monday. I know for a fact that those three just cannot be here over the weekend because of other commitments that they have.' Fred continued.

'Forgive me for interrupting. Do you know the nature of these commitments?' The Chairman interrupted.

'From Mr. Fitzgerald, Mr. Worthing, and Mr. Bridge? I personally do not, but Ms Charlston does because I know she has been working on it, since we were given the intimation of the dates for hearing from the GMC'. Fred replied. The Chairman did not appear to be happy with that explanation. I could not believe how this panel expected, such busy people, as a Chief Executive of a Trust or senior Orthopaedic Consultant, drop everything at a short notice, and come running for the convenience of the Panel.

The next problem was the objection from the GMC counsel about the number of witnesses we were producing. The Chairman turned to the GMC counsel and asked him for his comment.

'I do, yes. When we adjourned last time, we were told by the defence that there were going to be four witnesses. It was on that basis that we set aside four days so that we could conclude these proceedings, which is in everybody's interests, including of course Mr. Kasyapa's. We are now told that there are a number of other witnesses, some of whom cannot be here until Monday.' He clearly was not happy at the number of witnesses we were producing.

The Chairman suddenly decided to everyone's surprise that the panel would go into *camera*.

It was Sykes, who asked, 'Can I just ask: what is the application because at the moment you are not actually confronted with an application, except for a possible application tomorrow for an adjournment. I query what you are deciding.'

The Chairman explained that he had to discuss that morning's issues with his colleagues in the panel. In addition, obviously it had to be done in secret.

There we are. After about half an hour of what appeared to be wrangling and more waste of time about waste of time, we were asked to wait while the panel discuss in secret. We trooped out to the waiting room and again trooped back about forty-five minutes later. The Chairman made a long-winded statement, essentially laying the blame of the problem entirely on our legal team. He said that there is no need to call the witnesses to be present and that telephone interview would be sufficient except Mr. Bridge. That was not what I wanted to hear, and I was already having doubts about the outcome of this stage. Fred stood up.

'I am afraid that is simply not satisfactory. I do appreciate the kindness of Mr. Sykes's offer to agree the evidence, but Mr. Kasyapa wants you to hear from these witnesses in person. This is a question of whether or not he is currently fit to practise, and it is a crucial matter for him. He wants to leave no stone unturned and, in my respectful submission, that is an entirely reasonable position for him to take. I appreciate the time constraints. I am also conscious I am taking time as I speak now. I appreciate the time constraints, but this is not a case where there is any question of danger to the public; it is a question of justice for Mr. Kasyapa, and justice has to be seen to be done as well as being done. Mr. Kasyapa wants you to hear these witnesses in person. In our respectful submission, the difficulties posed by a hearing on the last Saturday and Sunday before Christmas are as they are. When we agreed the dates, all the legal teams were available, and here they are. We hoped that the witnesses would be available on Saturday and Sunday. The reality is that, in fact, they are not. That is the way it is. I am still optimistic that the matter can be dealt with. If, ultimately, it cannot be dealt with, well, that is truly unfortunate; it is particularly unfortunate for Mr. Kasyapa, but that is a burden he is prepared to shoulder. It does, respectfully, seem to me that the burden is far greater for him than for anyone else – the GMC, the public or indeed those of us who are here, to deal with the matter sitting round this table'. I could see Fred was getting more and irritated as he went on. All the Chairman could say for that was

'Thank you, Mr. Barnard. I am going to ask the Legal Assessor if he has any advice at this stage.'

It was time for Sykes to take the stage and come out with what the GMC wanted to do with me. My heart was in my mouth as he started. It was again rather long-winded statement and went on for about half an hour. He detailed the determination that was given by the panel already at the end of the last stage, and he then went on to describe, what was given in the GMC's Good Medical Practice guide. He quoted a couple of past cases where the judgement was made against the Doctor, and finished his submission by saying,

'It effectively means that you must look at the doctor's current practice as to the question of impairment. It is for that reason that I will not be objecting to any material, which Mr. Barnard wishes to put forward which is relevant to that issue. Having said that, you must still be careful, if I may so submit, to distinguish between what is pure testimonial evidence, such as 'I had a jolly good operation and I am very grateful to Mr. Kasyapa' and evidence which does actually go specifically to the question of his current practice. That evidence is plainly relevant to the question of whether Mr. Kasyapa's practice is currently impaired or not.'

Interesting choice of words, I thought. I had always thought that the aim of any physician's treatment is to make the patient better. Here, he is telling everyone that is not good enough. It was time for another break. As we filed back into the waiting room, understandably George was getting rather impatient.

'What is going on guys?'

'It is time for yet another break, and I think you will be called next'. I replied.

Fred took him aside to have another word with him about his statement that had been produced to the panel and his evidence.

It was nearly 12'O clock by the time George was sworn in. As we went back into the hearing room, the first thing we heard was that the GMC would not be producing any witnesses at this stage.

George was asked about his CV and how long he had known me. We went back to when I was a registrar in the 80's and George was a Senior Lecturer at the University. I did some work with him researching the biomechanics of elbow. He had helped me with my career in various stages, and we had developed a close friendship since then. All this came out during Fred's questioning. Fred also took him through the last eighteen months during which time; he had been nominated as a 'Supervisor' by the Interim Order's Panel. The GMC had decided that I was not safe to practice on my own without a supervisor as soon as the assessors had made the.

George reassured the panel that I had adhered to all the conditions that GMC had set out through the Interim Orders Panel. Fred specifically asked him about my Basic surgical skills and knowledge.

'Mr. Cooley, criticism was made of his basic surgical skill. Now, you have seen him actually operate. Does he lack basic surgical skill?' Fred asked.

'I think one of the important points is that surgery, since I became a consultant 24 years ago, has changed in that, we are no longer generalists, and we are now single limb surgeons or single joint surgeons, and so the repertoire of procedures is very narrow now, and the procedures that we carry out during those surgeries are relatively narrow. Certainly Mr. Kasyapa, does not lack any surgical skill in carrying out the techniques, required to perform the variety of operations he does.' George replied

'The assessors also came to the conclusion that he lacked basic surgical knowledge. From your observation of him over the last year and judging the position as it is today, does he lack basic surgical knowledge?' Fred continued.

'I have not certainly seen any evidence of that and so maybe the assessors --- I do not ..' George hesitating a bit with his words.

'No need to speculate.' Fred prompted

'I have not seen any evidence that he lacks basic surgical knowledge. I think quite the contrary actually; one or two of my colleagues would wish they could perform procedures the way he does and have said that to me.' George finished.

The session with Fred was finished with a statement

'I have never had any doubt about his fitness to practise in the work I have seen him carry out. I think that an impression may have been gained by some that he rushed surgical procedures, but I think in fact what I would like the panel to understand is that we all work differently and he is very efficient during surgery. His moves are efficient; he only picks up instruments he is going to use, not like some of us who pick them up and put them down and then choose another one. I think that that is why he is able I think to safely carry out a volume of work where others would struggle. In the outpatient clinic, I am impressed by the demeanour of the nursing staff as much as anything in that if everyone is happy and smiling and there is a relaxed atmosphere, which is the sort of clinic where I think patients relax and information can be exchanged better and people understand what is going on. I think the general impression I have gained is that, particularly during the last 18 months I have been looking closely at him, his practice is perfectly satisfactory.'

He looked at the panel Chairman before continuing.

'Yes. I might add that I think if colleagues ask you to treat them or members of their family, then it does imply a great deal of confidence and this remains today that he is consulted by colleagues and their families. I might also add that the two colleagues who were acting as mentor and supervisor have benefited from his experience recently on one or two cases I recall, one in particular, when one of my colleagues was having difficulty carrying out a hemi-arthroplasty on an elderly patient with a fracture; he then asked his other colleagues to help and both of them were in a lot of trouble, and finally Mr. Kasyapa was summoned and sorted it out. I was quite impressed with that. That is a case about two months ago. They know who to send for when they are in trouble.' He finished and that was about the time the Chairman decided that it was time for lunch break.

He reminded George that he was still under oath and that he is not allowed to discuss anything with anyone. It was Sykes's turn after lunch to grill George.

He concentrated on what I would do once the hearing finishes. He wondered, whether I would go back to the 'bad old days of doing a lot of operating.' He tried to discredit George's testimony by saying that he did not know anything about the allegations against me and he concentrated on that case of suspected Sudeck's dystrophy.

It was left to Fred to try to build it back up again. He started with the case of Sudeck's.

'Mr. Sykes has asked you about this Sudeck's dystrophy case. I think we had better look just very briefly at the notes in view of his questions. I think it might have been a case that you were involved in. Sir, this is C4 at page 96. Just to give you the background about this, there is no dispute, this was a lady who had been brought into the hospital on 29 May after a car crash in which she had suffered a series of injuries: fractures of left ribs and pneumothorax trauma, chest drain inserted, and so forth and so on. Then we have a note here on page 96A on 6 June 2006. Can you just read to us what that says?' Fred asked.

'Her left clavicle seems to be displaced since the original chest X-ray. If this is confirmed by X-ray examination of the left clavicle, then if she is fit for a GA, I would hope to be able to internally fix left clavicle tomorrow.' So I was suggesting another X-ray, and then if it was displaced, fixation. So I obviously did not think that she had Sudeck's.' George replied.

'Could I ask you to repeat that? You obviously ..' Chairman interrupted.

'I did not think she had Sudeck's atrophy or else I would not have made that comment.' George continued as if he was not interrupted.

'If you go to page 101B, we see that she was admitted on 12 July 2006 and was 'seen by Mr. Kasyapa and Mr. Schmidt – admitted for assessment by anaesthetist and? ..' Fred looked at George questioningly.

'Open reduction and internal fixation – '(ORIF) – left clavicle.'

'What was her condition then in July?' Fred asked.

'Again, Mr. Schmidt is a colleague of ours who like me specialises in upper limb surgery. So it would appear that Mr. Kasyapa and Mr. Schmidt felt that open reduction and internal fixation was required or was advisable if she was judged safe to carry out a general anaesthetic.' George replied.

'What, if anything, does that say about Sudeck's dystrophy?'

'Again, I do not think it could have been clinically overt at that time or else --- I think Mr. Kasyapa and Mr. Schmidt saw this patient again by the looks of it in that note.'

'Mr. Schmidt, what is his specialty?'

'Upper limb surgery.' George replied.

'I think we know from the notes that this lady was his patient. The operation was carried out on 20 July. We have that in another volume, page 99 of the main notes: exploration and trimming of left clavicle was carried out by Mr. Kasyapa.'

'Excision and debridement, yes. I see it. I think the Sudeck's atrophy was probably secondary to immobility as a consequence of her original injury. That then developed. I think that was the sequence of events by the looks of it. It was a secondary problem that developed later. You see, Sudeck's atrophy is a condition that does occur in response to injuries after a period of time. One of the important ways of avoiding or treating early Sudeck's atrophy is to start vigorously moving a limb in which it develops as soon as possible, so urgent physiotherapy is a way to treat the so-called regional sympathetic dystrophy; i.e. Sudeck's atrophy. It would seem to me, just reading this, that this lady had a problem, she had a clavicular fracture; she was not able to use her arm and later Sudeck's atrophy developed. I think it is perhaps unfair to say that she had full blown Sudeck's atrophy and then somebody did an operation on her arm.' George replied.

'Mr. Cooley, forgive me for interrupting. I am wondering what this is all about, frankly.' The Chairman interrupted. He obviously did not like to be told that the assessors got it badly wrong'.

That conveniently led on to the questioning by the panel members themselves. O'Neil confined himself to Audit and my database. He could not get much out of it. The reverend tried his hand on some of the basic surgical skills.

'You say that you observed Mr. Kasyapa's work in operating theatre, et cetera, and without his knowledge. Quite simply: you must have observed him there doing a tendon repair?' He wanted to know

'No. It is not something he would do in his elective practice, a tendon repair' George replied.

'I am sorry to interrupt you. Would it be true to say that you only attended ..' Reverend interrupted.

'No, I went to his trauma list as well but I never saw him do a tendon repair. We rarely have to carry that out as an orthopaedic surgeon.' George continued.

'But not never?' The reverend persisted.

'Not never, no. It is rare. We are dealing with really surgery of the limbs and the tendons that require repairing are often in the hands. If we had tendon problems in the hands, they would routinely go to the plastic surgical unit in the Royal Victoria Infirmary.' George replied.

"How about presumably you observed him knotting?' Reverend continued his questioning.

'Yes, of course we do.'

'Is he a good knotter?' I got a distinct impression that the panel was just having some fun. There was no intention of getting at the truth.

'Yes, fast.' George replied.

'He does good knots?' Reverend would not let it go.

'Yes. He does tie good knots. I can reassure you about that. The only trouble is in the fishing manuals they have a thing they call a surgeon's knot that I struggle with but surgeons never use it.' George tried to make light of the situation as well.

They then tried to make light of my preoperative templating and planning. Both the Reverend as well as the Chairman took one of the trauma lists that I had done a couple of months ago.

'Can you just go a little further on to 18 August? On the basis of what I said a moment ago that actually what I am interested in is how much time was spent in theatre, i.e. how much energy is expended, and how tired someone might become, you would agree, though, would you, that there are six procedures which Mr. Kasyapa has attended?' The Reverend asked.

'Yes, these are trauma procedures. I think he would be certainly sitting for the ankle fracture. The hemi-arthroplasty operations, that is half the joint, they are relatively short procedures.' George replied.

'To someone who winces at just reading the titles of what this might involve surgically, that seems to me like a pretty big day's work.' The Reverend insisted.

'You have two experienced people. Mr. Shekhar, I have got to say that he worked with me for a year, it is like having a consultant colleague working with you, and so if you are assisting him ..' The Reverend would let George finish his answer.

'I totally accept what you are saying and I totally accept the implication of what you are saying. My interest in a way, and there are a number of others I could take you to but I will not detain you any further, and my point is that whether he is assistant or primary, he is still doing six procedures here and spending six lots of time on longer and shorter cases.'

'Yes. They were trauma, so that was not the elective planned list. Those were patients requiring surgery.' George tried to tells them the trauma case had to be operated on no matter how many there were.

'Sure, but as for the pressure, as you said yourself, it is up to every surgeon to self-regulate. So presumably even under the conditions that now exist from the Interim Orders Panel and so on and so forth, Mr. Kasyapa is still doing on occasions a very long day's work?' The Reverend did not seem to understand the implications of 'Trauma' and 'Emergency.' How could he? He had never worked in a hospital and probably the only link with any hospital would be as a patient or a visitor.

'You would not want to put any of those patients off, as it were, those six; they were not elective patients. They need their operations.' George tried to make him understand.

'I fully accept that. The point I am making is a very narrow and simple one and I think you have got my drift.' He would not let go. I had given up hope of him understanding the working of hospitals and treating emergency patients by now.

'Yes.' George replied. I think he had given up as well. It was getting late for his flight and rushed off to Heathrow. It was my turn for more inquisitions after yet another coffee break. George had to rush to catch flight back home. Nancy had arranged for a taxi to be ready outside and he literally ran to the taxi. He barely managed to catch the flight with a few minutes to spare.

We settled back to the routine again after that bit of excitement. Fred took me through the period since the assessment was finished and the Interim Orders Panel had imposed restrictions on my practice eighteen months ago. We went through the interminable monthly meetings with the 'Support group' consisting of a Supervisor, mentor and the clinical director. Our service manager used to attend those meetings and kept minutes diligently. He took me through those notes and tried to impress on the panel that I had stuck to the instructions of the Interim Order's Panel. I had attended the Basic Surgical Skills course run by the Royal college of Surgeons and came out with flying colours. I had spent three weeks with Mr. Bridge at Marsden on Sea on a sabbatical and again had come out with an impressive report. Mr. Bridge was an extremely senior and highly respected Hip and Knee surgeon in the country. He would be giving evidence to this panel hopefully in the next couple of days.

He was so impressed with me that he came up to visit me and spend the whole day observing my operating and did a Procedure Based Assessment of the cases, as prescribed by the Royal College of Surgeons, that day. He gave an excellent report at the end of that day.

He took me through the pre-assessment procedure for joint replacements as I had developed it over the years. I tried to impress on the panel that I was one of the pioneers of this type of pre-assessment, which was now being followed widely by others not only in this country but also in other countries in Europe.

He then took me through the trauma list the Reverend had criticised earlier.

'Is this a sort of typical trauma list?' Fred asked showing me the list for 18th August, which was criticised earlier.

'No, it is not a typical trauma list. I remember that week. We had a very large number of admissions. We had to get through quite a lot of cases. Luckily, as Mr. Cooley was saying, I have Shekhar working with me and he is an extremely experienced chap. If he is actually doing a case, my work actually is very minimal. I just hold the retractor and he does most of the work. I think we finished probably about 7 o'clock that day in the unit. That was one of the beauties of a trauma list, there is no end point. You keep going until it is finished. Unfortunately, if you leave any of these case to the next day, two things happen: one, they become unwell and you cannot operate on them and the chances are they will never get better; and also there is plenty of evidence to show that particularly the elderly ladies with fractured hips, if you leave them for more than 24 hours for any other reason apart from medical reasons, the outcome is very poor. Therefore, we want to operate on them in the first 24 hours of admission. You try to do them as much as possible. Other fractures such as ankles fractures, if you leave it for 24 hours, you will not be able to operate on them because the ankle swells up. If you operate on them the next day, they have a high risk of complications such as infection.' I replied. 'We pick and choose those cases which can be left over for the next day; we will do them the next day. We try to manage most of the cases. Unfortunately, we are limited by the fact, and this does not happen frequently, it happens once in a blue moon, but when it does happen unfortunately you are in theatre all day from the morning to 8.30 or 9 o'clock in the evening.' I had hoped that I had cleared up any doubts about 'long lists.'

Rest of that day was spent in going over the details of day-to-day working in my unit. George took me through the consenting process, the Joint Care programme, record keeping in theatre and generally took me through the whole set up, as it existed then. He also took me through the follow up process where the outcomes are recorded by the Nurse Practitioner's independently – probably one of the first of the kind in the country. He took me through the criticisms that had been upheld by the panel and asked me how I would deal with similar situations. I had to say that I would do differently to what I had been doing before. I made it very clear that I would practice 'defensive medicine', even though it may not be the ethical way of managing certain patients.

I could see the attention of the panel was beginning to wane and it was not long before the Chairman said

'I am wondering if this is an appropriate time to adjourn for the day. Would you have any objection to our adjourning, Mr. Sykes? I suspect it will be panel questions.'

When no one objected, he turned around to Fred and asked

'Mr. Barnard, may I ask about your plans for tomorrow?'

'Sir, yes; we have been making urgent phone calls, as you would imagine, and trying to establish availability and if there is availability at all. I am not in a position to tell you at the moment how successful we have been but we are trying as hard as we possibly can to get as much as we can into tomorrow.' Fred replied

'Thank you. Have you any witnesses at the moment to call?' I think he was hoping that no one would be forthcoming.

'Yes. We have Mr. Menzies, who you have just heard mention of, Mr. Rayner and Mr. Gautam, who are all available tomorrow. What we are working on is those that we had listed for Monday: Mr. Fitzgerald, Mr. Worthing, and Mr. Bridge.' Fred replied. I could see the Chairman's face drop at that. They wanted to read the report by Mr. Bridge before starting next morning. With that, the hearing broke up for the day.

It was an odd day, I thought. I was not sure what to make of it. When George was going big guns this morning, I felt that everything was going my way. I was not so sure in the afternoon. It looked like we were going over the same old ground where we could not persuade the panel from their previous decision.

I was not allowed to talk to either Nancy or Fred as I was still under oath and hence there was nothing much for us to do once the proceedings were concluded for the day. We trudged back to the apartment, which I had rented in south London. We spent rest of the evening dissecting the day's events. Yadavi felt that the day had gone very well and she was very hopeful. We were due to start again next morning at 9.30. We were expecting Gautam and Howard Menzies to get to the GMC offices in the morning. Nancy had promised me that the travel arrangements would be paid for and I had asked Gautam to fly down to London with Howard. As we neared Piccadilly, there was a call from Gautam.

'Hi Upaas. Where are you? We are at the offices in Piccadilly. It looks deserted.' He sounded a bit surprised.

'We are walking down Euston road. We should be there in a few minutes. Help yourselves to the GMC coffee and thanks for coming.' I replied.

'Is Yadavi with you?'

'Yes. She is. Do you want to speak to her?'

'No. That is fine. I'll speak to her when you get here.' He replied.

Nancy was just getting in as we entered the front door. As we went up in the lift, I wanted to speak to her about a few things. However, I was reminded that I am not allowed to speak to her yet. Both Gautam and Howard were waiting in the waiting area. As we entered, I introduced Howard to Nancy.

'Good morning Howard. Thank you very much for coming along.'

'It is my pleasure boy. Anything to help you.' Howard said. He always called me 'Boy' for some reason. A term of endearment I suppose.

'This is Nancy. Our Solicitor. Nancy, this is Mr. Menzies.'

Nancy took Gautam and Howard to another room to brief them of the day's timetable. Just as we were getting on to our second cup of coffee, Douglas Rayner walked in. He recognised Lopa and spoke to her for a few minutes.

'I would not worry too much. I have an impression that this is only a formality. When they see the support Upaas has and his reputation, they will just close the case. I suspect they have to go through the motions to show that they are doing their job.'

'Thank you Douglas. It is very nice of you to come and help us.' Lopa replied.

'It is my pleasure to help Upaas in any way.' Douglas replied. The only thing we knew about the day's timetable was that Sykes would be cross-examining me first. I was not looking forward to that at all.

Fred walked in as we were called into the hearing room. We all trundled along to the hearing room behind the usher.

Fred started saying that he does not have many questions and began with my portfolio and the operative log. He took me through several days of the log and also through my diary. He picked up the project I dearly wanted to do – to assess the validity of the GMC's Surgical Knowledge Test for senior orthopaedic surgeons in the country.

'Let's go to Friday 8 August 2008 and that is the very last entry on that day. It is four months ago obviously and it predates the Panel's most recent findings but you wrote: 'I met up with Mr. Cooley in my office and went through the case notes audit we had done last year and beginning of this year. He agreed to take it away and complete the analysis. We also went through another project, to look at the validity of the GMC's performance assessment core knowledge test/postal questionnaire.' Can you tell us, please, what the purpose of this questionnaire was?' Sykes asked. I had to be careful here, I thought.

'I and my supervisor, Mr. Cooley, thought that it might be an idea to assess the validity of the surgical test that I went through. Mr. Cooley initially thought that it was probably a good idea and then on reflection we decided that it was not such a good idea because it is something that is not really within our remit; so we decided not to do that.' I replied. I could see Sykes's eyebrows raised and there was an immediate reaction from the panel as well. They were quite alert at this stage.

'Really, the purpose of this was to examine, as you put it, the validity of the core knowledge test which at this stage plainly you were still not accepting as being valid.' I could see the Chairman was looking rather surprised. They could not believe that I was questioning the GMC's test

'I am sorry?' I had to think fast. I was trying to buy some time to answer this. The last thing I want to do now is upset the panel.

'It appears from this that you still were not accepting in August of this year that the core knowledge test was valid as far as you were concerned.' Sykes persisted. He was almost accusing me of 'how dare you question the procedures of the GMC?'

'No, no. That was not the point of the exercise. The point of the exercise was to see how the general orthopaedic surgeons would feel about this thing. We did not have an opinion one way or the other at that stage.' I was backtracking very fast. I had hoped that I had done enough.

'You did not have an opinion on it?' Sykes continued.

'Whether it was good or bad. I did not have an opinion at that stage whether that was the right thing to go about doing because I was being frustrated, as you can understand, going through all this stressful process and all that. So, we brought up this idea but then we gave it up because we thought that was not really our role.' I had hoped that I had made that sound as contrite as possible and cursed the day I had put that down in the diary. The Chairman was not happy with this explanation and decided to intervene.

'I ask that you pause there. Perhaps I am not the only one who has not understood the question and the answer, so maybe I will just pick it up here. Mr. Kasyapa, what I am not understanding is what the project was. Was the project to put out a questionnaire to orthopaedic colleagues about their opinion of the core knowledge test which was part of your performance assessment?'

'No, no. I could not remember what the questions were obviously. We wanted to know what the role of such a test was in an orthopaedic surgeon's repertoire and also to see the knowledge at the stage of the practice. We were not trying to question the validity of what I had gone through. What we wanted to know was, for example, a surgeon who had just qualified and become a consultant and then a consultant who had been in practice for 10 to 20 years. We wanted to know the general knowledge of the consultant orthopaedic surgeons. We thought initially that it might be a good idea but then we thought that it was not really our role, it was the General Medical Council's role. So, we decided not to do that.' Sweat was pouring down my neck as I replied. The Panel was obviously very upset at my questioning the GMC yet again.

'I will leave it there. I confess that I would still like more clarity about this.' The Chairman said looking at me. It was a cue for Sykes to crucify me.

'I am going to pursue it slightly. Can we take it that this is not an idea that came from Mr. Cooley, it is an idea that must have come from you?'

'I am not sure who. During one of the discussions, we were discussing the core knowledge questions and things like that and we were trying to see what I knew and what I did not know and I was trying to find out what Mr. Cooley knew and what he did not know about the questions that I was asked. Then we decided, do you think we should ask other people what their knowledge of these questions would be? For example, intra-operative management of a diabetic patient or blood loss and that sort of thing. We just wanted to have an opinion.' I was trying desperately to make light of the issue.

'I understand that. You say that you cannot remember the questions that you were asked, but you plainly could remember the questions that you were asked because you had the assessment form and you were going through the procedure.' Sykes continued. He knew he had me by the balls and he was not going to let go of it lightly.

'No, I only had the headings.' I was clutching at straws now.

'Was the idea to set out approximately the questions you were asked to see who else could answer them?'

'No, no. Not the questions, we are talking about the topics/subjects.' I was quite taken aback by the accuracy of his assessment. He knew exactly what I had planned on doing.

'And to see how many passed, as it were, and how many failed?' He continued his drilling. He knew he had won this argument. He had that wry smile on his face as he said that.

'No. It was not a question of seeing how many passed. We wanted to know what level of knowledge they had. It was nothing to do with whether they passed or failed. I was not trying to replicate what the GMC did. That is not my role.' I knew by then I had lost this battle. I will have to try to make the most of patchwork to save my skin.

'Do you accept now that certainly so far as trauma work is concerned, the surgical core knowledge test is relevant?' Sykes was positively gleaming now.

'Yes. I am not sure that I made that clear as we have been through that before. These are essentially features of a general surgeon's knowledge base and he should know these things to a level where it can be managed with the help of a multidisciplinary team.' I had to retract and accept defeat. In addition, I hoped that when it came to make a decision the panel would not put too much weight on this part.

He then took me through the audit George had done and tried to pick holes in it. He then tried to catch me out on the practice of two surgeons operating on complex cases. How would I deal with it if the credit crunch make second consultant unavailable! By now, the panel obviously had enough for the morning and wanted to have a break. Soon after the break, the Chairman again brought up the subject of witnesses. He was still trying to stop us getting all our witnesses on the stand.

'Just before we resumes with questions of Mr. Kasyapa. Mr. Sykes and Mr. Barnard, I have had a discussion with my colleagues during the break. You will have seen that I am getting rather concerned about the time. The luxury of time is no longer with us. I would like to have submissions this afternoon but that leaves the question about Mr. Bridge. The panel has received and read the agreed statement of Mr. Bridge. I do not know what Mr. Bridge will be able to add were he here in person. For my own part, I cannot imagine what that might be. As I understand it Mr. Bridge is travelling, or making plans to travel, to be here in person tomorrow. I am wondering whether Mr. Barnard wants to reconsider the position given that I have asked for submissions this afternoon or whether I am just being wholly unrealistic.' The Chairman asked. He wanted to finish everything before Christmas and get back home.

'Can we simply see how we go, at least for the moment? I hear what you say and we will reflect on it. We remain keen that witnesses should be seen as well as heard.' Fred replied. It was becoming increasingly obvious that the panel just wanted to wrap this up as quickly as possible. They did not want to listen to any more witnesses as they probably had already made their minds up.

'Given the information in my possession, it was right to say something now. Mr. Sykes, can you make any observations?' The Chairman said. That was worrying. What was this 'information?'

'I agree with Mr. Barnard. Let us cross that bridge when we get to that bridge.' Sykes agreed with us to my surprise.

There was the questioning by the panel members. Again, O'Neil tried to undermine everything I had written down. He picked up on the number of cases that was being done on an average month. He tried to insinuate that I was still doing a large number of cases. Fred had to intervene at one stage, as it was getting out of hand.

'I am sorry to intervene, Dr O'Neil, but if these allegations are going to be pursued by the Panel, I think that they ought to be put fairly and squarely to this witness. The previous allegations were that clinics were being dealt with by junior staff. If that is the allegation, we want to know about it, we want it out on the table and we want this witness to have a chance to deal with it.' Fred was quite terse when he said that.

'It was just wanting clarity over what had been written in his log diary, Mr. Barnard that was all. It was because management workload in theatre was part of the learning plan, I wanted his take on how he managed his workload, and I quoted an example from over a year ago. It was no new allegation or anything else; it was about his learning plan and to see how things had developed from last year. That was all.' He had his Cheshire grin on his face. He was not going to back track on his questioning. This was more like inquisition than an enquiry. If I had thought that this panel was independent and were supposed to give an opinion based on facts presented by two parties, I was quite clearly completely wrong.

'Are you satisfied, Mr. Barnard?' The Chairman asked.

'I am concerned about the possibility of the Panel finding adversely to my client on an allegation that is in their minds which the witness has not fairly and squarely had an opportunity to answer. That is all. I hear what

Dr O'Neil says and I am not persisting on that point. I will see where we go from here.' Fred was clearly not very happy as I was.

The Chairman had a whispered conversation with the legal assessor and turned around to Fred. 'I have obviously just had a consultation with the Legal Assessor and the advice, Mr. Barnard, is that we should give Mr. Kasyapa the opportunity to explain what it is that Dr O'Neil has asked him and if at the end of that you are not satisfied, then you will tell me, please.' I think he was just making sure that he won't be caught out in a legal argument.

The Reverend tried to pick holes in George's role as a mentor and a supervisor. He tried to imply that as a 'friend' he could not be an effective supervisor. Luckily, the Chairman did not have any questions. A fair bit of wrangling went on after that to see who should be next. For one reason or the other, the Chairman insisted on getting the telephone interviews first. We had the Chief Exec on standby near a telephone. He had just returned from his honeymoon and was quite prepared to come down to London give evidence to support me.

He was sworn in over the telephone. George started his questioning first, as he was our witness. John confirmed that he acted as our 'Link Director' to the trust management when I was the Clinical Director for Orthopaedics. He then moved on to the workload, which had been roundly criticised by everyone acting for the GMC. Fred asked him if the workload has been reduced.

'What we have seen I think is a reduction in the workload that has been borne by individuals as a result of those two things: making the new appointments to the team, and the fact that we have successfully got on top of achieving the NHS targets.'

'Does that apply to operating lists and to clinics or to one or the other?' Fred asked.

'.the position we have got to with the orthopaedic surgeons is one where they have had an equal say in the discussions with the Trust about what they consider to be the right number of operating sessions that they have every week and the number of cases they should do on those list, and exactly the same applies to the number of patients they should see in their out-patient clinics so we get the right balance of new and follow-up patients. It applies to both sides.' a typical politician's answer I thought.

'The Panel will obviously be concerned that an excessive workload is not placed on Mr. Kasyapa. How satisfied are you that such an excessive workload will not occur in the future?' Fred continued.

'I am absolutely satisfied and confident that it will not occur in the future.' He reassured everyone there.

George asked him about supervision and mentorship within the hospital and if I was abiding by the restrictions placed by the Interim Orders Panel.

'Throughout the process of supervision we have put in place over the course of almost three years since Mr. Kasyapa started the Interim Orders Panel, or it may be two, we have been reducing the degree of supervision we have had. We have made sure that Mr. Kasyapa has complied absolutely to the letter of the restrictions placed on him by the Interim Orders Panel. That has worked successfully for him. I think Mr. Kasyapa has produced a portfolio of evidence now that, my deputy head of director, has described as absolutely the model of best practice. All that together points to the fact that we are working very closely with Mr. Kasyapa.' Ian explained.

George asked him about the question of two consultants operating on complex case, which again was seen with scepticism by Sykes as well as the Panel earlier.

'We have been told that for complex hip revision surgery the orthopaedic surgeons agree that there would be two surgeons on such a case at the same time. Does that apply to all the orthopaedic surgeons?' Fred asked.

'Yes. I think the issue for us as an organisation lies in two of the recent appointments that we have made to the team.' John replied confirming what I had said that morning.

It is at this point I thought Fred played his trump card. He asked Ian about my standing within the hospital as well as the community.

'So far as Mr. Kasyapa is concerned, can you say as the chief executive how he is regarded in terms of his practice and his safety by his professional colleagues?'

Ian took a deep breath before answering, 'His professional colleagues, specifically in the orthopaedic department but also broadly across the Trust, remain absolutely supportive of Mr. Kasyapa. When the original allegations were raised by Serpe, an investigation was carried out by the

Trust. The then Clinical Director of Orthopaedics and Trauma was, and still is, a consultant in emergency medicine, an A&E consultant, at that time the clinical director of orthopaedics. In his investigation into Mr. Kasyapa did not find anything out of the ordinary in terms of his revision rates and in terms of any complications or problems that occurred pre or post-operatively. There were certain infection rates, things like that, that were within the norms of the rest of the team. Mr. Kasyapa retains the support not just of his orthopaedic colleagues but colleagues' right across the surgical specialities and of the entire Trust board. Since that time more recently at the time that the Interim Orders Panel indicated that it was going to take a closer look at Mr. Kasyapa's work, the Trust also commissioned an independent review of Mr. Kasyapa's work. We asked Mr. John Worthing, who is an orthopaedic surgeon from Liverpool, to come and review his work. He provided the Trust with a report, which we have been very happy to provide to Mr. Kasyapa. I would be surprised if that does not form part of his portfolio of evidence. Mr. Worthing did find one or two issues with regard to some of the record keeping which had been identified by the Interim Orders Panel. In terms of the safety of Mr. Kasyapa everyone can be re-assured by the findings of Mr. Worthing's report.'

'What about other staff, nursing staff and the other staff of the hospital?'

'The staff of the hospital, right from the Trust board right down to the auxiliaries on the wards, all support Mr. Kasyapa. He is held in extremely high regard. He is a well-respected, well-liked member of the broad Trust and hospital team. The staff in theatres think the world of him. I can say that because in the past I have had the delight and the privilege of spending a day in theatre with Mr. Kasyapa so I have seen him interact on his territory with the theatre staff and with patients. I have seen it in practice myself. He is well liked, well respected, and well regarded by all staff right across the Trust who comes in contact with him. He is also absolutely held in the same respect by his patients. When we have had bits in the local press going through this process with the GMC we have had numerous letters of support, both in the press and that have come into me directly in the Trust, in direct support of Mr. Kasyapa.' John replied. I hoped that weight of this statement was not wasted on the panel.

Fred went on to ask him about any concerns he had about my practice.

'I see every single complaint that comes into my organisation. I sit down on a weekly basis and review those with the medical director, with the deputy medical director and our head of complaint and I cannot recall having seen a complaint about Mr. Kasyapa from a patient in that time. I cannot recall a complaint about Mr. Kasyapa in the three years I have been chief executive from a patient.' He replied.

'The question of whether Mr. Kasyapa is now fit to practice is obviously a matter for the panel but they may wish to know what the Trust's view of that is. Are you able to express it?' Fred continued

'If Mr. Kasyapa was not fit to practice he would not be practising.' John replied.

"Meaning?'

'Meaning if the Trust had any reason to believe that Mr. Kasyapa is not fit to practise as we stand here now he would not be allowed to practice. As I have said twice already, patient safety is absolutely paramount to my organisation. If there was any indication, any fear that patient safety had any risk of being compromised then Mr. Kasyapa would not be allowed to practise until this prosecution is finished. He would have been withdrawn from practise.' John replied with some firmness in his voice. There could not have been any doubt about what he said.

'We have notes that were made of the assessor's interview with you some two years and a month ago. In the course of that, you make reference to a member of your family. Is there anything that you could tell the panel about that?' Fred continued.

'Yes, I can. My mother actually remains under the active care of Mr. Kasyapa. My mother, I believe, was one of the last hip revisions that Mr. Kasyapa undertook. She had a hip that was originally done in 1977 which Mr. Kasyapa did the revision of about two years ago now. My mother has had five different orthopaedic operations, Mr. Kasyapa has done at least three of them, and she remains under his active care at the minute. Follow-up is done on that revision. She is one of those who absolutely has the utmost respect and regard for Mr. Kasyapa. When I told her about what I was doing at work and she has seen things in the press about it, she is absolutely astonished that Mr. Kasyapa finds himself in this position. It is difficult to explain to her sometimes how this is the case. My Mum would choose to go and see Mr. Kasyapa and I would do nothing to dissuade her from that.' Ian replied.

'A final matter from me, although there will be some more questions, is the rapid recovery programme which we are told is a flagship in the United Kingdom.' Fred asked.

'It is, yes.'

'How do you regard that?'

'A flagship is a good expression used to describe it. Mr. Kasyapa has worked closely with them. I was at the formal launch of the rapid recovery programme about 18 months ago now or slightly more than that. It has had certainly national interest. We have had visitors from all over the country from orthopaedic units who would consider themselves have be larger units than the one we have at Seaport who want to come and have a look at the work we have done. The benefits for patients is a tangible one. We get patients in and through the system; our length of stay is second to none locally, and it stands up to scrutiny if you compare it with national lengths of stay. It is a programme where the patients get actively involved in their own care themselves and they absolutely appreciate and enjoy that in the context of being able to take charge of some of their own care. Mr. Kasyapa has been instrumental in getting that set up. It is another thing that Seaport can be proud of and one of the great successes that we have in Seaport. Mr. Kasyapa is almost single-handedly responsible. It is something else that has put Seaport on the map and Mr. Kasyapa has been responsible for that.' I am not sure if this made any impact on the panel. They were sitting there with a monumental disinterest on their faces.

It was the Sykes's turn to ask questions. He asked John about the statements he had made during his 'third party interviews.'

'One matter that I wanted to ask you about – and again it arises in your third party interviews – is at page 32 where you say this: 'What I do know is that one of the accusations levelled against Kasyapa is whether or not he is always in his clinic when he is due to be or whether he sometimes delegates duties and responsibilities but, if he does do that, in my experience, he has always been round about in the hospital and he certainly does not leave the juniors unsupervised.' I just want to ask you again briefly about that and whether that has changed.' Sykes asked.

'With the benefit of the passage of time, I think that the more we have looked into that as an allegation, the more it seems to be another one of those that was raised by Mr. Serpe that was actually unfounded. I think that the allegation was that Mr. Serpe was away doing operating lists when he should have been in clinic and that he was leaving SpRs to run his clinics and, as I said in my third party interview, we have not been able to find anything that substantiates that allegation either at that time and certainly there is nothing that indicates that that is what is happening now.' John gave a firm answer. I hope that would put that allegation to rest.

When the questioning had completed, John asked if he was allowed to make a statement. The answer as expected was a 'No' both from Sykes as well as the Chairman. When he went on to make the statement despite that stating the whole process was a result of an 'embittered old man,' he was stopped short. That was a pity as I could see John was getting into this and was going to express how wrong all this was on the part of the GMC.

I grabbed Nancy and Fred at Lunchtime and wanted to know how things were progressing.

'I think I was on a very sticky wicket with the audit we were going to about Surgical Knowledge test. Did not do well at all.' I said.

'I would not let that worry you too much Upaas. Let me handle that in my submission. Leave it to me.' Fred replied.

'Don't worry Upaas. It has been fine. The most important part was your Chief Executive saying he has full confidence in you. At the end of the day, the buck stops with him. I don't think the GMC can take his witness lightly.' Nancy joined.

'I sincerely hope so. I have a bad feeling about this.' I replied.

'No. You should not. It is the Chief Executive who is finally held responsible for patient care. If he says that he has no reservation about your practice, I can't see how the GMC can say otherwise.' Fred added. That gave me some solace as we walked down to the local eatery for some sandwiches. Douglas Rayner, Gautam, and Howard Menzies joined us. Fred and Nancy decided to stay back to catch up on some paper work.

It was the turn of Douglas Rayner after Lunch. The idea of asking him as my witness was to give some weight to my training as that had been criticised by the assessors.

'Are you able to comment on his skills and knowledge as a surgeon at the time of his training?' Fred asked him.

'All I can say is that having been a consultant now for 25 years and having trained and been a trainer for that period of time, Mr. Kasyapa's skill as a surgeon during his period of training was very good, better than the average; he had good hand-eye co-ordination; he had a good appreciation of the clinical aspects of a case; he was able to evaluate a patient consistently in relationship to his level of training. He was also able, I think most importantly, to know when he had to refer to a consultant and when he was able to make a valid decision based on the training and his experience at that point in time. His clinical ward work was also good. I do not, and I do admit it is a long period of time away, remember – and I can definitely remember other specialist registrars in training – any problem in terms of note keeping, dictation of notes and the post-operative management of the cases. I do not remember myself having to become involved with any of the cases that Mr. Kasyapa had been involved in managing.' Douglas replied. In addition, went on to explain the Master's degree in orthopaedics where he had been my supervisor for the Thesis.

He was then taken on to his involvement with my work at present.

'In fact, even within the last six or seven months I have referred a case for advice from Mr. Kasyapa because it has been a difficult knee revision case, and it is one that I think probably calls for his expertise in that area – an expertise that I have been made aware of because, having gone to the meetings which he has outlined in his CV where I have been aware of the other orthopaedic surgeons internationally discussing things, Mr. Kasyapa has been in that discussion; it is quite obvious that he has knowledge. You can tell whether knowledge is based on reading a textbook or whether that knowledge comes from being actually clinically involved in a case – somebody speaking from knowledge as opposed to, yes, it is in the book. Therefore, in those sorts of international discussions you can tell straight away who knows what they are talking about and who has just read it. I have always been impressed with his ability to converse with knowledge, to actually talk about the use of the orthopaedic skills in those areas and to say that I have been more than happy to refer cases to him, I think underlines that.' He added.

'If you had reservations about his practice, would you have referred a case to him?' Fred asked him.

'Definitely not.' Douglas replied.

Sykes asked a couple of rather inconsequential questions about the number of time Douglas had been involved with me and where he heard about the problems. As soon as he said Newspapers, Sykes stopped.

O'Neil did not have any questions of significance. The Chairman asked him about my training again and Douglas reinforced what he had said to Fred. He also asked him about my Basic surgical skills and the Multi-disciplinary approach we take in managing patients.

'Mr. Kasyapa has explained to the panel that the environment in which he works is very multidisciplinary and so those particular problems, such as a patient having an insulin-dependency or so on, are not problems that he needs to deal with himself. He needs to be aware of the general issues but these are passed on to specialist inter-disciplinary teams. Is that an environment that you are familiar with?' The Chairman asked.

'Did I recognise? Undoubtedly. The majority is multidisciplinary work team. Somebody who is diabetic whilst I may be aware of it and there is the standard procedure that person would go first on the list, that person is managed first of all through pre-assessment for their surgery and contact with the diabetic multidisciplinary team while they are in and the anaesthetic. In the post-operative period, they are managed by the specialist nursing diabetes also. The actual management from an orthopaedic side, as a carpenter technician, is the same. The rest is overlaid on top with the multidisciplinary team and managed both pre and post-operatively by usually the diabetic nurse specialist and during the intra-operative period by the anaesthetist.' Douglas replied. I thought you could not get clearer than that about 'core knowledge.'

'I am going to ask you a similar question about your training of Mr. Kasyapa in terms of his specific surgical skills. I do not know to what extent orthopaedic surgeons develop their own techniques but would you be confident as a result of your training, and perhaps even your subsequent contacts with Mr. Kasyapa, that he could, for instance, tie secure surgical knots.' The Chairman continued.

'I would be confident at the end of that training period that he would have been able to. All I can say is that if he had not been able to, firstly, I would have noticed it by supervision and not just myself but my other two colleagues at time would have noticed it and drawn it to my attention or his attention. If somebody is there for a three-year period in training, you pick up problems. If not tying had been a problem or he had not been putting the screws in correctly when doing some sort of surgery or there had been fractured drills on a frequent occasions then these would have been highlighted to myself, as his main trainer at that time, but also the other consultants would have picked it up. In a three-year period, you would pick up the problems. When somebody changes post quickly whilst they are in training, you sometimes do not associate the problems so easily. If there had been problems within that three-year period, we would have picked them up. I do not remember picking them up and therefore I could say with confidence that those aspects were satisfactorily covered in the training.' Douglas replied.

'Along the same lines, I guess you form a view about someone you are training, about his dexterity, his facility with handling instruments. Did you, during the time Mr. Kasyapa was training with you, form a view as it how skilful he was likely to be? Did you have any concerns about his instrument handling?' The Chairman asked. I could see Douglas rolling his eyes up.

'I said earlier, and I may have not pronounced it correctly, I had felt that his hand eye co-ordination and use of instruments and his hand skills were good. I can say I have seen other specialist registrars who needed to specifically address that area and you would take them back a few steps and say, 'Hold on come back, let us revisit that area.' I remember specifically Mr. Kasyapa being good with hand eye co-ordination, treatment of tissues, dealing with bleeding blood vessels, dealing with the muscles and the ligaments and that his hand skill was good. That is particularly why I sent him away to Liverpool because I felt he needed to go through that final stage of completion of that training to do his MCh Orth which was, and still is, regarded as an exit exam' I could detect a tinge of exasperation in his voice.

Next to come was Howard Menzies. His evidence was quite short as he was requested as an outsider to give evidence on my capability as an orthopaedic surgeon. Fred mainly concentrated on how he was involved with me.

'Can you tell us the circumstances in which you came across Mr. Kasyapa?' Fred asked him.

'I have known Mr. Kasyapa as a colleague for approximately ten or 12 years, firstly every since he was appointed as a consultant at the St Edwards Hospital in Seaport. I have also been involved with him on clinical practice at clinical meetings both locally and abroad. On occasions I have been able to monitor or observe his clinical practice and on one particular occasion asked him to help me with a difficult case at hospital" I still remember that case where he needed some help with a difficult revision total knee replacement.' I was really grateful that he acknowledged my help in public, albeit small. He was very forthright man and spoke his mind. He had been tutored by Gautam over the last few days to temper his language during his replies. We did not want to upset the panel at this stage. He had felt all along the entire process that it was unjustified and called it a 'travesty of justice when incompetent fools are allowed to perform butchery on patients and a good surgeon is being crucified by malicious intent.'

O'Neil again wanted to know about managing blood loss and diabetes in surgical patients. Howard made it very clear that that is managed by the anaesthetist and physicians in no uncertain terms.

Next on stand was Gautam. His questioning went along similar lines to Howard. It was concentrated on the type of work he did and management of medical problems such as Diabetes, blood loss and pain control. Again similar to Howard, he made it clear to the panel that they are managed by anaesthetists and physicians and not by himself.

We were in a sort of limbo at that stage as we had finished all our witnesses who were available. We still had John Worthing and Simon Bridge to give witness. Nancy had been trying very hard to get hold of John Worthing to give evidence over the phone that day and we knew Mr. Bridge was coming to give evidence the next day. What the Chairman said next took all of us by surprise.

'Mr. Barnard, what would you next like to do, please?' The Chairman asked.

'I would like to have a couple of minutes to get Mr. Worthing teed-up to give evidence by telephone in the light of your indications earlier.' Fred replied looking a little confused. That is when the Chairman dropped a bombshell.

'Can I ask you, how shall I put this: my own impression, having listened to witnesses this afternoon, is rather than specifically to impairment of the evidence that we are now getting is diminishing. I wonder what it is you hope to cover with Mr. Worthing that has not already been covered?' There was a deathly silence for a minute before we all realised what he may be saying. I could not believe what I had just heard. Did he say that the evidence for impairment was diminishing?

Fred was the first to recover and said that we have to discuss the two reports by John Worthing prepared completely independently on my work. It turned out all he was trying to do was deflect Worthing's evidence completely so that the submissions could be made that afternoon or the next morning. I was beginning to understand the meaning of the term 'Kangaroo court' used by Fred Barnard a while ago to describe the Panel hearing. It looked like they were in a hurry to go somewhere! They probably wanted to finish off their last minute Christmas shopping in London.

By this time, Nancy had located John Worthing and he was sworn in over the phone after the lunch break.

He was asked to identify himself and confirm that he had written the two reports on my work at the behest of Seaport Health NHS trust independently. He was asked about his own CV – Consultant in Liverpool specialising in hip and knee replacements for the past 12 years. It also came out that he did about 250 joint replacements a year and approximately 12 joint replacements a week. I wondered if O'Neil was going to question him about that, as he was critical of me doing 21 joint replacements in a month. He was again asked similar questions to others about managing diabetes, blood loss and pain relief. He confirmed that the management is done by anaesthetists and physicians and his role is to oversee the management of the patient.

He was taken through his report. I got a faint suggestion from Sykes's questioning that he was alluding to the data as coming from me and not quite independent as it was made out. John Worthing went through the process where he spent a whole day at our hospital going through notes and x-rays randomly selected by a third party. He was criticised for not taking into account 'Basic surgical skills' in his report. They read out the paragraph in his report, which said;

'The only area that has not been fully addressed in Mr. Kasyapa's portfolio in relation to the Interim Orders Panel so far as I can see is the results of his surgery core knowledge test. Given the fact that the validity of these tests is open to question, that in orthopaedics we now work in the multidisciplinary team environment involving anaesthetics, intensivists and physicians to address basic peri-operative surgical complications such as the management of diabetic patients inter-operatively, I feel that Mr. Kasyapa has the necessary knowledge and skill base and insight to be allowed to continue to work as an orthopaedic surgeon with an interest in hip and knee replacements without having to undergo further basic surgical core knowledge tests.'

He paused for a minute as if to let what he said can be absorbed.

'I was more referring in this instance to the test themselves being that they are sort of an artificial test, if you like, of a surgeon's technical and clinical ability and operative ability and management of patients done in an artificial situation. To do these tests is often quite a stressful situation. It is in the College, it is using equipment on artificial patients, if you like, and the surgeons are asked to perform tests that they would not routinely do and in fact, some tests they have not done for many years in very stressful situations. So, it was actually the test that I was questioning rather than to do with the multidisciplinary team.' John Worthing finished. There was complete silence after that outburst. I could see Sykes was getting rather annoyed. He did not like this one bit. He decided to attack John Worthing.

'You are attacking the quality of the tests.' Sykes said.

'Yes. In my opinion, I think that there are probably better ways to assess a surgeon who performs hip and knee replacements regularly perhaps rather than testing them in an artificial situation using instruments that they do not commonly use. That was my main point.' John was not prepared to back down.

'And this is the surgery core knowledge test that you are referring to?' Sykes pursued.

'The whole test. How was it the surgical core knowledge test when the questions that he had was about the medical management of patients?' Worthing countered. The Chairman saw that it was getting out of hand and not going the way of his liking. Worthing was indirectly attacking the decisions so far made by the panel. He put a stop the questioning with; 'Can I ask you to pause, Mr. Sykes. I am just wondering where you are taking us. We are rather beyond this, are we not?'

Sykes had no option but to drop the line of questioning. I guess he was taken aback by the ferocity of Worthing's attack on the assessment process, and particularly the Core Knowledge Tests. He was trying to justify and probably defend the GMC assessors' action.

Once John Worthing's evidence was finished, the Chairman tried once again to stop Mr. Bridge coming personally. He was told the Mr. Bridge would be in the room before nine in the morning. With that 'day 24' was adjourned. 'Day 24' – I have been through this nightmare for 24 days now and there is still no end in sight as far as I can see. I had mixed feelings about the day's outcome. Everyone else felt that it had gone extremely well and the case was in our bag. Gautam and Howard did not have to rush back as they had booked seats on a late night train. We decided to show Howard a nice Indian restaurant in London. Unfortunately, that restaurant was closed for 'refurbishment' to the dismay of Swayambhu. It was quite late by the time we said goodbye to everyone and got back to our rental apartment that night.

As we wound our way back to the Council chambers for what would be the last time we can produce witness and do the submission, I had butterflies in my stomach. It was just like the first day of my first medical exam. I was hoping that the evidence of someone as powerful and as high up as Simon Bridge would swing the case towards me. Most of the previous night had been spent arguing about the questions that we should ask Fred to put to Mr. Bridge.

As we entered the building, Mr. Bridge was already there. As soon as he saw me, he got up and came towards me with his hand held forward in a friendly greeting. It was just like the first day in Marsden on Sea when he saw me in the hospital. This was someone who did not know me from Adam and his greeting that first day, was as if I was someone important and someone his equal. He made me welcome and at no time did he make me feel as if I was being assessed. He was sharp and he was assessing me all the time I was in Marsden on Sea. He would weigh up everything I did or said and analyse it without me suspecting anything.

'Hello Upaas. It is very nice to see you again after all this time. What a dreadful mess. I am sure it is all a misunderstanding. We'll get this cleared up in no time.' He said shaking me by the hand.

I introduced everyone to him. I was very pleased to see him there. It gave me a sense of confidence and lifted the feeling of foreboding that had lingered in my mind all these months. Fred took him to a conference room to discuss the issues of the day. By the time he came back, we were ushered into the hearing room. The Chairman appeared to be in a hurry. There was no time for pleasantries and he asked 'the witness to be brought in.' Mr. Bridge was brought in and sat in the witness box.

Fred started with 'Would you give your full name and your professional address, please?'

'I am Mr. Anthony Simon Bridge, and I am a consultant orthopaedic surgeon at Marsden on Sea Hospital.'

'Can you give us some idea of your experience and your current posts and functions and so on?' Fred continued.

'I was appointed as consultant orthopaedic surgeon in 1980, to Marsden on Sea Hospital. I have worked there ever since. I am a full-time consultant. I have been a member of the specialty advisory committee on the College of Surgeons, which is very much involved in training. I have been Chairman of the training committee for South West Thames, which is one of the largest training areas in the country. I do the annual appraisals for all the orthopaedic departments, which is 11 appraisals, to the GMC standard each year, and I have done that since it started. Further, I have trained specialist registrars in orthopaedics since I started in 1980. I have always been involved in training.' Mr. Bridge completed a short précis of an impressive career.

'Do you have a particular specialism within orthopaedics?' Fred asked.

'Yes, it is hip surgery and particularly hip revision surgery, replacement surgery. A bit like most orthopaedic surgeons of my generation, I have done most things in orthopaedics.' Mr. Bridge replied.

'We know that you had Mr. Kasyapa working with you for three weeks in July 2007: had you ever met Mr. Kasyapa before that?'

'No, I had not. I was introduced to him by I believe a request from the chief executive to my clinical director, would I look after an attachment, a consultant attachment, for three weeks, and I did.'

'The Panel has read your report, and, indeed, your letter of August 2007. I do not want to ask any particular questions about it but just this sole one: how satisfied can the Panel be that Mr. Kasyapa is currently fit to practise without any impairment?'

'Broadly speaking, there are two main elements to somebody gaining their CCT in surgery, their competence in surgery, and that is a knowledge test and a surgical skills test. Obviously, there are many other facets involved but those are the two main ones. The knowledge test is the fellowship exam, which of course Mr. Kasyapa has, but during the attachment with me, we talked continuously in outpatients, in theatre, about surgery, about his practice, my practice, and I found that his knowledge level in orthopaedics was certainly equal to my own. I did not have any doubt to question is knowledge level. The surgical skill question, which I received from the MPS I believe, I could not answer fully from his attachment with me because the chief exec precluded him from carrying out surgery himself when he was with me, and so he was assistant only. He was an excellent assistant, but I wanted to see surgical skill myself so I offered to go up to the Surgical Centre, St Edwards Hospital and observe him operate, and then carry out tests which I normally do on specialist registrars, and which are currently used as a means of testing registrars in their surgical skill, the competence assessment test, and I did that on total hip replacement and on arthroscopy, two arthroscopies, during the day that I spent with him at his centre. I took the opportunity on that day to quite separately, away from Mr. Kasyapa, talk to the theatre sister, and I talked to his staff-grade assistant, who is an experienced doctor, about Mr. Kasyapa, and I spoke to one colleague of his who happened to be in an adjacent operating theatre: all three gave me their views and unreservedly said that he was a good surgeon. So I believe that I have carried out as best I could a 360 degree appraisal of his surgery.' Mr. Bridge replied.

'Just to amplify what you have written in your letter of 12 December 2008, how did you find his skills as a surgeon?' Fred continued.

'They were fine. There was no problem that I observed at all with his surgical skill. He carried out a hip replacement in just over an hour in a manner that I would have been happy to do myself. I am quite certain that that hip will do well and that it was a safely performed operation. What was particularly obvious during the day that I spent at the centre was that there was a good rapport in theatre between theatre sister, anaesthetist, and Mr. Kasyapa. They worked together as a team. He went to see the patients before he operated on them. He chatted with them. There was obvious friendliness there. He checked the marking of the leg and so on in the proper manner, and afterwards talked to the patients again, these are all factors, which matter very much, and I have observed over years of training that somebody who bothers to talk to patients like that means they have a caring attitude, which is important. So I felt he was safe and careful and a good surgeon.' That I thought would convince the panel about both pre-operative assessment and operative skills as well as note keeping.

'Can you say anything about his manual dexterity, and in particular his closing of the wound, suturing and knotting, that sort of thing?'

'I would say he is quicker than average, but the average for me is a senior trainee, year 5/6 of their training, he is better than that. It is very difficult to compare speeds. I would say that he was probably as slick as I was.' I did not think one could be any more clearer than that about my surgical skill.

'Tissue handling?'

'Careful, yes.'

'Have you any reservations about his fitness to continue in practice as an orthopaedic hip and knee surgeon doing trauma from time to time?' Fred asked the crucial question. I was no quite surprised that the Chairman or Sykes did not object to this question.

'I do not have any reservations from my observations. I would like to make the point about the performance-based assessments that we do. They are supposed to be, and they are designed to be, a thorough examination of a person's knowledge about practising that particular operation from start to finish, so the performance-based assessment starts with 'Why are you doing the operation? What do you do before you even start operating?' right the way through to taking consent, marking the leg, putting them on the operating table; how they act in theatre; the communication between anaesthetist and surgeon and nurse; care of tissue handling is one of the aspects that we mark, and then finally the complications afterwards, knowledge of that and how they look after the patient in the post-operative room until they wake up. All that was checked by myself on the day I went up to the North East, and to a standard that I was quite happy to put grade four, which I rarely give to a trainee registrar. They work hard to get the top pass.' This is solid reinforcement from Mr. Bridge.

'Finally Mr. Bridge, I think you can confirm that you specifically have not seen the assessment performance report, and you are not familiar with the allegations that were made against Mr. Kasyapa?'

'No, I have knowledge of the allegations. I have not seen any performance report.' He finished.

To my surprise, Sykes did not have any questions.

'No, that last question was the only question I was going to ask you and you have answered it, so thank you very much.' And sat down.

The Chairman started with the questions this time

'May I clarify one point? Mr. Barnard has just dealt with this, but when you were answering Mr. Barnard, you used the phrase 'the performance-based assessments that we do.' The phrase 'performance-based assessments' might have a confusing meaning for this Panel. I take it you mean the performance-based assessments that you do when you are training registrars?'

'That is right. It is a little bit more confusing even because it used to be called 'performance-based assessment.' The College of Surgeons now wishes it to be called 'procedure-based assessment,' and there are reasons for that but it is the same test. It is a test, which was devised by others and myself as part of the OCAP process, the orthopaedic competence assessment project, which the College has embraced. It is now used for all orthopaedic trainees during their six years of training. It encompasses 20 operations at the moment but it may increase, and it is a test of their competence in all the different facets of orthopaedic surgery. The test has a common format in so much as it tests right from the start, the reason for doing the operation, all the way through the operation itself to the end result, the complications that can ensue. So that is the way we decided to act following the Bristol inquiry as to how we knew the surgeon was trained, and this has been accepted by the College of Surgeons now as the way that in orthopaedics we test and train surgeons.' I thought that was quite lucid description of the Royal College assessment, which I had passed.

'Thank you. You may have said this and I may have failed to pick it up. The scale is from what to what?'

'There are four skill levels that you can mark the test at and the highest level, grade four, is written down as a competence where I am not needed in the operation. I am observing. I felt that he could do the operation completely by himself without my actually having to give him verbal commands, suggestions, and that sort of thing, so he is able to do the operation. We are quite anxious not to make the PBA a certificate of competence to operate by yourself because these are still trainees, and we do not want to cross that line to say to a trainee, 'You have now done a hip replacement well enough to do any hip replacement on your own' otherwise I feel at some hospitals they will be left on their own, and trainees are trainees and should be supervised. So we have not gone as far as saying that the PBA is a passport to operate by yourself but the skill level of grade four is the highest level that we can assess to and that is the skill level that he got to, the best possible. There is not a higher one.'

'Thank you. That clarifies it very helpfully. I am going to check to see whether my fellow panelists have any questions. Dr O'Neil is the medical member of the Panel and he would like to ask some questions.

I was curious t see what line he would take. Audit again?

'At the beginning you were talking about the trainees having to pass a knowledge test and a surgical skills test, and perhaps, rightly, you have been concentrating on telling us about the surgical skills side of things.

How about the knowledge test? I presume the trainees have to have some basic knowledge of general medical conditions.'

'The passing out test is the Fellowship of the Royal College of Surgeons trauma and orthopaedics, which they take in their fourth or fifth years, and they can re-sit again if they do not get it, but that is a test of the knowledge that is required to be an orthopaedic surgeon in this country, and Mr. Kasyapa has the FRCS, so, I mean, his knowledge test, I think, has been tested. When he was with me, and during the operating day, I was talking to him about surgery the whole time, and I think I learned as much as I gave.' That I thought was very convincing and appropriate. Passing an FRCS exam is no mean feat. One had to be an expert in basic surgical knowledge, both theoretical and practical to pass the exam.

'To me surgery means the act of performing surgery.' O'Neil twisted the whole issue around. That was not what he said when he was questioning me. He insisted that the basic surgical knowledge was essential in everyone even at the level of senior consultant. Now he is saying it is 'performing surgery.'

'The act of performing surgery but also the reason for doing it and how would you treat this and that case. We saw some very difficult cases down in Marsden on Sea where I do a revision hip clinic and his opinion showed how much knowledge he had about that type of surgery.'

'Did you have any discussions about patients with co-morbidities, as they impinge on the orthopaedic surgeon?'

'Certainly we did, yes, that is almost invariably present in somebody having a revision of a hip done. They are nearly always more elderly than average and usually are co-morbidities.'

'Can you give me a flavour of that kind of discussion?' I got the impression that he was trying to trick Mr. Bridge.

'I suppose to put it in its most crude form, would this patient survive the operation was discussed; would this patient make use of the operation? Has he/she got 10 years of life left? Is it worth going through a life-threatening operation to do this procedure? That is what I ask myself every week, and that is the sort of thing that we were discussing. We get more advice than just us; it is not just the surgeon's view. Nowadays pre-operative assessments are done by anaesthetists as well and occasionally a case will be turned down that I thought was a good option, by an anaesthetist.'

'Thank you very much. That is very helpful.' O'Neil said that with his Cheshire grin and nodded at the Chairman to indicate that he had finished.

'The Reverend is a lay member of the Panel would like to ask a few questions.' The Chairmen continued.

'I have one very simply question following on from the question before you responded to Dr O'Neil. The test that you were referring to about orthopaedic competence, they are all on live patients?'

'Yes.' Was the short answer. I wish we could have used him to ask the assessors this question who insisted that such a test cannot be done and also that it was against the Royal College policy. Here is the representative of the Royal College saying exactly the opposite. They were trying to justify the artificial test in the Council as against assessing in live situation.

'Could you describe for me the process that trainees go through before you would feel you could let them loose on live patients, if I can put it crudely? Presumably you do not let them practice from day one?'

'When they come as specialist registrars they have done some time in hospital and they will have assisted at most of these operations. When they come to work with me I would, say, take a simple operation at first for them, such as carpal tunnel decompression, a simple operation on the hand, and they will have seen it with me several times; we would then start the PBA if they requested … Because it is a trainee-requested test this, 'Sir, I have done seven carpal tunnels with you, can I have a go at the next one please?' is often what happens, so we would then, first of all, check that he knew why he was doing the operation, and I would have talked to him about what he is going to do beforehand: I would then scrub with him/her to do the operation. Always, I would not do it without, and during the operation, I would frequently have to interfere in a trainee. I may even have to take over, and if I do take over he is grade one, he does not get … He maybe not even get a grade at all, it would be in effect a failure of the PBA because he was not able to complete the full operation, and so it moves up the scale. As they get more, senior so you would expect them to complete the operation and if you see them doing something stupid halfway through you interfere immediately, but, of course, that affects the grade. Therefore, I believe it is a safe way of doing it. It is not very different to a driving instructor letting him have his way in the car until he sees it is dangerous and taking over.'

'Yes, thank you, that is very helpful. Can I take you back to the stage before that? I understand that people coming as trainees are not coming straight out of Medical School obviously, but where would they practise their surgical skills before they are competent to practise on real people?'

'The college has set up in the South of England an opportunity to go to the college in the School of Surgery to practise on cadavers so you can operate on cadavers. In my own hospital, we have a session about every three months where surgeons give up their time to train juniors on sewing up wounds, making incisions, so they have some practice there working on animals – dead animals – so they get some skill in using instruments. But, when they are assisting a surgeon at an operation before they have a chance to do it themselves, they will be using instruments in an open wound, so they are shown how to retract and they are able to identify tissues. That is what you are doing with the trainee all the way through their training, asking them 'What is that, what is that, what do we cut now?' and so on. They are taught from a pretty lowly level. One of our bug bears at the moment is that the medical schools are producing doctors with very little anatomy training, really terribly important in surgery, and we are having to start almost again.'

'Thank you.'

The Chairman wanted to ask more questions.

'Mr. Bridge, I would like to turn to an area that Dr O'Neil touched upon. We have heard a great deal during the course of this hearing about multi-disciplinary contexts in which many orthopaedic surgeons currently practice. Can I first ask you if that is your experience, that is that orthopaedic surgeons now operate in multi-disciplinary environments?'

'To give you a direct example, this morning I should be at a combined clinic with a rheumatologist doing a clinic in which severely affected rheumatoid patients will need surgery. The decision to operate on a rheumatoid patient is complex because nearly every joint, in some patients, in their body will give them pain. It would be very easy as a surgeon to latch on and replace the one, or operate on the one, which you want to do, which is easiest. However, with a rheumatologist present, there is discussion about the pros and cons of doing whatever the surgeon is suggesting, so that is very much multi-disciplinary. To go on, nobody gets on to my operating list without a pre-operative assessment, which is organised and run by the anaesthetist. The anaesthetists often stop a patient getting any further than that by saying, 'There is a heart arrhythmia, there is a heart murmur,' they must have a cardiology opinion first, so the pathway gets stopped, and they go off on a side track.'

'Let us suppose for the moment that you are training one of your trainees and this trainee is presented with a patient that, for example, has insulin dependent diabetes. What would you expect a satisfactory trainee to do about that?'

'You would have had a letter from the GP, I hope, saying, 'This patient I am referring to you is diabetic.' They usually controlled or on insulin or whatever. That should be there. It is an absolute must in surgery to test the circulation, especially in diabetics. I have seen diabetics get into trouble time and again if you operate and not checked that the circulation is not adequate. Even when it is checked, it is still a risk, so it is something you discuss with the patient. I would certainly want to test the pulses in the legs and so on, feel the pulses. If I was in doubt, they would go off to a vascular surgeon to have an assessment about that. It is not at all uncommon after a major operation like this to find that the vascular blood flow into the foot, which may have been precarious before surgery, goes over the barrier and gangrene ensues, so it is very important to know about this up front. You try and then guide the patient as to whether the risk is worth taking. Sometimes you have to come off the fence and say 'yes' or 'no', but I think it should all be open with the patient, with the GP, with the vascular surgeon if he is involved. Having been made aware of the condition of this patient and having taken the decision to go ahead with the surgery, who would be responsible for the management of this patient in respect of his diabetes?'

'I would be the one who was responsible for saying, 'I am prepared to do the operation', knowing the risks, having discussed them with the patient, having taken informed consent. I am quite prepared to do that and often do that in people I know could die from the operation, but you have to make these decisions. As soon as, and if, trouble arises afterwards, then you get your colleagues' help, so I would go to the physician, the diabetic consultant in fact if it was a diabetic problem, but it is more likely to be a vascular problem so I would go to the vascular surgeon. I would involve my colleagues as and when needed, but beforehand, if I thought there was a high risk, I would involve them by asking their opinion.'

With that, the Chairman finished his questioning. I was feeling very happy at this. Both the questions and the answers made me feel that things were definitely looking good.

At this stage, Sykes had a couple of questions.

'First, you were asked by Dr O'Neil about co morbidities. Can you explain what a co morbidity is?'

'Somebody who has arthritis of the hip and needs a hip replacement may very well have angina, they may very well have had a past history of stroke, they may be diabetic, they may have other medical problems which make the operation more risky than if they were one hundred per cent fit.'

'By way of example, you were just being asked by the Chairman about insulin dependent diabetes. Is that what amounts to a co morbidity?'

'Yes.'

'Did you see any evidence that Mr. Kasyapa may have been limited in his knowledge of co morbidities or his understanding of how to deal with them?'

'No, to my knowledge we did discuss patients with co morbidities when he was with me in Marsden on Sea. I have one clinic for revision hip surgery, which is complex. It often takes one and a half hours, two hours or more, and most of the patients are fairly elderly. They will mostly have co morbidities, and we would have discussed the merits, pros, and cons of surgery in that context together, in fact, we did. I do sometimes advise patients that the risks are two great. Without them hearing I may well, say to my colleague, 'I honestly do not think this chap is going to live more than a couple of years, it is not right that we should be doing a major op on this patient', and so on. You have to make these judgment decisions. One thing I would like to say, and it is important to understand this, is that there may well be differences in opinion about whether somebody should undergo an operation or not. At the end of the day, the patient, if they are corpus mentis, has a right to make that decision, I believe. Sometimes the anaesthetist will turn down a patient, for example, because they are too fat, too over weight. I may know, the GP may know, the patient may know in their heart of hearts, that they are not going to get their weight down as much as the anaesthetist may like. Do you take the risk or not? I believe the patient has the right to say whether they are prepared to take the risk under those circumstances. Unlike my colleagues, I might operate on someone with a very high BMI that another surgeon might feel, 'I am not prepared to do that.' I appreciate their opinion; I think they also will appreciate mine.' Mr. Bridge stopped to take a breather and looked at Sykes.

'On the same topic, we have heard a lot of evidence over the last couple of days about the multi-disciplinary approach, largely in relation to dealing with co morbidity. I want to understand this. A surgeon, however specialised, has to have a basic knowledge, presumably, not only of in order to recognise what may amount to a co morbidity, but also strategies for dealing with them?' It was a parting shot from Sykes I thought.

'Certainly.'

'Although you work in a multi-disciplinary strategy team in order to form a strategy of dealing with co morbidities – therefore you will pass on, presumably, to a specialist very often when you have identified something; – the surgeon still has to have a core knowledge of how to deal with co morbidity?'

'Yes.'

'Did you see any lack of understanding so far as Mr. Kasyapa was concerned, by way of knowledge of dealing with any of the co morbidities that you did identify during the three weeks that he was with you'

'No, I can honestly say I did not pick up any inadequacy in that direction at all.'

'Thank you.'

'The Chairman asked you who would manage diabetes, and you explained you would take the responsibility. Who would actually prescribe treatment for your diabetic patient?' Fred asked.

Mr. Bridge smiled and said, 'GPs claim the right to look after diabetes in most patients, but some patients are difficult to control and they would then be referred to a diabetic clinic run by a diabetic consultant. The patient would often have trips to the hospital on a fairly regular basis to a Diabetic Clinic where they would probably not often see the consultant but most likely, they would see a diabetic nurse. They would have a protocol for checking the patient's blood sugars and so on.'

'I was thinking more specifically, when you have a patient who has come in for hip replacement or whatever and is diabetic and you make the decision, as you have explained, who actually prescribes insulin while the patient is in hospital to make sure they are getting the right amount and so on?' Fred persisted.

'The anaesthetist always takes over the control of the drugs. The anaesthetist will normally change someone from injections of insulin onto a drip in which insulin is put in over a long period of time, so it is an anaesthetic thing. If the anaesthetist felt control was wrong in the post-op period, I would think he would go to the diabetic consultant in the hospital for advice.' Mr. Bridge answered.

'Both the Chairman and Mr. Sykes asked you about the multi-disciplinary approach and you have given your explanation of that. We have heard reference to multi-disciplinary teams. What is a multi-disciplinary team in your experience?'

'In hospital we work in teams. I can only think it means the other consultants in the hospital. They are all part of my team and even the psychiatrist I have called on his help occasionally. You need each specialist in turn when they are needed and that is what a hospital is; it is a collection of experts.' I could see slight irritation in Mr. Bridge's voice.

'What about specialist nurses, for example you mentioned the diabetic nurse. Presumably there are other specialist nurses as well, how do they fit in?' Fred continued as if he had not noticed the irritation.

'It depends on the local arrangements, but it might well be the case that the diabetic nurse would call to the ward and check what system has been put in place by the anaesthetist for the diabetes control.'

'The final matter. The Chairman's initial questions were about the performance based assessment and you explained how that worked; that is the performance based assessment that you applied to Mr. Kasyapa earlier this month?'

'Yes.'

'If you look at your letter, it is D41.'

'I can remember it.'

'Could I ask that you should have a copy? You explain the form that is used in your first paragraph and then attached to that letter is the appraisal you carried out. Go past that and we come to the document, which is headed 'Trauma and Orthopaedics PBA 6: Total Hip Replacement?'

'That is the standard form which all centres training registrars use.'

'This is your handwriting on the typed form?'

'It is.'

'This is what you would apply to Mr. Kasyapa?'

'Yes.'

'We can see at the end the matter which our Chairman asked you about, on the very last page, "The level at which completed elements of the PBA were performed', and there are the four, five levels because there is a level '0' as well, set out?'

'Yes.'

'What would help me, and I should probably have asked you at the beginning but I am not sure whether it is controversial, is whether you could take us through your handwritten comment on the right hand column?'

'Yes, on the hip replacement?' Mr. Bridge wanted to know.

'Through all of them, if you would not mind.' As we had discussed earlier, Fred was trying to get the entire episode in detail so that it does not leave anything in doubt as far as the panel was concerned.

'Under the section 'Consent', I have ticked 'Satisfactory', the individual questions, but I have written in the comment: 'Patient given information leaflet pre-operatively and good pre-op notes taken.' Mr. Kasyapa gave me copies of the leaflet that he gives patients, an information leaflet, for those undergoing total hip replacement in this case. It is a well-put together document and it covers what is going to happen to the patient, how they should look after their hip in the post-operative period. We have copied that ourselves in our own hospital since he has given me a copy; it is good. It is not unusual to have this. There is in fact one on the internet you can download, but it is good that a surgeon actually goes to the trouble of giving a patient a leaflet they can read in their own time about the operation because in a half-hour's consultation it is difficult to get through all the points they may want to ask.'

'The next one is "Pre-operative planning?"

'On the screen in theatre, on the x-ray screen in theatre, when I went in was the x-ray of the patient we were going to operate on. He had put on to the osteo-arthritic hip a diagram of the hip he was going to replace, so that he had worked out the size that it was likely he was going to use. He had worked out the angles and the sizes, so we had a little discussion about that even before we started the operation. I thought that the planning of it had obviously taken place. He had thought about the operation before he started.'

'You have written: "Excellent pre-op planning on X-rays up in theatre.'

'I thought that was better than average. It might have been because I was going, but it was better than average to have drawn out the x-rays in such detail. It is what I do for revision surgery routinely. In primary hip surgery, you can usually be pretty certain what size it is going to be anyway, but this was nicely done. It could not have been improved on really.'

'You have another comment ..' But before he could finish Mr. Bridge continued.

'It is vitally important to operate on the right side, and there was a jolly good arrow on the leg that was being operated on. He had checked that pre-operatively and again in theatre. He was also present at the setting up of the patient as you have to put them in a good position to be able to operate safely.'

'Exposure and closure?'

'It was neat exposure.' Mr. Bridge continued.

'What does your comment say?'

'Good exposure, neat operation.' Oh yes, he was teaching the staff grade surgeon during the operation as well, so he was telling him what he was doing and so on."

'I cannot read what it says after 'Neat operation', it says?'

'Also teaches staff grade surgeon.' On the next page, the Intra Operative Technique was all satisfactory. The 'N' that I put in was because we did not have any complications on the hip replacement so it was not tested. During the operation the instructions to the sister and the assistant were clear instructions.' Mr. Bridge continued.

'Clear instruction to sister and assistant.' Fred asked.

'This is really what I meant about the rapport in theatre was excellent between all three of them, the anaesthetist, the assistant and the sister. The last comment I have made is, 'Yes, stable' – he checked that the hip was stable at the end of the operation and demonstrated to the staff grade who was helping him and to myself. Then he did something, which is a fairly new innovation for most surgeons, he typed up the operation notes in theatre. They have access to a dataset where they can put in the operation details immediately and it then goes on the patient's records and I believe that it sets up a copy that can go to the GP as well.' Mr. Bridge replied.

'Then, 'Global Summary'?'

''A well executed total hip replacement. Safe operation carefully done. I consider him to be a competent hip surgeon.' Mr. Bridge answered.

'And for 'arthroscopy,' can you read us your comments there.' Fred asked.

'The arthroscopy that I observed was a double: both knees needed to be done. This was a rheumatoid lady, so it was more complex and it took a little longer, a bilateral arthroscopy. Again, there was an information leaflet that was given to the patient and he talked to the patient before she went to sleep. I was observing that. Again, the knees were marked and consent was taken. We had a complication in this operation insomuch as the tourniquet failed. That is not really Mr. Kasyapa's fault; I suppose it is the tourniquet that fails but it is put on by the operating department assistant and I am afraid that they often do fail. When it fails, it makes the operation more complex because there is then bleeding inside the knee as in this case, but he dealt with that complication very ably, washed the knee out with a lot of fluid, and was able to finish the operation. The anaesthetist was told what was going on, so realised that the operation was going to take a bit longer and it all was handled very calmly. I have written, 'Good rapport with anaesthetist and scrub sister.' Lastly, 'Types up clear note in theatre.' My last comment is, 'Proficient arthroscopist and safe.' In a way, having that complication arise allowed me to see him act under a bit of pressure in adverse conditions. It is something that I would not have liked to happen to myself with an observer being present, but he handled that very well.' Mr. Bridge answered.

'Thank you very much, Mr. Bridge. I do not know if there are any questions arising out of that.' I thought that went extremely well. From this interlude, it should be clear to any impartial observer about my ability as a surgeon, I thought.

'We have no further questions for you, Mr. Bridge. I am sorry that you had to re-arrange your clinic in order to come here, especially so early. We are extremely grateful for your assistance. You are excused. Thank you very much.' The Chairman said to Mr. Bridge.

Once Mr. Bridge left the room, Fred introduced two more documents as 'witness.' One of them was a Petition raised by the staff of the hospital with over 200 signatures protesting the action that was happening against me. The Council did not object to its submission, made light of the petition saying it was 'only hearsay,' and cannot be counted as evidence of my fitness to practice. The second one was a letter written by one of patients imploring the Chief Executive of my trust the injustice that was being carried out.

When Fred said that he did not have any more witnesses, the Chairman asked Sykes if he was going to make his submission. That appeared to take Sykes by surprise and said he does not have a 'submission' and gave out an 'advise' instead. Fred wanted some time to make his submission and asked for a short break. When we came back from the break, the Legal Adviser gave his 'advise.' He droned on for about twenty minutes, literally repeating what was written in the rulebook of the Council.

Fred started off with the usual introduction to his submission reminding the panel of the rules of the council as it existed and then went to on to his submission highlighting his points of submission as a summary;

'There are four points there that I would like to make. The first is that both parties have had the opportunity to put in further evidence. The GMC has not put in further evidence. There is no further evidence on Mr. Kasyapa's fitness to practise as of now which the GMC has thought it appropriate to put before you. The only evidence that they rely on is the assessors' report of two years ago. The second point is that both parties are entitled to make submissions, and Mr. Sykes has made two uncontroversial and highly proper submissions as to the appropriate test and how to approach the problem. He reminded you in opening of your previous findings of fact. There is no submission, however – and this is important – there is no submission from the GMC that Mr. Kasyapa's fitness to practise is now impaired. That is not the case that is being advanced by the GMC. The third point is one that I know your Legal Assessor is going to raise in his legal advice, it is that any question of fitness to practise is on the basis of any facts found proved, so any allegations which are based on facts or allegations or hypotheses outside the facts that you found proved on the last occasion are irrelevant. It is only on those facts found proved that you are entitled to judge, and plus any further evidence, and all the evidence about Mr. Kasyapa, that you can judge whether his fitness to practise is now impaired. The fourth and final point is one, which is established in the cases of *Cohen* and *Zygmunt* and *Azzam* that had been in dispute before. The word is in the present tense, and that is, of course, the way that you and your colleagues have approached this: is the practitioner's fitness to practise now impaired? Now and into the future, not whether it was impaired: is it now?' I thought his second point was crucial – the Council has not made any submission as to the fitness to practice. Neither have they produced any witnesses to support that. I could not see how the panel could make a decision on something, which has not been asked for.

He clarified the four points and went on to his detailed submission based on the evidence gathered through the previous few days' witnesses. He started off with the last determination made by the panel and

'Can I attempt, in nine points, to say just a few words about each, to identify what those findings were that are critical of Mr. Kasyapa?' He went on to read out the nine points he was going to discuss.

'No pre-operative plan for Patient 31. Do you remember that was where the very poor transcription of the operation note recorded no strut graft? No explanation of why Mr. Kasyapa prescribed three weeks bed rest to Patient 39. A written but no oral warning of the risk of DVT in Patient 17. No assessment of the risk for or plan for prophylaxis for DVT in Patients 6 and 22. No warning of the risk of gout flaring up in Patient 43. You thought that the risk of operating on Patient 30 was too high. Operating in the presence of Sudeck's in Patient 35. Failing the surgical core knowledge test. Failing the basic skills test.'
'I have taken them slightly out of order so they are grouped in a sensible way.

I think that covers it. I have obviously paraphrased just to give you headlines, as it were, but I think that is the gist of what you have found as a basis of criticism of Mr. Kasyapa on the last occasion. That group of nine falls into two obvious categories, one is there is criticism in relation to the treatment of specific patients and the other is that there is a failure of tests which have been undertaken by Mr. Kasyapa. It is quite clear, and I will not take you to it again, that the assessors felt that the failure to perform well in those tests was <u>the</u> most critical thing. I am not diminishing the others but one suspect from the way it is written that that is what they felt was the most important. Anyway, it does not matter, I have got to deal with all of them whatever their relative importance or not.

There is one thing that can be said about all the patient cases, and that is compared to the very serious allegations that the Fitness to Practise Panel (whether this or others) often comes to deal with, these cannot be regarded as the most serious cases in the world.

Let me now say a word about each of them. We have not got the benefit of the transcript, or at least I have not had the benefit of the transcript either so I am just working on recollection here, but your memory no doubt is better than mine. Can I just summarise what we say about these various points? I think it is possible to group them yet further. If I give you the heading 'Pre-operative assessment and planning' and 'record keeping' it seems to me that that covers several of the issues, and by the time I get to the bottom of my headings I hope you will feel that I have dealt with all of them. So, 'Pre-operative assessment and planning' and 'record keeping' I hope, sir, that the Panel is now satisfied that this problem has now been sorted out. You heard from Mr. Kasyapa yesterday about the process of seeing the patients in outpatients; seeing them in the assessment clinic, and seeing them immediately pre-operatively as well. You have heard that he makes appropriate entries in the notes. You have heard about the templating, which is illustrated by D40, on the x-rays and the notes of components required. His operation note system has now improved dramatically, with the notes being made on the computer in the theatre on his own initiative.

You heard that the system for non-attending, failures to attend, DNAs, failures to attend at outpatients has been improved, and you have seen Mr. Cooley's and Mr. Worthing's survey, both surveys of the notes, which, although not perfect show a good system at work. You have also heard the way that Mr. Kasyapa has taken on board the criticisms that have been made. In our respectful submission, you cannot have – to use Mr. Sykes's phrase – substantial residual concerns about those matters.

The next heading is 'Assessment and warning of the risks of surgery' (which includes, obviously, DVT and gout, and so on). You have heard about the leaflets which are exemplary and have been copied by Mr. Bridge's hospital, and which have been continuously improved by Mr. Kasyapa. You had the older and the improved versions. As he made clear, he has taken on board your findings and the assessors' criticisms in relation to warnings on DVT and gout, and now will warn.

He and others have told you about the multi-disciplinary teams that deal with issues such as diabetes and deep vein thrombosis pre, peri and post-operation prophylactic measures and so forth, and the involvement of the anaesthetist and the relevant specialist nurses and so on. So, once again, there cannot be any substantial concern outstanding there.

There is then the high-risk patient: a simple and probably the only measure that Mr. Kasyapa could take he told you yesterday, he would consult a colleague in such a case.

You heard from Mr. Bridge today that, of course, surgeons are going to differ about how high a risk there has to be before a surgeon refuses to operate. But if two of them put their heads together (and that is what Mr. Kasyapa is going to do in a high-risk case), this Panel can be satisfied that there is no impairment of his fitness in that respect.

The next heading is the 'Operation in the presence of Sudeck's': Mr. Kasyapa told you he will not do that.

Then there is the basic skills issue, the failure of the basic skills course. Two points answer that: No. 1, he undertook such a course and he told you yesterday that he learned things which added to his repertoire, so that addresses that problem, but there is a second reassurance for the Panel as well and that is that there is not and never has been any evidence in practice of any such lack of skill pre or post the assessment. That is particular relevant when you have heard Mr. Bridge this morning who actually watched Mr. Kasyapa operate, or Mr. Rayner who taught him and who has operated with him since, and the others that have seen his work.

Then there is the question of surgical knowledge, the failure of the surgical knowledge test. There are four points here, of which the fourth is probably the least important but which is going to take me the biggest part of my time. The first three are the most important: No. 1, he gave you evidence yesterday that he had addressed that problem; he had had discussions with colleagues and he had learned lessons. No. 2, all the surgeons you have heard from have testified to the limited knowledge, which is required of an orthopaedic surgeon in comparison to the experts they have around them available in the multi-disciplinary teams. Of course, they need core knowledge but it is nonetheless limited, and it is quite clear that Mr. Kasyapa operates well in the multi-disciplinary team setting.

The third point once again is that there is no evidence in practice of any lack of basic surgical knowledge, or of basic medical knowledge; no evidence in practice, both pre and post assessment. There are no cases where there has been a failure because of a lack of basic knowledge.

The fourth point is a different one. As I say, it will take me a few minutes to develop this. Remember Mr. Worthing's report said that the only area he felt had not been addressed was core knowledge. He said that the validity of the tests that had been applied to Mr. Kasyapa were open to question. That is in his report. He, like others, pointed to the presence of multi-disciplinary teams as dealing with that issue.

There is, in fact, another point about the openness to question of the validity of the tests. It arises in this way. I made submissions on the last occasion, and for this, I wonder if I could invite the Panel.. I do not know if the Panel has my written submissions. Would it be possible to have them before you and, with it also, your own conclusions on the last occasion.' Fred paused and looked at the panel Chairman.

Once the relevant documents were produced, he again went through the incongruity of scoring used by the Council's assessors and pointed out the false conclusions drawn by the assessors as well as the Panel itself. He quoted some of the recent court cases to substantiate his submission as to how the panel cannot make a decision on current impairment based on some evidence, questionable at best, which was over two years old.

He later went on to elaborate the evidence of the leading orthopaedic consultants over the past few days telling the panel about my qualities as a surgeon and made a point of stressing on the fact that this was obtained by direct observation. The only reservation I had about this part of his submission was that he did not stress on the authority of these consultants, particularly Mr. Bridge.

He then went through the testimonial written by colleagues from various specialities who had worked with me in the past. They were all glowing references and all of them had said that they would have no hesitation in having me operate on them or anyone in their family.

I particularly liked his conclusion.

'Sir, I come to the conclusion, you will be happy to hear, of my submissions and I want to make these five observations about the evidence relating to Mr. Kasyapa's fitness to practise. The first point is this. The Assessors looked at some 50 cases. In no case has any harm to any patient been identified by an act or omission of Mr. Kasyapa. I say again, this is a remarkable case that a doctor's practice can come before the Fitness to Practise Panel and yet in not a single case is it said that his intervention or lack of it caused injury to any patient. That is my first point of five.

The second point is that there is no criticism of Mr. Kasyapa as a surgeon by anybody who has worked with him or seen his work save for Mr. Serpe and Pakshar. I made observations about the motivation of Mr. Serpe and so did Mr. Fitzgerald and I know that you will quite rightly not consider that relevant, but it is perhaps significant, only from this point of view, that the only person who criticised Mr. Kasyapa was a man who Mr. Fitzgerald regarded as being malevolent – I forget the adjective that he used. No other criticism.

The third point is that there is no evidence of any lack of clinical skills or clinical knowledge save for the curious outcome of the tests, which, as one of the Assessors agreed, was odd. The reason why it was odd is of course that none of the cases show any lack of surgical skill or surgical knowledge and neither does anybody who has ever worked with him suggest that there was any lack of skill or knowledge and I invite the Panel, as I have done on the previous occasion, to infer that it is simply inconceivable, whatever may have been the situation in the past, that Mr. Kasyapa lacks essential skill or knowledge which has not been detected in any of his cases or by any of the people from nurses to consultants who have seen him operate. The proof of the pudding is in the eating, we say.

The fourth point is that there is much evidence that Mr. Kasyapa, chastened by his experience to use Mr. Justice McCombe's word, has taken to heart the criticisms that were levelled against him and has sought to redress them and made improvements, not just by going on the basic surgical skills course and going on the placement with Mr. Bridge but in all sorts of other ways as well.

The fifth point that I make is that, as of today, there is no significant evidence that Mr. Kasyapa is not now fit to practise without any impairment at all. Those are the five points that I want to make.' Fred finished and paused for a moment for that to sink in before finally concluding with;

'This is a case therefore, sir, in which the criticisms which you have found which survive from the Assessors' report of two years ago have now been dealt with. There are, to quote Mr. Sykes, no substantial residual concerns, which this Panel ought to have. Mr. Sykes himself has not identified any substantial residual concern, which you ought to have. There is no sufficient evidence to sustain any substantial residual concern and, in those circumstances, I invite this Panel to find that Mr. Kasyapa's fitness to practise is not – *is not* – impaired.'

My mouth was dry as and I felt tired and at the same time oddly elated. It is very difficult to explain the emotions that go through someone who is being defended in public. It was also rather humbling experience to finally understand the high regard many of my colleagues had of me. They adjourned the hearing for the panel to go 'into camera' and deliberate. We were told to be available at half an hour's notice for determination.

Everyone was silent as we walked into the waiting room. Nancy said.

'No point waiting around Upaas. They will not give a determination until at least tomorrow afternoon. You might as well spend your time looking around London.' Fred thanked everyone and talked about his summer holiday when he had gone to Holland and spent time on a riverboat. There was a poignant moment as we were about to leave the building. Mr. Sykes came into our room and shook my hands and said;

'No hard feelings Mr. Kasyapa. It was nice knowing you. I cannot believe even this panel is going to find fault with you after what we have seen over the past few days.'

And left the room. Everyone in the room were taken aback and quiet for what seemed to be a long time. It was Fred who broke the silence with;

'That was nice of him. A thorough gentleman.' and he walked out as well. All of us trooped out behind him to the cold December evening in London. It was dark and damp and the traffic was as busy as usual. London was going through its business. This was just another event that had taken place among a million more. No one took notice of us as we walked along toward the tube station.

In fact, it turned out that Nancy was being very optimistic. The panel did not reach a conclusion not only the next day, but the day after. It was the day before Christmas Eve and London was bustling with shoppers. Shuchi took us around some of her haunts – mostly specialist Cake shops and Japanese savoury shops. It was well into the afternoon when I got a call from Nancy. I was actually in one of those cake shops when the call came through. I got out of the shop to take the call.

'It is not very good I am afraid.' Nancy started and before my heart could stop, she continued 'They have not come to a decision. They have set a date for February next year for determination. Obviously, we are all very disappointed. I thought it was 'cut and dry' after Mr. Bridge's evidence. It is not to be.' she did sound rather down beat.

I was relieved and at the same time furious. I would be kept hanging around for yet another three months. I wanted to know if there was anything that could be done in the meantime.

'I don't think so. It is now in their hands. We will just have to sit tight and wait. I am hoping that we will get it our way. I can't imagine that this panel would give a decision against you after all that solid evidence from some of the senior most surgeons in the country.' Nancy tried to cheer me up. I went back into the shop and gave the bad news to Lopa and the girls. We spent the next couple of hours wandering around the shops before making our way back to the car and back home. As usual, there was a lot of discussion among our friends and us. Gautam took the view that the panel will try to fudge the determination so that the GMC could not be sued. Swayambhu felt that the panel would probably decide on a 'slap on the wrist' so that the GMC will be seen to be doing something and that it had not wasted nearly a million pound on a wasted trial.

That must have been the dullest Christmas we have had in our house. The Damocles' sword was hanging over not just my head but also everyone else's. We made the most of it and the time seemed to drag waiting for February to come. There had been several phone calls from me to Nancy after the New Year asking about possible scenarios. Poor Nancy. She could not answer questions that I was asking. No one could. The only ones who knew the answers were the Panel members. Eventually I broached the subject. What would happen if the decision were against me? Where do we start? What do I do?

'We will have to take stock of the determination and go from there. It all depends on which way they swing. But, Upaas. I have a strong feeling that we have won. I think they are taking a long time to word the decision so that the GMC cannot be taken to court successfully.'

That brought some comfort to me and I tried to put the thought out of my mind and try to concentrate on my work.

23. What Next?

There I was, very impressed with the last stage of the inquisition reinforced by what Nancy had said. I was particularly impressed with Mr. Simon Bridge's deposition. After that, I did not think anyone would say anything wrong about me. I could not have been further from the truth. I had forgotten that I was dealing with three individuals who are the face of a large organisation with immense power. These are people who behave with impunity and apparently not answerable to anyone. Particularly, in the case of the lay Preacher not even to God. By now, I had the dates for the final stage of the hearing in February. They had earmarked three full days for that. I decided not to go and sit waiting in London and be stressed out. It was better, that I was preoccupied with the stress of work, and forgot the shenanigans of the Panel. I was doing what I enjoyed best – be with my friends at work and treat patients and make them better. The feeling you get when a patient says 'Thank you' after a Hip replacement is worth millions. I thrived on this and made me forget everything else. After the depositions and statements from some of the most senior orthopaedic surgeons in the country supporting me, I had no reason to believe that things could go wrong. In fact, I looked forward to getting back to 'normal' work. I was so confident of the outcome, that I sent Lopa off to India with her mother for some 'rest and relaxation'. I felt she could do with a decent break from the stress of the last five years; particularly the last two of them had been extremely stressful all around.

It was only a matter of time before I realised how wrong I was. February turned out to be one of the worst months in my life so far. Lopa had gone to India to see her mother all the children were away at the university, and I had the house to myself. I felt rather unusually lonely, and feeling sorry for myself at being left on my own. Just when I thought, things could not get any worse, fate dealt me with another blow. It was a Tuesday afternoon, and I was extremely busy in a clinic when a call came through from Nancy.

'It is not very good news, Upaas.'

My heart sank, and it took me a minute to grasp what she was saying.

'The panel has given a decision against us. I am utterly disgusted, and Fred is furious. We have to go to court. We'll not get any justice ..'

Nancy went on for a long time. By now, my mind was racing and I was not really hearing what she was saying. I was rather numb and distraught. The nurses in the clinic knew there was something wrong. I told Nancy that I would call her back after the clinic. I do not know how I finished the clinic that afternoon. It was nearly six in the evening, before I could get hold of Nancy again. She still did not have any details of the 'determination' and said she will call me as soon as she gets some more information. I had to wait until nearly eight at night before she called me with the details of the determination. By then I had a call from Dr Smiths from the MPS. He was furious and seething with anger. He was travelling back home on train and could not really be too explicit. I could sense his anger and sheer frustration in his voice. He said, 'The MPS will do everything in its power to avenge this nonsense. I have never seen any panel, which was as corrupt as this. I cannot speak in detail now as I am inside a train.' He went on to say that, he had instructed Nancy and Fred to take the GMC head on and he wanted all the money spent by the MPS on this case back.

'We have to get the costs back for the members of the MPS and you should be compensated as well.'

This statement coming from the Medical Adviser at the MPS was reassuring and dulled the pain slightly. By then I had sent text messages to Swayambhu and Gautam. As usual, Swayambhu wanted to know the full details of the determination, which I could not give, as I had not seen one yet. Nancy had promised to email me the determination as soon as she gets the document. It was nearly nine that night before I got the scanned image of the determination from Nancy. It was shocking reading. More I read angrier I got and rational thinking went out of the window. My mind was racing and was full of if's, but's and what next's. I could not think straight. I had not expected this bolt from the blue. I was only half prepared for this eventuality a few months ago. Nevertheless, the events of the previous couple of months had made me forget the worst-case scenario and I had cocooned myself in this shell of appreciation from all around me and slightly oblivious to the perversity of the GMC panel. The glowing support that was demonstrated by six of the senior most and highly respected orthopaedic surgeons in the country and made me feel invulnerable to assault as it were. I felt as If I was being trampled on and defiled in some way. I did not know whom to turn to. With so many people around me, I felt alone and slowly sinking with nothing to hold on to. I could see John Fitzgerald calling me up and asking me to leave. The little nest that I had built with a lot of blood and guts over the past twenty-six years was crashing down like a pack of cards in front of my eyes. Whenever I closed my eyes, there was this vision of despair and disaster of losing the house and everything I had worked so hard for and cherished so much. I was afraid to close my eyes as the vision kept coming back at me.

I could not sleep all night. I kept thinking about what would happen tomorrow when I go to work. Would there be a call from the Chief Executive to come to his office? Worse still, would I be summoned to his office in the middle of a clinic? Who would be in the Chief executive's office? How can I face my colleagues at work? What can I tell them? How would my friends at work react? Would I be ostracised by the people who had admired me all my working life? Would I be asked to clear my room and empty my desk? This would give more than enough ammunition to my erstwhile colleagues and no one could stop their tongues wagging. I am sure our new head of the department would be telling George, 'I told you so' with a satisfaction of winning a lottery. One or two of my colleagues would be rubbing their hands in glee and probably build their ego even higher, if that were possible.

What would I do when there is no payslip at the end of the month? How can I pay next month's mortgage? Can I sell the house quickly? Where would I live? How can I support the children still in the university? This will be the end of my career in this country! Can I get a job abroad quickly? Would they ask for a GMC registration if I apply for a job abroad? What would be Lopa's response when she finds out? Can I ever get back to work after this?

How can they FTP panel do this? Are they blind and deaf? As my mind started to wander towards the decision of the panel, I got angrier and angrier. I must have cursed them a million times that night. I must have cursed Pakshar, Serpe and the three assessors till the early hours of morning. I cursed the day I agreed to help Pakshar get out of the gutter he was stuck in India. If I had met any of them that night, I do not know what I would have done. At that moment in time, my world was collapsing around me and I felt that the whole world was against me. I could not see an end to this nightmare and I even felt that even Nancy and Fred were not working hard enough. For the second time during this nightmare, I was having serious doubts about the selection of the solicitor and the barrister. Finally, I had to get out of bed with a splitting headache at around 4'O clock in the morning. Two cups of coffee and four Paracetamol later, I decided to make my first move. I decided that, I would pre-empt any action by the Chief Executive by asking for a meeting. The brain started to think logically for the first time in the past eight hours. I sent an email to the Chief Executive's office asking for an urgent appointment at 4.30 in the morning! I was sure that would grab their attention when they get to the office in the morning.

Rest of the morning went rather quickly with taking Laika for a walk and my exercises. By the time I reached the hospital, there was a message waiting from the Chief Executive's secretary. She had arranged for me to see him in his office at lunchtime. I do not know how I went through the clinic that morning. It must be some sort of a reflex action and I was an automaton going through the motions. Come Lunchtime, I trudged out to the Chief Executive's office. As the secretary smiled and lead me into his office, my heart sank to see the Medical Director as well as the Divisional director. Next, my eye dropped on the table in front – there it was the dreaded decisions document from the FTP. I was rather taken aback to see that document, as I had only seen the document myself about an hour ago on my email from Nancy. Bad news travel fast. I was even more angry when I found out a little later that the Chief Executive had the document the previous night at eight – several hours before me. That just confirms the despicable Machiavellian behaviour of the FTP panel. The Chief Executive, John Fitzgerald started saying that he was sad to see the document from the GMC and that it arrived on his desk the night before. He offered me a cup of coffee and said

'Upaas, let me reiterate that you have the full support of the entire hospital and the Trust board.' and went on to say 'on a personal note I am one hundred percent behind you.'

I started to relax and some of my fears were laid to rest. The discussion of the text in the document started and things started to get worse. After about an hour of this, I asked him –

'Tell me what do you want me to do now?'

He turned politician, he rambled on for a few minutes before finally coming down to what he was actually going to say.

'I have to protect you from possible media attention and I don't want you to face awkward questions from any of the patients. As the Chief Executive of the Trust, I do have moral duty to protect the reputation and interests of the Trust as well as one of my most valued employee i.e. you.'

I could feel my mouth go dry and my hands started to sweat. However, rather unusually I was very calm on the outside. I was dreading what was coming next.

'I want you to stay away from work for a while until this blows over.'

There was deathly quiet in the room. No one spoke for a minute.

I said very calmly, 'I don't really want to stay at home not doing anything. I would rather be doing something.'

'Do you mean a Sabbatical?' John said.

I had to think very fast on my feet here to get out of a situation and not get cornered into a 'Gardening leave of absence.' So, I turned around and said

'Yes. I would rather be working somewhere to keep up my skills. Otherwise, once this is finished, the GMC can very well say that I am de-skilled and that I would need to go on further training.'

I could see all the three heads nodding at this suggestion. We spent next fifteen minutes discussing where would be the best place for me to go. I managed to get them to agree to let me arrange a Sabbatical at the local hospital in the Royal Hospital. I was desperate to stay at home and not travel out for lots of different reasons, mainly financial. I was rather disappointed when he turned around and said that I should not go to the clinic that afternoon — which had started about fifteen minutes ago. When I objected to leaving the clinic unmanned, all three of them chorused together

'.. all taken care off. Don't worry ..'

I left with all three of them shaking my hands and patting me on my back full of 'support.' John Fitzgerald said,

'Upaas, my door is always open to you and you can come and meet me anytime you want.'

I said my Thanks to everyone and left, rather bemused and a bit shell shocked. I was not sure what it all meant and how I will react to me sitting at home not doing anything. I had to go to the office to pick up my case. I was hoping against hope that I will not bump into anyone on the way. I called my friends Gautam and Swayambhu to tell them of the outcome of the meeting. I sent a text to Lopa telling her what happened. There was the usual anger and disappointment from every one. There was a lot of advice from Gautam and huge amount of indignation from Swayambhu.

When I returned to an empty house, it felt colder than usual and about an hour later, it all started to sink in. My feet became heavy the heart was pounding, my mouth was dry and tears welled up in my eyes and could not control myself. I felt that I was completely alone and no one to turn to. The house looked completely empty and huge. The situation as I saw at that stage was desperate. It suddenly dawned on me that the Trust might not want me back. May be I am an embarrassment to them now. Are they trying to tell me something that I could not catch during the meeting? I went through the conversation during the meeting several times in my own mind. More I thought of it the worse it became and by about sixth time, I was convinced that I have not only lost my job, but my career as well, as an orthopaedic surgeon. I had visions of losing the dearly loved house and having to sell all my prized possessions. I did not know what I would do if the salary stops coming in next month. Would I be able to keep up with the mortgage payments? Would I be able to support Sanvi and Akshaj through University? How am I going to afford to get the girls married with no income? Am I really a failure as all these so-called GMC experts are saying? I must be if so many of them are saying it. Where did I go wrong? Was I fooling myself that I was an internationally renowned surgeon? All those trips to Italy, Germany, Vienna, Spain, Saudi Arabia, Denmark, and Sweden must have all been a dream. All those reputed professors of orthopaedics coming from all over the world to learn from me must also have been a dream. Those numerous papers published and research that was recognised must be a figment of my imagination. All those international meetings where I stood and spoke about my experience must be a fantasy. The mind was raging with thousands of questions with no answers to any of them.

I paced up and down the house and started to search for something. After a few minutes of ever more desperate searching in the bedrooms, study, the loft, and even the garage, I stopped to think what I was looking for. I could not remember. I just realised that I had not lost anything physical and so I will not find it. This made it even more distressing. After about an hour I realised that, I was not getting anywhere and was at the end of my tether. I had lost interest in everything and all I wanted to do was to go to sleep and never wake up again. It was not to be, as I could not get to sleep. I decided to seek help from the GP to see if he could prescribe me something to get sleep.

I called up Lopa who was at her mother's in India at the time. The response was rather muted and she asked me if she should prepone her flight back. I did not see any point in preponing the trip by three days. I sat down, had a cup of coffee, and promptly fell asleep on the settee. I woke up about an hour later, bright as button and my brain in hyperdrive. I had thousands of ideas as to how to make the best of the situation and to start thinking about earning some money to top up my basic salary, which was promised by the CE. However, I was not sure where this was heading. There was a real threat that I might lose my job and hence my livelihood in this country. I needed to have contingency plans. My first thought was to give everything up and move to the Middle East. I sat in front of the computer and updated my CV, registered my name with numerous recruitment companies dealing with the Middle East. The discussions I used to have with Gautam, about relocating to India looked particularly attractive to me at that point in time. The internet was very useful and it picked up several corporate hospitals in Bangalore. I shot off my CV's to all the corporate hospitals asking for an appointment to visit. I visited the Website of my old Alma mata and tried to see if I was still registered in India.

I called Nancy and apprised her of the latest developments in the hospital. She was very disappointed, angry and rather surprised at the turn of events. I do not think she expected the Chief Executive to react the way he did. I asked her if there was any way we could stop the press from printing their version of the story like last time. Unfortunately, I was told that the 'Determination' goes on the website as it was being read out and was probably on public domain before we got the determination in our hands. I had made my mind up by then – this FTP panel is corrupt and I am not going to get any justice from them. The only option available to me was the High Court. I still had some faith in the British Justice system being fair and just, despite the fact that one facet of the British Justice was found to be far from being fair or just. I asked Nancy to start the proceedings for a Judicial Review of the FTP process. She said we would have to ask the GMC first if they would reverse their decision before going to the High Court. She called it a 'Pre-action Protocol letter.' It apparently lays out the mistakes made by the GMC during the process and asks them to change their decision. The GMC will get fourteen days to answer and then we lodge a case at the High Court.

A good three hours later, I felt a bit satisfied and hungry. Best thing to keep my mind occupied is cooking. I decided to cook, looked up one of the recipe books, and started to cook with a glass of wine in my hand. By the time I finished cooking, I was slightly tipsy but the mind was settled. By this time, I had had several phone calls and many more SMS texts from all of my close friends. I finished eating and went to Swayambhu's house for more wine and more discussions on our future steps. It was very late by the time I got back home, very tired and emotionally completely drained. I did not have any problem falling asleep that night.

However, woke up a couple of hours later, profusely sweating, and thought I had a nightmare. However, it was not a nightmare, it was as real as can be, and it was not going to disappear when I open my eyes. I could not sleep after that. Got up and went down to have a glass of orange juice. There was the welcoming Laika with her tail wagging furiously and I thought she was smiling at me. If there was one person (I am sure I can be forgiven for calling our Laika a 'person') who was always happy to see me and who always filled me with a sense of pride, it was Laika our newly acquired Black Labrador puppy. I gave her some food and took her out for a walk. It did not matter that it was only 4'O clock in the morning; she was bright as a button and eager to run after a ball on the town moor.

We came back by about six in the morning and had some breakfast. It was my usual practice to plan my day during my walk in the morning. Today, I was at a loss! There was nothing to plan to. No hospital to go to. No one to meet. No deadlines. No operating lists. No meetings. No nothing! This was Thursday and I would be rushing to get into theatre, see the patients, and worry about if they had filled in the pre-op score sheets. The whole day was an empty void that I could not fill. My heart started to get heavy again and eyes started to fill up. The sense of desperation and depression started to set in again. For the first time in my life, I did not have anything to do and did not feel like doing anything. Nothing to look forward to but more disillusionment and more anguish. The sense of desperation would not go whatever I tried to do. The house looked emptier than before and it looked as empty as my mind at the time.

I had to think of something to fill my day and not get into this rut of self-pity and sense of disenchantment. I had to do it fast before I go completely round the bend. I decided to see if I could lose myself in another of my favourite pastimes – woodwork. I brought a half-finished Tea trolley from the loft down to the garage. Took the whole thing apart and started to get the project finished and see if anyone wanted it. It had been languishing in the loft for over two years, as Lopa hated it. Spent rest of the day sanding it down to a fine finish and started to apply first coat of oil. It was late afternoon by the time I had finished. I was physically tired and mentally exhausted. My mind still was in a huge turmoil and I could not settle down.

There had been several phone calls from Swayambhu and Gautam in the meantime. I do not think I had ever felt as lonely as I did then. I could understand the concerns showed by my close friends. If not for the moral support by such friends, I am not sure I would have been able to withstand the pressure I was under at that stage. Days passed by agonisingly slowly and that weekend, Lopa came back. There were many discussions with Lopa and my close circle of friends. There were recriminations from Lopa. She felt that I should not have gone to see the Chief Executive and I would have been OK if I had not gone to see him. Any attempts at trying to explain the process a hospital Chief Executive would undertake in such circumstance was just pointless. She had made her mind up and when she makes her mind up, even God cannot change it.

It just occurred to me that I had not read the determination in any detail. It was too painful to read at that stage. Gautam said,

'Upaas. Leave the damn thing for a few days. It will just get you angry and depressed. You need a clear mind to think of the next step.'

In fact, I did not read the document properly for nearly a month.

The next six months were probably the longest in my life. It took a while for the fact that I do not have a job to go to sink in. All my friends rallied around and tried to support me as much as they could. They all wanted me to immerse myself into my woodwork and take up painting that I had given up a few years ago. At the end of the day, they all had their lives to lead and their work to go to. I was left alone at home every day and it became more and more painful to say bye to Lopa every morning when she went to work. I used to look forward to the call from Swayambhu to go for lunch on those days he was free. It became the highlight of every week – going to lunch with Swayambhu and sometimes with Pavaki to the local Italian restaurant. Sale Pepe became an oasis for me in the middle of a huge void. That was the cure for emptiness and loneliness. It was Mother Teresa, who said 'Loneliness and the feeling of being unwanted is the most terrible poverty' and I was at that time a pauper. There I was, alone and feeling completely unwanted and felt completely useless. I tried to go into the garage to start my woodwork that had come to a halt because of all the pressures. Picked up a half-finished coffee table, but could not carry on. The mind was not in it and I could not think of the steps that needed to get a good finish. I did not want to ruin a half-finished project and gave up. Picked up a half-finished watercolour and did spend some time on it. Listening to an old Mukesh tape and the mood I was in, helped get the right effect on the surrealist type of painting I was doing. After a few hours of that, I suddenly realised that the day was up and it was dark outside when I heard the door open and Lopa came in. I must have looked terrible at that time. Lopa wanted to know if I was all right.

The days passed extremely slowly and painfully. When you do not have anything to do, the minutes feel like hours. The mind plays tricks on you when one is idle. Leonardo d Vinci said 'Time stays long enough for anyone who will use it' and in my case, the time appears to be never ending without any use for it. Weeks passed when Sanvi came home with news that an Allotment had been allocated to her. At the time, I did not know what a boon it was until she took me to see it. As soon as I saw the allotment, my eyes lit up and for the first time in weeks, I started to feel a purpose for my time. However, there were strict instructions from Sanvi as to what I can and cannot do with it. From then on, I spent most days in the allotment trying to get piece of land back to life. It was hard work, but I could see the result as the weeks passed. I surfed through the web and got a lot of information on growing vegetables and looking after an allotment. I dug up the weeds, built raised patches, cleared paths, and generally made it all look professional. I might have been a slightly over enthusiastic as there were a few disapproving noises from Sanvi. It was therapeutic for my loneliness and felt that I was achieving something after what seemed to me a very long time. It was also during this time that Sanvi came with a very high score with her exams at her veterinary course and she was offered a place in Cambridge for clinical veterinary course. I was beginning to feel that the wheel might be turning in my favour! Clutching at straws comes to mind. However, I could do with some good news.

During this period, there was a regular phone call from dear old Nancy who tried her best to put the positive slant to everything. She even tried to intervene with the Chief executive with rather an unexpected rebuff from the Trust. He threatened to take me through the 'disciplinary route' if we did not like his recommendation. Swayambhu, Gautam, and everyone else tried to get me to see the positive side of this debacle. I for one could not see what the positive side to the whole mess was.

I decided that my days at Seaport may be numbered and I should look for alternatives. I spent the next couple of weeks re-visiting some of the recruitment agencies specialising in doctors for the Middle Eastern countries. It was not too long before I was called for an interview for a hospital at Abudhabi. It was a telephone interview with three orthopaedic consultants sitting in the other side of the world with associated management types. It lasted nearly forty-five minutes and was very thorough. I was quite impressed by the whole process. It ended with the chief executive of the hospital telling me that he will contact me soon. A couple of weeks later an offer came and to me looked quite impressive. Next few days there were a lot of discussions on the pros and cons of accepting the offer. I got the distinct impression that no one was keen on me going away to the Middle East. My argument for going away was partly financial and partly the fact that I may not want to work with individuals of dubious faith to say the least. Lopa's and some of my friends argument was that, if I wanted to go, I should, after clearing my name. After an agonising couple of weeks, I turned down the offer. I would only realise some months later how big a mistake that was. After that, there were a couple of more interviews and offers, which I turned down again. By this time my financial situation, which was already in dire straits plummeted further, and I was getting rather desperate. I had to think of ways of boosting my income one way or the other. Since the Interim Orders Panel stopped my private practice in March 2007, the income had halved, but the expenses had not changed. The debts were mounting up and I was too proud to admit to anyone. Unfortunately, Lopa could not understand the situation as she failed to understand how I do not have any 'savings.' The fact that we were spending more than what I was earning, was a difficult concept for her.

One of the avenues, which had dried up a few years ago, was writing medical reports for those involved in road traffic accidents. I could not face the 'clients' who were blatantly misusing the system for financial gain. It is extremely difficult to sit in front of an adult telling you that he or she cannot do anything after a minor accident few years ago. In majority of cases, no pathology is detected or demonstrated. However, I had reached a situation where I could not be ruled by my principles. As someone cleverer than me once said, the principle of looking after oneself and one's family overrides all other principles. I started surfing the web again looking for the numerous agencies dealing with such claims and registered my name to do medical reports. Nothing happened for a few months and the requests started to trickle in slowly. I managed to hire a room at the local clinic once a week. I decided to do my own secretarial work, as I could not afford a secretary to do the work. Moreover, these companies normally took up to a year or more to pay. It would take me couple of hours to type one medical report and I was spending more and more time on the email and telephone answering queries and setting up appointments. If there was something that I had lots of, it was time.

When Samuel Johnson said, "It is better to suffer wrong than to do it, and happier to be sometimes cheated than not to trust", he definitely had not come across either Serpe or Pakshar. I had trusted both and helped them both only to be cheated by the two. Whenever I thought about my plight at that stage and looked at my life just two years ago, my heart would sink and depression set in. There I was going around the world demonstrating my surgical skills to experts in the field in Europe and outside. I was going around the world lecturing and teaching specialised surgical techniques. Everyone in the hospital looked up to me and everyone wanted me to treat them or their families. Here I am now, typing out dull and meaningless medical reports trying to earn an extra dollar. The emotions that were going through me were a mixture of anger, frustration, and depression. There were thoughts of recriminations and retribution almost every day.

It was a phone call from Nancy, which brought me back into the realms of the problems with GMC. She wanted us to have a meeting to discuss further action. She said

'How are you Upaas? I know it must be hard for you to be sitting at home. I am rather disappointed at your Chief Executive and quite surprised. From his support during the hearing, this reaction was least expected. Anyway, the MPS council has approved our request for applying for Judicial Review of the GMC process. We will have to sit down and discuss a plan of action. When can you come down to Leeds so that we can discuss this with Dr Smiths and Fred Barnard?'

I was rather touched by the sincerity in her voice.

'I have all the time in the world now. You name the date and time and I'll be there Nancy.'

'OK. I will set up a meeting probably next week. How are you bearing up? I am quite confident that we will get through the next stage without any sanctions.'

That was the first time the word 'Sanctions' reared up. I had no idea what the next stage involved.

'What does the next stage in GMC mean? What can they do?'

'Well. The worst-case scenario is that they can strike your name off the register. That is extremely unlikely. They may decide not to do anything or issue a warning.' Nancy replied. 'Or they might take the route of further training or sabbatical or put some restriction over your practice over a set period of time.'

'Nancy we can't let them get away with this. We have to do something.'

'I know. Fred has recruited an assistant, Harshad Singh for the Judicial Review as well as the next stage at the GMC. We are going at them all guns blazing. The MPS is fully behind the fight. We will not let them get away with it. Don't worry.'

It was all very well for Nancy telling me to stop worrying. However, she had been behind me and my sheet anchor at worst of times. She had always had my best interests at heart. After about half an hour of that it was decided that, I will come over to their offices in Leeds in a couple of weeks and discuss both the Judicial Review and the last stage of GMC hearing.

I thought I better read the determination in some detail. It was painful to read it the second time. I spent the next few hours dissecting out the determination, cross-referencing with the thousands of pages of cross-examination and all the evidence that was produced in front of the panel over 28 days of hearing. I made several pages of comment. I had mixed feelings about the impending Judicial Review. One part of me was asking me to have faith in the British Fair play and justice system. However, my experience so far was not filling me with any hope.

The meeting in Leeds went quite well I thought. By now, these meetings had become routine. I let Nancy and Fred do most of the talking. The Judicial Review was entirely new to me. I was not sure of the actual process and I had my own doubts about how anyone could go through 10,000 pages of evidence, listen to the arguments of two barristers, and come to a balanced decision all in one day. Well, that was awaiting me in London's Royal Courts of Justice.

The whole rigmarole of Nancy sending the GMC the pre-action protocol and the inevitable reply of denial by the GMC took over two months. It took several more weeks before we could get a date for the hearing in London.

24. 'Never allow someone to be your priority while allowing yourself to be their option'

Mark Twain

The period after I was sent away on the 'gardening leave' as it were proved to be filled with several issues and events, not all of them to my liking. It all started with a meeting I had with our Divisional Director along with George one Friday morning. We met up in the department's research lab. He made us all coffee, and it was extremely cordial and friendly. The Director started asking me what the next steps with the GMC were.

'I will not be going back to the GMC if I win the Judicial Review.' I said. He looked at me for a moment and said,

'We will have to work on your sabbatical at Oxford. George tells me that Peter in Oxford was quite keen on you coming over there and operate on his patients'. He looked at George.

'Peter is a good friend of mine and he was particularly enthusiastic about it when I mentioned your name. He does not have much sympathy for the GMC and its activities. He feels empathy towards your cause.'

George was getting into his rhythm – bit surprisingly for that time of the morning I thought.

'He welcomed the idea of you operating on his patients as it would give him some free time! Everyone knows about his fabled wine cellar. At least you will get some excellent wine.'

George looked at me with a wide grin on his face.

'Upaas, take me through the next stage in the process.' The Director intervened.

'Well, from what I gather, our barrister does a submission to the Judge at the High court followed by a rebuttal submission from the GMC barrister. The Judge may then follow up with questions to both of them, and withdraw to make a decision'. I tried to explain, in the best legal tone I could muster.

'And what would be the likely outcomes, Upaas?' The Director wanted to now.

'The Judge has two options, one is to say that the GMC was wrong, which we are hoping for, or he can turn around and say the GMC was right in their process.'

George intervened with;

'What would happen if the Judge says that the GMC got it wrong?'

'That would mean the end of the GMC case and it would be ordered to quash its decision of impairment.' I replied.

There was an audible silence at this stage. I am not sure if the Director did realise that this might be an outcome of the next stage of this process. He was clearly trying to find out where to go next. I had the distinct impression that he had come to that meeting with some instructions, and he had little leeway in discussions.

'I am sure the GMC will take its time to quash its decision after the Judge's verdict surely?' He soliloquised.

'I have no idea how long the GMC will take to reverse its decision, but I intend to get back to work if I win the case in the High Court.' I insisted.

'Upaas, I think it would be a good idea for you to spend some time at Oxford even if you win the case. That will tick all the boxes, and you can come back to practice unhindered'. I was quite sure then, that this was someone higher up than him, talking to me through him. I am being told that I had better go to Oxford for 'retraining' or else.

I could feel some warmth under my collar slowly creeping up.

'I am sorry; I don't see what boxes I need to tick before I get back to work. The GMC has made a perverse decision based on dubious assessment by assessors whose qualifications are highly questionable. If their decision is quashed, my name is clear, and I should be allowed to get back to work with no restrictions'. The words came out in a rush. I kept saying to myself to calm down as otherwise it might be counter-productive.

He was not going to stop;

'There have been Chinese whispers and tittle tattle within the department, and we want to put a stop to it.'

George intervened again at this stage.

'And what are these whispers? We have to stop it.'

'Two of your colleagues came and said something about concerns about your practice and that you should not come back unless you get some training in certain aspects. There was also a mention of you not going through recognised training programme ..'

I could see George's ears getting red and hot and nostrils flaring as he spoke at this stage;

'Hang on a second please. That is unfair. It is not for want of trying that he did not go through senior registrar programme. He was short-listed several times and was told he was 'overqualified' on each of these occasions. Upaas was appointed to the local teaching hospital as a consultant and the chief executive of that trust was extremely reluctant to let Upaas go when he applied for a job in Seaport. He did everything he could to stop him going for the interview. Upaas has gone through a proper appointments advisory committee, he was appointed to this post in open competition, and he is recognised as a Trainer by the Specialist

Advisory Committee. His appointment has been ratified by no less a person than the President of Royal College at the time. You should ask them to substantiate their claims.'

George was talking about the additional ratification that was obtained for my appointment as the Chief Exec of the previous Trust had put in an objection. The Director was beginning to look a bit uncomfortable now.

'We did ask them to show some evidence for their claims. When they did not bring anything over a few weeks, I had to remind them to. Only to be told that the evidence had gone to the Chief Executive. On looking at their 'evidence,' it was not worth the paper it was written on. We did an internal audit of everyone's work over the last few months. Three outliers were identified and you were not one of them.' I could see he was trying to fight desperately to keep his corner.

By this time I had managed to calm myself down to some extent and said;

'I still don't see why I should go anywhere before returning to work if I am cleared by the GMC.'

'Upaas that is exactly what John wants. A clearance from the GMC. However, you know how long these things take. You do not want to be out of clinical practice for such a long time. I was going to suggest sending an email to all your colleagues to write to me about any concerns they have on your practice and show evidence for it. What would they expect you to do before returning to full practice?'

I was slowly beginning to get the picture. I could see the hands of some of my colleagues behind this decision. I could see the threat behind his words. It reminded me of the famous American freelance writer, Chuck Palahniuk's words, and 'The unreal is more powerful than the real, because nothing is as perfect as you can imagine it.' What I am not seeing is what I should imagine and rest assured I am not going to get any help. I left the meeting with more questions than when I started that morning. George took me along to the surgery centre cafe for a cup of coffee. Both of us were rather quiet on the way there. It is not like George to stay quiet for long.

'Upaas, we have to get those b****** and I need your help. To think we appointed them and gave them not only help but a role in the department'

I was not going to commit myself to anything. My aim at present is to get out of this mess and get back on to my own two feet without any encumbrances. I appear to be gathering a lot of dead weight and luggage on the way.

I was looking forward to the Judicial Review as for the first time in this nightmare; I can put forward my case to an authority outside the GMC.

I had heard and read so much about the "fairness" of the British justice system. I did not have any cause to think otherwise, as did all of my friends. There was a lot of expectation from the Judicial Review as we were certain that we would get a decision in our favour.

The exclusion from work was causing untold damage to my confidence and esteem and I made that very clear to Fred Barnard and co. I insisted that we get an expedited date for a hearing. It took a robust application by Fred to get the courts to agree to bring the date of hearing forward. It was not long before we got the date for a judicial review. As had been my practice, I booked an apartment in London and we drove down the night before. It coincided with Sanvi's graduation from Veterinary science at the Royal veterinary College. We were all a bit excited at the prospect of trying to get some justice outside the GMC and Sanvi's graduation. There was a lot of excited discussion in the car on the way down.

Sanvi, who is normally pragmatic, was the only one who was cautioning us to be more circumspect.

'I am not too sure. The judge will not have had a chance to see or read everything.'

'Well. He has had all the documents now for over a week. I think that should be enough for anyone to digest it.' I argued.

'There are over 10,000 pages of documents from both sides to go through. He will not only have to do some reading but also analyse the arguments from both sides and weight up the evidence from both sides.' Sanvi appeared to be thinking aloud.

'I can only see one problem. He may say that we are too premature as the final sanction stage at the GMC has not occurred yet.' I was beginning to feel a little less optimistic.

Next morning we took the tube from Canary wharf to the Royal Courts of Justice. As we were waiting for a taxi outside the tube station, my mobile rang. It was Swayambhu 'Where are you Upaas? I am in a taxi probably ten minutes from the courts.'

'We are waiting for a taxi and should be in the court in ten minutes as well.'

Both the taxis arrived at the court almost at the same time to see Nancy waiting at the steps. She was blooming and appeared radiant as one would at eighth month of pregnancy! I was glad to see her, as I was not sure that she would be able to make it because of the proximity of date of delivery. She always filled me with confidence and it was good to see her at the court.

The Royal Courts was an imposing Victorian Gothic building, designed by G E Street, opened by Queen Victoria in 1882, the architect's finest achievement, and the last major Gothic revival building in London. It was opened by Queen Victoria in 1882 and was said to contain 1000 rooms and 3.5 miles of corridors. The stress of its construction was said to have killed its architect. Most of the serious civil cases were heard in its chambers whereas the criminal cases are heard in the Old Bailey. It was home to a large number of high profile cases in history. We entered through a security-controlled door into a large equally impressive gothic hall with granite flooring and Portland stone walls. The high walls decorate with famous figures from legal history. Nancy took us to the far end of the hall through open double doors into a maze of corridors and soon we found ourselves in a waiting room at Court no 21. It was sparsely furnished with a large oak desk and two oak benches. One thing I noticed was the absence of sound. I suspect the Portland stone absorbs sound to some extent and every one talking in hushed voices. We were ten minute early and if this was anything similar to the GMC hearings, we will be waiting for another hour at least. I was wrong.

A gentleman in robes came out of the court exactly five minutes before ten and said

'This is the case of Kasyapa v GMC. Are both parties here?' He was looking at our team who were sitting at the desk and the GMC barrister who was sitting across the room on a chair. I assumed that it must be Mrs Palmer, barrister for the GMC. Both Fred Barnard and Mrs Palmer nodded their heads. I could not see any one with the GMC Barrister.

'Please come in and make yourself comfortable. Justice Magarvey will be in shortly.' The clerk of the court said. We were a bit taken aback at the promptness of it. We had been used to spending hours waiting for the FTP panel to turn up over the previous two and half years. The courtroom itself was not what I expected. Maybe because we have been conditioned by watching courtroom dramas on the TV with ornate wood panelling and furniture. Again, it was rather sparsely furnished. The Judge's seat was on a high platform at one end of the room with a desk running the full length of the room. The clerk and the short hand typist sat in front to a side of the desk and there were four rows of old oak benches with desktops for the rest of us at the rear end of the room. The benches reminded me of my school days in Bangalore. The only difference was that these benches had cushions on them. The furniture probably went back a hundred years as well. The two barristers took their seat on the front row and I along with Nancy and Harshad Singh sat in the second row. Swayambhu, Lopa, and Sanvi sat in the third row. Fred Barnard was wearing robes of a Queen's Counsel – black silk gown with a flap collar and long sleeves and the wig. He looked an archetypical Barrister. He had his folder neatly arranged on top of the desk, clearly indexed, and marked. Nancy and Harshad had copies of all the documents that Fred might need in the second row next to me. There were the customary bottles of water on all the desks.

'All rise' the usher promptly shouted on the dot at 10'O clock! We all stood up as Justice Magarvey entered. He bowed to everyone in the room and sat down. All of us reciprocated before sitting down. The clerk of the Justice read out the case number and title of the case.

'Good morning everyone. I have had the chance of going through the large bundles of documents over the weekend and I have formed some views about the application. But I would like to hear what you have to say. Mrs Palmer, if you would like to start?' Justice Magarvey said looking at the GMC barrister. Mrs Palmer stood up bowed to the Judge and thanked him for the opportunity. She briefly went through the case, very similar to presentation of Bill Sykes in the FTP hearing, highlighting the deficiencies noted by the FTP in their last determination six weeks previously. She also said

'Mr Kasyapa's application is premature as the final sanctions stage has not been reached. The panel might or might not impose any sanctions on the Doctor's registration. If they don't impose any sanctions, this would be a wasted exercise.'

'However Mrs Palmer, if the panel does not impose any sanctions, the Doctor does not have any avenues of appeal.' said the Judge.

It turns out that if the GMC panel does not impose any sanctions on me, I cannot go to court to clear my name. Even though I would be allowed to continue practicing, I would not be able to get rid of the taint that has been attached to my name by the GMC panel – 'Fitness to practice is impaired.'

'I agree your honour. But the GMC feels that this application is premature and should not be allowed.'

The Judge asked a few more questions to clarify before asking her to sit down.

'Mr Barnard. Let's hear what you have to say about your application now.' The Judge said looking at Fred Barnard.

Fred stood up adjusted his glasses and set off on what has now become a very familiar argument. His argument was based on four main categories – Irrationality of referral to Fitness to Practice Panel, Procedural impropriety on the grounds of bias, use of Wrong test by the Panel and irrationality of decision by the Panel.

The next two hours were fascinating to say the least. If I were not, so tense at the situation I was in I would have enjoyed myself. I had been a fan of Perry Mason as a teenager. It was just like watching one of those arguments between Fred on one side saying how badly the GMC had behaved during the hearing and Mrs Palmer saying the GMC behaviour was within the laws and the Judge moderating in between. There were several 'Objections My lord' and 'Objections over ruled' or 'Objection sustained' on several occasions.

Fred started with the rationality of the entire case itself. There was a sense of Déjà vu when he said that the rationale for referral was skewed. He pointed the judge to look at the paragraph in the first bundle, which included the GMC's rationale for referring me to the panel.

'Due to the extensive concerns raised by Mr. Kasyapa, the case examiners consider that the case should be referred to Fitness to Practise Panel for consideration. In other words, their finding was that because of the doctor's concerns the matter should be referred to Fitness to Practise Panel for consideration. They are not relying on the findings against the doctor by the assessment panel but by referring to the concerns which he himself had raised.'

I could see the Judge was interested in this.

'Let me get this straight. Do you mean to say that the GMC was saying that the Doctor should be put through this hearing because he complained against their assessment?' He raised his eyebrows and looked at closely at Fred.

'In short. Yes your Honour.' Fred answered "And when the doctor's solicitors questioned their judgement the reply was in the affirmative. The GMC replied thus – '...and it is considered that the case examiners rationale, as it stands, is irrational and impermissible.'

He then went on to tell the judge about the copies of emails we found after a request for documents using Freedom of Information act. As he came to the email where one of the GMC officers was asking the author of the letter to change it to 'Concerns raised *against* Mr. Kasyapa' instead of '*by* Mr. Kasyapa.' He went on to highlight all the irregularities in the process including the deleted and blacked out internal emails by the officers of the GMC. At this stage Mrs. Palmer stood up and objected saying;

'Objection your Honour. That ship has sailed your Honour. If the Doctor is objecting to that, he should have asked for a judicial review then and not after the event. I respectfully submit that this argument should not be taken any further.'

The Judge smiled at this.

'I know what you are getting at Mrs. Palmer and you as well Mr. Barnard. But, Mrs. Palmer is right. I suggest that you leave that part of your argument out. I am surprised that you did not go for a Judicial Review at that stage.'

'Thank you. Your Honour. We did raise this issue and made a submission to the Panel itself as we thought it would be more appropriate to do so. However, our submission was turned down.'

'That's all very well Mrs. Palmer. But you cannot submit the rationale reason now as it is too late.' The Judge continued. 'This is a hearing about the process of the hearing and we cannot go back to the beginning.'

I could see Fred was a bit disheartened, as the wind had been blown out of his sail. He changed his tactic to the assessment process. He highlighted all the irregularities within the assessment process mainly concentrating on the mistakes made by the assessors while marking the test paper and the misinterpretation of surgical procedure by the assessors. He spent some time showing the court how we managed to find most of the records within the clinical notes of patients.' which had been marked as 'Missing records' by the assessors.

He then went on to highlight the fact there the entire proceeding was done without an adequate Specialist Adviser and that the two of the assessors that were appointed by the GMC had to be recused because of blatant bias. Mrs. Palmer again interrupted with;

'Your Honour. The very fact that these Specialist Advisers were recused highlights the fact that the hearing was unbiased.'

The Judge looked rather bemused by this outburst and he said.

'Thank you Mrs. Palmer. Let me make my own mind on that.'

Fred then went on to the test score and spent some time on the mechanics of the scoring by the assessors. He was trying to highlight the gross discrepancy between the scores awarded by the two assessors, which were at time diametrically opposite. I felt that at this point he should have spent more time showing the mistakes made by the assessors in marking the answers. Their process was so wrong at times that they do not appear to have read the instructions that went with each question.

At this stage, there appeared to be a lot of activity going on in the background around the GMC Barrister. Someone in a dark, rather dishevelled suit had joined the bench just after lunchtime. There was a lot of exchange of pieces of paper going on. The Judge had glared at Mrs. Palmer a couple of times with no effect.

I could see that the GMC Barrister was a bit rattled at the response of the Judge to the exposure of numerous mistakes made by the assessors – missing notes, mistakes during the Core surgical knowledge tests, mistakes during hearing and admission of several mistakes by the assessors during the hearing etc. When Fred pointed out that the GMC did not produce any witnesses apart from the report by the assessors, which was over two years old, I could see Mrs. Palmer exchange several notes with the man in dark suit in the back. It was nearly five in the evening by the time Fred finished his submission. The day was adjourned to hear GMC barrister's rebuttal in the morning.

The day ended with what I thought was a good day for us. I felt that the Judge was very receptive and appeared to grasp the gist of the situation very well despite having had a very short time to look at thousands of pages of evidence.

We were asked to resume the next morning at ten. I could not eat anything the night before or this morning. I had knots in my stomach and I had not slept very much through the night thinking about possible outcomes. We had spent several hours the night before discussing the day's events. Swayambhu had managed to find a nice Italian restaurant in the west end of London and we had walked for an hour after dinner in the pleasant surroundings of the west end of London. It was quite late by the time we had got back to the rented flat and continued the discussions well into the night. The general opinion was that the day had gone very well and everyone was very impressed by the grasp of the contents of the case by the Judge. Swayambhu felt quite positive and he kept saying the Judge would quash the GMC panel's decision. I was not so sure.

As we took our seats in the courtroom, the Judge walked in promptly at ten to the sound of 'All rise' by the usher.

The Judge sat down and adjusted his glasses before saying.

'Good morning to all of you. I hope you have had a restful evening.'

There were some discussions about the content of Fred's submission and the Judge said that we would get a copy of his decision in a few days time once he has corrected it.

Finally, when it came of the rebuttal by Mrs. Palmer, her main argument was that the Judicial Challenge was both premature and too late. It was too late for a judicial review of the rationale for the panel hearing and too premature for a Judicial Review on the decision of the panel. She repeated the fact that the application for a judicial review was not made until the very last date of time allowed for such an application. She argued that the GMC did not need anything apart from the assessment to show that my fitness to practice is impaired.

While this was going on the man in the dark suit had vanished only to return about an hour later and passed a note to Mrs. Palmer.

'Your Honour. I have just been handed a note by the officials of the GMC that the GMC accepts that if the Judicial Review is brought as soon as practicable and within 3 months and there is a decision not to impose a sanction such a claim would be deemed as being brought in time. And the GMC accepts that appeal can be pursued in a section 40 appear or a Judicial Review, if brought as soon as practicable if the Panel impose no sanction.'

This came as a shock to everyone. Nancy whispered

'This is unprecedented. I have never in all of my years of practice come across GMC acceding to his.'

'Let me get this straight. The GMC is now saying that the Doctor can appeal or ask for a Judicial Review even if the Panel does not impose any sanctions. Is that right?' The judge asked. I could see surprise written all over his face. She went on to explain the process of Section 40 when the Judge interrupted;

'I know what Section 40 is, with due respect Mrs. Palmer and I am sure Mr. Barnard does as well.'

I think this took Fred by surprise as well and he was lost for words – for the first time since the trial began, I must admit. She went on to elaborate the reasons for her rebuttal and went through all the reasons Sykes and Miss Norsworth had gone through in the past. She had changed the words here and there, but the essence was the same. The GMC's case was that they have done everything 'by the book' and there was no need for a Judicial Review. She almost said that the Judge is wasting his time and everyone else's time by letting this carry on.

It was lunchtime before she finished her submission refuting everything Fred had put in his submission. The Judge adjourned the hearing for lunch and asked us to come back by three in the afternoon.

We all went back to the court with a lot of trepidation and dry mouths all around. Nancy felt that the 'concession' has given the Judge a way out. She was quite sure there is going to be fudge.

'I hope he is brave enough to give an honest judgement. But, I have suspicion he is going to take the easy way out. The Judges are very reluctant to give decisions against these large Quango's.' She said with a tinge of sarcasm in her voice.

'I sincerely hope you are wrong Nancy. I am sick and tired of these hearings. It will be too soon if I never see another court room again in my life.' I replied.

'I can understand your frustration. However just think you are on the home stretch now. It won't be long now.' It was Fred who was talking. He was walking in front of us and still must have heard everything that we had said.

We had sat in the courtroom for not more than five minutes before the Judge walked in to the usual 'All rise' shout from the usher of the court.

'Good afternoon. I am going to read my determination out as it were, going through the evidence at the same time. I have not actually written down the determination and so it will be a few days before a copy is available to you.' He said looking at both Fred and Mrs. Palmer. He asked all of us to sit down and that he will give his decision.

I was quite impressed with the way he went through thousands of pages of evidence that both sides had produced so far. He agreed that the first to reasons quoted by Fred was relevant;

'The first two grounds are in principle matters which could be the subject of Judicial Review if they are made out and brought at the appropriate time. They may have the consequences of aborting the proceedings.' And he went on to say, 'The grounds for referral suggested that the matter had been referred because of Mr. Kasyapa's complaints about the assessors and not the other way around. Whether or not there was merit in that contention, if it was to be raised as a challenge by way of Judicial Review it should have been done within three months of the 16 October 2008 and before the panel considered the case on 28 April 2008.' He concluded that

'It is too late now for the claimant to bring for Judicial Review on that ground.'

He then went on to the second ground of bias. He felt that the two Specialist Advisers were recused because of bias they had showed during the hearing and it shows 'exemplary behaviour of the Panel.' He went on to address the apparent bas showed by the GP during his questioning and said 'questions about commercial arrangements between the claimant and the providers of prosthesis and his arrangements for junior staff. The topics were not relevant to the charges and the questions were better not asked but there was insufficient to amount to bias.' and he refused permission for Judicial Review on the first two grounds.

He then amalgamated the next two grounds together and said

'The Court has heard submissions on grounds 3 and 4 and he has formed a provisional view in particular in respect of ground 4 the irrationality of the panel.' However, he felt that as the GMC had give a concession to allow for appeal or apply for a Judicial Review, the application for Judicial Review at this stage could be considered premature. The way it was covered was quite extraordinary;

'The court accepts that parties cannot extend the time for claiming Judicial Review under the CPR however in this case the Statement of Principle has been made by the Regulatory Authority the GMC and accepted by the Court. The Judge accepts this concession in this capacity. It will avoid any duplication of litigation and give certainty. He has no hesitation in accepting the GMC's concessions and his acceptance should give reassurance to other practitioners. If the Panel does not impose a sanction the practitioner can bring claim for Judicial Review and this will not be rejected on the grounds of delay.'

He paused there for a moment and my heart sank when he then went on to say;

'In summary therefore permission to apply for Judicial Review is refused, on grounds 3 and 4 as the claim is premature.' He then went on to discuss the claim for costs of the hearing by the GMC and refused their claim on grounds that the permission for Judicial Review was turned down essentially because of the GMC's concession today. "If they had made this concession earlier then the expense of this hearing may not have been necessary.'

He did a parting shot in the end of 'In respect of grounds 4 this is the matter which has formed the heart of the case against the GMC and his mind has shifted.'

This gave me some solace as I read it as that he would have quashed the GMC's decision if it had not been for the concession shown by the GMC at the last minute. As we walked out of the court into the July sunshine of London, my heart was rather heavy and I was quite depressed.

'I think this has not been a bad decision in some ways.' Nancy said.

'I agree. This leaves the door open for us to go for a judicial review after next month's final stage at the GMC whatever the outcome is. I only hope we get the same Judge to sit on that hearing as well.' Fred said.

'I am not so sure Fred. I am getting more than a bit fed up of the whole situation. This has tested my patience and sanity for the last few years. I cannot see any end to my troubles.' I said.

'Just hang in there. You have been through all the worst bits of the trial and we are near the end. I am quite confident we will come out well next month.' Fred tried to reassure me. My heart was not there and I found it difficult get out of the gloom that appears to be facing me. We said our goodbyes to Fred and Nancy and made our way back to the car park for the long drive back home.

Swayambhu said we should have a cup of coffee before we set off.

'Do you want me to drive Upaas?'

I said I was all right and started to look for a familiar coffee shop in the neighbourhood. The next couple of hours in the coffee shop were spent dissecting the previous two days happenings. All of them felt that the result was a good one and if we can get the same Judge when we re-apply for a Judicial Review after next month, we are sure to win. It was with mixed feelings that I drove back in silence all the way back home while the others slept in the car.

25. And Finally...

I was not looking forward to this trip down to Manchester. I was extremely nervous and apprehensive. It was August 2009 and 18 months since the hearing had begun. I was sure the panel would have heard of my attempt at Judicial Review and the result of the review. I was also quite sure of their response. There was no reason why they would look at my case favourably as I had complained to the court against them. Nancy tried her hardest to convince me that the panel are supposed to be independent, and they will not make decisions, borne on such actions. My argument was that the panel at the end of the day was made of human beings, and no one likes to be told that they are wrong.

'But, Upaas. If they do give a judgement against you, we can go to the court, and the courts will have no excuse but to act on it.'

'After the last visit to the High Court I am not sure if that is going to achieve anything constructive. I don't seem to have the same confidence as you on our courts" I am sure she could detect a hint of desperation in my voice. She tried her best to calm my nerves.

"We will have to get some people to give evidence to the panel for the next stage. Ideally we will need your medical Director, your mentor during the last two years and anyone else who would vouch for you.' Nancy continued.

'The medical director is also the Mentor at present and my Supervisor is George. I will have to ask them if they would give evidence'. I said with some trepidation.

'I will do that for you. It is probably better the request coming from me rather than you. All I need is permission to contact them.'

'OK. I will speak to them and ask them if it is OK for you to contact them.'

'Please let me know as soon as you have done. We will have to get them prepared and get their availability.'

I was not looking forward to asking the Medical Director for help. However, I was not in a position of option. I will have to swallow my pride and do the necessary. It took me a couple of days to work up enough determination and 'hard skin' to contact the Medical Director. He was quite friendly and was extremely sympathetic which made it even worse.

'Not to worry Upaas. I will be more than happy to support you. Please be reassured that the whole Trust Board is behind you. I am sure you will look at this someday, in the future as a learning experience'. For him, everything was a 'Learning experience'. He had always been terribly keen on teaching and learning. He was well recognised Clinical

Tutor for the Royal College of Physicians, and he took the job extremely seriously. He had been instrumental in building up the 'Learning Protocol' for me over the past two years. He was tremendously impressed with the portfolio that I had built up over the past two years. He would take every opportunity to tell everyone that, 'Upaas' Portfolio is a model for Revalidation with the GMC in the future.'

'Thank you very much. I am truly grateful. Nancy is going to contact you, over the next few days, and brief you about the next stage of the hearing, and what you could expect the panel would ask on the day'.

After that, speaking to George was a piece of cake. I called him up that evening, and he was full of sympathy for me, and could not believe that this still has not been finished and cleared.

'I can't believe that this is still going on. I thought after the evidence of some of the biggest authorities in orthopaedics supporting you no one could cast any aspersions on your practice. This is simply unbelievable. What do you want me to do Old boy?'

'The panel would want to ask you some more questions during the next stage as you are my Supervisor. They probably want to make sure that I have been behaving myself over the last two years.'

'No problem Upaas. I will do anything you want.' George continued. Conversation with George never finished less than half an hour. Nevertheless, these interludes always lifted my spirits up and made me happy and 'comfortable.'

I called Nancy the next day and told her about both George and the Medical director. I also gave her their personal phone numbers so that she can talk to them. She called me up a few days later that everything was sorted out, and she was waiting for the GMC to come back with some dates. She thought it would not be before July or August. That would make it 18 months of hearing and nearly six years of nightmare.

Helen called me up one evening a few days later. She was her usual cheerful self. She wanted to know everything as usual. When she starts to talk, it is like opening a floodgate. There is a torrent of words coming out non-stop. It was several minutes before I could find out that, the staffs in the theatre were planning on a demonstration, in front of Chief executive's office, and there was even a suggestion to go in front of the GMC offices.

I had visions of a large number of nurses going in front of the GMC offices in Manchester, with placards with my name on it. It suddenly filled me with dread. The last thing I want now is to upset the panel members and get them to pass an adverse judgement against me.

'That is very kind of you, and everyone else. But, that may not help. It may even upset the panel and pass a judgement against me.'

'But Upaas, if they do that we'll escalate the protest. We won't stop until you are back at work.' Helen continued. She has always been hard to change once her mind was made up. She always saw things as black and white. Grey tones of the world around us seem to have escaped her. She could not believe what was happening to me and what I had been put through by people who I had helped. I took me a while to convince her that this protest idea is not going to help me.

'Well, Upaas. If you change your mind, give me a tinkle, and we will mobilise everyone. Everyone here, are thinking of you, and keep asking about you.'

This filled me with some hope and faith in humanity once again. It was not long before I started to notice some changes around me. There was a distinctive difference in the way I was treated, by a number of my colleagues and friends. It was extremely subtle at first, and I thought I was being paranoid. When people started to 'forgot to invite' us for family occasions, I did not think much of it. When people started to speak to me in monosyllabic language with a forced smile on their faces, I was totally oblivious. Gradually, I began to realise that I had a lot more time on my hands at home and not only because I was not working but also because the there was nothing for me to do. I realised how many hours I must have spent on reading, analysing, reporting on the GMC hearing over the past few years.

I could see the change in attitudes towards me from everyone. Part of it may be my paranoia, but mostly many did not want to be associated with me. The number of texts I used to get, dwindled gradually down to trickle. I even began to think that my loved ones were distancing me. Paranoia plays its tricks on one's mind, and I started to think of the negative side of every conversation with everyone. No one wants to be linked with "failures". Here, I was, judged as a failure by the GMC and now the courts have reinforced the verdict.

It must be the lowest point of my life at that stage. I did not know who to turn to or what to do. I started to feel that there did not seem to be any help from those who I cared about, in dealing with the situation. It was as if 'you got into his mess, and you get out of it'.

Nancy called me a few days later, giving me the dates, for the next stage of the hearing. It was a dreadful day as I remember. This was something I was not looking forward to. This was the day where three individuals were going to decide my future. These are the three men whose only experience with a NHS hospital would be as patients. None of them had ever worked or spent any time within a hospital to know how the hospital works. The GP Dr O'Neil might have spent a few months during his house job working in a hospital. That would be the extent of the Panel's expertise. They had no idea of the issues that were dealt everyday of life by nurses and doctors at the front line – issues of clinical, time restraints, cost restraints and managerial restraints. They had never had to make a decision on whether to offer a patient life changing treatment or not. These patients are someone's mother, father, wife, husband, son, or daughter. The decisions taken by doctors and nurses everyday had far-reaching consequences to several people every time they make a decision. I suspect the biggest such decision these people would ever had to make would probably be, who was going to buy the next round in the pub.

I was not looking forward to the decision at all. I could not sleep or eat properly during the waiting months. My health suffered in consequence. I was getting more and shorter tempered. I was taking my frustration out on everyone else. There were several moments during those months, where I had entirely given up and wanted to end it forever. Nevertheless, it was not to be. One had to have a certain mind-set to do such things.

The day of decision came, and we tripped down to Manchester this time. It was quite a humid August morning in 2009, as it had not rained for quite a few days, and there was the usual 'hose pipe ban' in progress, in several counties. This is a country of extremes of weather in one sense without the dramatics of earthquakes or volcanoes or tsunamis. We have wet weather most of the year with drizzle for rain almost throughout the year. There is no 'Rainy season' and there are contrasts of now and then of extreme dry weather, when everything dries up – rivers and lakes with quite a water shortage.

As we reached the offices of GMC on Oxford Road, Nancy was already there, and we were waiting for Fred. No one was saying very much, and everyone tried to avoid eye contact with me.

'Hi Nancy. Have you got the phone numbers for Mr Cooley and the Medical director? Fred asked as it was beginning to get slightly uncomfortable.

'Yes Fred. Both of them are on notice. The Medical Director is waiting in his office for my call, and we should be able to get Mr Cooley soon afterwards. Mind you, he has a clinic in the afternoon.' Nancy replied

'We should be able to get to him before lunch time. I am sure.' Fred sounded supremely confident. The usher called us into the hearing room just after ten. First change I noticed was that Miss Norsworth had taken the place of Sykes again for this stage.

The Chairman again started with his usual welcome to everyone except me. He still refused to recognise my presence. I think Fred had under estimated the process of these panels. He immediately went to the legal Assessor for his advice. Both Miss Norsworth and Fred looked at each other and wondered what the advice was about.

The legal adviser took out a large sheaf of papers and went into his spiel about the rules of the GMC and the powers of the panel and so forth. It took him over an hour to get through all that. The Chairman turned to Miss Norsworth and asked her to make her submission. Miss Norsworth stood up to make her submission.

'The GMC has completed the case and would like to make a submission regarding sanctions ..'

Fred immediately stood up and raised his hands.

'I am sorry Mr Chairman. This is out of order. The GMC has completed its case at the last stage. As far as the GMC is concerned, the case is closed and they have made their bid. It is now Dr Kasyapa to defend the accusations.' I could see there was quite consternation in the face of the Chairman as well as the other panellists. The Chairman covered the microphone, spent a few minutes in an animated discussion with the legal assessor, and then turned around to announce that the panel would like advice from the Legal Assessor.

'I will have to agree with Mr Barnard in this matter. The GMC had the chance to submit its case and has done so. It is now up to Dr Kasyapa to show what effort he has done to merit sanctions if any.' He went on for another ten minutes justifying what he said using examples and legal jargon.

'The panel will go into camera to discuss this issue. We will have a short break and reconvene in 30 minutes.' The Chairman decidedly looked unhappy. This is not good. I did not want the panel to be 'unhappy' at this stage. My life depends on them being 'happy' at this stage so that they do not take it out on me. It was a rather silent coffee break. I kept asking both Fred and Nancy what is likely to happen. My anxiety must have shown and both of them tried to reassure me as much as they could. I was having difficulty controlling my emotions. Could not drink my coffee and it must have been the longest 30 minutes of my life. The ubiquitous usher eventually called us back into the hearing room again.

I tried to assess the mood of the panel as we walked in. I could not make out anything from the Chairman's face. The reverend's face was hiding behind his beard and the GP; Dr O'Neil had his permanent Cheshire grin on as a disguise. The Chairman once again welcomed everyone back and asked Fred to start his submission.

Fred adjusted his glasses and started off with;

'Thank you, sir. I would like to start off by saying that we have two witnesses who will be giving Telephone evidence on behalf of Mr Kasyapa.'

'I see. Miss Norsworth, does GMC have any objection to this?'

'No sir. Mr Barnard mentioned it this morning and I have taken instructions from the GMC. It is perfectly acceptable to the GMC.' Miss Norsworth replied.

'Thank you. You may continue Mr Barnard. What time do you expect to call your witnesses?'

'I am hoping to call them before Lunch time. They are the Medical Director of the Trust and Mr Cooley who has been the Supervisor for Mr Kasyapa for the last couple of years while this investigation has been going on.'

Fred continued with the usual arguments about the improper proceedings of the trial and the mistakes made by the assessors before the Chairman stopped him again.

'That ship has sailed now Mr Barnard. Can you please tell us what you have to support Mr Kasyapa now?'

'Yes sir. My apologies for that. I could not resist that temptation to voice my frustration.' Fred replied and then went on to enumerate all the details in my huge three-volume portfolio that I had constructed painstakingly over the previous two years. I had filled in the diary everyday about my time in the hospital in detail. I have had to go through every case with George and get his approval and his signature for every operation I had done. There were details of every operation done over the previous two years and their results. There were details of every meeting that I had attended within the hospital as well as outside the hospital. It had letters from my colleagues within the hospital and outside extolling my qualities as a surgeon. There were numerous testimonials from patients. There were testimonials from visiting professionals who had come to learn techniques of surgery in the knee and hip – leading surgeons and professors from this country as well as Europe – leaders in their own right and in their own countries. It had copies of the numerous publications I had published in reputed peer reviewed journals and details of presentations in several international orthopaedic meetings. I had included the extract of my database, which had every joint replacement done by me since taking up the post as a consultant surgeon over fifteen years ago. It showed that I had performed over 3000 major hip and knee replacements including complex revision surgery with independently recorded results. There were copies of independent audit done by external auditors on my work. He next went on to show the entire course that I had taken over the previous twelve months to 'improve' my 'basic skills' as it were. I had spent hours on end reading up and taking online-based tests set up by British medical Association, The Royal College of Surgeons, and American Academy of Orthopaedic Surgeons as well as Royal College of Anaesthetists. I had spent a large amount of time with George in trying to select the right modules. George had taken upon himself to choose those modules, which would address the criticisms raised by the assessors as well as the FTP panel members. It was a mammoth task to sift through over a thousand pages of document and identify every 'deficit' that had been identified. He wanted to address even the slightest criticism that had been raised over the previous three years. He pointed out yet again how I had passed with flying colours the Basic Surgical Skills conducted by the Royal College of Surgeons barely couple of months after the so-called 'assessment.'

It was after lunch break before George was called to give evidence. He was in the middle of an outpatient clinic when the telephone conference was set up. He was grilled about the 'supervision' over the previous couple of years and my compliance with the restrictions imposed on me by the Interim Orders Panel. They spent some time asking him about how I would cope with the work and skills if I were 'allowed to go back to work tomorrow.' George was excellent in his response and made quite sure that I would be supported in my work and that I have enough sense not to perform any complicated procedures and end up in the same situation again. The interview took over 20 minutes. I could imagine the outpatient nurses getting stressed about 'waiting times' for the patients that afternoon.

Then it was the turn of the Medical director' who was also the Chairman of the 'Support group' which had kept an 'eye on the progress' over the previous three years. He was again asked the similar questions. He also reinforced that the Trust would do the best to integrate me fully into the service over a period. He reassured the panel that a senior middle grade doctor would be support me by during the first few months, and that the group will keep an eye on the progress and support wherever it was necessary. I was looking at the panel members during the questioning quite intently. Their faces were blank and I could not see if any of the statement was registering any reaction from the panel.

This was followed by concluding remarks by Fred. He reminded the panel again about the enormous work that I had done over the years and the amount of new 'training' that I had gone through over the previous couple of years and the vast support I enjoyed within the hospital and the community. It was nearly four in the afternoon by the time he sat down. Miss Norsworth did not have anything else to say. The Chairman for inexplicable reason asked the Legal adviser for his opinion. He did not have anything to add to what he had already said that morning. The Chairman decided that the panel would 'go into camera' to make their decision and we were excused till next morning.

As we walked out of the building, no one was saying anything. Judging from previous submissions and 'final outcomes', no one was prepared to guess how the day went and what the outcome would be. It was quite a sombre group as we went back to our respective hotels for the night. Nancy asked us to be ready by about 10 in the morning and she would let us know.

It was nearly 11'O clock next morning before Nancy called.

'They are still not ready. I suspect it would be after lunch. We have been excused till 1.00 PM. Why don't we meet up at the GMC offices after lunch?'

'That is fine Nancy. What do you think is going to happen?' I was shooting in the dark.

'There is no point worrying about it now Upaas. We will address whatever they throw at us.' She tried her best to reassure me, but it was not working. We went out into the Piccadilly centre and after going around a couple of time wandering aimlessly, we went into a cafe and tried to have some lunch. I could not bring myself to eat anything. As we reached the GMC offices just before 1'O clock, Nancy and Fred were already there.

It was probably the first time in the entire process that we were called into the room promptly at 1'O clock.

The chairman started off without any preamble

'Mr Kasyapa, the order imposed by the Interim Orders Panel is hereby revoked.'

I could hear a tiny intake of breath by Nancy and I looked up. She was smiling and had her thumbs up. I did not understand.

He went on;

'The Panel must now determine what sanction if any should impose on your registration.' He rambled on for next half an hour going through submissions of both the GMC and Fred Barnard. He stressed on some of the evidence produced by Fred Barnard.

'Mr Barnard also referred the panel to the Audits of your work that have been undertaken. He also commended to the panel the evidence of Mr Fitzgerald, Chief Executive at the Trust, and also the supportive testimonials, petition and other documentation all of which demonstrate the high regard in which you are held. Mr Barnard told the panel of the effect that these proceedings have had upon you. Mr Barnard submitted that you have complied with everything that has been asked of you, in particular the conditions imposed by the Interim Orders Panel and that is now time, in the public interest and for the benefit of your employing Trust for you to return to surgical practice.'

He then went into the legal issues within the statute of the GMC just as I was feeling good about myself listening to the positive things that were being said about me. He returned to the issue again with

'The panel has reminded itself of the content of the numerous letters and "thank you" cards from patients as well as unambiguous support of your professional colleagues including your Chief Executive and Medical Director. It is obvious that even now you are held in high regard by those with whom you work and the patients to whom you have provided care. It is said that these proceedings, resulting in your being placed on leave by your Trust, have had a 'devastating and demoralising' effect upon you. The panel has heard that you have worked for some 15 years and undertaken over 3000 major joint replacement operations. There is no evidence before the Panel of any complaint throughout this time prior to the matter giving rise to these proceedings.'

He spent the next fifteen minutes again going through the requirements and implication of Sanctions guide from the GMC before coming back to

'The Panel considers that this is an exceptional case' and then went on to enumerate all the points raised by Fred and the evidence provided so far in support before saying

'The Panel is satisfied that any risk to patients by your phased return to medical practice is negligible. Therefore, conditions on your registration are unnecessary. The Panel therefore concludes your case by taking no action. That concludes the case.'

There was a deep sigh of relief from Nancy. I was quite numb. I did not know how to react. Fred was not looking at anyone. He was busy collecting all his papers. Nancy just got up, was getting ready to leave the room, and signalled me to do the same.

'Don't make any eye contact with anyone. There is no need to thank them. Do not say anything. Do not give them the satisfaction of seeing you as grateful. Just get up and walk out. We will talk outside.' Fred had not lifted his head and said the whole thing under his breath. I just got up and walked out of the room without looking at anyone. I was so desperate to say my piece at the end of the hearing. I had spent a lot of time thinking about what I wanted to say to the Panel and the GMC publicly. I had prepared a long speech telling them about how unfair and wrong the whole proceedings were and I wanted to question their qualification to judge my work and me. It was not to be.

As we gathered outside Nancy was the first one to come and give me a hug and said;

'Congratulations. I knew we were going to win, but I did not want to say anything in case of getting jinxed. I think you should take some time off now and don't rush back to work.' She congratulated Lopa as well who was looking somewhat relieved. I could see that she was holding back tears.

Fred turned to me and said shaking hands;

'Well done Upaas. Do not dwell on what has happened. Look forward to future and develop your career again.' He was beaming from ear to ear. He was obviously pleased at the outcome. 'This Panel must be one of the worst I have come across in my 30 year career. They did not have any other option than to give the decision that they have. I am sure even they knew there would be serious problems if they had decided against you. The statement was a fudge of sorts and they have taken a lot of effort and time to formulate the words in that determination. I am sure they would have had legal help in writing that determination. They have been clever and covered their tracks well.'

'I have to thank you Fred, for the excellent work you have done throughout the case. Without yours and Nancy's hard work, I do not think we would have won. I am deeply grateful to both of you for all the hard work you have done.'

I thanked both of them again and after asking them to keep in touch, we both started to walk back to the car park. On the way, I sent SMS texts to all my friends about the outcome of the day. I was not sure what the reaction would be from my friends. I did not have to wait for long. The phone did not stop ringing. As I was driving back from Manchester, Lopa was on the phone for almost the entire journey talking to numerous people and Pavaki had asked us to go to their house for dinner and a small celebration. It was quite late by the time I said good night to everyone and reached home. After a long time I slept without waking up until morning.

Did I really 'Win?' I am not so sure. It has taken a huge toll of my life and health and my family. Did the GMC win? Did it protect the people from a 'bad doctor?' I think it was at the end, a triumph of mediocrity over excellence, and a blow to development and progress.

I honestly believe this has affected large population of Seaport who were denied of my expertise and skill that were built over the past twenty odd years. I am not the only doctor who has been hauled over the coal for no good reason. I agree there has to be a mechanism and process to make sure the community gets a good and honest service from the medical profession. However, the process and mechanism as it exists now is too cumbersome, convoluted, and buried in bureaucracy. The tests are too artificial and do not really assess the doctor's skill and ability. The quality and skill of the assessors and the panellists leaves a lot to be desired. I blame the remuneration that is paid to these people is woefully inadequate to attract high calibre surgeons and doctors become involved. Pay for a whole day's work is less than what an orthopaedic surgeon is paid for an arthroscopy of the knee and slightly more than half of that for a hip replacement in a private sector. The issues are difficult, but not insurmountable. Until the medical profession takes ownership of their own regulation, this is going to continue.

It is not easy to sum up those five traumatic years of my life. There is a lesson for everyone in my story, whether one is in health care or not. In short the entire saga can be summarised in seven short paragraphs;

I tried to help a colleague improve his life and make a career within the health service. I literally lifted him out of a 'career gutter' and gave him a life and career. In response, he reported me to the General medical Council with trumped up accusations. Is the moral 'never to help anyone who may construe you to be a competition in the future?' There is a saying in Rig-Veda, an ancient Hindu scripture that says, 'Harm will befall of helping an unworthy person.' This was written over 4000 years ago and how true it is even today. Not everyone can be helped or should be helped. One has to be circumspect and choose who one helps in their hour of need. The history is surfeit with numerous traitors who backstabbed their benefactors.

Once you are reported to a regulatory body such as General Medical Council, it is best to consider yourself convicted before the trial begins. I took it rather lightly and had over confidence in myself. I assumed that the process would follow in a fair and honest fashion. It is more likely than not that, some assessors will be sent to assess you, who have very little if anything to do with your repertoire at work. I was too naive in believing my advisors and the assessors and took the 'test' too lightly. I could have made it more air tight by preparing for the test as one should be.

Do not for one moment believe anyone who says, 'It is just your day to day work that will be assessed.' The assessment has very little to do with one's present day practice and more to do with what you learnt in the school or the beginning of one's career. It is like asking a Criminal Barrister of 15 years experience questions about conveyance basics or assessing a Ship's captain of 15 yrs experience on basics of building a rowboat. One has to be extremely lucky to get out of such a scenario unscathed. Preparation and preparation and more preparation are the name of the game if one has to get out alive.

If the regulatory body accuses you of wrongdoing, accept it and look for a compromise way out. Never send a 95-page response highlighting the mistakes done by the assessment. It can be very expensive as it happened to me. The '95 page response' was thrown at my face numerous times during the trial. It was to say, 'How dare you question our authority?' No one likes their competence questioned, especially a regulatory body. It is an unwritten dictum that a Regulatory body can never do wrong. As Justice Magarvey said, I should have gone for a Judicial Review at that stage. I was concerned about waiting 'four to six months.' In the end, I waited nearly two years for an outcome. I should have had more faith in my own convictions. If I had asked for a judicial review at that stage, who knows what might have happened? The nightmare could have ended then and I may never have had this permanent stain on my name.

Building one's career without outshining others can be risky and lead one into trouble as it did for me. Mediocrity is roundly appreciated and encouraged in medicine as it is; I am sure, in other fields. No one likes a smart ass. The suppression of daring research is rampant and it is a miracle that the world is actually progressing forward, albeit slowly. If one wants to outshine others, make sure one builds a wall of security around with powerful people. One of the mistakes, I made was that I did not cultivate friendships of powerful people.

Friends, friends, and more friends. I was extremely lucky in having an enormous circle of very good friends around me. All of them with one or two minor exceptions stood beside me. A trial such as this is extremely taxing and stressful beyond imagination. It caused stress not just for me, but also for all my near and dear ones over the years. It is unrelenting and deepens as the time goes on. There were a number of times, I had come close to ending it all and take the 'easy way out.' The strength of friends and their loyalty gave me more strength to go through the difficult period. It is not easy to make good friends, but the effort pays off in the long run many times over.

Personal effort helped me to a significant extent. I did all the research work trailing through hundreds of clinical records, going through several audit processes to get my portfolio not only up to date but make it so that no one can find a fault with it. The hard work paid off when the Medical director told the Panel that my portfolio was an example for future revalidation process for all doctors. Thousands of dreary hours spent in producing the portfolio was worth its weight in gold.

I believe one has to have an inner strength to fight such a battle and win without going over the edge. One has to belief in oneself to get this strength. I thank my father, whose belief's I followed and gave me this strength. I firmly believed that there is some good in everyone and treat everyone as I would want them to treat me. I do not know if there is a God or not, but my belief that there is something I can rely on as a crutch helped me through periods of depression and despair.

Coming to the gang of four, who were instrumental in trying to destroy my family and me; what did they achieve by trying to nearly destroy my life and career? Did they win? They certainly caused severe hardships to hundreds of my patients in my district. They destroyed my reputation to a large extent. I am back at work trying my best to rebuild my life and career. I was never a believer of 'What goes around comes around.'

However, one of them was diagnosed with cancer within a year of the case going to trial and died two years later. Second one ended up in a psychiatric institution for a period of time within a year of start of my trial. The third one ended up getting a warning and had to retire to a life of ignominy and isolation. The fourth one however is still going strong even though he and his family have been completely ostracised by the community. I will let the reader make his or her own conclusions.

I will have to spend a considerable amount of time and effort over the next few years to re-build my tattered career and life. Nevertheless, I am happy that I still have my huge circle of very good friends to help me do that.

ABOUT THE AUTHOR

Shankar N Kashyap works as a Consultant Orthopaedic Surgeon in Gateshead, United Kingdom. He has published numerous scientific articles in peer reviewed scientific journals over the last 25 years. This is the first foray into literature. A series of books based on Harappan culture in 2500 BC is due to be released soon by the same author. He lives in Newcastle upon Tyne, married with three children.

CPSIA information can be obtained
at www.ICGtesting.com
Printed in the USA
LVOW10s1126070617

537254LV00004B/487/P

9 781468 081336